ADVERTISEMENT FOR A MAN

Braven tore down San Francisco's muddy streets, chasing down the infuriating, beautiful Rivalree. As she finished tacking the handbill in place and stepped back to admire her handiwork, Braven reached out and snatched the poster down.

"'Will pay for the right man to guide me into the Sierras,'" he read aloud, and swore. "Don't you ever stop to think before you do anything?"

Rivalree whirled, outrage etched on her face. "Don't you realize I don't have to answer to you?"

"You may not want to," he hissed, "but I'll make you!"

Braven dragged her down the sidewalk, her small fists pummeling his ribs, his chest, anywhere they could reach. He caught her hand, and pressed her into a doorway, bringing his lips down on hers, hard and uncompromising.

"No," she sobbed.

"Oh, yes," he growled, deepening the kiss and tightening his hold on her slender, nubile body . . .

D1553314

GOLDEN LIES

TERRY VALENTINE

ZEBRA BOOKS
KENSINGTON PUBLISHING CORP.

ZEBRA BOOKS

are published by

Kensington Publishing Corp.
475 Park Avenue South
New York, NY 10016

First printing: May 1988

Printed in the United States of America

To Darwin Reynolds, for being more than a father but a friend as well, always there when I need you, and for making the days of the Gold Rush come alive for me.

Chapter One

Charity, New Jersey
January 19, 1851

Cr-r-rack!

The loud detonation plagued Rivalree's sleep-ladened mind. Shivering beneath the pile of covers, she rolled to her side. Frigid air nipped at her nose and cheeks, the only parts of her not encompassed in the quilts. Dawn would be here soon. She scrunched up her nose and sniffed. Another day would begin—livestock to feed and water, the cow to milk with hands so cold the animal kicked in protest.

She almost wished the sun would never rise. No, that wasn't true. What she wanted was winter to be gone, never to return again. How she hated the cold, the snow, and the way her fingers and toes never got warm, even now nestled deep in the bedclothes. Leaden eyelids framed in a thick layer of dark lashes eased down over her amber eyes as a dream of warm sun and green grass carried her down the tunnel of sleep.

Cr-r-rack!

Her eyes flew wide, all remnants of languor vanishing. *What was that? Ma never rose this early, and if she did, she was as quiet as a church mouse, careful not to*

7

waken anyone.

"Jesse! Oh, my God, please no."

At the sound of her mother's frightened voice, so full of pain, Rivalree's heart pounded a tempo in her neck making it impossible to swallow.

"Ma?" she eked out of her constricted throat. Rivalree's stockinged feet hit the cold floor. Without a second thought she threw back the covers and stumbled in the darkness toward the door. From the corner of her eye a flicker of light caught her attention. What a strange illumination outside. Not sunrise, much too fiery. She recrossed the room at a run, pushing back the honey-colored tresses falling into her eyes.

Trying to see past the barrier, she clawed at the wool curtain tacked to the window frame, there to keep the north wind from seeping through the precious pane of glass.

"Angie!" Her father's voice sliced through the silence, followed by a bloodcurdling scream that could only be her mother's.

The curtain gave way, and, for a moment, Rivalree wished it hadn't. The flickering light was fire, the barn and smokehouse undulating in the licking tongues of destruction.

"Oh, my God, the animals," she muttered as she whipped around feeling for the chair holding her clothes. She dragged the woolen skirt over her nightgown, ignoring the blouse.

"My shoes? Where are my shoes?" On hands and knees she felt across the floor, discovering the leather laces of her boots. Settling back on her haunches, she tugged on her shoes and cinched them enough to keep from tripping over loose ties.

"The runaways," she panted as she took the steep stairs down to the kitchen as fast as she could. "How many times did Pa tell those Negroes not to use fire in the hayloft, no matter how cold they got?" It was obvious they hadn't listened to his warning.

Cr-r-rack! The sound brought Rivalree's feet to a halt at the bottom of the stairs. Gunfire. *Who would Pa shoot at when there was a fire? The only people who would show would be neighbors willing to help put out the flames. Why . . . ?*

"Jesse, help me." Her mother's voice held a plea as if she feared for her life.

Rivalree whirled, and her eyes skimmed over the shadows dancing against the mantel from the eerie light filtering in from the outside. Pa's gun still hung over the fireplace. *If Pa wasn't shooting, then who was?*

She clumped across the room and stretched on tiptoes to take the flintlock rifle down from its pegs. With shaky hands she managed to load it, the time the process took seeming like hours as she primed the gun, rammed the shot down the barrel, then tamped the wadding after it.

The sound she heard next stilled the blood racing through her veins—cruel laughter of several men. Her mother's scream rent the air again and ended with a gurgling moan as the roar of a gunshot reverberated through the ice-nipped air.

"Mother," Rivalree gasped as she tucked the weapon under her arm and lifted her skirt with the other hand.

Frost-rent air slammed into her as she threw the front door open. Hostile stares riveted on her as she stepped over the threshold, legs braced wide apart, the rifle raised against her shoulder.

Her gaze skipped over the nightmare scene, her mother curled on the frozen earth, her father pinned to the ground a few yards away, a man standing over him with his foot raised to kick his unprotected body. The remains of the barn snapped and cracked with the all-consuming flames as the roof crumbled into the fire. A group of dark-skinned men and women crowded against an unfamiliar wagon, chains binding their hands and feet. A Negro child, clutching one of the women, whimpered with his head buried against her ragged skirt. There were chains around the thin, black ankles making the boy appear even smaller.

"Well, I'll be damned," drawled a voice to her right. She swiveled, pointing the rifle at a lanky man, a mass of greasy hair framing his face, a pair of piercing, blue eyes boring into her. Looking back over his shoulder, he growled, "Your daughter, Richards?"

"Damn you, leave her alone, you son of a bitch," her father demanded.

Rivalree started at the pain and venom in his voice, but she held the rifle straight and firm and beaded on the man who eyed her with cold delight.

"Come here, li'l missy, and let me take a better look at you." The man took a step toward her.

She lifted the rifle higher, laying her head against the butt taking better aim.

"Now, you won't shoot ole Silas Guntree, would ya?" His hand stretched out as he took another step toward her.

"Stop, or I will shoot you," she whispered.

"Run, Rivalree. Go get help," her father urged.

"Shut that bastard up," Guntree snapped.

The point of her rifle darted to the other man as he pulled back the hammer of the pistol aimed at her father's head. *What do I do?* her mind screamed as indecision ripped through her. She only had one shot. The pistol leveled; she pulled the trigger of the rifle.

The explosion next to her ears made them pop, and her head whirled. The butt of the gun slammed into her shoulder. Tomorrow she would have a bruise as evidence of her actions, but the enemy crumbled to the ground in silence. At least her pa still lived.

The gun ripped through her fingers. Silas Guntree. She had forgotten about him. Her hands flew out to recapture her empty weapon, her only form of defense.

"I should have known you weren't no lady. You abolitionist trash." Guntree grabbed her by the wrists and slammed her against his heaving chest. "You got a lesson to learn. That ain't how you deal with a southern gentleman." His hands grasped her shoulder, and the flannel of her nightgown tore away. The cold air pricked at her exposed skin like sharp needles.

"Now, Richards, you watch. You watch real good," he sneered over his shoulder at her father. "This lesson is meant for you as well, you nigger-stealin' Yankee. You take what belongs to a man, and he'll take what you find precious."

Fear rolled like thunder through her insides. Her gaze flew to the rag-doll figure of her mother. Why did she lie so quiet and pale? Rivalree met the cruel, blue stare of Silas Guntree.

With the instincts of a woman, even as young and innocent as she was, she knew what he planned to do. Twisting like a captured wild hare, she squealed and tried to wrench her arms from his fingers. "No, no. Pa, help me."

The sounds of struggle coming from behind her gave her courage to continue her fight.

"Ain't no use, little girl. Silas Guntree always gets what he wants. You watchin', Richards?" With a shove he sent her crashing to the ground. Tiny sparks filled her vision as a pointed rock contacted with her skull.

No, this can't be happening to me, she thought as blackness engulfed her sending an unnatural warmth surging through her limbs.

"What a shame. She was such a promising child."

Rivalree's mind raced to the surface. She neither moved nor opened her eyes.

"I know, Amy. She was so pretty and sweet. Why would

11

anyone do this to her?"

Why did they speak of her as if she were dead?

"*Why* doesn't matter," the clipped voice answered. "She's soiled, Prudence. No man will have her now."

A cool cloth pressed against her fevered brow, and her eyelids lifted under the protection of the terry cloth.

"Nonsense, Amy. It weren't the girl's fault. Her father was a fool. Involved in the underground railroad after the law was passed making it a crime to help runaway slaves escape to Canada. If anyone should be punished, he should be."

"Cain't punish a dead man. Fool or no, he done what he felt was his moral obligation. The girl should've stayed in the house and hid under her bed."

"Just as I'm sure you would have, Amy."

"Humph," the other woman grunted. "At least I wouldn't be a woman with no future like her."

The gentle hand dabbed at Rivalree's forehead, and the cloth lifted unexpectedly. She snapped her eyes shut and made her breath remain slow and even. What did Amy Lyles mean when she said she had no future? What had happened to her?

"Ssh, Amy, I think the girl's comin' around. She's had enough tragedy in her life without your predictions of doom."

There was no sense in pretending. The two women waited for her to awaken. With a sigh, Rivalree opened her amber eyes. Prudence Bankhurst's motherly face studied her, concern creasing the broad, peasant features. Amy Lyles's countenance was drawn in a slight frown as her eyes darted around the room refusing to settle on any one item.

"How do you feel, child?" Prudence asked, her hand again descending with the damp cloth to pat at the sweat popping up unbidden on Rivalree's forehead.

"Sore and bruised," she answered as her hand wandered

12

up to the livid mark on her shoulder—the bruise from where the butt of the rifle had slammed into her tender flesh.

The rifle. Her mother and father. Rivalree sat straight up in the bed, unable to stop the moan that slipped from her lips. The man with the piercing blue eyes and the syrupy southern accent. His was a face she would never forget as long as she lived. "Ma? Pa? Where are they?"

The women exchanged reluctant looks. Amy Lyles turned her back, grumbling.

Prudence leaned over the bed and lifted Rivalree's hand in hers. "They're gone, girl. By the time our menfolk saw the fire and reached your place, it was all over. Your poor ma was blessedly out of her misery, and your pa too far gone to save. He managed to tell Mr. Bankhurst the story of what happened before he died. His last words were ones of concern for you. He sobbed as he described what that southern trash did to you and your mother."

Rivalree blinked in confusion. The woman's words were clear enough, but her emotions refused to allow her brain to understand what they meant. "Ma? Pa?" she mouthed, the sound as soft as the coo of a dove. She pushed up from the bed onto her knees. "I want to see them. Where are they?"

Prudence urged her back down on the bed. "They're buried, child. Yesterday. You've been out for two days. There was no helpin' it. We done what was necessary and decent. They're restin' side by side under the elm tree in the pasture. I remember how partial your ma was to that elm tree."

Rivalree didn't resist the pressure pushing her back against the pillow, and she closed her eyes. Her parents were dead. She would never see them again. And the man who had done this to them? What of him? Her eyes popped back open. "Silas Guntree," she murmured. "Did they hang him?"

"Who, child?"

"The man who did this to us. What happened to him?"

"Don't rightly know. The sheriff caught up with the man your father described. He claimed he was defendin' himself and his property. Your pa shot one of his men first, you know. The sheriff had to let him go as there was no one to say it happened different. Besides, he had the law on his side. Jesse done wrong hidin' them nigras. If your pa had lived he would have gone to jail."

A sour taste rose in her throat. Her pa was a good man. He was no criminal. He had done what God had directed him to do, help others in need, just as Reverend Cox had told him was his moral obligation. She clamped her lips tight. Prudence Bankhurst, for all her kindness, would never understand. How could the law be so wrong to allow a murderer to walk free while her life fell like shattered glass around her? What would she do now, alone and, as Amy Lyles had so bluntly put it, a woman without a future?

Rivalree pushed open the door of the house, so quiet and lifeless—so empty without the boom of her father's voice asking her if she'd finished her chores, so unfriendly without the chirp of the copper kettle her mother left warming throughout the day for a cup of hot sassafras tea. She sniffed the air hoping to catch a whiff of the potent smells that usually assaulted her as she walked through the door. Her shoulders sagged in disappointment. Nothing greeted her but an abandoned house. Her father's chair sat in his favorite corner of the room. Her mother's kettle perched silently on the cold stove. The pegs above the mantel hung empty. What had happened to the rifle she had taken from them that morning two weeks ago?

She glanced around the room. "Why, God?" she

demanded in anger. "Why have you done this to me?"

The silence remained unbroken except for her harsh breathing.

"What am I supposed to do now?"

If only Judd were here. He'd help her make a decision. *Judd Baker*, she thought. *How I wish you were home when I need you most.* Her head dropped in silence. He was a world away in California trying to make it rich in the gold fields so he could come back and carry her to a land of milk and honey. She smiled at the thought. That was just how he had described what their life would be like once he returned and they married. A land of milk and honey.

She had always teased him as he dreamed. A land of cows and bees. Sounded like a lot of work and pain to her. But Judd had laughed at her cynicism and promised to buy her the finest carriage with a pair of matching horses, all as golden as her hair. Then his eyes would get that faraway look as he whispered the word "gold."

The last she had heard from him was over two months ago. He and his partner were close to finding a bonanza. Yes, that was the word he had used. Maybe she would hear from him soon that he was headed home. Her pulse quickened.

If she wrote to him and explained what had happened, he might send for her, or better yet, return for her. But how could she tell him in a letter that she had been . . . ? She had trouble thinking the word rape; she would never be able to explain on paper. She wasn't even sure she had the courage to confess to his face. What would his reaction be when he did find out? If his parents were any indication, it wouldn't be good. Her mouth curved down in a frown.

Yesterday in church had been one of the worst days of her life. Most people had avoided her, their eyes cast down in an attempt not to look at her. They had treated her as if she deserved disdain. And Judd's parents. Before, they had treated her like a daughter. Yesterday, Mr. Baker had pulled his wife along as the silent sympathy had radiated from Mrs. Baker's face. But she had said nothing and averted her eyes at her husband's command.

The only person who didn't ostracize her was Prudence Bankhurst. The woman threatened her standing in the community each time she stood up for Rivalree. How could she let her problems taint the kind woman? She owed her too much.

Taking the steps two at a time, she headed upstairs to the bedrooms. She had no choice. It was time to leave Charity and go where no one knew about her past. But where? She had heard the women whispering, Amy Lyles the ringleader. They predicted she would end up in the big city leading the life of sin and corruption.

Her jaws clamped in resolution. Reaching the corridor, she opened the hall closet, took down the rawhide valise, and continued toward her room. As she passed her parents' door, she quietly reached for the handle and closed the heart-wrenching sight from her view. She couldn't look at what that room held. Not yet. The wound was too fresh.

Once in her bedroom, she tossed the bag onto the bed, still mussed the way she had left it that morning, the quilts trailing on the floor, her blouse draped over the chair, the curtain dangling from the window. *Who do I think I'm kidding?* She turned back to the bed. *I don't have anywhere to go or any means to get there, even if I wanted to leave.* If she stayed here and continued to work the farm, she could survive until she heard from Judd. But the livestock had all been lost in the fire, the precious seed her father had stored for the spring planting destroyed as well. She would never make it on her own, not here or anywhere.

She tossed herself down on the bed beside the forgotten traveling bag. *Maybe if I close my eyes, this nightmare will go away. Or if I'm lucky I'll die and go to heaven, or . . .*

"Rivalree? Rivalree Richards?" Prudence Bankhurst's voice filtered from below.

With an exaggerated sigh she rose from the bed and stepped out of the door. "Up here, Prudence. I'm upstairs."

Feet pattered up the steps. Prudence waved an envelope. "A letter for you, girl. From California. Thought you might want it right away."

Rivalree's heart skipped a beat. Judd. It had to be a letter from Judd. She raced down the hallway to take the missive from the outstretched fingers. Her hands trembled as she tore the envelope open. The neatly creased paper dropped into her palm. Shooting a glance at Prudence's encouraging face, she unfolded the pages.

"Well, child, what does he say?"

She dipped her head back down to discover a printed ticket for a ship leaving New York Harbor February 11, a little over a week away. Clutching the ticket—a miracle, her salvation—in her fist, she read the words he wrote.

Her gaze lifted, seeking approval from Prudence. "He wants me to join him in San Francisco. He says the gold is starting to come in, but it could be a while before he returns to Charity. He misses me and wants me there as his wife."

Rivalree swirled across the floorboards, her thoughts spinning faster than her feet. California and Judd. God had answered her prayers.

"You can't go out there by yourself. What is that boy thinking of? Propriety won't allow it, girl."

She finished her circling dance and faced the other woman. "There's no propriety for me now, remember? No one will care. Admit it, Prudence. For all your kindness, you'll be better off, too, if I leave. I know the abuse and ridicule you've taken on my account. I will always be in

17

your debt. There's no way I can repay you." She unstrapped the valise.

"But what about the farm? You can't walk away and leave it."

"Can't I?" She laid the few items she planned to take with her in the open bag. She would be leaving her entire life behind, everything she had cherished and loved for eighteen years. No matter. The promise of a new and better life with Judd lay ahead. Raising her chin in confidence, she tucked the letter and ticket into a side pocket of the bag. Judd loved her. He would accept her as she was. She just prayed she'd join him before news from his parents reached him with a tainted story of what had happened.

"Rivalree, what about the farm?"

Her head snapped up as she closed the valise. "I'll sell it. It's good land. There'll be those in the community who'll want to buy it."

Prudence nodded. "Including Mr. Bankhurst. Your land adjoins ours. I'll speak to him and see what we can offer you. It won't be much; God knows we aren't rich folks."

Rivalree circled the woman's shoulders, her friend, the closest thing to family she had now. "Whatever you can come up with will be fine. Pa and Ma would be pleased to know the land is in such capable hands."

Prudence drew the golden curls to her breast. Her fingers traced the dark slash of brow over the amber eyes. "You're a good girl, Rivalree. You remember that. Life will give you only what you offer it back." She cupped the firm, young chin in her hands. "You write me, you hear? Remember what your ma and pa taught you about right and wrong."

Rivalree nodded as the woman released her. *I'll remember*, she vowed inwardly. *I'll keep in mind the way people treated me when I lost everything. Most of all, I'll never forget the cruel blue eyes and the mocking southern accent of the man who took it from me. May God help any southern "gentlemen" I might meet,* she sneered in her mind. *They'll be sorry they had the misfortune of crossing my path. They will pay for the deeds of their brethren.*

She smiled sweetly at Prudence. "I'll remember," she promised.

Chapter Two

San Francisco Bay
July 15, 1851

Rivalree's shoulders lifted with a whimsical sigh as she leaned against the brass rail of the clipper. The wind whipped her honey-colored hair from the tight knot at the back of her neck under the French chip bonnet she wore. She pushed back the offending tendrils with her palm and held them plastered to her neck.

How she had survived the past five months, the only woman aboard ship, she wasn't sure, but she had. She had endured bad food, foul weather, and worst of all, the advances of the male passengers who had assumed that a woman traveling alone to California could only be one kind of female.

She glanced at the tall man standing next to her. If it hadn't been for John Masters, she would still be enduring the crass comments. The precisely dressed gentleman had boarded in Panama. As if he had sensed her plight, he had taken her under his wing, and the other passengers had ceased their harrassment.

Her gaze skittered away as his face turned toward her, so open and boyish, so like Judd's. She stared across the bay the ship entered, her hair still held back by her hand.

"The Golden Gates," she breathed in excitement. "Somehow I expected them to look more like the pearly gates of heaven."

Masters laughed, a short bark of a sound, as his dark eyes studied her profile. "More like the gates of hell, dear lady. Believe me, San Francisco is anything but heavenly."

Under lowered lashes, she cast him a doubtful look. Anything would be heavenly after five months aboard a smelly, rolling ship. She wrinkled her nose, and her free hand touched her stomach, but she kept her thoughts to herself and took in the scenery inching into view.

"Then, Mr. Masters, if it's so horrid, why do you return?"

"Because it's home," he answered with a crooked grin.

She smiled, winning her point. "Just as it will become home to me."

Shaking his head, he grunted. "We'll wait and see, Miss Richards. We'll have to wait and see. But now, I need to go below and check on my roulette wheel." He raised a dark eyebrow. "If I find one scratch on it, I'll take it out of the captain's hide. Will you be all right on your own for a few minutes?" He doffed his wideawake hat.

Rivalree nodded her assent and watched him pick his way across the deck. The roulette wheel he spoke of was one he had gone to New Orleans to purchase for his casino in San Francisco. John Masters was a gambler, a breed of man she should have nothing to do with. Yet he had been nothing but considerate. She tore her eyes from his receding figure. But a gambler, nonetheless. She shouldn't look at the man, much less think about him. She had Judd to look forward to.

Her heart began to race as she tried to picture their reunion in her mind. Judd would be standing on the docks searching for her, his brown hair tousled in that boyish way she remembered, a contagious grin on his face. What would his first words to her be? She tried to believe they would be romantic, but knowing Judd, he would more than likely make a joke—a comment about the way her bonnet sat askew on her head. Her hands flew up to check the angle. Or to tell her she had dirt on her nose. She scrubbed at the tip, erasing any smudges, real or imaginary, that might be there.

The snap of lowering sail brought her out of her reverie. She lifted her head as gray and white sea gulls discovered the ship, swooping and screeching for attention. From a distance the harbor came into view, the activity on the docks appearing like moving specks of sand. Judd would be there anticipating the ship's arrival, just as she watched the piers grow closer. The thought sent a rush of excitement through her. Raising her hand, she waved, knowing full well no one could see the movement. She could imagine Judd doing the same from the other end.

"You know, Miss Richards, no one could have possibly seen that gesture from the shore."

Her head whipped around at the sound of John Masters's voice. How foolish she felt knowing he had observed her. "Did you find your . . . cargo secure, Mr. Masters?" she asked, ignoring his comment.

"Tight as a pie-eyed drunk. I also think the double eagles I slipped into several hands will assure the wheel's safe delivery to the Veta Madre," he boasted.

Rivalree smiled, indulgence lifting the corners of her mouth. The man had given out twenty-dollar gold pieces as if they were plugged nickels. She couldn't imagine having that much money to waste. She considered the funds tucked away in the bottom of her trunk, five hundred and twenty-one dollars, the culmination of everything she owned. The five hundred was from the sale of the farm to the Bankhursts, all they could scrape together to give her; the twenty-one dollars, her parents' life savings kept hidden in a crock by the stove. It wasn't much, but she'd make it do, a dowry for her and Judd. If things were going as well as he made them sound in his last letter, the money wouldn't matter much anyway.

"Is someone waiting to meet you in San Francisco?" Masters's resonant timbre broke into her thoughts.

"Yes, in fact, someone is. My fiancé."

Masters pushed back his hat from his forehead, his boyish face considering her. "Surely you're not one of those advertised-for brides. I always pictured them sapless and plain."

"No," she explained. "Judd and I have known each other all our lives. We were promised long before he left for the goldfields. He and a partner are working a mine in the Sierras."

"Well, dear lady, if you ever find yourself in trouble look me up." He slipped a visiting card into her hand. "You'll find me here most days and nights."

"Trouble, Mr Masters? What possible trouble could there be?"

"Haven't you heard the *Miner's Prayer?*"

She shook her head.

With a chuckle he recited:

> Dear God, tonight I ask of thee
> To help me keep my sanity,
> To place my pan in waters great
> Where golden nuggets lie in wait,
> To keep my loved ones safe back east
> Until these fevers in me cease.
> But most of all I do plea
> Protect me from partner treachery.

"But Judd trusts his partner completely," she defended.

"Of course he does. They all do, and most end up victims of a mining accident the minute they strike it rich."

24

She glanced down at the ornate lettering on the card. John Masters, Proprietor, The Veta Madre, Kearny Street, Portsmouth Square. "Thank you, Mr. Masters. I'll keep what you've said in mind. You've been more than kind. I don't know how to repay you."

He pushed his hat at a rakish angle. "Come by my place," he said, mischief sparkling in his eyes. "I'm sure we can figure out something."

"Mr. Masters," she protested, raising one eyebrow at his obvious jesting. "Now you sound like all the other men aboard this ship." *He is kidding, isn't he?* Suspicion nagged at her.

He grinned disarmingly.

Of course he is, she thought.

He placed his hand over hers clutching his card. "No jokes, Miss Richards. You come see me if you find yourself in need of anything. There's always a place at one of my tables for a lovely woman like you."

Rivalree Richards working in a gambling house? How ludicrous. No respectable woman would do that. She would maintain respectability, no matter what. The man meant well with his sincere offer of help. "Thank you, sir." She tucked the card in her reticule, dismissing it as unimportant. "I'll keep what you said in mind."

She cast her eyes back across the waves of the bay, the activity she witnessed holding her in rapt attention. Her pointing finger pursued her glance. "Why are all of those boats coming toward us? Is something wrong?" A feeling of foreboding sent a chill down her spine.

Masters's look followed her direction. His distinctive chuckle washed over her. "Well, let's see. The large boat out front—that's the quarantine official. He'll board first and make sure we're not carrying the plague or something."

Rivalree frowned at the amusement in his voice. How could he joke about something so serious?

"The boat just behind him—the customs man here to get any money due him on goods the ship carries. But old Higgins is smart. He'll hold back until we've passed quarantine. The rest of the craft carry merchants mostly, each determined to reach the captain first and inspect the cargo. These are desperate times, dear lady, and those," he explained with a sweep of his hand, "are desperate men."

"I don't understand. Are supplies so short?"

Again he chuckled. "I once saw a man give a gold eagle for an egg. One single egg, mind you."

Rivalree's eyes narrowed in disbelief. "No one pays ten dollars for an egg."

"They will when they haven't seen one for a year. And the chicken that laid it, the captain got a hundred dollars for it."

She studied the humanity converging on the ship. Did money mean so little to these people? A hundred dollars for a chicken? Just how far would her money get her? She shivered, thankful she would never have to find out.

"A few of the boats carry anxious relatives and friends looking for passengers. Maybe you'll find your fiancé among them."

Her heart beat faster against her ribs, and she leaned as far over the rail as she dared. Judd. Was he among the strangers? In frustration she canvassed the blurred faces bobbing toward the ship, but the people were too far away to distinguish one from another. She straightened, yet her hands clutched the rail to keep the excitement making them tremble under a facade of calmness.

The next fifteen minutes seemed longer than the five months it had taken to reach San Francisco. Would they never reach the docking area?

John Masters's hand whipped up, and he called a name. For the hundredth time Rivalree scanned the boats moving toward the vessel. Irritated that the man standing beside her had discovered someone he knew, she tried to will Judd's face among the unfamiliar ones.

The only acknowledgment she received were several crude suggestions shouted up to her by men with hands cupped around their mouths. She ignored what they said.

As the ship neared the docks, the scream of sea gulls blended with the squeal of lowering sail and taut ropes. As the quarantine official stepped from the deck, he lifted his thumbs in a signal of approval. A roar of enthusiasm from the craft surrounding the ship drowned out the other noises.

She studied the sea of strangers boarding the ship and on the dock. Why couldn't she find Judd? The captain was soon surrounded, and, as if an auction took place, merchants shouted bids at him for his cargo.

Amid the confusion, the anchor was lowered and securing lines tossed from the ship to the shore. The gangplank soon followed. Rivalree clutched her bonnet as if it was a lifeline as the wind, plastering her skirts to her legs, whipped around her, creating a melody. Then she saw the assembling band of mismatched players beginning a marching tune on a platform at the other end of the docks. What a strange welcoming committee.

Desperation battering her insides like moths caught in a jar, she searched the crowd. What if Judd had never received her letter confirming her arrival in San Francisco? What would she do? Where would she go? Fear set in.

A hand touched her arm raised to hold her bonnet in place. "You see your intended, Miss Richards?" Masters shouted over the din of confusion.

She shook her head. "But he'll be here," she answered his question and her private anxiety.

"Don't worry, dear lady. I won't leave until you find him."

She smiled her heartfelt gratitude. Her pulse slowed to a steady rhythm. She clung to the rail.

Again her eyes touched all the faces around the ship and

27

on the dock. Tight groups of people met and hugged as friends and relatives were reunited. Others spoke in earnest dialogue, hands flying to emphasize what they said, merchants and buyers. Only one person stood alone at the bottom of the gangplank watching the people cross over. She strained forward. No. The man was not Judd. She would recognize him no matter how much he might have changed. The man searched each passing face much as she knew she was doing.

Rivalree's amber eyes collided with the startling azure of his. Never had she seen such blue eyes. Her stare skimmed over the rest of the man. His face was hidden behind a brush of unruly beard as blond as the curls on his head. His clothes looked expensive but were dirty, wrinkled from more than one day's wearing. Though torn and poorly mended at one shoulder, his shirt was made from expensive linen. *A man down and out,* she decided. *A man without a woman.*

He nodded his head at her. Tearing her eyes away from his figure, she gasped. How dare the man. She shouldn't have stared at him in the first place. He must have misunderstood her intentions. Her face reddened in embarrassment. Where was Judd? He should be here by now.

She snuck another peek at the man standing at the end of the gangplank. He still studied her. If she went down the plank, she would have to pass right by him. No telling what he would say to her. Holding her ground, she continued to search the thinning crowd. *Oh, God, please let Judd get here soon.*

With a sinking heart she knew at that moment Judd wouldn't be coming. Self-pity welled up inside her, followed closely by panic. How could Judd do this to her? Why had he forgotten to come and get her? She lowered her head into her open palms, the desire to cry out her frustrations so strong she clamped her teeth together to keep silent.

A throat cleared behind her. She startled at the unexpected sound and raised her head, her vision sliding over the place where the stranger had been standing. He was gone. She whipped her head around. The man stood behind her, his hat held in his strong, sun-baked hands. His fingers twisted the dirty felt brim adding more soot to it.

"Excuse me, ma'am," he drawled, his intonation strong with a southern accent. "Would you happen to be Miss Richards? Miss Rivalree Richards?"

The lapis lazuli irises bore into her reminding her of another set of blue eyes. The southern accent brought back memories, unwanted images of Silas Guntree and the nightmare her life had become in New Jersey. Remembering the vow she had made to herself before leaving Charity, she narrowed her eyes and set her jaw at a determined angle. "Who I am is none of your business."

With a lift of her chin, she presented her back to the southern "gentleman."

The wide-brimmed hat came to a halt in Braven Blackwood's hands. Realizing his mouth hung open, he clamped his teeth together so hard a bolt of pain shot through his jaw.

He considered his actions of the last few minutes; the respectful nod of acknowledgment he had exchanged with the woman from the bottom of the gangplank; the gentlemanly way he had removed his hat before addressing her; the mannerly words he had spoken, asking her name. There was no reason for her response, so curt and angry. He had been the perfect southern gentleman.

Damn Judd for encouraging a woman to come to California in these times. He should be here, himself, to meet this woman. Braven cursed the Fates that forced him to take his friend's place.

He cleared his throat a second time, determined to try again.

"I'm sorry, ma'am, if I've upset you, but I must know. Are you Rivalree Richards?"

The woman whirled back to face him, the color of her eyes changing from an amber to a brown flecked with gold. Fear shone in those unusual eyes, something he hadn't noticed before.

He took a step back and lifted his hands in a nonthreatening gesture.

"And what if I am? What is it to you?" she demanded, her small stature raised to its full height.

"My name's Braven Blackwood. I'm Judd Baker's partner. I'm here to meet you."

Long lashes brushed down over her eyes revealing brandy-colored pools as they lifted. The fear swimming there intensified. "Where is Judd? Why didn't he come himself?"

Braven analyzed the woman before him. So unusually pretty. Gold hair, dark brows and lashes, a pert, upturned nose, and a mouth that was beautiful even as it quivered in what—fear, anger? Probably both emotions. Her body was slim but with every necessary curve to make her desirable. Just as Judd had described her night after night, month after month, before the fire in the cabin. If anything she was more attractive than his partner had admitted. He smiled inwardly at the thought, and the grin reached his face.

Seeing her mouth lower into a frown, he tightened his lips, and the light went out of his eyes. *Damn you, Judd Baker, for being so careless. This woman needs you.*

"Perhaps we can go somewhere and talk. A cup of coffee or tea? It's a long story."

The woman swayed in obvious indecision.

"Look, if you brought a companion with you, she can

come along, too."

"A companion?" Rivalree faltered. "No, I'm alone. A restaurant, somewhere close, someplace public. I . . ."

Braven offered her his arm. Instead of accepting it, the girl turned and looked around the ship as if she sought someone.

"I thought you said you were alone."

The proud head whipped up. "I am, sir. I thought I should see to my baggage before I leave the ship."

"There'll be time for that later, after we talk," he suggested. Her baggage would never leave the ship. Once he told her Judd was dead, there would be no need for her to stay ashore. She'd return to Charity, New Jersey, to the safety of her home and friends, back to where she belonged.

Chapter Three

"The beam fell on top of him, crushing his chest. We tried. God knows we tried to save Judd," Braven paused as if seeking the right words to say, "but there was nothing we could do. I think a rib must have punctured his lung." He eyed her up and down. "And so, Miss Richards, under the circumstances, I think it would be best if you returned home."

Rivalree stared into the muddy mixture that had once been tea. Lifting the pitcher beside her hand, she poured more cream into the mug, watching the brown and white liquids intermingle. She brought the drink to her lips; the tea was cold, cold as the blood in her veins, doing nothing to erase the sour taste in her mouth or to soothe the ache at the back of her throat.

First her mother and father, and now Judd. To die in a stupid mining accident, to leave her when she most needed him.

A whimper of despair formed in her chest, and she swallowed hard to keep the sound from surfacing. Glancing up, she stared into the blue eyes of Braven Blackwood. His gaze offered sympathy, and worse, it revealed pity, an emotion she couldn't tolerate, especially from this—this southern gentleman. The thought made the taste in her mouth turn even more bitter.

The miner's prayer John Masters had recited fluttered on the edge of her consciousness, the final words echoing in her head. "Protect me from partner's treachery." She examined the man sitting before her, this man with his syrupy words and piercing eyes. Was he responsible for Judd's death? Did he stab his trusting partner in the back?

She sat the mug down and toyed with the tin spoon beside it. Go home? She almost laughed aloud. She had no home to go back to. There was nothing but her valise and the small trunk holding everything in the world she owned plus five hundred and twenty-one dollars. How long would she survive? She didn't know, but she had no choice except to try and make her way here in San Francisco.

"No, Mr. Blackwood," she answered, twisting the spoon until it lay at a precise angle to the mug. "I'll be staying here in California."

Braven gulped so loud she could hear the sound from across the table. As he coughed and choked on the hot coffee he drank, she had a moment to study him unnoticed.

The blond hair falling over his face softened his features. She wondered what he would look like without the beard.

"You can't do that," he managed to rasp out as he tried to catch his breath. "This is no place for someone like you."

The hairs on the back of her neck stiffened. "Just what do you mean by that?"

His eyes took in hers and held them. "Look. There's only one kind of woman who makes it on her own in San Francisco, in fact, anywhere in California. Unless I've misjudged you, you aren't the type."

Rivalree bristled even more at what he insinuated. "Oh, come now, Mr. Blackwood. I know there must be

34

shopkeepers and seamstresses or women who do laundry in San Francisco.''

''Of course, but they're somebody's wives or daughters.''

''But that's not fair.''

''Fair or not, that's how it is.''

She rose from her chair, and it scraped against the floor. She didn't want to hear anything this man had to say. ''Mr. Blackwood. I appreciate the information.'' What she really wanted was to cram the words down his throat. ''I will make it here in San Francisco on my own and with respectability despite what you say.''

Without giving him a chance to refute her words, she swept from the restaurant and into the street.

Rivalree stared down at what remained of her shoes. Ruined. The mud was caked on the soft leather and had oozed onto her stockings. Resting against the signpost, she lifted her head to survey the street before her. It had to be crossed just like the dozen or so behind her.

Glancing at the card in her hand, John Masters's calling card, she stepped off the wooden sidewalk, her skirts held high to keep them out of the muck. She couldn't afford to spoil her dress as well. The mire squished around her lowered foot, easing up over the shoe.

''Ugh,'' she groaned, lifting her skirts as high as she dared.

Masculine laughter and a ribald catcall from behind her did nothing to ease her discomfort. ''Men,'' she mumbled under her breath. ''They're all the same.'' She refused to lower her dress, even though her trim ankles and the beginnings of her calves showed. ''I'll not ruin this dress, even for the likes of you.''

She pushed on toward the other side of the street, the quagmire getting deeper with each step she took. Halfway across, her mistake became evident. She would never reach the other side. Her dress dragged in the slime sucking at her calves, and still she sank lower. In frustration she gathered her skirts higher and trailed them over her arm much as the ladies of old draped their trains while dancing. But this was no dance. In fact, she couldn't move at all. She was stuck in the mud in the middle of the street somewhere in godforsaken San Francisco.

Casting about, she sought assistance. The broad chest of a snorting horse bore down on her. A scream ripped through her body as she threw her hands up in defense. She would be trampled in the mud by a steed from hell. Her skirts billowed around her and settled in the mire. *Please, God*, she prayed, *let death be quick and painless*.

A viselike grip wrapped around her chest under her raised arms lifting her high in the air. Wet skirts wrapped around her equally muddy legs. Her face rested against a firm thigh, which she clutched, thankful for its presence.

As her feet brushed against solid ground, she released her hold on the leg. Lifting her chin to pour out her gratitude to her rescuer, the words stilled on her tongue.

From atop his horse Braven Blackwood stared down at her, his mouth twisted into an outrageous smirk. "Didn't anyone teach you to read in New Jersey?"

"Didn't anyone teach you enough manners not to run a a person down in the middle of the street?" Her arms fell to her sides, and in vain, she attempted to straighten her dress, ruined beyond hope. "And, yes, for your information, I read quite well."

"Then, why didn't you take note of the sign before you tried to cross this street?"

Her eyes followed to where he pointed. The signpost she had rested against before she had stepped into the road read: 'This street impassable, not even Jackassable'. She had stood next to it, but had not looked up to read its warning.

"I didn't see it," she answered in a small voice.

"Hell, you leaned against it for a good five minutes. How stupid can you get?"

"Mr. Blackwood, you needn't use such foul language around me. I didn't see the sign. However, that doesn't give you the right to trample me in the road."

"Seems to me, sugar," he answered from high in the saddle, "I saved you. For somebody who claimed she could take care of herself, you sure aren't doing very well."

Rivalree's face flushed with the heat of anger. "Believe me, Mr. Blackwood, you're no knight in shining armor. I'll manage fine without further assistance from you. Now, if you don't mind, I have a few more blocks to go before I reach Kearny Street." She turned her back on his smirking face. If he wasn't atop that cursed animal, she would slap the smug expression from his mouth.

Her ruined shoes thudded against the wooden sidewalk as she picked her way down the street. Clip-clop. The horse followed close behind. Why didn't the man leave her alone? She quickened her steps, the beast picked up speed as well.

"Miss Richards" came the dreaded voice. "Already you need my help again."

"Damn you, mister," she screeched, whirling to face his persistence. "Leave me alone."

Pushing his hat back from his face, he arched one blond eyebrow at her. "There's no need to use such foul language, ma'am," he drawled, and turned the horse in the middle of the sidewalk. "But you're going in the wrong direction. You'll never reach Kearny Street that way." He touched the sides of the steed with the heels of his worn but sturdy boots.

Rivalree glanced around. If this wasn't the way to Portsmouth Square, then which was was? She threw her worried gaze after the horse and rider, now in the street, pulling away from her. Which way should she go? She lifted Masters's card, studying it. Then her eyes skimmed over the rutted mud of the thoroughfare, and back to Braven Blackwood's retreating figure. A few more steps he would be out of earshot. "Mr. Blackwood," she called as loud as she could. *Please let him hear me.*

The big bay came to a halt; the man twisted in the saddle to stare back at her. He waited for her to speak without offering encouragement.

"Which way is it, then?"

Braven reined the horse around and urged it back in her direction. Rivalree's shoulders slumped in unprideful relief as he slid down to stand beside her.

"Depends on where you're trying to go. What address are you looking for?"

She glanced down at the card in her hand. "Portsmouth Square," she blurted. "The Veta Madre."

"John Masters's place? Why are you going there?"

Rivalree puffed to her full height. "I see no reason to explain that to you. But if you must know, Mr. Masters is a friend of mine."

His eyes narrowed in disbelief. "Did Judd know you kept company with scum like Masters?"

Rivalree let out a squeal of frustration. "Just show me the way, will you please."

Braven pointed down an unfamiliar road. "Two blocks straight and turn left. That's Kearny Street. You can't miss the Veta Madre." He lifted his hat from his head in farewell. "I'll come around to see you, darlin'. How much do you plan to charge?"

She blinked at him, not comprehending what he meant. "Charge? Charge for what?"

"Why your favors. Hold out for at least a wine glassful of dust. I do believe you're worth it." Bounding into the saddle, he took off down the street.

Damn the man for his foul thoughts. She was not a whore. Before she would resort to using her body to survive, she would die. "Go to hell, Braven Blackwood," she shouted to his retreating back, not sure if he had heard her or not.

The Veta Madre. The sign flapped in the breeze like a broken shutter. Using the edge of the sidewalk's rough boarding, Rivalree scraped as much of the mud from her shoes as she could. With her hand she managed to dislodge most of the grime from the hem of her dress, but the edges were ragged and stained.

At least her skirts covered her mud-caked legs and ankles. John Masters would probably laugh her out of his establishment, but she had no choice except to enter the swinging half doors and try to look as dignified as she could. Her shoulders lifted and straightened.

The squeak of the door hinges was so loud that all eyes in the dark room swiveled to her. Smoke swirled around her. Unused to the reek, her eyes smarted and began to water. The odor wasn't pleasant like the sweet tobacco of her father's pipe, but strong and stale, smelling as if the haze never dissipated. It took her eyes a few moments to adjust to the darkness, and she stood poised in the door feeling tattered and mousy compared to the women dressed in ribbons and lace, their hair piled ornately on their heads.

Her hands flew to her bonnet, which sat askew. These people must think her a country bumpkin. Why did she think she would fit in here?

She turned, determined to leave, when a husky but feminine voice called to her. "Where are you goin', sweetie? Decide you're too good for the likes of us?"

Rivalree halted, an angry retort forming in her mind when John Masters's barking laugh reached her ears reminding her of her goal. She had nowhere else to go.

Lifting her chin she spun to face the willowy redhead standing with arms akimbo, her chest thrust forward in the low-cut dress she wore.

"John Masters," Rivalree piped out. "I would like to see John Masters."

The woman scrutinized her, and a blush crept up her neck and face. "What would Johnny want with a little mouse like you?"

Rivalree bristled. It was one thing to think of herself as mousy, but hearing the words from the brazen woman was unacceptable.

"I'm Rivalree Richards. I think you'll find Mr. Masters and I are friends."

"Mr. Masters?" The redhead laughed. "You haven't been in town long, have you?" The woman slanted her catlike eyes.

"Not long, but long enough to . . ."

"Miss Richards?" John Masters's familiar voice came as a relief, and she shifted her attention to his approaching figure. "Carla, why didn't you let me know Miss Richards was here?"

She tore her eyes from Rivalree and gave Masters a pouty look. "I would've, Johnny. I was just screenin' her for ya."

"I bet you were, Carla." Ignoring the frilly-dressed girl, he turned toward Rivalree. "I didn't think I'd see you again. After your fiancé met you, and you left the ship—may I remind you without saying good-bye—I figured you were on your way to marital bliss. Your man looked capable of fulfilling your needs. Have your first fight so soon?"

She studied his face. Was he being snide in his remarks? *Of course not*, she answered her own question as she took in his open countenance.

"Fortunately, that was not my intended, only his business partner." Glancing around at the curious people listening to her explanation, she fell silent, not wanting to share her predicament with a roomful of strangers, especially Carla.

As if sensing her hesitation, Masters placed a hand in the small of her back. "Come, Miss Richards, let's go in my office where it's a bit more private."

With relief, she followed where he led.

Once the door was shut, cutting off the voices and music in the main room, she slumped her shoulders. Self-pity welled inside her, and she couldn't stop the small noise of frustration from slipping past her lips. Masters lowered her on a seat in front of his desk and stood next to her, rubbing the back of her neck and across her shoulders. She shouldn't allow him to touch her so intimately, but her tense muscles responded to his fingers.

"Tell me, dear lady. What can I do for you?"

The story spilled from her mouth between unbidden sobs and hiccups. She related all that had occurred in the last few months. It was easy to tell this man towering behind her, erasing the tension from her stiff shoulders. Somehow she knew he wouldn't condemn her for what had happened in New Jersey.

"And so you see," she finished, letting out a rush of air, "I can't go back. I have to make my way here in California."

"What is it you want from me? A grubstake to get started?" He crossed to his desk and opened a side drawer with a key attached to his waistcoat.

Her eyes grew large in disbelief. He was willing to give her money? Though the offer was most tempting, she couldn't accept a handout. She raised her hand in protest. "Oh, no, Mr. Masters. I don't want your charity. I'm willing to work for the money." Dear God, what had she just said? She had actually suggested she might work for a gambler in a casino.

Returning in front of her, his finger traced her uplifted chin. "Rivalree—you don't mind if I call you that, do you?"

She nodded her approval. It felt good to be familiar with someone.

"Good." He smiled. "Are you sure you know what you're saying? As one of my pretty waiter girls, it's necessary to dress the part. Are you willing to throw your modesty out the window?"

She hesitated. Was she willing to dress like Carla, her legs exposed from the calves down, her breasts offered up to the view of every customer who walked into the establishment? Did she have another choice? She could starve or swallow her pride. Charity was not something she would accept, but wouldn't her dignity suffer if she displayed herself before strangers? No. If she kept her head held high, that was how she would maintain dignity. It wasn't as if she was selling herself. She drew the line there. As long as the men didn't expect to touch her.

Masters sat before her on the desk and placed his hands in his lap. "Don't worry, Rivalree. I'll not ask you to do anything you don't want. You don't have to accept any proposition a customer offers you. They will offer them, though, and you will have to be tactful. All I ask is that you talk to them, make them feel at home, and keep the drinks rolling. Do you think you can handle that?" His question was so gentle and made the offer sound so harmless.

Could it be that hard to be friendly? She caught her bottom lip between her teeth.

"The job pays a double eagle a week, plus whatever tips you make."

Still Rivalree hesitated. The money would be enough to pay for a room and to eat sparsely.

"You drive a hard bargain, dear lady. I'll tell you what," he offered with a chuckle. "I'll throw in a room in the

42

back, and you can enjoy the daily buffet I serve my customers."

Her heart accelerated. She could save all the money she made, and, in a short time, she could have enough to move on to someplace quiet and respectable. How could she refuse his generous offer? Her mouth lifted in a smile. "All right, Mr. Masters, I'll accept your job."

"Johnny, dear lady, please call me Johnny."

That's what Carla called him. It sounded too intimate to her ears. "John," she offered. "When do I begin?"

He rose and crossed to the door. Sticking his head out, he called, "Carla get in here." Turning back, he asked, "Your luggage, is it in the front room?"

She jumped up. Her trunk and valise? How could she have forgotten them? "They're still on the ship. I . . ."

"Don't worry. I'll send someone down to retrieve them."

The redhead slipped through the door, a frown on her face.

"Carla, see to Rivalree. She's joining us. She'll start working the floor tonight. See she gets the necessary clothes, and teach her everything she needs to know."

"Everything, Johnny?" the woman offered insolently. "Are you sure I shouldn't save some instructions for you?"

Ignoring her remark, he offered Rivalree a hand up out of the chair. Carla snickered, and Masters shot her a frown over Rivalree's head. "Carla is in charge of the floor. You'll take your directions from her." He patted Rivalree's back as she stepped from the office.

She glanced at the other woman's tight face. Carla didn't like her; there was no doubt in her mind. But why? She'd done nothing to her.

As the woman led her through a door in the rear, she studied her back. There was no way around the fact, she would have to get along with Carla. She trusted John Masters. He had promised he wouldn't make her do anything she didn't want to do.

Carla turned on her once they entered the solitude of the hallway. "All right, you ignorant little bitch. These are the rules. Satisfy the customers; keep them drinking no matter what you have to do. If you don't, I'll personally see you lose your job. But the number one rule is this: keep your sweet, innocent eyes off Johnny. He's mine."

Chapter Four

Determined to cover as much of herself as possible, Rivalree tugged at the neckline of the sapphire blue satin of the dress she wore. Her gesture did no good. As the scanty neckline rose, the hemline followed, revealing more of her shapely calves. Grabbing the bodice, she jerked the gown back in place. She felt exposed, but there was no helping it.

Lifting the tray of glasses and bottles, she recalled where each drink went: the mug of beer to the tall gentleman by the faro table, the bottle of whiskey to the loner in the corner, the glass of champagne to the man winning big at the roulette wheel. She hoped she had it right.

The smiling face of the bartender offered her encouragement. "You're doing fine, kid."

The corners of her mouth curved upward in response as she stepped from the bar and headed across the room to deliver her orders.

Only a couple of hours had passed, and already her feet hurt in the high-heeled shoes she wore. She would never make it to the end of the night much less day in and day out until God knew when. The tray teetered in her hand, and she snapped her attention back to what she was doing.

"Rivalree" came the sharp call across the room. "Pick

up your feet. We have thirsty men here."

She glanced at Carla's hard face. There was no pleasing the woman. No matter how she tried, Carla demanded more. Narrowing her eyes, she shot the redhead a glare, but quickened her steps all the same. Carla could make her lose her job. She couldn't afford to let that happen. *Give yourself time,* she thought. *Things will get easier.* They couldn't get worse.

Placing the champagne before the big winner at the wheel, she skirted by him before he had a chance to comment. As long as the man gambled, his drinks were free. The man who had been by the faro table had moved, and it took her a few minutes to locate him at another table, sitting down to play. She managed to serve him before he could speak, and, with a groan of relief, she started toward the loner in the back. Hopefully he wouldn't look up before she set the whiskey in front of him.

"Hey, girlie," a man slurred, grabbing her about the waist. If she hadn't lunged for the bottle of whiskey, it would have crashed to the floor. "What does a fella have to do to get a drink around here?"

She forced a smile. "What's your pleasure, sir?"

The miner eyed her up and down and pulled a pouch from his hip pocket. He hefted it in his hand, offering it to her. "Enough, li'l darlin'?"

Rivalree ignored his offer. "More than enough for a dozen drinks, sir, but not near enough for anything else you have in mind." Oh, how she hated the propositions, the endless propositions. She dreaded dealing with each and every one of them.

The man gaffawed. "Boy, honey, you must know somethin' special about belly bumpin' I ain't never heard of. Ain't no woman worth as much as you ask. Tits and ass are all the same once you get the clothes off."

She cringed at the vulgar words as the miner walked

away, but at least he had left her alone. She continued on her way to the loner in the back of the room. On silent feet she approached, hoping not to arouse his interest.

The man's head shot up as she drew nearer. He saw her. She sat the bottle and glass on the table, given no choice but to wait as he paid her.

"Ten dollars, sir," she told him and cast her eyes to the floor. The clink of coins caught her ear as he fumbled in his pocket. Five double eagles hit her tray.

"That's for the bottle and the rest of your evening," the loner rasped.

Rivalree dumped the money back on the table and picked up one coin. "I'm not for sale, mister. I'll bring you back your change." She spun and headed toward the bar. She wouldn't be able to take this much longer. Soon she would run screaming out the front doors.

Braven ran his work-roughened hand over his shaven face, then placed his boot on the porch in front of the saloon. The Veta Madre. The mother lode. Lord, he wished gold would be this easy to find. What in the hell was he doing here? Why did he care what happened to the little snip of a girl he had left in the middle of the muddy street earlier? He must be an idiot to make sure she had found her way safely. Closing his eyes, he shook his head. He couldn't deny he owed Judd that much. The girl was a fish out of water in San Francisco; even he could see how green she was.

Decided in his action, he shouldered the swinging doors and stepped into the ill-lit gambling house. The smell of stale smoke and even staler, cheap perfume assaulted his nostrils. He blinked and waited for his eyes to adjust to the dimness.

Voices buzzed, women giggled, and the call of triumph as someone won at the gaming tables were the sounds bombarding him. A woman's high-pitched squeal as her backside was slapped brought his head around. He prayed it wasn't Rivalree. Sweet, innocent Rivalree.

A familiar figure dressed in blue satin backed toward him and away from a man sitting in a corner. Damn, she was pretty, even costumed as she was. As she turned, her cheeks glowed with rouge, and her lips looked moist and inviting from the color smeared on them. His body tightened with desire as her lush breasts pressed against the front of her gown. She didn't belong here. His brows knitted together, and he hardened his mind. She had chosen to come to this place instead of going home. He had every right to take advantage of the situation and enjoy the display she offered—he glanced around the room and noticed the look of lust on several men's faces— to him and every man who cared to look. It was his responsibility to get her out of this place no matter what he had to do or say.

With the doggedness of the desperate, Rivalree lifted her chin and continued across the room to the bar, another list of drink orders churning in her head. Carla's eyes shadowed her, disapproving, spiteful, and looking for every mistake she made. Other stares groped her, but she had become immune to them, the first step to accepting her new way of life. Someone watched her, probed her very soul, somehow different from the other lustful looks. A chill rushed down her spine. Turning her head, she sought the eyes causing the strange sensation. She didn't like the feeling of being dissected.

Rivalree groaned as her gaze locked with the azure orbs of Braven Blackwood—clean-shaven and dressed in new clothes—but there was no doubt in her mind it was he. What was he doing here? She wished he would leave her alone. Why did he have to look so handsome?

She glared back at him, hating him for all he stood for: southern heritage. If only he had been the one killed, not Judd. A single tear slid down her cheek. She dashed it away. Tears would do her no good. She had shed a river full when her parents died. No! They had been brutally murdered by a man just like Braven Blackwood.

Whirling, she tore her gaze from his glower. Maybe if she ignored him, he would go away along with the doubt nagging at her. Something about the story he had related to her describing Judd's death didn't ring true. Partner's treachery. John Masters's words resounded in her mind. Like a sharp stone in her shoe, they bit into her consciousness.

Reaching the bar, and the one person in the room who had sympathy for her, she smiled up at Dusty as he wiped moisture from the counter. "Back again so soon?" the bartender asked.

She dropped her head and repeated her drink order. A warm hand touched her bare shoulder, and she grumbled under her breath, formulating a sharp retort for the drunken miner she expected to find. She spun and choked on her words. Braven stared down at her, the scowl on his handsome face still intact.

"Miss Richards," he acknowledged with a nod. He didn't bother to remove his hat. Instead, his hand dipped into his shirt pocket. Taking out a leather pouch, he dropped it down the front of her low-cut gown. "I'd like to buy your company for the rest of the night."

Heat rushed to her face. She fumbled in her cleavage and removed the bag of gold dust. The man had his nerve. Tossing the pouch back at him, it hit his chest before plummeting to the floor. "No thank you, sir. I've had a dozen offers better than yours this evening. I'm not interested." Confronting Dusty, she ignored the look of amusement on his face.

Braven's hand reached over her shoulder and plunked

49

the pouch on her tray still sitting on the bar. "I'm sure you have received numerable offers for your invaluable time and talent, but I just want to talk, here in the bar, with plenty of witnesses. What you do after the casino closes is no concern of mine. I'm sure within no time you've built up an impressive clientele."

How dare he speak to her that way. Her hand flew back to erase the smug look she knew contorted his features.

"I wouldn't if I were you, kid." Dusty's warning sliced through her red haze as his hand stopped her flying palm. "Carla's watching. She'd love an excuse like this to fire you. The gentleman wants to talk." He nodded toward Braven. "That's the rules. If they want your company over a drink, it's your job to sit and listen. Accept his money with gratitude."

"Take his advice, Miss Richards," Braven coaxed, again lowering the gold pouch into her cleavage. He grabbed the wrist of the hand that had moments ago threatened to slap him.

Given no other choice, she followed. "Don't you dare try to make me sit in your lap," she said, eyeing several other girls draped across the knees of customers.

Braven stopped before an empty table and stretched out on one of the chairs, his leg extended. "If that's where I want you, that's where you'll sit. You're bought and paid for, remember?"

She jerked her hand from his relaxed grip and slapped the gold pouch on the table. "No, I won't," she choked. "I don't want your filthy, ill-gotten money."

He straightened in his seat with a sigh. "Sit down, Rivalree."

Her back stiff and unyielding as the wood underneath her, she complied. She would sit, but she wouldn't listen to anything he said. Nobody could force her to listen. The drumming of his fingers on the tabletop set her teeth on edge.

"You know, you won't last a week in this job if you

don't learn to relax and, at least, pretend to enjoy yourself. Your attitude doesn't do much for business. John Masters won't tolerate your behavior even if he is your friend," he quipped.

"John told me I didn't have to do anything I didn't want to do."

"John? John! Now you're on first-name basis with the son of a—? Tomorrow I imagine you'll share his bed."

Rivalree shot straight up from the chair. "Look, Mr. Blackwood, you have no right to talk to me like that."

"Sit down, Rivalree. You're drawing unwanted attention to yourself." With a nod he indicated Carla.

She dropped back into her seat, her lips drawn in a taut line.

"I'm not trying to upset you," he explained, placing both of his hands on the table before him. "I thought to give you relief. Just being a gentleman trying to protect a lady. I know how rough miners can be."

Doubtful of his intentions, she stared back. Which was worse? The blunt propositions of strangers, or the disapproval on the hard-planed face before her? She closed her eyes to escape his soul-searching gaze.

God, her feet hurt. It felt good to get off them. She slipped her toes from the tight slipper and rubbed her bare foot against the opposite leg. She groaned. There was no way she could force her swollen foot back into the shoe. What did it matter who she sat with as long as she sat? Her shoulders slumped forward, and her head drifted to cradle in her tired hands.

His fingers wrapped around her wrist. As if she had been touched by a flame, his hand seared hers. Lifting her head, she met his gaze burning into her brain.

"Give it up. Go home. You don't belong here," he urged softly.

Rivalree swallowed the self-pity scalding the back of her throat. "No," she whispered. "You don't understand. I

51

can't go back. I have no home. I can't . . ."

Her lips clamped over her betraying tongue. Her problems were her own. How could he understand about her or what she had suffered? "Take your money back and leave me alone. I don't need your help or sympathy." She rose to leave.

His grip tightened on her arm. "You'll never make it here unless you become like them." He nodded his head at the other women, laughing, drinking, catering to the men who had bought them for the evening. "They rarely go to bed alone at night, you know. You owe Judd more than that."

His words tore through her, intensifying the guilt nagging at her heart. She swayed in indecision. No. She had no choice. She must stay in San Francisco.

Braven stood, towering over her, his chest inches from her uplifted face. From inside his leather vest he drew out another pouch clinking with gold coins. He tossed it on the table before her.

She eyed the bag, her suspicion returning. What was he offering her money for now? "You expect me to take you back to my room, am I right?" she asked, her question spoken as soft as satin.

"No, Rivalree," he countered as he twisted away.

Then if he didn't want her body, what did he want? Her eyes slanted in skepticism. Was the money a bribe? "Do you honestly think I'd take your blood money?"

Braven whipped back around. Their gazes locked, doing battle. The look in his eyes turned from one of confusion to a cold, deadly stare.

She smiled, triumph shining from her eyes. He understood exactly what she insinuated, and she was right. This man had murdered Judd for his share of the mine. Her heart turned to stone in her chest. Murdering southern bastard. Not caring what the consequences of her actions were, she rose to leave the table. She wouldn't remain at the same table with the man who had murdered Judd.

Braven stepped in front of her. "Take the money. It's yours."

Her eyes narrowed in disbelief. Was this a confession of guilt?

"Take it," he continued, "and go set up somewhere respectable. It's Judd's portion of the money. Before he died he told me to give you his share of the mine. It's not much now, but enough to see you through a few months. I'll send more when we strike another vein." He moved away, guilt contorting his features.

Confused, she stared at the money bag. How much did it hold? A thousand, two thousand? No doubt more money than she had seen in a lifetime. If he gave her this much, how much more did he have stashed away for himself? Her gaze followed his retreating back. She couldn't let him think he had paid for her silence or the acceptance of the situation. Judd had spent three years of his life in the gold fields so they could marry in comfort. She couldn't let Braven Blackwood walk away with the rewards of Judd's hard work. If she did, she allowed him to destroy what was left of her life and dignity. Somehow she had to get to that mine and prove his guilt. Braven Blackwood, whose heart was as black as his name, must pay for his heinous crime.

"You killed him, didn't you?" she taunted in a loud voice across the barroom.

People turned and stared, her accusation crackling the air.

Braven heard, too. He wheeled, anger distorting his face.

"Judd worked like a slave for three years. He trusted you and you stabbed him in the back."

"Shut your ignorant mouth. You don't know what you're saying."

"Don't I? I heard about the *Miner's Prayer*. 'But most of

53

all I do plea, protect me from partner treachery'," she mocked.

"Don't press, Miss Richards. Take the money and be grateful."

"You'd like that, wouldn't you? Buy me off with a pittance to keep my mouth shut, and retain the majority of the earnings for yourself. I won't let you. You said I own half of the mine, now. Are you prepared to get rid of me, too?"

"Don't tempt me." A slight smile curved his lips. "How do you plan to prove what you say?"

"I'm going to the mine."

The smile dissolved. He gaped at her, disbelief mirrored in his eyes. "No. No way. A single woman with all those miners. You're better off here in a saloon. I won't take you." He laughed and started for the door.

"I'm not asking you to take me. The law must be interested in what you've done. I'll see that there's an investigation."

"Go ahead, Miss Richards, try. This isn't New Jersey. The law here could care less what happens high in the Sierras."

"Laugh now, Mr. Blackwood. Tomorrow will be a different story when I show up with the sheriff."

He snorted. "Just where do you think you'll find me?"

Her breath hitched in her chest. She had no idea where he was staying.

"St. Francis Hotel," he offered. "Room two-eleven. I look forward to seeing you again, tomorrow." He scooped up the bag of gold coins, her share of the profits, then tipped his hat.

"You'll pay," she swore under her breath. "You'll pay for everything you, and every other southern blackguard, has done to me." She limped back to where she had left her shoe. Tomorrow morning she would find the sheriff, as well as a means to get to the mine. *Her* mine, now. The only thing she had left of the dreams she and Judd had shared. Picking up the pouch of gold dust Braven left, she squeezed the cinched neck as if it belonged to him. She'd avenge Judd and make his murderer pay. With his life, if at all possible.

Braven studied the drink in his hand. The room was dark and sinister—the image of the man to whom it belonged. How had he gotten himself in this mess? All his twenty-five years he'd been sucked in by stray dogs and helpless females. He chuckled to himself. Rivalree Richards helpless? She was about as incapable of taking care of herself as a polecat. It was bad enough he had offered her the sack of gold coins, not Judd's share of the profits as he had told her, but all they had accumulated in six months. The worst part was that he had lied and told the little chit she owned half the mine. Judd had never had a chance to say what he wanted done with his share.

What a fool he'd been to think the girl would accept the money and leave. A fortune hunter if he'd ever seen one, and her greed glimmered like gold. She wanted to get as much as she could. Why else would she demand to go to the mine?

He slammed his fist down against the chair arm then ran his fingers through his cornsilk-colored hair. All he needed was the law detaining him from returning to the mine. He had no doubt she would stoop to accusing him of murder to get what she wanted.

Damn the little bitch. Damn the way she had stood before him, defying him, her breasts spilling forth begging to be caressed. Didn't she know how she affected him?

Where had she gotten the crazy notion he had murdered Judd? The younger man had been closer to him than a brother. They had worked side by side scraping away at the mountain to earn what little they made. When Judd died a part of his heart had gone with his friend.

He shook his head, weariness seeping into his bones. Tomorrow early he would head to the sheriff's office and explain before she got there. He didn't want the law to give her a hard time, and the man would. Good Lord, she was fresh off the boat spouting a wild story of murder. The sheriff would assume the worst about her.

If he packed up and left San Francisco tonight, he'd be better off. He'd do himself a favor if he forgot all about Rivalree Richards, but he owed Judd, including his life. His friend had seen something in the girl. Judd's dying words had been about her, making Braven swear to see she was cared for. He didn't want the responsibility of the woman, but he had promised. If nothing else in his life, he was a gentleman of his word. He wasn't sure how he would keep his pledge, but he would even if he had to marry the little baggage.

The creak of the door opening behind him brought him to his feet.

"Braven Blackwood. A pleasure to see you again."

Braven responded with stony silence as he faced the man who entered. He didn't like the bastard before him—he never had—but he was given no choice except to be here.

The figure in the shadows chuckled, a short barking sound. "Wondered when you'd come around with my third of the money."

Braven tossed a leather pouch onto the desk. "Your share, as we agreed."

"I understand we've lost our other partner. What about his share? You plan to keep it for yourself?"

Braven bristled. "We agreed to one third. That's all. What I do with Judd's share is none of your goddamn business."

The shadowy figure laughed again. "Just wondered." Weighing the pouch in his palm, the man continued.

"Not much of a profit, it seems, for a whole season of work. I'm surprised you'd dirty your gentleman's hands for such a small amount. Not holding out on me, are you, Blackwood?"

Braven's hand clenched in a ball. He'd had his fill of being accused of crooked dealing. He'd be damned if he'd take it from this scum. "Go to hell for all I care. Take it or leave it. That's all you're entitled to."

Pushing past the other man, Braven left the office and headed for the alley door determined to put an end to all his problems, especially Rivalree Richards.

Chapter Five

Rain. Bone-chilling, mist-hung rain. Rivalree glanced through the swinging doors to the street beyond. Maybe she should forget the entire affair. She cut her eyes back to the empty barroom. The only people in sight were John Masters and Carla, heads pressed close together over an accounting book, adding up the evening before's profits. Everyone else probably still slept.

"Nasty day to go shopping," Masters called from across the room.

Rivalree flinched at the unexpected words. With a quick smile she nodded, making up her mind. She must see the sheriff before Braven Blackwood had a chance to leave town. "I know," she answered, and stepped through the doors.

"Be back by eleven. I'll need you on the floor by noon."

"I'll be here." Three hours. That should be long enough to find the sheriff's office Dusty had given her directions to last night and file a complaint against the blackhearted man who had murdered Judd.

The sheriff's office was only a few blocks away, but Rivalree was soaked by the time she reached the porch steps. Slipping the cloak from her shoulders, she glanced down at her damp dress, the hem mud-stained—but that condition was expected in San Francisco.

Stepping through the front door, she entered an office cluttered with wanted posters and a tray of dirty plates. No one was there. She waited, thinking the lawman would appear. Finally losing patience, she cleared her throat and called out, "Anyone here?"

"Be with ya in a minute," came the answer from a back room.

She plumped down on a straight-back chair and waited, rehearsing in her mind what she planned to say to the sheriff.

A gray-haired man stepped from the opening in the rear and nodded. "Can I help ya?" He eyed her with curiosity as if he knew what she was about to say.

The badge pinned to the front of his shirt proclaimed him the man she sought. "Yes, please. I'd like to report a murder."

Stone-faced he asked, "A murder? When did this alleged crime take place?"

She paused to think. When had it happened? The tips of her fingers touched her temples as she tried to place an approximate date to the event. "I'm not sure. A few weeks ago, I would guess."

"If you saw the murder two weeks ago, why wouldn't you know when it happened, and why wait this long to report it?"

"I didn't see it," she explained. "I wasn't in San Francisco at the time."

"Then how do you know there was a murder?"

"The murderer told me about it," she answered, exasperated, rising from the chair.

"Are you telling me that you heard about a murder from the person who committed the crime?"

"Well, not exactly," she admitted. "He told me about the death, but I just know it was murder." The sheriff didn't move. "They were partners in a gold mine," she clarified. "I was coming out here to meet my intended, and Mr. Blackwood murdered him for his share of the gold."

The man sighed. "Look, lady," He cast her a doubtful look that she deserved the title. "Do you have any proof of what you're telling me?"

Rivalree began to shiver. How lame her story sounded even to her ears. She had no proof; she had nothing but a feeling inside her. No wonder Braven Blackwood had laughed at her last night with such cock-sureness. She eyed the man standing before her. He must believe her; he had to help her. "No," she answered in a small voice, "I have no proof. But if you would investigate what I've told you . . ."

"Look, ma'am, I'd like to help you. But I have got to have something besides the story of an hysterical woman. Where is the body?"

"At the mine, the Louisiana Mine. Judd's mail came from a place called La Porte," she informed him.

"That's out of my jurisdiction, ma'am. There's nothing I can do for you."

"But there has to be somebody who cares if a man is murdered."

"Look, lady, let it rest. Chances are there was no murder. Men skip out on their wives all the time. He's probably moved on and doesn't want you to know where he is."

"Oh, no, not Judd," she insisted, horrified.

He took her elbow and showed her to the door. "I'm sorry."

"Please, you must help me."

"Go home, ma'am."

She stood there, dazed, the familiar words—go home—ringing in her ears. The law wasn't going to do anything. He didn't care. The sheriff just wanted to be rid of her. She jerked her arm from his guiding hand. "Then, if you won't do something about it, I'll do something myself."

"Lady, if you shoot anybody, I'll toss you in the clink so

61

fast your head'll spin. Don't you do nothin' foolish," the sheriff warned.

"You'd throw me in jail and do nothing about the real villain?"

"Go home," he repeated, and gave her a final push toward the door.

"Please, there must be somebody who can help me reach the mine and get the proof you need."

"Good luck, lady. Every able-bodied man who knows these hills will have no time to escort a woman. It's pannin' season. They only have a few months before the mountains are snowbound. When the fever hits a fella, he thinks of nothing else. You ain't got a prayer in hell of findin' a guide."

Rivalree turned and flounced from the office. There had to be a way to get to that mine. She would do whatever it took to get there, including making a pact with the devil himself.

"She's gone now, Mr. Blackwood. You can come out."

Braven stepped from the back room and joined the sheriff. "Thank you for going easy on her."

"It's a good thing you came by first. With a story like that, I would have taken her for a whore with a vengeance for sure. She's lucky to have such an understandin' adversary. So what are you plannin' to do now?"

Braven smiled at the other man. "I guess I'll have to marry her so she can't testify against me, won't I?"

"Sounds to me like you're takin' on a mighty big burden."

"Perhaps. But if I leave her here she'll wind up in more trouble than she's worth."

The other man grinned. "She's a purty little thing, but I'm glad she's your problem, not mine."

"At times I wish to God it was the other way around myself."

Braven watched Rivalree pick her way from the newspaper office, a bundle under one arm. What was she up to now? At least the rain had stopped. He followed, keeping his distance. Stepping into the building she had left moments before, tenacity drove him to find out the answers to his questions no matter who he had to bribe or threaten.

The smell of drying ink and the clickity-clack of the printing press greeted him. Sizing up the little man wearing an ink-blackened apron over black trousers and an immaculate white shirt, he chose his approach.

"Yes, sir," the man offered with a smile as he wiped his stained hands on an equally spotted cloth. "What can I do for you?"

Braven took one final perusal of the man and selected his words. Directness would be the best approach with the open face before him. "The lady that was just in here, what did she want?"

The journalist seemed taken aback. "Can't rightly say that's any of your business."

"She's my wife." The words stuck in Braven's throat like a toothpick caught sideways.

The man studied him as if trying to decide what to say. He wiped his hands again and pivoted to face a small desk behind him. Picking up a piece of paper, he turned back and laid it on the counter before Braven. "She wanted to run this ad in tomorrow's paper. Paid me for a whole week in advance."

Braven's eyes skimmed the words. The advertisement announced her need for a guide into the Sierras and her willingness to pay well "for the right man." Damn her.

What a stupid thing to do. He crumpled the paper in his hand. "There'll be no need for you to run this."

"But, sir, she's paid me, and I'm obliged to print it."

"No need. The position's filled. Understand?" Braven knitted his brows together and slapped his hand on the counter.

The man nodded, shaken by the intensity of his words.

Braven revolved, determined to find Rivalree and end this ridiculous game. If she wanted to go to the mine, then, by damn, he'd take her. She'd be a hell of a lot safer in his grasp than running around San Francisco doing idiotic things like advertising for a man.

"Mister," the newspaperman called.

Braven stopped, his hand on the door.

"She also had two dozen handbills printed with the same thing on 'em."

"God damn her," he growled, never looking back at the other man. He must stop her before she distributed the fliers.

He started down the street the way he had seen her go. The first handbill hung on a post before a general store. Braven ripped it down and cast his gaze about looking for another. He discovered it across the street and down two buildings, in front of a bank. "The stupid chit!"

Around the corner he caught sight of her in front of a saloon putting up another one.

Ignoring the mud and ruts, Braven tore down the street. As she finished tacking the handbill in place and stepped back to admire her handiwork, he reached out and snatched the poster down. "Don't you ever stop to think before you do anything?"

Rivalree whirled, fury etched on her face. "Don't you realize I don't have to answer to you?"

Anger twisted his mouth as he jerked the remaining fliers from her grasp. "Don't you know what kind of men will answer an ad like this?" He shook the posters under her uplifted nose.

She grimaced. "Murderers and rapists, just like you?"

His fists balled, and he forced them to remain at his side. Never in his life had any woman stirred such fury in him. My God, he actually considered hitting her. The look of triumph on her face as her words twisted his guts was too much. One deep breath, two. *A gentleman didn't have such thoughts about a lady*, he reminded himself. *A gentleman treated a lady with respect and genteel persuasion. Damn it to hell, a lady didn't go about advertising for a man!*

Braven grabbed the crook of her elbow and started down the street, still clutching the handbills. *What in hell did you do with a woman who refuses to act like a lady?* The need to dominate her, to force her to accept his authority rose like bile in his throat.

"Let me go," she hissed, her fingernails biting into the flesh of his grip.

"Not on your life."

The Veta Madre loomed two doors away. He dragged her down the sidewalk, her small fists punching him in the ribs, the chest, anywhere they could reach, leaving stings like annoying flies. What should he do with her? He stopped before the casino. Her fist pummeled again, and he caught it in his larger hand, pressing her backward. She reminded him of a whore, hitting and scratching, demanding. Then, by damn, that was how he would treat her. His lips descended down on hers, hard and uncompromising. He swept his tongue into her mouth, plundering every hidden recess. Her clenched hand, still encompassed in his, began to shake, and he grasped it harder.

"No," she sobbed, the words muffled by the violence of his kiss.

Her softness, the acknowledgment of his superior strength, fingered its way into the red haze in his brain. His mouth curved sensuously against hers, the anger turning to need as he urged her tongue to dance with his. She complied, and her body sagged against the rock-hard plane of his, asking for support. Finding her shoulders, he sought the curve of her back, so tiny and frail beneath his strong fingers. His arms curled tighter about her, locating one soft breast, and even beneath the layers of fabric between them, he felt her nipple harden and pucker against his palm.

His lashes lifted to find her watching him as if he were the slime of the earth. He jerked back, and her eyes narrowed in contempt.

"Satisfied?" she rasped. "You may be stronger than I am, but you'll never change how I feel about you."

"Damn you for the bitch you are," he snarled, wrath returning to dominate his senses.

Reaching the Veta Madre, he shoved her through the entrance. As she landed in a sprawl on the floor, undisguised hate distorting her features, he towered over her, the swinging doors held out of his way by his powerful hand. The sunlight poured in behind him casting an aureola around him, like a blond deity above her, his anger like that of the ancient Greek gods.

"If the life of a whore is what you want, then, by damn, stay here." He whirled away.

"I'll go to that mine," she vowed through racking sobs. "You can't stop me."

He stilled the doors slapping back and forth. "Can't I?"

"I'm half owner, your legal partner now. You won't keep me away from what is mine. Judd gave it to me; you can't deny me."

Over his shoulder he studied the crumpled woman on the floor. Her chin was lifted in defiance. Even in the face of defeat she didn't give up. Damn her for the way she made him lose control.

"You can't stop me," she repeated, air rushing from her trembling body.

Pushing the doors back open, he stared long and hard at her. "There's only one way I'll let you near the Louisiana Mine." A sardonic grin creased his face. "As my wife."

Rivalree's eyelids fluttered, disbelief molding her features. "No, never. How could you even suggest it?"

"You know where I'm staying. I'm leaving in three days. If you change your mind, let me know. Otherwise, stay away from my mine." He stormed out of the casino as stunned as she that he had made such a ludicrous demand.

The bare shoulder of the brunette peeked from the sheet and shone like white alabaster. Braven studied it, dissected it, and rolled as far from it as he could. The woman's cheap perfume drifted toward him to become a permanent odor of the room.

He sighed, the anger drained from him by the act he had committed with the whore beside him, the tasteless sexual act that stirred no more excitement in him than washing his hands.

As if sensing his change of mood, the woman twisted toward him and placed one leg over his. "What's the matter, honey. I never figured once would be enough for a man like you."

Braven glanced down at the face. Beneath the layer of paint, there was nothing but a girl, no older than Rivalree.

She twisted an experienced finger in the blond fur on his chest. "You're just like the other southern men I've known. Underneath the proper clothes, the 'ma'ams,' and the gentleman's facade lurks a baser side." She rolled to her back, a laugh gurgling from her throat. "But then I prefer my men brutish."

A brute, dear God, that's exactly how he'd acted with Rivalree.

"If you want to do it again, we can. This time it'll be on me," she purred in his ear.

Braven rose, disgusted with himself, the words of a dying man ringing in his head.

"Take care of her for me, Braven. She's like a wild spirit, but she's innocent and good. Don't let the jackals of San Francisco destroy her. She'll make you a good woman, my friend."

"Judd, she's your woman. I can't take what belongs to you."

"Please, Braven, promise me. I can't die easy unless I know you'll take care of her." The boyish face twisted in pain, and he gasped for each breath he took.

"Judd, I . . ."

"Promise me, damn you. Don't let me die with this on my conscience." His hand gripped Braven's with a surprising strength.

"I swear, my friend. I'll see that either she goes back to New Jersey, or I'll make her mine."

"Thank you," Judd breathed with relief. "You two were made for each . . ." The light left his eyes, a slight smile curving his swollen lips.

"I promise, God damn you." Braven rested his head on the broken body of his partner.

"I promise you," he muttered into his hands covering his face.

"What do you promise, honey?" The whore's words shattered his thoughts.

He looked at her seeing the reality of who she was, a girl with no other way of surviving.

He remembered Rivalree's lush curves in the clinging satin, and the lusty stares she had received. How could he have ignored the hunger he'd witnessed in John Masters's eyes as he had watched her move across the room?

The rap on the door threw him into action. He wasn't expecting anyone, but the fact someone sought him out didn't surprise him. Scrambling from the bed, he reached for his pants. "Cover up, Lil," he snapped at the woman sprawled in the twisted sheets.

Prepared to face the demons of hell, he jerked the door open. Instead a young ruffian greeted him, his fist raised to pound on the wood again.

Braven's bare chest rose and fell in expectation as he eyed the boy through slit lids.

"You Mr. Blackwood?"

Braven nodded curtly, and the boy's hand darted out, a folded piece of paper offered up. He dug a few coins out of his pants pocket and exchanged them for the note in silence. Both parties satisfied, he closed the door.

Somehow he knew the message would be about Rivalree. He was right. The note read: "If Rivalree Richards means anything to you, come and get her before it's too late."

He dropped the paper unaware where it landed. Then he finished dressing as fast as he could. *Damn it*, he cursed himself. He had left her there in the clutches of the biggest jackal of them all—John Masters. The man would make his move and make it soon if he hadn't already. There was no doubt in Braven's mind she would find herself tonight in another situation she couldn't handle. Why had he let his anger get the best of him?

Once she had told him he was no knight in shining armor. Maybe not, but he would rescue her again, even if he had to do it over her sharp tongue.

A manicured hand slipped around his waist as he sat on the bed to pull on his boots. "You aren't leaving so soon, are you?"

"Sorry, Lily," he answered the brunette. "I have a damsel in distress who needs a knight."

Rivalree pulled the pins from her hair and shook her head. Her golden mane tumbled around her shoulders. It felt good to be herself again. Leaning forward, she studied her painted face in the cracked mirror. Flooded with embarrassment, she glanced away and rose from the rickety bench. The makeup was only a mask, she reminded herself. The real Rivalree was still here, just in hiding. The words Braven Blackwood had shouted at her earlier in the day still stung. *Whore* he had called her. She covered her ears trying to still the echo in her head. No, never. The man was exactly what she thought he was, a brute under the pretense of civility—the same as Silas Guntree.

Glancing around the room, hers now, she raised her head. It smelled of inexpensive perfume and—what? There was a muskiness emanating from the bed that set her nerves on edge. She could almost see the countless women, and men, who had spent endless nights there.

Stepping behind the dressing screen, the only piece of furniture of value in the room, she began unhooking the buttons on the side of her dress. She was tired. Bone-tired. But most of all she wanted to escape the nightmare her life had become. Perhaps she could dream of soft grass and the softer down of baby chicks. Maybe . . .

A pounding on her door shattered her musing. Fumbling with the buttons under her arm, she refastened them. She wasn't expecting anyone. Had some drunken miner confused her room with one of the other girls? "Yes, who is it?" she challenged.

"Rivalree? It's John Masters. Just wanted to check and make sure you're all right. First few nights are always tough no matter how seasoned you are."

Her shoulders lowered in relief. It was nice to know someone cared how she felt. Stepping to the door, she opened it enough to see the man in the shadows on the other side. "I appreciate your concern." She cast her eyes down demurely. "However, I was getting ready to retire."

John Masters grinned at her. "I know you must be hungry. You didn't touch a thing all night." He offered her his hand. "Come on, I had us a late-night fea[s] prepared."

Rivalree hesitated. His offer seemed so innocent. He ha[s] never acted anything but proper with her. "Well, all righ[t]. Just give me a minute to get into something mor[e] appropriate. I don't feel right in my working clothes. Als[o] I don't have on any shoes."

His laughter rumbled. "Your clothes are fine. And, if i[t] will make you feel more comfortable, I'll take off m[y] shoes, too. Come on, dear lady, the food will get cold if yo[u] don't."

His eyes glistened from the darkened hallway, so hones[t] looking. She could trust him. Braven Blackwood had trie[d] to scare her with his remarks about John Masters. Th[e] blackguard didn't know what he was talking abou[t]. Besides, she was starving. Offering him her fingertips, sh[e] smiled up at his boyish face.

He guided her out the door and down the hall. Sh[e] giggled in reponse to his reassuring smile as he patted he[r] hand resting in the crook of his elbow. The privacy of th[e] corridor was shattered as Carla stepped out of one of th[e] closed doors, her dress unlaced and her breasts spillin[g] from the bodice. The merriment died in Rivalree's throa[t] as the other woman glared at her then tossed her eyes o[n] Masters. "Time for a little private instructions, Johnny?[''

"Go to bed, Carla," he demanded, passing the woma[n] and urging Rivalree down the hallway.

"When the prude turns you down, you know where [I] am."

Masters ignored the redhead's remark.

"It's no use, honey. He'll tire of you and come back t[o] me. He always does," Carla shrilled.

Rivalree's back stiffened at the other woman's words[.] "What does she mean, John?"

His fingers tightened over hers. "She's just jealous, dea[r]

71

ady. She's like an alley cat. Ignore her. It's not often I invite one of my employees to dinner." He smiled down at her and squeezed her fingers. "But you're special. You're more like a friend."

His words were soothing, and she relaxed as his fingers rubbed the palm of her aching hand.

He guided her into a small but elegant room. A table was set for two, and a graceful divan faced the empty hearth.

"It's a shame it's so warm. A fire would have been so cozy," he crooned.

As the door clicked behind them, a disquieting feeling slithered down her spine. Something wasn't right.

Masters led her around the table to the sofa. "Sit, Rivalree," he said, narrowing his eyes. "I'll fix you something to drink."

Stiff and alarmed, she sat on the edge of the divan, Carla's words running through her mind. The shiver began in her knees and traveled upward. She wished she were back in her room. Better yet, she yearned for the safety of home and New Jersey.

Braven pushed the barrier of the door out of his way, then stormed past the bartender finishing up his glasses.

"Hey, mister," Dusty called. "We're closed for the night. The girls have chosen their paramours for the evening."

Braven turned, revealing his face and recognition beamed from Dusty's eyes. "Oh, yeah, you. I thought you might be back for her. She don't belong here, you know."

"I know," Braven answered. "Which way to her room?"

Dusty pointed toward a closed door in the back. "Third room to the left."

Braven didn't wait. His fist connected with the obstruction, and it moved out of his way. The dim hallway was empty except for Carla draped in a doorway, her head lowered and her shoulders shaking.

He touched her arm, and she looked up. She didn't seem surprised to see him. In fact, she appeared relieved.

"Is she with him?" Braven asked.

"End of the hall and to the right. The damn girl's so innocent I don't think she knows what he's up to."

Braven nodded his thanks and widened his steps. God, he hoped he reached her in time. If John Masters harmed one hair on her golden head, he'd kill him.

The door to the room swung open. All Braven could see of Rivalree was blue satin spread across the foot of the divan. Masters's long body covered the rest of her.

"Set the meal on the table, Enrique," came Masters's muffled voice, "and get out." The man didn't bother to look up.

"I don't think so, Masters," Braven growled. "Let her go."

Masters's head flew up level with the back of the couch, his hair mussed over his brow. "What the hell do you want?"

Braven glared at the figure in blue draped on the divan. What was wrong with her? Why didn't she resist? Had he been mistaken about her all along? He hesitated to approach her dreading the contempt he would find staring back at him.

"Get off of her, you son of a bitch."

Masters rose and shrugged his shoulders. "Gladly. I would have anyway. The dumb chit fainted."

Skirting the sofa in three strides, Braven shoved the other man away. She lay so still and pale, as if she had been frightened to death. Beads of perspiration coated the fine hairs around her temples and forehead. "What did you do to her?" he demanded, whirling on Masters.

"Nothing, I swear. All I did was try to kiss her and shove her down on the couch. When the door crashed open, she went limp. I looked down, she was out. Hell, I've had women scream and scratch, but never pass out on me."

Braven pushed the man further back. "Get out of my way." Scooping up the still figure, he cradled her against his chest and carried her out the door and down the hall, stopping long enough to gather up her few possessions strewn around the room.

Masters followed him. "What the hell do you think you're doing?"

"Just see to it her trunk is sent to the St. Francis Hotel and up to my room, two-eleven. You sorry son of a bitch, I ought to kill you."

Shouldering his way back into the hall, Braven carried his precious burden out into the dark street.

As Rivalree's cheek jostled against the hard chest, stark fear set in. John Masters. He was carrying her to his bed to . . . to . . .

"No," she screamed, slapping at the arms holding her prisoner. She wouldn't let him. She had been molested once in her life, she wouldn't let it happen again. Her palm contacted with a jaw in the dark. "Let me go," she demanded.

"Be still, sugar," a voice with a southern accent insisted.

Oh, God, her worst nightmare had caught up with her. Silas Guntree had her. How had he found her? She bucked in the restraining arms. Her hands balled, slamming over and over into solid flesh. Each grunt of pain her captor made worked like adrenaline in her veins. Her fists pummeled anything they could find.

"Damn it, Rivalree. Have you lost your mind?"

Her feet slammed against solid ground sending sparks of pain up her legs. She groaned in agony, but regardless, twisted to escape the man who held her. But where was she? How had she gotten outside and in the street? The building before her glistened. The St. Francis Hotel. The name sounded familiar. Why did it seem a haven of safety to her? She struggled against the iron grip restraining her, keeping her from escaping into the security the hotel offered.

Her abductor pulled her back against his chest and held her without compromise. "Be still, damn it. I'm not going to hurt you. I promise no one will hurt you, ever."

Torn between the comfort and the fear the words evoked, she continued to battle.

"Ssh, ssh, sugar. Everything's all right now." His arm circled around her shoulders in an attempt to soothe.

She trembled like an autumn leaf in a breeze, unsure she should relent. Her eyes followed the man's throat and watched his Adam's apple bob once before she continued to trace the line of his chin. The front door of the hotel opened and light poured out revealing the lapis lazuli blue of Braven Blackwood's eyes. Their gazes locked and held for an eternal moment. When his mouth lowered toward hers, her lips parted in anticipation of the oral contact. No, she couldn't allow him to kiss her. She stumbled backward, and he released her. "Where did you come from?" She glanced around, unsure. "Where are you taking me?"

"I'm taking you where you'll be safe. Then I'm giving you a choice. Marry me, and I'll take you to the mine, or I'm putting you back on a ship to New Jersey in the morning."

"No, you have no right." Gone was the momentary surrender she'd felt.

"Perhaps not, but you've got no other choice. Make up your mind, and make it up now!"

His eyes gave no quarter. His commanding voice brooked no defiance from her. She had no alternative except to accept his terms. But marriage to the man who had possibly murdered Judd? In her heart she knew he would do what he threatened, put her on a ship back East.

He would also continue to thwart her every attempt to reach the mine on her own. Here he was offering to take her. Once there, she could find the proof of his deception and bring this man to his knees. What better way to know what he was up to than to be with him day and night? Chances were that was the same reason he had for marrying her, a way to keep up with her.

Fine, she thought. *If that's the way you want it.* Her head nodded. "I agree." She lifted her hand in restraint. "But you have to agree to stay away from me. I want no part of . . . you."

Braven's eyes narrowed, studying her, as if trying to read her mind and draw out the horrors she held hidden there.

"Agreed, for now. As soon as your trunk gets here, you can change. We'll find a preacher." A look of fleeting triumph crossed his face.

She followed his lead into the hotel. *You haven't won yet, Braven Blackwood. I'll be a burr in your side until I can prove your guilt.*

"And do you, Rivalree Annette, take this man in holy matrimony, to honor, love, and obey, until death do you part?"

The words were so ominous. How could she vow to do those things? How could she honor, love, and obey a man who stood for all she despised? A man who had murdered?

Braven squeezed her cold hand. "Answer him," he warned, the pressure of his grip demanding compliance.

"I do," she responded. *My God, what have I agreed to?* She stared down at her hand as Braven slipped the simple gold band on her finger. How ironic that the symbol of this marriage was forged in gold. *I accept my body is soiled; there is nothing I can do about that. I was given no choice. But now, I choose to break a solemn vow before God. Never will I be a true wife to Braven Blackwood. I*

76

cannot love, honor, or obey the southern hypocrite. She glanced up at him; his gaze was hard as granite. Would he keep his vow he'd made before God to love, honor, and protect, any more than she would? He didn't look any happier about the situation than she did. Then why force her into this marriage?

"I pronounce you man and wife," the preacher thundered. "Those whom God hath joined together, let no man put asunder."

Braven's mouth descended. Shock tore through her as his lips touched hers. Turning her head, he captured her cheek wet with tears of self-condemnation. His kiss blazed a trail across her face leaving her breathless. *No,* she screamed inwardly, *I feel nothing for this man but contempt. I will not let him woo me from my goal with his suave southern charm.*

Chapter Six

The shrill of the steamer's whistle pierced through her like a needle. Once, twice, three times. With a great whoosh the mighty paddle wheel sliced into the gray water of the Sacramento River churning up plant life and debris with the force of a tornado.

Sitting on the temporary seat her battered trunk afforded her, Rivalree watched the other passengers scurry around her as the boat got underway. Off to the left her husband negotiated with the steward making arrangements for their accommodations.

Her husband. The word sat sourly on her tongue. She was no longer Rivalree Richards, but Mrs. Braven Blackwood. The words spoken over them earlier that morning had changed more than her name. She was now the wife of a man she knew nothing about and had no way of knowing if she could trust—someone she was determined to prove a murderer and a thief.

She pressed her palms against her temples, the total bewilderment of her thoughts causing her head to pound. Headed up river on the first leg of their journey, it would be several days before they reached his mine. *Their* mine, she corrected herself, forcing her body to sit up straight. That gold mine was as much hers as his.

The late-afternoon sun beat down on her, and the dry heat left her breathless. Wiping her face with the back of her hand, she wished Braven would hurry. She wanted to get out of the glare, which made her eyes squint and her head throb.

Braven glanced in her direction, an unreadable grin slashed across his face, as he continued speaking with the uniformed officer. The two men shook hands. Gold coins slipped from her husband's fingers into the steward's eager ones and objects she could only assume were the keys to their separate cabins placed back in Braven's.

Thank God. She let her rigid shoulders slump forward. She would have the privacy of her own quarters. She couldn't bear the thought of sharing a room with him, even if he was her husband. In name only, she reminded herself.

She rose as he ambled toward her, that silly, irritating grin plastered on his face. Without a word he picked up her trunk and hefted it upon his shoulder.

"Were you successful?" she asked, following him across the deck, his long strides forcing her into a run.

"You might say so," he answered, never looking back at her.

Skirting in front of him, she demanded his attention. "Just what do you mean?"

He stopped, the trunk bolstered on his broad shoulder. "I mean we managed to get a private cabin."

"One cabin?"

"One. We were lucky to get that and not have to share with a half dozen other passengers. Believe me, it cost me plenty."

"You and I are sharing quarters?"

"That's right, Mrs. Blackwood." His voice full of exasperation, he shifted the weight of the burden on his shoulder.

Blinking in disbelief, she attempted to clear her throat.

She would feel safer in a cabin filled with a dozen strangers than alone with Braven Blackwood.

"Then I'll sleep on deck," she stated matter-of-factly and turned to walk away.

"The hell you will." Grasping her elbow, he pulled her along as if she were a feather.

His grip on her arm didn't release until they reached the nondescript door of their accommodations. Dropping the trunk like a barrier behind her legs, he worked the key in the rusty lock until with a creak of protest the door sprung open.

The musty cabin wasn't what she expected. So tiny, barely room to turn around, it was crowded with a bed not nearly large enough for two, a night table, a washbasin that was cracked and chipped, and a small cabinet meant to serve as a wardrobe.

Braven managed to squeeze her trunk through the door and, by setting it up on one end, stashed it in a corner. Her gaze followed his actions. Impossible. Two people couldn't be expected to share this cabin. There was nowhere to sit except the bed. She eyed him suspiciously. He had insinuated that some cabins had as many as six occupants. He was lying; he had to be.

Braven turned, the mischievous glint still in his eyes.

"You planned this, didn't you?" she accused.

"No. But it seems to me it's the will of nature. You are my wife, you know."

"Not by choice!" Rivalree backed out of the doorway and retraced her steps. She wouldn't submit to him. He had agreed to her terms. Her feet picked up speed as she bumped and pushed her way across the crowded deck.

How dare he go back on his promise not to touch her. But was he any worse than she? She was breaking a vow, too. A solemn one she had made before God. As she walked her head hung lower and lower.

She stumbled. Glaring down at the coil of rope she had

ipped over, confusion overcame her. She glanced around
the strange surroundings discovering that a mountain
f kegs and flour sacks as high as her head caged her in.
ow how had she managed to get in here?

She turned to go back the way she'd come to find the end
f the box canyon blocked. Braven's imposing figure
eaned against a stack of kegs, his arms crossed victori-
usly on his chest, one leg stretched across the other, his
veight resting on the toe of his propped boot. But it was
he way he looked at her that unnerved her. His stare bore
hrough her, undressing her until she felt naked before
im. She placed her arms over her chest in a futile attempt
f defense.

Did he plan to take his conjugal rights here on the ship's
leck in full view of the passengers and crew? She
wallowed hard knowing if that was what he wanted to do,
he wouldn't be able to stop him.

One step back, two steps back, her feet lifted and edged
er away. Again she tripped over the same coil of rope she
ad tangled with moments before. Reaching out her
ands to steady herself, she considered her chances of
larting around his imposing figure. Didn't look promis-
ng.

Braven's hand snapped up and displayed a dangling key
winging on a bit of twine.

"Please," she rasped in utter confusion, "let me by."

His dark look melted with her plea. "Here," he scowled,
hoving the key at her, "take the damned thing. Go back to
he cabin. If anyone sleeps on deck, it'll be me."

Her eyes narrowed at him, unsure how to take his
offering. *And why not?* she thought. *I didn't make the
stupid arrangements for quarters; he did.* She stepped
orward and accepted the offered key. "Thank you."

Slipping around him, she sped toward the cabin, the
single key gripped to her bosom. Her heart lurched. One
key? She was sure she had seen at least two pressed into

Braven's hand by the steward. That meant he had a key also. So, he planned to trick her. Once she was settled in the room, he would come barging in. Her stomach rolled in indignation.

"Over my dead body," she mumbled, her sprint of escape slowing to a march of determination.

Braven downed the last of the watered whiskey in his glass, the third he'd had in the last thirty minutes while he waited. Accepting the scarred tray from the waiter, he edged his way through the dining room crowded to overflowing with dirty miners. The once elegant room was now a shambles, the rose-colored velvet curtains torn and tattered and coated with a thick layer of grime.

The only female in sight was a rotund woman who served as a barmaid, but Braven observed her, detecting her real purpose as she scouted the table where a dandified gambler sat cheating three marks with the woman's aid. As she served them drinks she signaled to her partner what cards they held in their hands. It was an old trick, one he had fallen for himself the first time he'd traveled to the gold fields.

What held his attention about the woman was the yellow flower pinned in her hair. Braven stared down at the bleak tray he held. The blossom would brighten up the plate of mundane food he was taking to Rivalree. Maybe the barmaid would sell it to him.

Crossing the hot, smelly room, he shook his head. Flowers had once been a natural part of his existence. His mother's greenhouse had sported flora from around the world, and the house, no matter what season, had been filled with the aroma and color of the many specimens. While plucking a rosebud or daisy to put in his lapel before setting out each day, he had taken her floriculture for granted.

He sighed, fingering the gold coin in his palm. Now he was willing to spend a small fortune on one sad, wilted poppy.

The woman's sharp gaze brushed him as he stepped nearer, the tray held above his head to protect it from the shoulders and elbows of the rowdy occupants in the room. He reconsidered his foolish actions. Even if Rivalree accepted the tray of food, the flower would probably go unnoticed. Yet he pressed on through the crowd. If his gesture made her see him through slightly kinder eyes, his effort would be worthwhile.

Why was her approval so important? There was more to his feelings than he wanted to admit. More than the need to keep his promise to Judd to watch out for Rivalree. Earlier she had in no uncertain terms reminded him she hadn't married him by choice. Her words still stung like angry hornets. But she was right, he had forced her hand. Why?

Bemused, he considered each of their past encounters. First, the ship docking and the hostile way she reacted to him, then later, the meeting in the muddy street. Chance hadn't brought him to her rescue. He had followed her every step from the restaurant, but he hadn't interfered until she needed his help. The spunk and fire had flashed in her eyes each time, and that intrigued him. What confused him was the way he had found her with John Masters, so frightened she had fainted, so vulnerable and helpless. Why? Her reaction went against all he knew about her nature, a fighter at heart. What had happened in her past to make her react so uncharacteristically?

A few hours ago he hadn't missed the stark fear in her eyes once she discovered they would share a cabin. He frowned and ran his fingers through his thick blond hair. He had always considered himself somewhat attractive to women, but Rivalree repulsed his very touch. In fact, she had despised him the moment she had first seen him. Why?

84

And where had she gotten the crazy notion he ha
murdered Judd? He would have given his right han
before harming the man who had been like a brother t
him. The need to gain her trust and prove his innocence t
her boiled in his gut. It was important. Why, he wasn'
sure. But it was essential.

Why? Why? Why? The multifaceted question pounde
against his temples. That damn woman was so infuri
ating. What gall to insist he keep his distance. What a foo
he had been to agree. He had a right to her, but he ha
given his word. His blood pulsated angrily in his head. I
nothing else in his life, he was a man of his word.

"Yeah, you want somethin'?"

Braven deflected the barmaid's skepticism. Remember
ing the reason he had approached her, he flipped the coi
he held onto her tray. "The poppy in your hair. I'd like t
buy it."

Her head flew back in laughter. "Are you serious
mister?" Her hand fumbled in her brassy hair. "Hell," sh
said huskily, "for that much money you can have mor
than the flower, if you want." She gave him the blossom

Braven rolled the broken stem of the flower between hi
fingers. "No. I just want the poppy."

"Suit yourself." Turning, she melted into the mass o
humanity.

The cool night breeze struck his sweating face as he lef
the crowded room. He lowered the tray and arranged the
poppy to lie across the utensils. No matter what hi
reasons in the beginning, now that he had committed
himself to this marriage, he would make it work. For
better or for worse, the preacher had pronounced. He
wouldn't give up until he broke through the barrier she
had thrown up between them. He would earn her trust and
devotion. He would prove to her he was a gentleman of
honor.

*　　　*　　　*

Rivalree's eyes flew open. The darkness swallowed her up; the only sound she could hear was the rhythm of her own heart hammering against her chest. She had no idea what had awoken her nor how long she had been asleep.

The small noise came again—the grind of a key forcing an unwilling lock. She had been right. Braven had come as she had predicted. She blinked in an attempt to see better, but the darkness remained—ungiving—severe—total.

The door scraped open. "Damn," muttered a familiar voice as he stumbled against the trunk she had shoved against the portal in a desperate attempt to keep him out. "What in the hell do you have in front of the door?"

Rivalree pushed up from her lying position onto her knees and crouched, ready to spring from the bed in self-defense. Outlined in the light pouring through the opening, Braven hesitated, a tray balanced in his hands.

She didn't say a word. In fact, she held her breath, keeping the scream threatening to burst forth trapped in her throat. She waited to see what he would do, to find out what he wanted, as if she didn't already know. The moment she dreaded had arrived.

"Damn it all, woman, are you in here?"

She refused to answer.

A match flared, throwing an eerie light across the bed as it touched the wick of the lone candle in the room. She squinted as her hand came up to shade her eyes.

He lowered his burden and stared at her, up and down, then he turned and sat the tray on the night table close to where she huddled on the bed. "You look like a scared kitten with your back all hunched up that way." The candlelight caught the humor glinting in his eyes.

A scared kitten! How dare he compare her to a small helpless animal. "Perhaps, sir. But you'll find out just how sharp this kitten's claws are if you come one step closer."

"It's not your claws or your sharp tongue I'm looking to

provoke. It would be much more amusing to see you pu[n]
under my most ardent tutelage."

Braven lowered his body on the edge of the bed and gav[e]
the door a light push with this foot. The barrier close[d]
with a click sounding like thunderous doom to her ears.
He leaned closer, as if he dared her to follow through with
her threat, and studied her with an intensity sending [a]
blush from her toes to her ears. Why did he have to look a[t]
her that way, as though he wished to devour her? Or was i[t]
only the effect of the dancing candlelight? Why did he[r]
body tingle wherever his gaze touched, almost as if sh[e]
wanted him to follow through with his cocksure challeng[e]
that he could make her respond to his touch?

She slipped back on her haunches, freeing her hands t[o]
rise to her defense, unsure whom she needed protectio[n]
from, him or herself. With a conscious effort sh[e]
straightened her back remembering his cutting remar[k]
about how she looked. The movement thrust her rounde[d]
breasts forward. There was no doubt in her mind that h[e]
thought she flouted defiance of his words as his eye[s]
dipped down to take in their gentle swells.

"What do you want?" The words squeaked by dry lips i[n]
an attempt to break his concentrated stare. Her tongu[e]
darted out to moisten them. She might look like a scare[d]
kitten, but he reminded her of a starved tomcat after a long
lonely winter.

His eyes flicked away. "Nothing, at the moment[.]
Instead, I brought you something." He pulled a checkere[d]
cloth from the tray bulging with delicious sights an[d]
smells. His eyes touched hers and the lust she had swor[n]
she had seen seconds before was gone. "I thought yo[u]
might be hungry."

Her mouth watered; her empty stomach flipped i[n]
complaint. She hadn't eaten since early that morning. Th[e]
hunger assaulting her was undeniable, but the fear of th[e]
man who offered her food was just as strong. What did h[e]

want in payment?

"No, thank you," she whispered, her stomach growling in protest to her words.

As he rose, her heart jumped to her throat. His eyes locked with her, a fleeting look of exoneration crossing his face. He spun and stepped over the trunk, the ridiculous barrier she had thought might stop him. Opening the door, he faced her. "Then I'll leave the tray while you and your stomach make up your mind."

Her mouth tightened.

"You know, Rivalree. One day you're going to have to trust me. I'm a tolerant man, but eventually my patience will wear thin. Eat. You'll need your strength for the next few weeks if you plan on fighting me the entire way to the Louisiana Mine." The door closed with a click leaving her alone and confused.

Her eyes flew down to the ladened tray, and a wilted, yellow flower stared back at her. She blinked in surprise. Where had he gotten it?

She plucked the blossom up and twirled the stem as she studied the closed door. What kind of man was Braven Blackwood? Was he sincere or trying to get her to lower her guard? She would watch and wait and stay alert. The next move would be his.

Ow-weeeee. Ow-weeeee. The boat's whistle shrilled. The floor beneath Rivalree's bed shuddered as the mighty side paddle changed direction, slowing the protesting steamer down. Her eyes flew open. The morning sun peeked through the tiny porthole above her bed, casting a beam of light alive with dancing dust particles.

She raised to a sitting position. Good Lord, what time was it? Not much past dawn. She fisted her eyes to erase the haze of sleep from them. The floor shuddered again, and the paddle wheel groaned as it came to a halt. They must have reached their destination.

The thought sent blood coursing through her body, and she scurried from the sheets. At last she could escape the confines of this horrid cabin. Anything was better than being in here, alone and isolated. Not once had she seen Braven. The only evidence he existed were the trays of food that had unfailingly arrived at each mealtime. The man was a perfect gentleman, but his undying courtesy stuck in her throat. John Masters had been polite, but look what trusting him had brought her to. She wished Braven would show his hand, then she could be as certain about him.

The knock on the door captured her attention as she finished buttoning up the front of the clean dress she had donned. Her hair that fell to her hips in natural, golden waves was still uncoifed, but brushed. She coiled it on top of her head and stabbed two hairpins in the thick knot to keep it there until she put on her bonnet.

"Miz Blackwood?" called an unfamiliar voice.

It took her a moment to realize the person spoke to her. "Yes, I'll be right there," she answered.

The face greeting her as she cracked the door was just as unknown as the voice. The boy stared back as if she were something to behold, his eyes wide drinking in every detail about her he could see, which wasn't much. "Yes, ma'am. I got a message for ya from Mr. Blackwood. He says you're to hurry up and join him at the boarding plank."

"But what about my trunk?"

The boy's eyes brightened. "Not to worry, ma'am. I'll see to your luggage.

"It's awfully heavy for such a small boy," she warned.

He grinned his confident appreciation. "I'm to guard it until the steward sees to its removal."

She hesitated. Everything she owned in the world was in that trunk, including the money she had brought with her from back East. Her eyes flicked over the slim figure, assessing his worthiness.

"Mr. Blackwood also said to tell you if you didn't hurry, he'll leave without ya," he added, embarrassment shading his face.

No doubt about it, the boy was here at Braven's orders. Only her husband would send such a curt message. She pushed the door open all the way and, grabbing her bonnet, crushed it on her head. As she tied the dangling ribbons in a bow under her chin, each movement she made announced the anger boiling inside her. How dare he threaten her with abandonment. She was tempted to stall to let him cool his heels and learn he didn't control her life. However, if he did leave without her, what would she do? She wasn't even sure what town they were in.

With a stately grace she left the room, strolling with a slowness betraying no alarm. Braven Blackwood could wait a few moments. What was his rush anyway?

A strange feeling assaulted her as she navigated the crowded deck. People stared at her, or was it only her imagination? Her hand fingered the front of her dress making sure the buttons were secured as her gaze touched her hem to check if it lay evenly. Everything was in order. She wasn't mistaken, the other passengers and crew, all male, did eye her oddly.

With relief she caught sight of Braven's imposing figure standing at the boarding plank. One booted foot rested high on the bottom rung of the railing as he leaned his arm across his upraised knee, his hand drumming his thigh with impatience. He stared out over the city never once checking for her arrival, so sure of himself and the fact she would come at his command. Damn him. Why didn't he look at her?

As if he sensed her presence, he lowered his foot and whirled to confront her. "Took you long enough." He reached for her elbow as he guided her down the gangplank.

"Think so? Then next time I'll see to it I take longer, just for your benefit," she answered sweetly.

His fingers clamped her arm so tightly it hurt.

"Well, I'll be damned," called a voice from behind them. "She *is* real."

On the dock Braven turned to confront the speaker.

"You know, there was a bet going on that this little lady didn't exist. She sure is a pretty little filly, Blackwood." The man grinned and doffed his battered hat. "'Scuse me, ma'am, but your presence cost me twenty dollars." He glanced back at Braven. "We all figured that cabin was full of polecats the way you avoided it, man."

Braven stiffened beside her. "She's no filly, Sawyer. She's my wife, and don't you forget it." He whipped her about face and continued down the dock, pulling her at a neck-breaking speed.

She planted her heels and jerked her elbow from his grip.

"Now what the hell," he groaned in exasperation.

"What was that man talking about back there?" she demanded.

His eyes traveled the length of her. She wished he'd look in some other direction. "Why, can't you guess? No one believed I had my new wife stashed in that cabin. What man in his right mind would sleep on the deck instead of with his bride? They figured I was lying and the room held a newfangled gold-panning invention. Either that or you were ugly as sin, and I was too embarrassed to let you out."

"That's why everyone stared at me?"

"Wives are a rare commodity around here. Why, one fella swore I had an elephant hidden in there."

"An elephant? Good Lord, why an elephant?"

"The saying goes, when a man sees the elephant he's ready to quit the gold fields and go home. This fella figured I was taking an elephant back to the hills to get rid of the competition."

Laughter burst from her compressed lips. He grinned back as they shared the hilarity of the situation, the first time they had cooperated in anything. Then her eyes narrowed in suspicion. "You're teasing me."

"Am I, sugar?" He raised one eyebrow high in self-defense. "Perhaps so," he confessed as he reached for her elbow and continued their march down the main street.

"Where are we?"

"Sacramento."

"Are we close to the mine, now?"

"Hardly. As close as an elephant is to a jackass . . ." He cut his words short. "No, we're a long ways away yet."

"Then why are we rushing?"

"Doesn't your mouth ever stop? If we don't hurry, we'll never get a seat on the Marysville stagecoach, which only runs once a week."

"But what about my trunk?" She stumbled as he pulled her along.

He stopped, issuing a deep sigh as he helped her straighten up. "Look. Once we have our tickets, I'll gladly answer all your questions. Right now, concentrate on keeping up with me," he said with pointed politeness.

She clamped her mouth tight. He could go to the devil if he thought she'd ask him one more question. Damn him for his stupid courtesy. Why did he have to be her only means of survival in this insane, gold-crazed world?

Chapter Seven

Rivalree thought her insides would be jarred loose as the crowded Concorde bucked and swayed its way out of town. She laid her head back against the cracked leather seat and tried to concentrate on anything but the motion beneath her and the five other bodies pressing against her in the confines of the vehicle.

What a madhouse Sacramento had been. By the time Braven had dragged her to the ticket office, sweat rolled down her face and her feet hurt. But the nightmare had only begun. The ticket office had been a swarm of humanity as experienced miners fought tenderfoots for the limited spaces on the stage to Marysville. Six inside and ten on top.

"Damn it," Braven muttered under his breath as he left her under the thin shade of a scraggly tree. "Stay here and go along with whatever I say." His stare forced her submission. "Understand?"

She nodded dumbly as she leaned in relief against the rough bark of the twisted oak and lifted one foot to rub the blister on her heel. She didn't care what he did as long as she could rest.

He edged forward, taking the steps up on the porch of the building and pushed his felt hat back revealing a red band mark across his forehead. Smiling, he spoke to several of the men and turned to gesture toward her, blowing her a kiss.

Dumbstruck, she smiled in return. What *was* he up to?

Slowly the crowd parted as he spoke to individuals, and, within minutes, Braven stood at the front of the line. Again, he turned and waved, giving her a big smile.

How had he managed that? What did he say to those men?

The throng, all male, set up a clamor as the ticket seller opened the window and began to disperse tickets. Braven waved two above the heads of the miners as he pushed his way back to her.

He placed his hand on her arm as he whispered in her ear. "Just do as I say. Smile and be polite. They're expecting it."

"Who's expecting it?" She glanced at him in bewilderment.

The ticket agent held up his hands and shouted, "Sorry, folks, we're all sold out until next week. We open at eight, but I'd advise you to be here by six if you want a chance at a seat."

The crowd of disappointed men seemed to turn in unison to stare at her. Again that feeling she was some kind of freak.

"Keep smiling, Rivalree," Braven whispered in her ear. "All they want is to see you, talk to you, and get your blessing for luck in the gold fields."

"My blessing . . .?" she gasped loudly.

"But, of course," he answered in a booming voice. "I told them how your father was a healing preacher and a good-luck charm to his congregation. Don't be embarrassed, sugar." He clutched her arm. "You know how the gift was passed down to you from your father."

Humiliation crowded her thoughts. The man was impossible. What an absurd story. "My father . . ." she

94

began through clenched teeth.

". . . was a generous man, just as you are, my dear wife."
He tipped his hat to the surging crowd. "Be gracious,
Rivalree," he again hissed into her ear. "They'll tear us
apart if you give our little charade away."

How had she managed to get into this situation? Her
eyes slid to the tall, blond man beside her. A thief, a
murderer, and a liar to boot. She'd get even with him for
this one.

And get even she would. She winced as the coach hit a
hard rut in the road nearly tossing her into the lap of the
man across from her. The man's burly arms encircled her
and lifted her back into her seat.

"Sorry," she mumbled.

"No problem, ma'am. It's an honor to help someone
like you. Just give me your blessin', and I'll be repaid.
Ain't every day a man like me gets to do somethin' for the
Sierra Angel."

"Who?"

"Why, the Sierra Angel. That's you, ma'am."

Braven Blackwood and his wild story again. Rivalree
sighed and clenched her fists hidden in her skirts. If only
he was in this carriage with her, instead of on the top, she'd
give him a piece of her mind. Sierra Angel. The blessing
bestower to miners. Where had he come up with that
name?

She smiled wearily at the miner, and he gave her a
gapped-tooth grin in return. "You know, ma'am, you sort
of remind me of my Lily." Sadness shaded his features.

"Is that your wife?"

"My wife? Oh no, Bessie died givin' birth to Lily."

"Then she's your daughter."

"I should've left her in Indiana, but I was a fool and let
her badger me into bringin' her along."

"If you brought her to California, where is she now?"

"Back in San Francisco. I left her in the care of a family

there in forty-nine. Didn't see her for nearly three years. First she took a job as one of them pretty waiter girls. Said she just wanted the money to go home. She didn't like it here. I didn't have enough to even get back to the city much less to send her home. I wrote her a letter beggin' her not to take the job, I'd give her the money the minute I struck it rich."

The big man edged his shoulders forward into a hunch. "Didn't never strike it big. Last time I seen her, just a few weeks ago, she had a crib on the Barbary Coast on Pacific Street." He made a defeated sound that almost was a laugh. "Terrific Street the boys call it. She told me to go away and leave her be. She didn't need a loser like me hangin' around."

The impact of the man's story struck her full in the face. She had been headed down the same path as his Lily. If it hadn't been for Braven Blackwood's persistence . . . Rivalree hung her head. She owed him so much. He didn't have to tell her Judd had left his part of the mine to her. Instead, he could have walked away and left her at the Veta Madre. But he hadn't.

She reached over and patted the big man's laced fingers. "You'll make it big this time. I just know it. Then you can go back, get your Lily and take her home."

The big man's eyes lit up. "Why thank ya, ma'am. With your blessin' I know it will happen this time. Please bless my Lily, too, if you will."

She nodded silently. Was it so wrong? She had given the big man hope and sympathy when there was nothing else to offer. Smiling, she thought of Braven spinning his story on the steps of the ticket office. The Sierra Angel. He had done what he must to get them tickets and, at the same time, given those men a boost. Her eyes glanced up at the ceiling of the swaying coach, and she pictured him sitting on top. Maybe she was wrong about him. Perhaps he had told her the truth about Judd's death. It was an accident.

96

But that would mean that she would have to admit she had entered this marriage for all the wrong reasons. She prayed she hadn't made a mistake that would ruin both of their lives.

Braven sat relaxed, swaying with the rhythm of the coach. He couldn't count the number of times he had ridden on the stage from Sacramento to Marysville in the last few years. He probably should have joined Rivalree inside the vehicle, but he had no desire to crouch in the stuffy confines and bear the brunt of her insolent glare. He rationalized his actions as a means of avoiding an unpleasant scene in public, as a gentleman didn't bicker with a lady in a crowd.

Remembering the look of surprise on Rivalree's face as he handed her into the stage and had stepped back, for a moment he had thought he had seen regret in her eyes. Was she beginning to depend on him? Then the regret had turned to the familiar look of distrust as he had tipped his hat and closed the door.

He studied the rolling foothills of the Sierras as the horses labored under the heavy-handed whip of the driver. The land was gentle and clean, like a soft, emerald carpet, a place of immense beauty, so much more appealing than the overpowering green growing on the flat river land of home.

Home, he thought. *Now, why would I think about there?* It had been ages since he had reminisced about Louisiana and his family. He wondered what they would think about his new wife. Would they see the beauty and spirit he saw in Rivalree? How could they not? She was everything he had searched for in a woman—brave, proud, and willing to fight for what she believed in; not like the simpering girls of the South. He guessed he should be fair. It wasn't their fault he found them boring. Society dictated their behavior. Southern belles didn't know there was any other way to be. Social balls and gowns were the only things they seemed to think about.

And the way of life itself. The masters reaped the benefits of the laboring slaves. Even as a child, he had known something was wrong with the system—one too easily taken advantage of by the greedy and the lazy. He'd have no part of it. He'd earned what he got by his own sweat and work, not the life blood of another individual, man, woman, or child, something his father and older brother Brent just couldn't understand. They were not cruel by the standards of the day, but they couldn't understand what was wrong with one man owning another and treating him like prize stock.

Braven smiled to himself. He would never forget the day he had given Carter, his playmate and friend from birth, his freedom. His father had turned the Negro's papers over to Braven as a ten-year birthday gift telling him this was his start to success, his first slave. Without hesitation, Braven had signed the papers over to the other boy and declared him emancipated. His father had been furious. In fact, he could still feel the sting of his razor strop against his backside, but he had refused to relent. Carter had remained free, and Braven had shared his allowance with his friend until they had parted ways eight years ago, each seeking to make his fortune. He smiled broader as he thought about Carter, clutching his freedom papers and heading North. He wondered if his friend had made it.

With a teeth-jarring thud the wheel under Braven hit a a pothole nearly throwing him from the moving vehicle. The man beside him grabbed his arm. "Better pay mind, mister, if you don't want to lose your seat."

Braven nodded his gratitude. "Yeah, I guess I was daydreaming."

The man grinned back. "Maybe you should have taken that seat inside with your pretty little lady."

"No, I don't like the closeness in there."

"I know what you mean."

Braven returned to his musing, this time with one eye cocked on the road ahead. Remembering how soft and vulnerable Rivalree looked early in the mornings when he had quietly entered the riverboat cabin to leave her a tray of food, his heart contracted in his chest. Then he pictured the determination in her eyes at the ticket office as the miners had surged around her. Sierra Angel. The name fit her well. It would give her a stigma of saintliness in this wild country where decent women were rarer than polar bears. Just as important, his scheme had gotten them tickets on the morning stage. The hotels in Sacramento were places of horror. He hadn't wanted to subject her to them.

With luck they would reach Marysville in plenty of time to gather up the wagon and prearranged supplies. Marysville hostelries made Sacramento look heavenly. They could stop for the night once they were on the trail. At last he would be alone with his wife.

As the coach jerked again, Braven snapped his attention to the road ahead. From here on, the trail was steep and rough. He'd need his full wits about him to maintain his balance.

Hoping they would rest for the night before catching the next stagecoach, Rivalree trudged behind Braven through the dusty streets of Marysville. She had never seen such a raw, thrown-together place in her life. Most of the buildings were mere shacks constructed of whatever the builders could find, crates, wagons, and local timber. None of the material had been used with an eye to aesthetics. Several of the buildings were nothing more than tents with lean-tos attached to the rear and, perhaps, a false, wooden front. She had lived her entire life appreciating handmade items from furniture to table-ware, but she was unprepared for the disregard in which Marysville had been tossed together as if the citizens didn't expect the town to survive overnight. How could people live so temporarily?

Braven's steps led them down the main street and then through a crooked alley to a side entrance of one building. Expecting the inside of the establishment to equal the shabby outside, she expressed delight as they entered the rough plank door. The contents of the store were organized, nary a speck of dust in sight. The merchandise was neatly displayed on shelves and in bins. Rolls of beautiful material were wrinkle-free, and to Rivalree's amazement, the current issues of *Harper's Magazine* and *Godey's Lady's Book* completed the picturesque scene. The mercantile was nicer than anything she had seen in Charity, New Jersey.

"Braven? Braven Blackwood?" called a man from across the room, rising from a ledger and tucking a pencil stub behind his ear. "Been expecting you the last few days." The man, obviously the proprietor of the store, stuck out his hand in greeting, and Braven pumped it eagerly. "Just get in on the Sacramento stage?" His gaze flicked over Rivalree, and a warm smile parted his lips. Then, he turned and called through an open door. "Janet. Janet, come out here. Braven Blackwood's back, and he appears to have brought a surprise."

A tall, angular woman stepped from the back room, wiping her hands on a stiff, white apron, a sincere smile of greeting on her face. "Why, Mr. Blackwood, so good to see ya'll again," she offered in a soft, southern slur. Her gaze slid to Rivalree, a look of hunger on her attractive face. "And who might this be?"

Braven laughed. "Why, Janet Longstreet, who would I bring with me but my wife. Rivalree, meet one of the finest ladies in all of California."

"Your wife," Janet squealed. "Confirmed bachelor of all times, Braven Blackwood, with a wife?" She slipped her hand into Rivalree's and began leading her away. "You must tell me how you managed such a mighty coup."

"You can't have her long, Miz Janet. I want to leave town as soon as the wagon is loaded," Braven warned.

"That's enough time for a pot of tea and a decent conversation." She gave Rivalree a conspiratorial wink. "You don't know how long it's been since I've talked to another woman. They're far and few between in these parts."

Graciously Rivalree smiled.

"Where are you from, my dear?" Janet asked.

"Back East. New Jersey."

"New Jersey!" Janet tittered. "Now how did a Yankee end up with a dyed-in-the-wool southerner like Braven Blackwood?"

The woman led her through the door to her private quarters. Rivalree wished to avoid the question, as she wasn't sure how to explain the complicated circumstances that had brought about her marriage to Braven.

Janet didn't give her a chance to answer. She indicated a ladder-back chair at the round, oak table in the tiny kitchen as she turned to start a pot of water on the stove. As she stoked the ashes and added a couple chunks of wood, she began chattering again.

"You know, Rivalree—my, what an unusual name— I've known Braven Blackwood all my life. I guess I should say I've known *of* him all my life." She sat the kettle over the rejuvenated flame. "Everybody in Shreveport knows who the Blackwoods of Blackhaven in Bentley are." She turned and gave Rivalree a knowing nod. "That's in Louisiana, you know." She returned to her work.

Rivalree nodded in bewilderment at the speed at which the woman spoke. She never paused to take a breath.

"Do you know him well?" Janet spun to face her, and her speech came to a sudden halt.

Rivalree's lids fluttered, taken by surprise. The woman waited for an answer. "No. I met him not long ago in San Francisco. I was there to meet my fiancé and . . ."

"And you married Braven instead? How romantic and exciting. I imagine Braven must have just swept you off your feet."

"Well, not quite . . ."

"You know, my dear, he's quite a catch. Even if he doesn't make it in the gold fields, he has his family plantation and money to go home to." Janet swirled, the pot of steeped tea in her hands, and sat two delicate china cups on the table.

What was the woman saying? Braven didn't need the money from the mine. Then why would he murder Judd? Revelation hit her stomach with a sickening thump. He would have no reason. Oh, my God, what had she done?

The other woman lowered herself into the chair opposite Rivalree and stopped to finally catch her breath. "But regardless of all that, he's a good man, an honorable man. Why I do believe I would trust my virgin little sister in his care." She giggled. "But I'm sure ya'll know his nature." She leaned forward on propped elbows. "What I really want is all the news from back East, and don't you dare leave out a thing." She waited expectantly.

Rivalree's head spun with all the information she had acquired in the last few moments. She had been wrong, so very wrong, about Braven. She glanced up at Janet's questioning eyes. "I'm sorry," she offered lamely. "I'm afraid I'm not that knowledgeable . . ."

"Is it true," Janet interrupted. "Are women really wearing those outrageous underpants introduced by Amelia Bloomer. I've seen pictures of them in *Godey's.*"

Rivalree sighed. It would be a long afternoon. Janet chatted on unaware she had lost her audience. The woman

102

would trust her virgin baby sister with Braven. In her heart she knew he was all he professed to be, an honorable man, a man to be trusted, a man who deserved better than a woman with a tainted background.

She was the one who deserved contempt. She had married him under false pretenses with revenge on her mind. How would she explain her sordid past to him? Would he be angry and disgusted and walk away from her? She admitted his reaction was vital to her, more important than anything else in her life.

Her chin lifted. She must tell him about her past before this marriage went a step further. But how? How could she confess that she was not the innocent wife he expected?

Braven clucked his tongue at the team, and the wagon picked up speed with a jerk. The late-afternoon sun skimmed the tops of the mountains, shooting vibrant beams across the clouding sky. Darkness came early in the foothills of the Sierras where the mountains pointed like long fingers at the vast blueness.

The canvas-covered wagon overflowed with supplies of every nature, enough to feed an army through a long siege. In fact, he carried provisions for several others, as well as for his camp.

The horses fell into a jaunty rhythm on the familiar road, and Braven fingered the reins resting on his knee as he leaned back against the seat and turned his attention to the woman beside him. "I hope Janet didn't talk your ear off," he said with a grin, hoping to put Rivalree at ease. "That's one woman I imagine must talk in her sleep. I don't know how George Longstreet tolerates it."

Rivalree smiled back knowingly. "She is rather long-winded, but I think she means well. How did her husband get an opportunity to propose? She doesn't give a person a chance to say a word."

He chuckled. "Mail-order bride. She was a pig in a poke. George didn't know about her nonstop mouth until she got here."

"She said she's a longtime acquaintance of yours, from before California."

Braven shot her a surprised glance. Was there a touch of jealousy in her voice or just curiosity? "Can't say I knew her. We happen to come from the same part of the country, that's all."

"Oh." She laced her fingers together. "She seems to regard you highly." She looked at him from the corner of her eye. "In fact, she said she'd trust her little sister to your care. She thinks a lot of your integrity."

Braven tossed his head back as laughter spilled from his mouth. "She does, does she?"

"That's what she said." Her gaze dropped back to her lap. "I think she's right. I feel safe in your care." Her fingers plucked at the fabric of her skirt.

Was Rivalree coming to accept him? He watched her fingers pick at the threads of her dress. Aware of the difficulty she had saying those words to him, he reached out with his free hand, closing his fingers around hers to still them. "I do believe that's the nicest thing you've said about me since we've met."

When she refused to look at him, he turned his attention to the team and gave them a nudge with the reins to keep their pace even.

"You know, Braven, I owe you an explanation for the way I've acted."

Braven. She had called him Braven. Not Mr. Blackwood or sir or some other formal form of address, but Braven. He liked the way her mouth formed his name and the way the air rushed from her lungs as the word tripped over her tongue. "If this is an apology," he said, hoping to make her speech easier for her, "then apology accepted."

Her eyes clouded in an emotion he couldn't quite

104

decipher. Pain, fear, or perhaps dread? She had more to say, he knew, and he offered her encouragement with his gaze to continue.

"There are many things in my past you know nothing about," she said softly.

Braven slipped his arm around her, offering reassurance. Relief flowed through him when she didn't resist. "That's true about both of us. But we have time, time to learn all we need to know about each other."

He watched her, waiting for her to return his look, but she didn't. He wondered what she had to say that made her act uncharacteristically shy.

Her hands began their kneading of her skirt again. "I grew up in a community so different than yours. I never saw a black person until I was ten. My father was a conductor for the underground railroad." At last she glanced up at him, her eyes seeking signs of disapproval.

Braven's brow twitched in surprise, but he said nothing.

"Before I heard from Judd, asking me to join him . . ."

Her bottom lip quivered slightly. She was near to tears. His eyes misted with compassion for the struggle going on inside her.

She lifted her chin. "We had runaways hidden in the barn," she continued stiffly. "When the slave hunters came . . ." She swallowed hard. "They killed my mother and father and destroyed the farm. I . . ."

He tugged her closer into the protection of his shoulder. "Jesus Christ, Rivalree. Is this what the problem's all about?" He pulled the horses to a stop and turned in the seat giving her his full attention. "I don't care what your political views are on slavery." He tucked her head under his chin. "Slave hunters are the scum of the earth." Warm, silent tears pebbled his neck where her face touched him. "I'm sorry, so sorry. Had I known, I would have broken the news about Judd so much gentler. No wonder you jumped to the conclusion I might have had a hand in his death." He patted her head like she was a small, frightened child. "I didn't, Rivalree. I swear to God. I loved Judd too much to ever harm him."

Little sobs racked her shaking body. He stroked her back, yearning to hold her like the woman she was and kiss the sorrow coursing through her soft form. But he didn't dare, fearing she would turn away.

The dripping tears tickled as they traced a path down his collarbone to soak into his shirt. "I'm here," he whispered hoarsely. "You aren't alone anymore."

She had suffered more than she admitted the day her parents died, of that he was sure. He could imagine the class of men she had faced. Slave hunters were all the same, filthy, uncaring sons of bitches. No wonder she had an unnatural dread of men. It was a fear he had seen countless times etched across her beautiful face, a terror he must help her overcome. "I won't hurt you, sugar," he whispered. She relaxed as if she took comfort in his words.

The horses nickered and snorted as the darkness edged around them. It was time to stop before the blackness became so complete he wouldn't be able to see to make camp. A finger of lightning seared the sky. Thunder rumbled in the distance. One of the animals shied, bumping into the other horse. Rivalree shivered in his arms, and he pulled her closer.

He couldn't deny she had a siren's mien about her, an allure that left his mouth dry, but what he felt for her was more than lust. There was a cure for that simple need. He wanted to see her smile and laugh, to witness that something special in her eyes each time she looked at him. What had begun as a debt to his friend Judd, to see that she was unharmed, had turned into a personal hunger to earn her . . . What? Her love? His mind protested the very thought. Then if it wasn't for love, why had he cornered her into a marriage she did not want? For the challenge, to see her want him as much as he desired her. Since that day he had discovered her standing so haughtily on the deck of the ship, the defiance had been there. She had thrown down the gauntlet, and he had taken it up. The drive to win was stong in his blood.

He glanced at her unaware face. No matter how he denied it, he cared for her. It was essential she learn how it was between a man and woman, and it was up to him, her husband, to teach her. He vowed he would take each step slowly, but he would begin the lessons tonight and make her the wife she should have been from the beginning.

Chapter Eight

The campfire undulated gently in the cool breeze skirting around the backdrop of boulders arched in a semicircle around the wagon. Rivalree glanced toward the rear of the Conestoga where Braven had disappeared behind the canvas flap moments before.

What a coward she was. She should have completed her story to him when she had the chance earlier. Yearning to know him better, to discover more about the man who had held her compassionately as the tale of her past tumbled over her trembling lips, she waited at the bottom of the wagon steps. She had misjudged him from the start. He was nothing like Silas Guntree. No longer fearing the man, she worried what his reaction would be when he discovered the sordid truth about her . . . lack of innocence. Would he turn away from her in disgust when he found out she was not a virgin? The thought brought newfound fears in focus. She had tried to keep the truth from him, but how? There was no way unless she forced him to keep his distance as he had once promised he would.

"You cook?" Braven asked from deep inside the wagon. Pots and pans banged in a chorus as he shuffled around.

"Well enough," she responded. "Depends on what I have to work with."

His head poked out the canvas covering. "Guess I should've checked you out first before I married you," he commented with a grin, dropping a large pot on the ground at her feet.

"Too late now, sir. You get what you get." She smiled lightheartedly. "Besides, it's not every man who marries the Sierra Angel." The jesting made her relax, and she thanked Braven in her heart for being so kind.

"So what other accomplishments do you boast, fair lady?" He stepped down from the vehicle.

Holding out her wrinkled skirt, she dipped him a demure curtsy. "Why, sir, besides cooking, I sew and spin, can milk the cow and churn butter. I handle a rifle manageably. Oh, and yes, I bless miners." She rose from her bow and fluttered her lashes at him.

"Seems to me you're a fair catch." He eyed her up and down, then he handed her a potpourri of different kinds of dried beans and a small slab of salt pork. "See if your blessing can make something palatable out of these."

"I can make a nine bean soup that will melt in your mouth, but I wish I had an onion." She set about the task of preparing a meager meal by the light of the fire. "Braven, I need some water," she called into the darkness where he had disappeared moments before. *Braven*, she thought. *What a strong name, just like the man.*

Lightning seared the night sky giving an illusion of daylight. Braven approached, a bucket of water in one hand. "There's a stream not far away. Thought you might need water to cook with."

Running a hand across her grimy neck, she smiled her gratitude. She could picture the river swirling around her, washing away the dust and dirt of the last few days. A bath, what she wouldn't do for a bath. She glanced up at Braven as he set the bucket beside her. Did she dare ask him to show her the stream? What if he mistook the meaning of her request? She shivered, and decided to test her theory before she said something.

"Smells good," he offered. His eyes dipped down to take in the curve of her breast pressing against her inner arm.

She noticed where his gaze strayed. Fascinated, she watched him moisten his dry lips. She raised her arm to wipe the sweat from her brow, aware her bosom molded against the bodice of her dress. She teased him, and she knew it, yet she couldn't resist the little thrill coursing down her spine as she did so. Glad she hadn't mentioned the bath, she lowered her arm and moved away before the situation got out of hand.

Braven dragged his eyes away as if it took all his effort. She swallowed hard as it dawned on her that she was totally alone with him. If he decided to press the issue, there was no one around to rescue her. She must be more careful in the future, but lordy, she'd like to take a bath.

"Think I'll go back down to the stream and cool off," he mumbled, standing up. The muscles in his arms and chest pressed against his plaid shirt, as if he held himself stiffly. "I won't be long."

Rivalree watched him turn, hoping he would offer to include her. She glanced at the bubbling pot looking for a reason why she couldn't go. It would be a good half an hour before the beans were soft enough to eat. Her gaze shot up at his retreating back and then to the fire. Fear of the situation and desire to be clean played a game of tug-of-war in her mind. As he edged toward the darkness rimming the campfire light, she knew she had to say something now, or hold her peace.

"Braven," she chirped.

He glanced back, the flames casting dancing shadows on his taut face muscles. Was it anger etched on his countenance?

"Maybe I could go, too."

His eyes narrowed, and his mouth slackened in surprise.

"I thought a bath might be nice. It will be a while before

111

the meal is ready. I could let it simmer . . ." she faltered.

"You're willing to take a bath with me?"

"Oh, no," she gasped. He did mistake her meaning. "There must be a spot, secluded, where I could have a little privacy. It's been so long since I've washed."

"Jesus, God, woman. What do you take me for? A saint?" He ran his fingers through his hair, his chest expanding and falling as if he had been running.

"No, I only thought . . ." She rose from her kneeling position and presented her rigid spine.

In three strides, Braven was behind her. He clamped his fingers over her upper arm and spun her around, their harsh breathing the only sounds except the snapping of the flames.

The flush of desire swept across his features like a flash of fire leaving a blazed trail in its wake. "I can't keep my promise, if you ask things like that of me. I want you, Rivalree. I've wanted you from the moment I laid eyes on you. How long do you think this charade can continue?"

Confusion clouded her mind as she glanced from his expectant face to his fingers crushing the flesh of her arm. He was right. She did bait him, and she was close to falling into her own trap.

His hand came up and untied the bonnet ribbons under her chin. Her confusion congealed into a need to survive. She tried to pull her arm away.

"You have nothing to fear from me. I'm not an ogre or a slave hunter."

As he ran a finger down the curve of her chin, her skin tingled.

"I'm a man, your husband."

The bonnet slipped from her head and trailed to the ground. Her golden hair followed down her back, wet tendrils framing her face. Appreciating the picture she presented, his features softened.

Closer his face drew. He planned to kiss her. Did she

want him to? Vivid memories of the two times he had kissed her in the past flashed in her thoughts. Those kisses had ravaged her senses, demanding a like response from her. She waited in brazen anticipation for his mouth to claim hers. What harm could one kiss do?

His warm breath brushed the corner of her mouth, and she twisted her face until her seeking lips met his with equal ardor, a golden fervor taking her breath away. Welcoming his probing tongue, she fenced with familiarity when he demanded she do so. The thrill coursing through her was intoxicating, and she melted when his strong arms pulled her close against his torso. She even allowed her fingers to dance across his shoulders to the soft brush of hair along the nape of his neck.

His hand drew a swirling pattern down her spine, leaving sparks in its path. She pressed against him, reveling in the new sensations spiraling through her belly with a tautness that took her breath away. Down his hand moved until he gripped her buttocks and welded her lower body against his groin. The rigid column of his manhood beckoned blatantly to her through the protection of their clothing. Her body tensed. This was going much further than she intended. She twisted her thoroughly plundered mouth away from his, shoving against his pounding chest. "Please, no."

Braven stepped back, the fire in his blood reflected in his gaze. She stumbled as he removed his supporting arms. She hadn't realized she had leaned so heavily against him. His eyes hardened like icy blue stones, wiping away the tenderness that had been there, and he raked her figure with what she thought was contempt.

"Come on," he grumbled. When she didn't follow, he glanced back. "You can trust me."

Following at a safe distance, she stumbled in the darkness. He gripped her arm and pulled her along. "If you don't want to get lost, stay close."

Lightning fingered the sky, and she caught a glimpse of the shimmering water not far ahead. As they reached the edge of the bank, thunder rumbled doom in the distance. "Stay here," he said in a voice as ominous as the fulmination overhead. "I'll be a little farther downstream. Bathe and be quick about it. We don't have long before the storm hits."

She waited until his steps drew dim, then nil. An electric flash cut across the sky. Her gaze darted from tree to tree. He was gone. Without a second thought she stripped off her dress and underclothing and slipped into the cool water. He had said to hurry. She would as she didn't want him to find her unclad—or did she? She washed as efficiently as she could and doused her head to wet her hair.

A flash lit the sky in front of her, revealing the curve of the stream below. Standing in the middle of the water up to his thighs was Braven, his hand scrubbing his chest and stomach. She sucked in her bottom lip as the darkness closed around her, the faraway thunder filling her ears. What a wondrous sight he made. So tall and regal, hair highlighting his body like spun gold.

Again the lightning ripped through the blackness. She glanced expectantly in his direction. He rose from the water like a phoenix, never once glancing in her direction. Was he aware that she watched him? Before the night fell like a curtain with a crash, she caught a look at the full length of him—his stomach and loins, his virile staff. It was the first time she had seen a man unclothed, and the sight unnerved her. She tore her eyes away from his direction determined not to spy any longer. Finishing her bath, she waded to shore where she had dropped her clothing and dressed, unable to stop the images of Braven's nude body from filling her thoughts.

"We'd better hurry back," he announced close beside her. She jumped, guilt of her voyeurism sending a blush across her face.

By the time they reached the camp, the fire hissed and sputtered in protest as large drops of rain splattered the flames. The bean soup sent out a heavenly smell as Braven grabbed the hot handle with his shirttail. He pointed the pot toward the wagon, and she took the lead.

The tiny cubbyhole he had cleared in the back of the vehicle was barely large enough for the two of them to sit. He placed the pan of beans on a crate between them. Producing two spoons, he handed one to her. They ate in silence, sharing the food. Tension crackled the air between them.

"This is good, How did you do it?" Braven lifted one blond brow in surprise.

She studied him across the short span, the crisp, golden hair of his chest peeking out of the vee of his shirt. With vividness she recalled how he looked standing in the stream, masculine and unabashed. Did he know she had spied on him? The face he presented was friendly and open, no sign of what he thought.

The rain began a steady thudding on the canvas covering. She glanced around the crowded wagon, then at him, unable to decide if he thought they would share the confines of the shelter all night. As if he read her thoughts, he wiped his mouth with the back of his hand and rose, grabbing a slicker. He turned the collar of his shirt up and slipped the coat on.

"Are you leaving?" she asked.

"There are blankets up there." He pointed toward the front of the wagon. "If you crawl on top of those flour sacks, you'll have a fairly comfortable bed."

"But what about you?" Her hand reached out and grasped his arm, the first time she had touched him voluntarily.

He studied her for a moment as if trying to read her thoughts. "I'll scrounge shelter around the rocks." He lifted the canvas flap, and the wind gusted in, flecking everything with drops of water.

She shouldn't let him go out, but the close confines of the wagon was too intimate. It would be unwise to allow him to stay. Not wishing to watch as he stepped down out of the shelter, she twisted away, guilt creeping into her unwilling mind.

The sound of his feet splashing in the puddles mingled with the drumming of the rain. *It's warm,* she reasoned. *He'll find a dry spot. He's a grown man; he can take care of himself.*

Facing the stack of flour sacks, she picked the spot that looked most inviting and arranged the blankets to her satisfaction. With a quick rush of air she extinguished the flickering light of the lantern. Donning a clean nightgown she retrieved from her trunk, she inched under the light covering.

Lying in the solace of her bed, her mind refused to allow her rest. Was Braven all right? Had he found a place to get out of the rain? Crawling from the blankets, she peeked through the back flap. She caught a quick glimpse of him as the lightning flashed and thundered. The slicker he wore jackknifed in the wind over his huddled figure beside the boulders. She closed the flap unable to watch him any longer.

Cymbals crashed overhead, and the outside grew momentarily bright. The wagon shuddered with the electrifying force. Rivalree covered her ears and trembled in the lonely darkness of the wagon. That had been close. Too close. Rushing back to check on Braven, her heart pounded in her throat. He wasn't safe outside with the lightning. His hunched figure hadn't moved. How could he be so unaffected by the storm? Did he never lose his self-control?

She wished she hadn't snuffed the flame in the lantern. The light would have been a comfort to her frayed nerves.

116

Cr-r-rack!

A fireworks of sparks showered around the tiny wagon.

"No," she screamed, the word spilling from her mouth before she had a chance to stop it.

The shrill neighing of the frightened horses undid her. The night was familiar, as if she had lived it once before. The smell of smoke filled her nostrils. The animals, the barn. The suppressed nightmare began again. The gun, she had to find her father's rifle. Blindly she felt around the wagon, stumbling over crates and trunks. *I can't let the slave hunter find me again. He mustn't touch me. I won't . . .*

Arms wrapped around her from the rear. She twisted, claws extended ready to defend herself from Silas Guntree.

The hands turned her to face their owner. Oh, God, this time she would be awake and aware of what happened to her. She screamed in the darkness. "Take your filthy southern hands off me."

Lightning flashed again, and blazing blue eyes bore into her. She swung with all her might, knowing she must escape at all cost. But the arms clung to her refusing to release her. Her fingernails ripped at warm flesh, and her teeth sunk into the captive grip.

"Damn it, Rivalree. Stop it." Her captor shook her until her teeth rattled.

"No, I won't let you this time," she shrilled. Her struggle intensified.

"I don't want to hurt you," answered the pained voice of the man who held her.

The impact of his palm across her face turned her screams into confused sobs.

"I'm sorry. I didn't want to do that," Braven whispered into her hair as he pulled her against his wet chest. His mouth brushed her throbbing temple.

The pain in her cheek receded, and she came swirling back from the past. The touch of Braven's lips worked like a miracle, calming her, soothing her. She remembered where she was, in a wagon, in the refuge of her husband's embrace. With a deep groan, she wrapped her arms around his damp neck and clung to the safety he offered from her inner fears.

His hands moved over her shoulders and feathered across her cheeks as he raised her head. "I didn't want to hurt you," he choked.

Her fingers twined in the soft hair at the nape of his neck. The storm gentled to a steady drip on the canvas above their heads. His moist lips moved as he spoke, and Rivalree's attention centered on them. So inviting and protective. She needed something to erase what had happened so long ago in New Jersey.

She pulled his head down to meet hers. Would his kiss be the balm she needed? When would he stop this gallant charade of his? Danger kindled to a fire of need inside her.

Sparks flew behind her closed lids as his mouth descended on hers. At first he let them touch, tentatively, easily. Then his mouth moved and opened over hers and seemed to suck the breath from her body. As if the lightning from the sky had entered her, electric shocks traveled up and down her spine to fragment in the pit of her stomach when his tongue explored her receptive mouth.

His fingers plucked at the buttons of her gown, slipping them from the security of the holes. Her hand moved up to stop him, grasping the gaping material together.

"Let me," he whispered in her ear, his very breath sending swirling sensations down her back. Loosening her hold, her hands dropped to her side.

He cupped her bare breast, and it tightened as he rubbed his palm over the nipple. She moaned with sheer pleasure and willed him to do the same to its mate. His hand moved to comply with her mental command. At the same time he pushed the nightgown down her shoulders. As the fabric

118

bunched around her waist and the cool air touched her unfettered bosom, she stiffened. What madness had struck her? She was allowing him to do the very thing she didn't want. Or did she? No, she couldn't let him. He would never forgive her for not being pure and untouched.

Ripping her mouth from his, her hands covered her nudity.

As if fevered, he panted over her, his breath like hot, fragrant steam against her face.

"I'm sorry, Braven. I shouldn't have done that. I didn't mean to let you think . . ."

"God damn it, you vixen." His aura of control splintered like the lightning struck tree outside the wagon. "You can't experiment with me this way. I'm flesh and blood." His fingers dug into her bare shoulders and pulled her close. "I will have you. It's what you've asked for and deserve." He swung her up into his arms and tossed her onto the makeshift bed. "But most of all, it's what you need."

Her arms were caught in the tangle of her gown. She could do nothing about her uncovered breasts beckoning to him with each breath she took. She lifted her chin defiantly—daring him to carry through with his threat. Their eyes locked, and as she watched, he stripped the wet clothing from his body.

He was right, she had toyed with his emotions. God help her, but she liked the fire he stirred in her, and she savored the sensation of power she held over him.

She couldn't tear her eyes from his naked body or the evidence of his determination to consummate this marriage. There was no denying she wanted to become a whole woman in his arms, but she feared she would lose him if she gave in to her desires. He would discover her lack of virginity.

But how would he know?

She mulled the question in her mind. Was there

physical evidence to attest to the fact? Or was it merely a matter of how she acted that would give away the truth?

She knew the mechanics of mating. How could she not, having grown up on a farm. There was no evidence when an inexperienced mare was given to the stud that she had never bred before, except for a bewildered skittishness as the stallion nipped and coerced the filly into compliance. Was it the same between man and woman? If she acted shy and uncertain, perhaps he would never know. She prayed she was right. Besides, she wouldn't be acting. Lost in a new world of swirling sensations, she was unsure. No memory of what had happened to her so long ago remained. Even if she wasn't virgin of body, she was virgin of mind. That was all that mattered, she told herself over and over.

Her chin lifted a notch higher, this time in determination. Don't let him know the difference, she prayed. She struggled in the confines of her nightgown, but the fabric twisted tighter. The flour sacks beneath her bunched and compressed as Braven stretched out beside her. Again she squirmed in attempt to free her arms, and he watched her tussle, not helping, not hindering, in fact lying so close his breath caressed her rippling breasts, yet not touching her. With the despairing whimper of quarry cornered and caught with no hope of escape, she ceased her senseless flight, both with her clothing and with her nervousness.

Like a cat understands when its prey has surrendered to the inevitability of death, he chuckled deep in his chest, one hand reaching out to stroke her quivering flesh, round and round each erect nipple, until with a groan of defeat, she succumbed to the feelings he evoked from her very core. "Don't be frightened, Rivalree. There's nothing to fear. Love between a man and a woman is wondrous, a thing of joy."

Love? she pondered. He speaks of love? Was it love that left her feeling breathless and hopelessly entangled in a web of deceit, or was it some other illicit emotion? Why else would she care what he thought of her and her past?

Gently he traced a liquid line down her exposed ribs until he reached the buttons of her gown that held her in its torturous grip. "Maybe I should leave you as you are, bound and suppliant, at the mercy of my whim."

Her eyes widened in genuine uncertainty. Surely he wouldn't do that to her. She began to struggle again.

His hand came to rest on the first button, and he pressed his palm against her rising and falling belly, an impish grin on his face.

"You wouldn't," she protested as his head lowered, his mouth encircling one bare breast. His tongue curled around the hardened knob of flesh her nipple had become, kneading it, flicking it, pulling it deep into his mouth.

She arched toward him, unconcerned he held her captive, uncaring until he lifted away from her.

"I would if I thought it necessary, but I don't think I need to bind you. You seem quite willing to me."

Her elevated senses came crashing down. Did she appear too willing? She stiffened, her shoulders and arms held rigid with fear.

Braven lifted one blond brow at the turn of events.

His fingers released the button pressing into her waist. "What is it, Rivalree? Do I frighten you? Or is it the difference between your body and mine?"

No, he didn't frighten her. But what answer did he wait for? Was this some kind of test? She lowered her lashes in what she hoped showed chasteness, and nodded her head. If shy, retiring virgin was what he wanted, she would gladly play the part.

"I suspect you've never seen a nude man before. Am I right?"

She hesitated for a moment remembering how he looked in the water. She nodded, the lie making her heart race in her chest.

He chuckled, and his fingers released the next button. "I could have sworn you got your eyes full earlier while we bathed."

Squirming, she pulled her arms free of the material and pushed up on her elbows. "You knew I was watching?" She blushed at the revelation.

"I was hoping you were." He ran his palms up and down her bare arms. "I would have done the same thing, if the situation had been reversed."

What did he want from her? She lay back against the makeshift bed, forcing her body to remain unmoving, keeping her breath at a low, even pace. She glanced his way once to find his gaze drinking in the lush curves and valleys of her body exposed from the navel up to his view. His hand crossed over her to find her upturned palm. Drawing nonsensical patterns from her fingers to her wrist, up her arm to the dip in front of her elbow, he left a glowing path in his wake. She lay there, breath held deep in her lungs, attempting to show no reaction to his caresses. His touch continued up her arm, over her shoulder, and down to capture one breast.

Bending over her, his mouth pressed down in her compressed lips, his tongue demanding access to the sweet crevice. She willingly kissed him, feeling safe with the action. Yet he continued to tease the soft mound he held, and her body screamed to arch against his cupped hand, but she kept herself in check, lying perfectly still, compliant. As if to torture her, his palm massaged the engorged nipple. She swallowed the wanton groan demanding release from her throat. She couldn't lie there and accept his sweet torture much longer.

"No, please," she begged, escaping his kiss for a moment as she covered his hand with hers. "I won't fight you, Braven. I'll let you have your way. Just please don't torture me that way."

"If you think this is torture, sugar," he said, dipping

down to take her breast into his mouth, "then be warned, I've only just begun. I want you writhing beneath my touch, begging for more, not for me to stop."

Her heart thudded against his palm. "But that wouldn't be proper."

"I don't care, Rivalree." His tongue dotted each upthrusted nipple, then seared a trail between her ribs. "I want the real you, woman, not some preconceived notion you might have as to how you should act." He lapped at the crevice of her navel, the muscles quivering wherever he touched. "Show me the passion I know is there. Be damned your virginity. You won't be that way for long, I promise you."

Was he saying he didn't care if she was untouched or not? Or did he say those things because he was confident he was the first man to take her?

His mouth continued to blaze a path downward. Half crazed, she threw her inhibitions to the wind and opened her legs to his insistent invasion, her hands entangling in the softness of his hair, wanting more, demanding much more.

"Ah, Rivalree," he breathed against the inside of her thigh, "you're all the woman I hoped you would be. All the woman I need."

Arousing her womanhood until she thought she would burst into a million pieces, his hand replaced his mouth as he rose away from her. Unabashed, she sobbed her frustration as he left her unfulfilled. His weight shifted, and he pulled her underneath him. Poised above her, his chest rose and fell in time with hers. "I don't want to hurt you," he said, his words pricking the rosy haze in her mind, "but there's no other way. I'll be as gentle as I can."

With restrained pressure he entered her, her body grasping his rigid flesh with undeniable need. The pain caught her by surprise, so sharp and blinding for a split second of time. She tried to pull away, but he held her .

pinned to the blanket, not moving, yet not retreating, gently soothing her with words of encouragement. "Relax, my love. The pain will go away if you don't fight me so."

The searing agony was quickly replaced with exquisite pleasure the moment she relented. Sensing her surrender, he thrust once, filling her completely. Again he paused, giving her a chance to experience the new stimuli swirling through every nerve in her body. Soon impatience to complete what they had started set her hips in motion. He matched her rhythm, never forcing her, yet urging her to a faster pace. The tingle at the crux of her being ignited to blinding white pleasure until she thought she could take no more, and still, it climbed.

She opened her eyes to find him watching her, fascination clearly etched on his features. Her lashes lowered as waves of sensation rocked her to the point of no return. With a final thrust, she dropped over a sheer cliff of bliss, a sob of newfound fulfillment bubbling in her throat. His mouth captured hers, stifling the sound before it emerged.

Plunging down into the lull of climactic satisfaction, she felt his body stiffen, his mouth pressed against her collarbone as he moaned, "Jesus, Rivalree, but I love you."

Realizing the implication of his words and that he experienced the same peak as she, her arms tightened around the taut muscles of his back as she marveled at what they had shared. The pain had been nothing compared to the pleasure, and she would embrace it over and over to reach that point of earthshaking joy.

"I hope I didn't hurt you too badly," he rasped, his heart slowing to mirror the soft thuds of her own.

She framed his face with her hands. "The pain is nothing, not when it's followed by such . . ." There were no words to describe what she had experienced. She lowered her hands until her palms rested on his chest. "I'd gladly endure it a thousand times."

His fingers stroked her jaw. "Your compliment to my prowess is gladly accepted, but you won't have to go through pain again, not ever, only the first time."

She blinked, unsure she had heard him right. Only the first time? But that's impossible. Her mind skimmed over the last few minutes. Was the pain real, or had she imagined it? Had his warning she would go through discomfort make her feel it? Confused she tried to relive that second of agony. She knew what she had felt. But most important, real or imaginary, she had been convincing. He believed her virginal. That was all that mattered. She breathed relief and nestled in the muscled contour of his offered shoulder, closing her eyes. She would work out the puzzle at another time when she wasn't so euphoric.

Chapter Nine

La Porte. She wasn't sure what she expected, but it wasn't the tidy, rough-hewn town sprawled before her. It was as if the mountain air had purged the dirt and grime of mining, washing it down the summits to the foothills below. She shivered in the cool July temperature, aware that the normal heat of summer had been unable to locate this hidden corner of the world. Taking a deep breath, the scent of pines waved toward her. So clean and fresh—like the pineland of New Jersey.

Glancing up, she found Braven watching her intently. "Pretty, isn't it?" He never once looked around at their surroundings, and she wondered if he referred to the landscape.

She nodded. "Yes."

"By September it will turn cold, and the snow won't begin until October, if we're lucky. Summer doesn't last long here." He pulled the wagon to a stop before a building that appeared to be the center of activity, "Jackson's" printed across its front. "Post office, general store, and just about everything else of importance around here," Braven offered.

Rivalree shot a look at the loaded wagon bed behind them. "General store? Then why all these supplies if you can get them here?"

Braven laughed, a deep, rich sound she had come to admire. "Most of what is in the wagon is for Jackson."

"I don't understand."

"Whenever anyone goes down below, we bring our wagon back full, share with Jackson, and charge no freight. He passes the savings on to his customers. That way we all save. We're a community here. We take care of our own."

"Oh," she answered in a small voice. Another act of kindness to chalk up to him. How could she have misjudged him so in the beginning? Then based on that misconception she had married him, thinking she was getting no better than she gave.

The events that stormy night on the trail three days ago still left her bewildered. Somehow in her need to convince him of her purity she had fooled herself as well. She had felt the hurt, but she had heard of people who could control their minds so well they were able to make pain disappear. Why not the other way around. She had made the pangs seem real in her mind. There could be no other explanation.

She cut her eyes to his tall, straight figure on the seat beside her. It was wrong to deceive him, she knew that keenly in her heart, but she didn't have the courage to reveal the truth to him. Not now, not when she had discovered this seedling of feelings for him that sprouted in her soul. But at the same time, she took great pains to keep her distance. She was almost afraid to reexperience lovemaking with him. What if she felt pain again? What if she didn't? It was easier standing on the abyss of not knowing than facing the truth about herself. She was deceiving and sinful, not deserving of his trusting nature. She wasn't comfortable with the loving, kind Braven. She was more at ease when he bullied and force compliance from her.

Damn him! Why couldn't he remain in the slot she had

placed him in—a murdering southern hypocrite controlled by his greed?

A barrel-chested man stepped through the rough-hewn threshold, a brown-stained smile of delight creasing his weathered face. "Sure as hell, it is you, Blackwood. Damn, it's good to see you, man." Dark eyes flicked over her, then passed back to Braven. "Looks like that wagon is filled to burstin'."

Braven wrapped the reins around the brake handle and offered her a quick, encouraging smile as he slid down from the seat, then turned his attention to the other man. "Longstreet did right by us, as usual."

"I'd say better than usual. That Janet Longstreet has a soft spot in her heart for you. You always come back with more than the others."

Braven's glance slid back up to Rivalree. "Miz Longstreet just thinks I'm a trustworthy fellow, that's all." He grinned conspiratorially at her and winked.

"Humph. More like she wouldn't mind fingering the front of your britches." Sheepishly the shopkeeper whipped a look at her. "Sorry, missy," he mumbled. "Didn't mean to offend."

"My wife, Eloy. Rivalree, Eloy Jackson."

Jackson's eyes took her worth, and he aimed a stream of brown spittle at the back hooves of the team.

Rivalree sighed. Why did everyone find it so amazing that Braven Blackwood had married? She nodded acknowledgement. Disgusted by the crudeness of the storekeeper's actions and words, she tightened her mouth until it became a slash against her face.

Braven circled to her side of the wagon and offered her a hand. "Might as well get down, sugar. It'll take a while to unload Eloy's share of the supplies."

Braven frowned, his hand remaining raised in the air toward her. "Step down, Rivalree."

She wouldn't. Jackson was horrible. Spitting tobacco

juice in the road. How could she have ever thought La Porte was clean and beautiful?

Eloy Jackson stepped up beside Braven. "I'm sorry, ma'am. Didn't mean no offense by my words. We're just not used to watching our tongues around here. Don't meet pretty ladies every day." He grinned, a tobacco-stained, gap-toothed smile. "There's a nice rocking chair by the Franklin, a pot of fresh coffee perkin' on top. You're welcome to help yourself."

Rivalree accepted Braven's hand. What else could she do? Her fingers were icy, and a chill invaded the thin material of her dress. The warmth of the fire sounded much more comfortable than sitting on the seat of the wagon. At least in the store, she wouldn't have to look at the uncouth Mr. Jackson. "Then, if that's the case, I'll accept."

The inside of the store was remarkably clean. The coffee sent out an irresistable aroma. She inhaled, catching the smell of new leather and licorice—homey, earthy scents.

A crowd gathered around Braven and the shopkeeper as the two men unloaded the wagon. Ribald laughter drifted through the open doorway. Busying herself with pouring a cup of the dark brew, she tried to ignore the few distinct syllables filtering to her. "Whore" and "hanging" were two words she clearly understood.

She sipped the hot liquid, her hands wrapped around the mug to absorb the warmth radiating through the ceramic. "I shouldn't listen," she mumbled, but the silence of the store made that impossible. She sat down on the rocker hoping it would squeak and drown out the men's conversation. It didn't.

"Well, I heard the story different," rang out Eloy Jackson's voice.

Rivalree gave up the pretense, rose from the chair, and edged toward the door.

"I hear tell, Juanita weren't no whore. She was

130

defindin' her home and her man from thieves and no 'counts. They hung her big with child and sent her man packin'."

Rivalree gulped. Where had they hung a woman? Here in La Porte?

Braven's eyes swept up and caught hers. She scurried back across the store. She shouldn't have been eavesdropping. God help her, but she didn't know what had possessed her to come to this wild, untamed country with a man she hardly knew. Judd, she reminded herself. She had to see the place where he had lived—she swallowed a mouthful of coffee—and died. She would put flowers on his grave and be close to the one person who had been her friend all her life. She would . . .

"Rivalree?"

She glanced up at Braven standing before her.

"You heard?"

She nodded, her head bobbing like a cork.

"I'm sorry. This is a raw, ungoverned country . . ."

"I know. I was just telling myself the same thing."

"There's no justice here except what the miners create for themselves."

"But a woman? They hung a woman here?"

"No, not in this town. Downieville, on the other side of the mountain."

"By men, like the ones who fawned and cooed over me a few days ago. They could hang me, too, on any trumped up charge."

Braven's arm circled her shoulders. "Good Lord, girl. I'd never let that happen to you. Don't you know that yet?"

She clung to him, wishing she could be sure of his sincerity. Insecurity buzzed around her like a swarm of gnats, never giving her a moment's rest, never letting her completely trust the tall southerner who offered his gallant protection. What if he was lying, trying to get her to lower her defenses? What if he planned to take her high

131

in the mountains and kill her, to rid himself of an unwanted partner? Her body stiffened, and as if he sensed her change in mood, he released her.

"Are we almost to the mine?"

Braven chuckled in a fatherly fashion. "We're close. Maybe thirty more miles. But thirty miles of wilderness over the roughest terrain you'll ever see." His hand reached out and lifted her lowered chin, concern written on his face. "Are you sorry you've come?"

She shook her head quickly. No, she wasn't sorry she was here. She had chosen to come, and she would do the same thing if she had to do it over again. What she was sorry about was the circumstances of her dilemma. What if Judd were alive? Would she still feel this strange attraction to Braven Blackwood? The thought horrified her, and she thrust the images from her mind. She would keep her distance from him. That way she would be safe from his possible deceit and from her guilt-ridden cogitations. "No, I'll just be glad when we get there."

"If we're lucky, we'll be there in two days. You'll see, Rivalree. We'll be happy."

In her heart she wished she could believe what he said, but deep down she doubted they would ever know true contentment.

The wagon creaked as if mortally wounded; the horses snorted in protest, stamping and kicking as they pulled the noisy monster up the steep grade. They would never make this long, arduous trip. Rivalree was sure. She strained to sit as close to the center of the seat as she could, even though it meant pressing next to Braven. So much for the vow she had made earlier that day to keep her distance from him. The view from the seat's edge was much more threatening than sitting close to him. She didn't want to look again, but morbid fascination stretched her neck to

132

glance over the side of the wagon. No more than six inches of ground stood between the rocking vehicle and the sheer cliff dropping to the valley so far below that the mighty pines and oaks looked like specks of green. She swallowed slowly and pressed harder against Braven, even though the rational side of her mind told her if the wgon wheel slipped, she would be tossed to her death no matter where she sat.

She glanced at Braven's profile. He sat easy and relaxed, yet alert to each time the team stumbled over loose rocks or shied at imaginary dangers on the trail. His arm crept around her in comfort, and she leaned into his shoulder, chastising herself for needing the security he offered. But his support remained only for a moment until he needed both hands to keep the skittish animals in line.

She entertained the idea of asking him to stop and let her down. She would walk the rest of the way. Then, she reconsidered. The trail was steep; she wouldn't last a mile on foot. More than likely he would laugh at her and make her feel ridiculous. Besides, if the wagon were to slip from the trail and be lost, the thought of being alone in the wilds of the Sierras wasn't a notion she relished. No, she'd much rather go with Braven and take her chances with him. He seemed at ease and unafraid; the least she could do was show him her spine was as sturdy as his.

His eyes slid in her direction. Chuckling as if he read her thought, he declared, "Don't worry, Rivalree. The horses know this trail well. We've never once lost a wagon."

She pulled away from him, embarrassed that he had so easily seen her fear.

"Maybe I should tell you different. I liked it much better with you close to me. Come back or I'll . . ."

The ground below one wheel crumbled, and the wagon tilted slightly. Rivalree scrambled back to press herself against his shoulder.

"Good," he exclaimed. His hand reached down and

patted her knee. "Promise me you'll stay here, and I'll keep the wagon close to the mountainside."

She nodded in ready agreement, her head pressed against his arm, the movement ruffling the fabric of his shirt.

As the late afternoon sun dimmed, her throat grew dry and parched from the fear clutching at her heart since they had left the small settlement of Howland Flats nestled in a high valley of long, green grass. The last thing she'd expected was sheer cliffs, but they were barely out of the community before the trail angled as it wound around the mountain peak. She fervently wished they would reach the end of their journey.

The air was sharp and thin, and she opened her mouth, taking deep breaths to ease her dizzyness. Her thirst intensified to the point she found it hard to swallow. Glancing at the man beside her, she refused to mention her discomfort. She would not display another weakness to his amused scrutiny.

A sound rang in her ears, a musical noise, a liquid tinkling that drove her need for a drink to a high-pitched intensity. Thirst was driving her out of her mind and causing her to hear sounds that didn't exist.

Braven's arm tensed under her fingertips. "Whoa," he ordered the horses as they snorted and flared their nostrils, their feet pawing impatiently at the dusty trail. Without another word he stepped down from the seat and patted the sweat-shiny rump of the nearest animal as he passed it and disappeared behind a wall of rocks. He returned carrying a deep bucket which he set before one of the horses. "Watering hole," he announced, offering her a knowing smile. "You thirsty?"

She was so parched she would have gladly dunked her head in the pail he lifted and offered the other steed. She scooted to the protected side of the wagon, but before she could descend, Braven was there, his hands circling her waist as he assisted her to the ground. As if a steel band gripped her, she fidgeted. He spun and settled her in the road. A mountain breeze eddied around them, lifting her skirts and wrapping them around his legs as well. It was if the wind was trying to bind them together regardless of her turbulent thoughts.

"Thank you," she whispered hoarsely, as much from her parchedness as from the confusion swirling in her mind.

He smiled and gave her a little shove toward the rocks. "Go drink. You sound as dry as a desert wind. I'll join you as soon as the horses have their fill."

Foreboding tugged at her heart, as strong as the thirst demanding to be quenched. She hesitated, glancing over her shoulder at the man she knew so little about. This would be a perfect place to get rid of her, if he wanted to. He busied himself checking the harnesses and hooves of the horses, as if she wasn't there. Was his nonchalant attitude a cover for his plans? The water gurgled just ahead, beckoning to her, reminding her how dry she was and how vulnerable she was to the man she called husband. She couldn't deny her thirst, but she could keep alert and ready for him to make a sudden move against her. She stumbled toward the liquid music, rounding the jut of rock she had seen Braven disappear behind earlier.

There she discovered a deep basin set back in the mountain the size of a washbowl, a steady trickle of moisture coming from some unknown origin to fill it. As the water overflowed the lip of the basin, it ran down the mossy rocks to again disappear deep in the bowels of the earth. *How strange*, she thought as she dipped her hand into the water to carry it to her lips, but by the time her cupped palm reached her mouth only a slight dampness remained, not near enough to quench her overpowering thirst. She tried two hands, but the angle of the basin was such that it was impossible to use her clasped fingers and

135

maintain her balance. Then she saw the gourd dipper suspended from a bit of twine overhead. Stretching on tiptoes, she removed it from the root from which it hung and eased it under the water. As she brought the dipper to her lips, she thought of Braven's mouth pressed to the gourd's lips moments before. She hestitated to touch it and glanced behind her, but her need was so intense it could no longer be denied. She drank remembering the feel of his caresses, denying the emotions they had wrought from her.

The iciness of the water cooled her fevered thoughts and her burning throat. There was a sweetness about it she couldn't identify. She never knew water could taste so good. She smacked her lips and lowered the dipper to fill again.

A wheezing little grunt floated down on her. She tossed her gaze upward, water dripping from her chin like a startled wild doe. Her heart drummed against her ribs. Was Braven somewhere above her, waiting to catch her unaware? Her eyes followed the rim of rocks. Again the plaintive cry sounded, so soft and small she swore she had imagined it. A scraggly pine clinging to a crack in the boulders to her left shivered, and her eyes traveled up its twisted trunk to find a furry, black ball swaying precariously on one crooked branch.

Her first instinct was to scream, but the fur ball squeaked again, and two button black eyes blinked at her in fear. She giggled in delight at her find, a small bear cub, clutching his perilous perch.

Without thinking, she rose and followed the line of boulders until she discovered a way to reach the tree. *How precious,* she thought, as she edged her way up the side of the rock formation. *How helpless. The poor thing could fall and hurt itself.* She identified with the tiny creature, a victim of circumstances much as she was.

As she reached the base of the tree, the cub hugged the

branch tighter, crying pitifully the closer she came. She clucked her tongue in a sound meant to soothe and lifted her arms. "I won't hurt you, baby. I promise. I just want to help you down."

Where had she heard similar words? Braven had said them to her as they had stood in front of the St. Francis Hotel just prior to their marriage.

"Rivalree?" Braven called in alarm from below.

She turned her back to the cub and shouted down to where he circled the rocks to join her at the water basin. "Up here. Do you see it? Isn't he cute? I thought I would help him . . ."

"Rivalree. Damn you. Look out." Braven's face bloated in fear.

"But, Braven, it's only a baby."

The cub's grunts had risen to high-pitched squealing as its little paws circled the bobbing limb.

Braven moved with lightning speed up the wall of the mountain. "Behind you," he yelled. "The cub's mother."

She turned at his command to find a tower of black fur a dozen yards away, the giant bear's nose lifted to the breeze, sniffing, its front paws as large as three of her hands flaying the air.

Rivalree screamed and backed away. Oh, God, the cub's mother. How could she have been so stupid?

The she-bear opened her mouth, her mighty teeth gleaming white as she roared in defense of her baby.

"Braven," Rivalree screamed, the word echoing around her as she froze, petrified with fear.

The bear held its ground, sizing her up, deciding how best to handle the intruder. God in heaven, it could kill her with one swipe of its powerful paw.

Braven's hand clasped her ankle, and he squeezed until the pain registered in her brain. "Slowly, Rivalree, back down here with me. If I show myself, it will probably attack. Come on," he encouraged. "Back down. I won't let

137

you fall. Trust me."

Trust me—trust me. The words echoed softly in her head. She had no other choice. If he wanted to get rid of her, now was the perfect time. He couldn't have planned it better. All he had to do was thrust her forward into the waiting jaws of death. She stumbled as she twisted to join him.

"Easy, sugar. Not so fast. Slow, smooth movements."

She knelt, her eyes glued to the mountain of flesh and fur, fearing if she glanced away the animal would pounce. Braven clasped her waist and swung her down on the ledge where he stood. "Go on down as quick as you can."

She hesitated, realizing he planned to stand his ground between her and the wild beast.

"Go on," he urged.

Her hands shook as she gripped the stones and backed down the way she had so blithely come. The bear roared, and the cub squealed. She had to bite her tongue to keep from screaming in response.

Back beside the water basin, she shot her gaze up to Braven. Only a few yards behind her, he scrambled to join her on the ledge.

"I'm sorry," she muttered, attempting to throw her arms around him.

He gripped her wrists. "We aren't out of this, yet. Come on."

The bear jutted its long nose over the cliffs and grunted as it watched them skirt the rocks back to the wagon. The horses trembled and snorted as they caught the scent of the bear, one nipping at its harness mate in terror.

"I'm sorry," she said again, falling against the wagon.

"Up with you. We're still not safe."

She didn't protest as he shoved her into the seat and joined her, edging the team away from the rocks and down the trail.

"Braven, I didn't know. I . . ." she choked. He cared

138

about her. He had saved her when he could have just as easily pushed her to her death. Or worse, left her to fend for herself. What a little fool she was, what an unworthy liar. Deep sobs tumbled from her mouth. She couldn't stop them, and didn't try. Braven Blackwood deserved so much better than she offered. "I'm sorry," she wept again. "I'm sorry for everything."

His arm came around her, so warm and understanding. "Ssh. It's over, sugar. What you did wasn't so terrible that you need to cry about it."

But it was. He didn't know. She had to keep him from ever learning about her secret. A liar, a cheat, used goods. Somehow she had to keep him from discovering her past.

The cabin was tiny, the room smaller still. And the bed, it was so narrow her heart quickened in her chest forming a tight knot. There was no way to avoid the fact she must share a room, if not the bed with her husband.

Braven entered the deserted cabin, her valise in one hand, his boot heels musically clicking a rhythm she had learned to recognize. Her heart raced in tempo to his long strides.

She turned, not sure what to say. *Say anything*, she chided herself, to cover up the tension electrifying the air like the sparks of a hammer against an anvil.

"It was kind of your friends to allow us to stay the night here," she offered against the backdrop of the pie-faced moon silvering the darkness outside as he pushed the door closed.

He studied her for a moment, something he did a lot the last few days, as if trying to decipher the hidden meaning of her words and appeared to take them at face value. "The cabin was empty, deserted by its previous owner. Besides," he grinned crookedly, "I don't think I could take another night on the damp ground."

She flinched at the undercurrent of his barb. Since that one unforgettable night on the trail, she had made him stay away from her. Until now, he had not made one mention of their separate sleeping quarters. She had assumed he had accepted that one night of intimacy as a fluke, something that wouldn't be repeated.

She swirled, busying herself with spreading the bedding that had been given to her over the bare ticking of the bed. "No," she answered, the only words she was capable of uttering at the moment, "I guess not."

Behind her Braven took a deep breath and eased it out. "Don't worry, sugar. I have no intentions of pushing myself on you again. As soon as you're settled I'll go back to the wagon."

"No," she said quickly, spinning to face him. "You don't need to do that. What would your friends think?" Now, what had possessed her to say that?

He shrugged his wide shoulders, his gaze following the line of her hip outlined in the curve of her dress, a skeptical glint in his eyes. "And does it matter to you what the people of Poker Flat think?"

Did it matter? she wondered. If it did, why? She glanced down, busying her hands again with the thin blanket. These people liked Braven, respected him. She had no right to take those things away from him. "Yes, of course," she answered, her words as crisp as the cool evening air.

"What are you saying?"

Her hands stilled, his question an echo of her own thoughts. She pressed the wrinkles from the bedding. "I'm saying that this community is a small one. Everyone would be aware you had left the cabin. We have our problems, Braven, but there's no need to share them with others."

She turned to face him. Their eyes locked, hers radiating pride, his curiosity.

"Besides, after this afternoon and the bear," she continued, snapping her eyes away, "I owe you that much."

"And am I to sleep on the floor, or does your debt go further?"

"We're two adults, and I know you're a man of your word." She placed two flour sack covered pillows side by side on the bed. "I think I can trust you." But could she trust herself? Her glance dared him to deny what she said.

"All right, Rivalree. We'll do this your way, at least for now." Braven began unbuttoning his shirt.

She drew her mouth in a thin line.

"Now what?" His hands came to a halt. "Do you expect me to sleep fully clothed? I imagine with my boots on as well. Aren't you afraid someone will peek through the window and see I'm not properly clad—or unclad, I should say—for bed?" There was derision in his voice.

"Sleep anyway you want." She cupped her hand around the waning candle on the night table and snuffed it out. Why couldn't he just accept her the way she was? Why did he have to push—always push—for a reaction from her? She listened to the sounds he made undressing. What should she do now? Disrobe and put on her nightgown or remain clothed?

She started with her shoes, slowly unlacing the ties, hoping a solution to her dilemma would come to mind. She could hear his boots drop on the wooden floor, succeeded by the swoosh of material as his shirt and pants followed. She had no idea what a man wore underneath his clothes. She knew nothing under his shirt, as she had caught a glimpse of his bare chest furred with crisp, blond hairs only moments before. She prayed he wore something under his pants.

Still standing with one shoestring loosened, the leather mattress supports creaked as his weight eased onto the bed. Her heart jumped, and she had trouble swallowing the racing pulse back down. Pushing off her shoe, she let her fear and indecision trail behind. The situation must be faced, if not now, then sooner or later. She would have to make it clear her body was her own, and he had no right to touch her. She fingered the thin material of her dress. The clothing would mean nothing if he decided to disregard her demands, but if she removed everything she wore to put on her nightgown, wouldn't she be asking for trouble? The safest thing was to remain as she was, but the dress was binding and she would never get a wink of sleep, so she might as well remove the gown and be comfortable. Besides, in the dark he wouldn't be able to see what she wore—a dress, a nightgown, or chemise.

Her gown settled around her ankles. The moon swam from behind a cloud splashing the room with shadow-laced illumination. She glanced at the man reclined on the bed, and in that few seconds of light she read the turmoil battling across his features. His hands were tucked behind his head, his eyes drinking in the sight of her clad in her chemise. He wanted her, and he didn't understand her reluctance to continue where they had left off that night in the wagon.

Thankfully the darkness swallowed them up as the lunar orb dipped back in hiding, separating them in the close confines of the bedroom. She hesitated, afraid to lie so close to him, positive her resolve would crumble like a sand castle in the wake of his overpowering tide of desire.

"Come to bed," he urged softly. Too softly, too intimately, much too intimately.

She lowered her weight, ruffling the bedclothes with no more force than a feather as close to the edge as she could. Then, in precaution she placed her pillow between their bodies, a barrier to remind him how she felt. She wished now she hadn't stopped him from sleeping in the wagon. What a fool she had been to insist he stay with her.

His fingers joined hers on the crest of the pillow, and he

squeezed the down-stuffed bolster as if tempted to dash the barrier to the floor. She pulled her hand back to the safety of her side and tensed, ready to escape if he came closer.

Their unmatched breathing sawed back and forth, hers rasping in fear, and his? In anger, exasperation, or, even, determination? The moments inched by, neither moving, and she wondered if she misinterpreted him. Maybe he slept while she fought an imaginary battle with the dragons in her head.

The thought irked her that he would give up so easily. Then she chided herself for being like a petulant child demanding all and wanting nothing. She should be relieved he was willing to leave her alone.

Her heart slowed its wild maneuvers within the cage of her chest, and an inconsolable yawn stretched her jaws allowing the tiny sigh of discontentment to escape. Her hand edged to the pillow between them to check and make sure it remained firmly lodged. She brushed his hard fist still clutching the down-filled partition. Her fingers begged to explore his warm flesh, but she jerked them back to the safety of her side. He was not sleeping, he was waiting—but for what? Her heart resumed its mad hammering. As if she were a trapped hare, suspended in time, until the golden mountain lion became bored with the game, she froze in abject fear, unable to move, not even able to breathe, knowing the motion would set her predator into action.

He rolled, so swiftly she had no time to utter a sound of protest, trapping her beneath his weight. His mouth descended, covering hers, drowning the denial on the tip of her tongue. At least this was better than the waiting. Now she knew her enemy and his plan of attack. Her body tightened, and her fists clenched, swung, and drummed against his back.

He lifted his head, his warm breath fanning her face. Smoldering desire sparked deep inside her, but she snuffed

143

it quickly. "No," she murmured, pressing her fists against his furred chest.

"Why not, Rivalree? Why all this demure acting with me?" He lowered his head and again captured her quivering mouth, which opened the moment he insisted, his tongue sweeping against hers bringing her flesh to life.

He ended the kiss, his lips so close to hers she dared not move or she would reinitiate the contact. "You say no, but your body says something else. You want me just as I want you," he whispered. His words ripped through her. She lowered her fists, allowing them to unfurl. Turning her palms down, she gripped the bedding again and again. God help her, but he spoke the truth. She *did* want him to caress her, kiss her, and ignite the spark tightening her belly with waves of indisputable pleasure. But she couldn't give in to her desire or he could discover the secret of her past. If he learned of her tainted history he might turn away from her as everyone in her life had. She couldn't risk that happening, not now when she knew without a doubt in her heart she cared for him.

"Please," she moaned, hoping to appeal to the gentleman she knew lurked inside him. "Please stop."

Braven's finger traced her jaw and lingered at the corner of her eye, the lashes splashed with tears of regret. With a groan he rolled from her, his breathing harsh and labored. Aware it had taken all his willpower to grant her wish, she had to tell him something. She couldn't let him think she didn't care how he felt. She did. More than she would admit, even to herself.

"Braven, I . . ."

"Why, Rivalree?" He grasped the flattened pillow and tossed it across the room. "Why do you throw a barrier between us?"

She swallowed hard. What could she tell him?

"Is it Judd? Do you still feel a loyalty to him?"

144

Without knowing it, he had given her the perfect excuse. "Yes," she confirmed breathlessly. "Judd. Somehow it's as if he isn't dead. It's as if he still waits for me to come to him. As if . . ."

His hand closed around hers, and he squeezed gently. "All right, sugar. I'll give you time to accept what is."

Her lies tasted bitter. Judd was no more to her than a friend, a brother, a loss she would store in a special place in her heart to be forgotten in time. And though the realization riddled her with arrows of guilt, she shoved the confession to the wayside. Braven. She had to keep him. She would lie, steal, cheat, even him, to keep him by her side. How long would his patience last? How long before her own desires betrayed her reason? How long before he would be lose to her forever?

The solution waited for her at the end of this trip, an inner voice whispered. Once they reached the mine, she would be able to see her way clear and give answers to the fears and insecurities tearing her asunder. She would make amends for her devious actions, yet save the one shining aspiration that drove her relentlessly—her love for Braven Blackwood.

The road curved as they crossed the rippling water and started up a small incline. Once they forded Canyon Creek, they were only a few minutes from the mine, Braven had informed her over and over throughout the day. Rivalree's heart fluttered, and she wondered how many minutes constituted a few.

She glanced at him beside her on the wagon seat, and she strained forward to see as far around the bend as she could.

"Almost there," he answered her unspoken question, a wide grin splitting his face. "The last stretch of a journey is always the longest."

She smiled, then giggled in excitement. *The end—no, the beginning,* she assured herself. *The answers are waiting here for me.*

The horses whinnied and tossed their sweat-flicked manes. They recognized home. Their pace quickened as eager as she to get there, but he held them in check.

Braven pointed down the road. "Just around the next curve."

Smoke curled and danced above the trees ahead, a sign of life in the vast wilderness. Rivalree clapped her hands, then circled his arm, hugging like an excited child.

"Yahoo," he shouted, tossing his hat into the air, "we're home."

The trees cleared making way on the left to rough-cut fencing. A cow and a nanny goat lifted their heads, still chewing as they watched in lazy curiosity as the wagon passed.

"Nelly," he announced. "The cow. That's Nelly. And the goat is Clementine." Excitement laced his every word.

"Clementine?" she exclaimed with a chuckle. "You mean, oh my darling, Clementine?"

His laughter overrode the plodding hooves and jingling harness. The sound was music to her ears. She liked to see him smiling and happy. His radiant face made him look more approachable.

The pasture ended abruptly, followed by a woodpile of enormous girth.

"Winter's long here. I mean to try and stay through it if the mine's producing."

She nodded, not thinking about what he said. Not really caring, just loving the exuberance bubbling from him.

The cabin rose like a dark fortress, rough and solid, a reminder that nature was no tame entity here in the Sierras. A wide porch circled the front, six rough-hewn timbers tiered to make steps up to the weatherworn planks. A big black caldron sporting an array of colorful wildflowers squatted between two of the four support posts holding up the roof. A touch of civilization. She glanced at Braven. Had he planted them? She would like to think he had.

A left turn, down a short incline, they passed a gaping chasm in the side of the mountain that must be the mine entrance. Braven brought the wagon to a halt near another wagon of slightly smaller dimensions, its tongue propped upon a log, empty, a string of four horses tied between two trees.

"Damn," Braven muttered, glancing at her from the corners of his eyes.

Rivalree sat straight in her seat, taking in every detail of the yard. "What's wrong?"

He pinned his gaze on the rumps of the team as he wrapped the reins around the brake handle. "Nothing, I hope." Dropping from the wagon seat, he circled in front of the horses. "Where in the hell is everybody," he called.

A face—funny and wrinkled in an impish way, looking as if it belonged to a leprechaun—popped out of the front door of the cabin. "By all that's green in Ireland, me boyo, it is you." The little man laughed in a delightfully musical voice.

Whoever he was, Rivalree knew she would like him, and she smiled when he looked her way.

"Your timing couldn't've been better." The little man grinned. "We have visitors."

"Is it who I think it is?" Braven asked, a slight catch in his voice.

"More 'n likely," the Irishman answered.

Braven groaned. "This is all I need."

The little man's eyes traveled to take in Rivalree still perched high on the seat. "And who might ye be, colleen?"

Without thinking she responded to his good-naturedness, "Rivalree. Rivalree Richards."

"Juddy boy's little lass?" He flicked a glance at Braven. "I thought you were sending her home?"

"Rivalree Blackwood," Braven corrected. "We're married now. Rivalree, this is Pat O'Grady, our . . ."

Pat slapped his knee and guffawed loud. "Now I understand your reluctance to greet our guests."

Boisterous laughter filtered from the open cabin door. Deep masculine sounds mixed with higher pitched giggles. Rivalree sat up alert.

A flutter of a bright red dress filled the doorway. The woman who wore it squealed in pleasure and hurried out on the porch, her skirts held high to free her running legs, her brassy hair flying behind her. Just as quickly she took the steps to the ground and raced to Braven. He stiffened, his arms close to his sides as if he expected to be attacked.

The woman's arms opened wide as she ran and encircled Braven's neck before she came to a complete stop. Her rosy mouth planted itself on his as she pressed as tightly to him as she could, as if she wanted nothing separating them, as if she knew him intimately.

Rivalree couldn't believe what she saw. The kiss went on, deepening, and Braven did nothing to stop the woman. In fact, his hands came up and gripped her bare shoulders almost in a caress.

Rivalree's eyes widened with an emotion she didn't understand. An emotion so strong she wanted to rip the tight red curls from the woman's head. Not caring that her skirts rose higher than they should, or that anyone would witness the horror twisting her features, she pushed down from the wagon. She stumbled as her feet hit the ground, unsure which way to run. But escape she must. Her husband embraced another woman. She couldn't watch the shattering of the dreams that meant the answer to her problems. This woman was no solution, just another obstacle.

Gathering her skirts, she glanced at her surroundings and discovered the river down the hill to her left. She spun away, strong emotions clogging her throat.

"Hello, Beth Ann," she heard Braven say.

"Welcome home, Braven, my love," the woman responded. "It's good to see you back."

Chapter Ten

Rivalree's thoughts swirled like the uncensored river rushing around the boulders and rocks blocking its path. She took a deep breath for composure and to slow the racing of her heart which sounded as if it had taken residency in her ears. Bewilderment gripped at her insides like icy fingers. The emotion was similar to fear, yet mixed with a variety of other sentiments: betrayal, anger, and confusion. Betrayal that Braven allowed that woman to press herself so intimately against him. Anger at the woman for daring to touch the man who belonged to her. And confusion with herself for being upset because of the situation.

She glanced behind her, but a stand of low trees blocked her view of the wagon and the cabin porch. Who was the woman in red? She had greeted Braven like a lovesick wife or mistress. Not once had he glanced in Rivalree's direction to catch her reaction. Infuriation and frustration battled for supremacy. Again that strange feeling clutched her insides and twisted.

Oh, God, she thought, *what if the woman is his wife, too?* She had heard about men who claimed a privilege to more than one partner in life. It was a known fact that many of these Mormons were in the gold fields seeking their fortune. No, she wouldn't share him no matter what he thought God had given him a right to have.

At the crunch of boots on rock shards, her head whipped around. Braven threaded his way down the side of the gentle hill to where she stood. She shook with fear and dread at what he would tell her, how he would explain the other woman.

He smiled, his gaze seeking reaction to his presence, and halted a few feet from her. She didn't return the expression. Instead, she stared, her eyes unwavering, waiting for him to speak.

"Mind if I join you?"

She faced away from him. "If you want."

His aura of body heat preceded him, caressing her as he stopped a hairbreath away, yet not touching. The water swirled on, oblivious to the emotions renting the air. He bent and stopped up a handful of pebbles, and, kneeling, began tossing the stones one at a time into the river. She sidestepped to escape his overpowering essence. She needed a level head to contend with what he would say.

"You left before I could explain." A stone clipped the water, sending out rippling waves.

"You don't have to justify anything to me," she snapped.

His rhythm of pitching the rocks never faltered. "You're my wife; you're entitled to know the truth."

Dear God, she didn't want to hear this. She couldn't bear to know how much he cared about that woman, nor be reminded that she had forced his hand in San Francisco by refusing to return to New Jersey. She had given him no choice but to marry her. Remembering the stone-cold regret in his eyes as he had slipped the wedding band on her finger, she glanced down at her hands, the golden ring mocking her and her newfound sentiments.

"Beth Ann is a—"

Oh, please, Braven, don't say it.

152

"—whore."

She blinked in disbelief at his words. "A *what?*"

"She and six other women travel to the mining camps during the warm months to . . . accommodate the men."

Relief flooded her. Beth Ann was nothing to him. He didn't love her. Then that other feeling rushed in. How dare he flaunt his harlots in front of her. He had kissed and fondled that woman right in her face. Anger flashed like daggers from her eyes. "And she's your favorite, am I right?"

He took a deep breath and let it out a wisp at a time. His hands clutched in his lap, the remaining pebbles slipping from his fingers to the ground. "I had no idea she would be here. Usually the wagon has come and gone by now."

"You didn't answer my question," she said softly.

"And I won't, Rivalree. What in the hell do you expect?" He raked his fingers through his hair. "By God, I'm a man like any other. I get lonely, too. When I left here weeks ago to meet you in San Francisco for Judd, I had no idea I would bring you back as my wife." His gaze snapped with righteousness. "By God, you're right. I don't owe you any explanations." He rose to his feet, towering over her, his determination to prove himself blameless as strong as hers.

She slanted her eyes and crossed her arms over her chest, a little "humph" of indignation puffing from her mouth.

He lifted one eyebrow, then the other, erasing the angry lines wrinkling the bridge of his nose. The rest of his face relaxed, and a mischievous twinkle shone from his eyes. He began to laugh, a low rumble erupting from his chest. "You're jealous," he stated in amazement.

"No, I'm not," she defended hotly, pivoting so she didn't have to witness the smug look on his face.

He clamped her around the waist, lifted her as if she were no more than a leaf in the breeze, and swung her around. "That's it, isn't it? You're jealous."

Her head shook in denial until she thought she would faint from dizziness. Never would she confess her feelings with him gloating over her. Never!

"Keep your pretty head still, sugar. I want to see that green-eyed monster lurking behind those amber eyes of yours." His hand captured her stiffly held chin between his thumb and forefinger. As hard as she tried to trap the passion behind her expression, she couldn't. The look of amusement on his features confirmed his words. "I didn't think you cared that much."

Lowering his mouth, he entrapped hers. His lashes closed with a flutter, yet the memory of his laughing eyes lingered to haunt her.

Her fists curled in protest against his chest, then rose on their own accord to entwine around his neck. She kissed him back with a hunger of astonishing proportion, leaving her breathless.

Lids opening to reveal the vivid blue orbs, his mouth lifted momentarily. The amusement she had seen seconds ago melted into something quite different and definitely more exciting.

His lips dipped to reclaim her eager mouth, and she inhaled catching a wisp of cheap perfume clinging to his shirt. Beth Ann's perfume, no doubt. He had been kissing that woman only moments ago, and now he had the nerve to come to her and demand the same.

"No," she choked, pulling away as she remembered how the woman had wound her arms around him just as she did. "No! Don't come to me straight from your whore."

Braven's arms dropped like lead to his sides. The hurt in his eyes was as if she had struck him with her fists not words. "Whore or no, you wouldn't let me near you anyway, Rivalree. This marriage is nothing but a farce. To hell with you and your inability to accept things the way they are. I've run out of patience." He spun and started up the hill.

"Braven," she demanded. "What do you plan to do?"

"I plan to make love to a woman tonight." He raised one eyebrow in taunt. "Will it be you?"

She gasped, openmouthed, unable to believe the crassness of his words. He wouldn't really turn to that other woman, would he? Not if he truly loved *her*. But the threat in his gaze told her differently. She squeezed her eyes shut, blocking out the fury directed at her. Heartbroken, she shook her head, rejecting his demands.

"Then, that means I'm free to do what I want, when I want, and with whomever I want. And, by damn, I will."

Oh, Braven, her mind sobbed in protest. *Please don't do this. Don't ruin what has taken so long to grow between us.* She opened her eyes and mouth to stop him, but he had vanished. "Gone," she groaned. "Gone to Beth Ann."

Standing on the porch at the front door of the cabin, Rivalree wasn't sure what to do. Should she knock and wait for permission to enter, or walk through the door as if she had every right? If she entered, uninvited, God only knew what she would find. Could it be worse than what she'd experienced at the Veta Madre? Yes, it could. She might find Braven locked in the arms of Beth Ann. She clamped her mouth tight and raised her fist, rapping, not timidly but with a boldness of one who knew she had right on her side.

Expecting voices, she was instead greeted by the frantic barking of a dog as its claws scratched at the wood between them demanding to be released. Braven had never mentioned he had a dog, but then he hadn't told her he had a whore, either. She stepped back, unsure.

The Irish lilt of Pat O'Grady's voice ordered the beast back as the door popped open, and his elfin face peered around it. "That you knockin', colleen?"

She nodded.

The doorway widened. "There's no sense to that. Seems to me you're the mistress of the house. Don't need to knock on your own door."

Rivalree reddened with his words. She didn't feel like the mistress of anything, much less this cabin. She felt like an outsider, an unwelcome intruder. The dog crouched in a dark corner, a growl vibrating from deep in its chest. Yes, an invader with no right to be there.

"I wasn't sure what to expect," she offered lamely, keeping vigilance on the dog.

The little man lifted one bottle-brush eyebrow as he glanced outside the door, up and down the porch, and across the cleared yard. "Where's Braven?"

Where, indeed. She shrugged her shoulders. "I'm not sure. We argued . . . He lost his temper and stormed off."

"By all the saints, never seen him act this way before," Pat lilted as he scrutinized her, then chuckled, clutching his stomach, again reminding her of a leprechaun. "Come in, come in. Make yourself to home."

Rivalree hesitated on the threshold, squinting in the dark shadows of the building after the bright sunshine. Her eyes adjusted, and she glanced around.

The cabin was large with a high ceiling. To one side a sturdy staircase led up to a loft. The fireplace dominated the far wall, its beam mantel running almost the length, a battery of crude chairs and benches arching around the hearth. To her right, a long, rustic dining table with slab benches around it made the other furniture appear insignificant. To her left squatted a wood-burning cookstove. On the wall above, one small window with no curtain allowed a minimal amount of light to illuminate the floor in front of the stove. No matter how she looked at it, the room was bleak and musty, reminding her of a cave. She shivered, not sure she could spend a lifetime in such a dismal place, especially with Braven Blackwood.

Oil lamps were situated around the room giving off an eerie light. The chairs surrounding the empty hearth sported an assortment of occupants, five women and a dozen men, all at ease with each other. The only comfort she received from the curious stares was that none of the people were Braven or Beth Ann. Which only meant one thing, they were somewhere together. *Oh God, he meant what he said. He is with that woman at this moment.*

Fingers touched her elbow, and she glanced around to find Pat watching her, concern on his face. "Beth Ann took one of the boys to the tent out back. Braven's probably down in the tunnels."

Uncanny. How had the little man known what she was thinking?

" 'Tis a power all we O'Gradys have," he answered her mental question. "You'll get used to it in time."

She wasn't sure she could adjust to someone probing her thoughts. It was unnerving, especially when you had secrets to keep. She smiled, warily, hoping he couldn't read every notion zipping through her mind.

"Well, you must excuse me. I have to get back to my cookpots. It'll be time for supper soon."

"You prepare the meals?" she asked, surprised.

"That and I do. Somebody has to. Ever since I hurt me back last year, I'm not much help in the tunnels." He grinned and did a little jig toward the stove.

Her uneasy gaze drifted around the room. The dog, a multicolored mutt with brooding black eyes, curled in one corner, a man's red bandana circling its neck. The group around the hearth shot her strange stares when they thought she wasn't looking. If she sat down with them, what would she say? Her feet shuffled self-consciously. Damn Braven for leaving her that way. She wanted to wring his neck.

"Sit at the table and keep me company," Pat offered from behind her.

The old man had done it again. But this time she welcomed his abilities and readily did what he suggested.

"Don't worry, colleen," the Irishman assured. "They'll be gone in a day or two, and everything will be back to normal."

Her shoulders slumped, and she hoped he was right. She wasn't sure what normal was, but anything was better than suspecting her husband was with another woman.

The clink of flatware rang in the air. Plates rattled, and the noise of hungry people filling their bellies dominated the room. Braven savored the Irish stew before him. It was good to be back at the mine. He hadn't realized how much he missed Pat's cooking until now.

He eyed his infuriatingly unpredictable wife from across the table. Her fork lifted with the pretense of eating, but she merely pushed her food around her plate. Why was it, when a woman was upset she had no appetite? No doubt she was uncomfortable and feeling out of place. Damn it all, it was her own fault. If she would act more like a wife, he would find it easier to portray the part of caring husband. How long would she play this maddening charade with him, one minute coy and untouchable, the next as wanton as any of the other women in the room?

As if reminding him she was there and available, Beth Ann's thigh pressed hard against him. The redhead had seen to it she sat next to him on the bench at the dinner table. He hadn't objected. Cupping her hand around his ear, she blew softly as she whispered, her eyes darting to take in Rivalree across the table. "Is she really your wife? Didn't never think no woman would claim that honor."

He nodded and grinned. Out of the corner of his eye, he caught Rivalree's piqued reaction. She tensed, then jabbed a piece of meat with the fork she clutched. He knew she was stabbing him in her mind. *Good, let her wonder what*

*we're talking about. Let jealousy force her into making up
her mind about what she wants from me.*

"That seems to be the case," he answered.

The bottle of whiskey made another circle around the
table and was pushed into Rivalree's unwilling hands. She
passed the offending liquor to Pat, who sat beside her like
a guardian angel. What was the Irishman's problem? Why
did the old man glare at him as if he had just beat the living
daylights out of her? Damn that Irish ability to pierce into
a man's brain. He wasn't wrong to force her hand. It was
time to either make this marriage work or . . . He didn't
want to think about the alternative.

The circulating spirits reached Braven, and he caught
Rivalree's eye and took a gulping swig. *There, let her stew
on that.* Wiping his mouth with the back of his hand, the
crudest gesture he could think of at the moment, he
challenged her with a look. He had had more than enough
whiskey, he knew, but the satisfaction he received
watching the scowl of disapproval clouding her amber
eyes each time he drank outweighed the hangover he'd
battle in the morning. Unfortunately she was worth
everything he had suffered since the day he'd first laid eyes
on her. *Damn her,* he thought.

Beth Ann's experienced hand crept to rest between his
aching thighs, a longing centering on the golden-haired
beauty across from him. The gesture was a familiar one
between them, one he usually found stimulating. But now
it served as a source of irritation. He didn't want the
willing woman beside him, he desired the unwilling one
within arm's reach across the wide planks of the table.

In an overt movement he patted Beth Ann's creeping
hand as it fluttered to rest in his lap. "Oh, sugar," he
drawled. "You do know how to please a man." Staring at
his wife, he continued. "Something some women could
take lessons in."

Rivalree nearly fell from her seat, his meaning striking a

159

sensitive cord. For a moment he thought he'd gone too far as she looked ready to attack him over the table. Instead, she turned to Pat and offered him a sweet smile. "Can I help you with the dishes?"

Rising, she began gathering the plates from the table to carry them to the dry sink tucked in the corner next to the cookstove. She circled the diners, saying nothing, her face blank, unreadable.

From the corner of his line of vision Braven noticed his dog stiffen with each step Rivalree took toward him. The faithful animal seemed to sense a danger, a knack she'd had since the day he'd taken her in, battered and hungry. His gaze switched from dog to wife and back. How much of a threat could Rivalree present? A reverberating growl erupted from Zoey. Ignoring the warning, he grumbled to himself and accepted the bottle as it was handed to him.

He studied his wife as she skirted the far end of the table. "Seems to me Zoey doesn't like you."

Rivalree continued as if he hadn't spoken.

"Seems to me, I have a way of attracting jealous females."

Beth Ann giggled nervously. Rivalree placed another plate on the growing stack in her hands. There was a gleam in her eye he hadn't noticed before.

Tilting his head back to take a healthy swig, he dismissed the notion she was up to something. She continued to work down the table toward him innocently removing dishes. *Damn, but she's cool.* Aware Beth Ann's hand still rested in his lap, he didn't bother to remove it. *Let her see. She needs to know other women find me attractive.*

The burning liquor worked its way down his throat. Beth Ann squealed, and her caressing hand flew up and away from him, knocking the bottle from his hand.

"What the hell," he sputtered as he twisted to a standing position.

160

Congealed Irish stew dripped from her brassy hair. Whiskey plastered his shirt to his chest. Rivalree stood behind them, an angelic look he knew wasn't genuine on her face.

He rose to his full height beside Beth Ann, who was attempting to wipe the gravy from her face. "Damn you, Rivalree. You did that on purpose."

She smiled sweetly, but her eyes narrowed in triumph. "Sorry," she offered to the other woman. Then she swirled and walked away. As she passed Zoey, the dog growled again and stood on stiffened legs.

"Shut up, Zoey," he snapped. "Lie down."

The dog's ears lifted, and her big, brown eyes pleaded with him to let her tear into her enemy, her rival. With a whine, the animal obeyed, but her gaze continued to follow every step Rivalree took.

Tempted to turn the dog loose and let her corner Rivalree, he would enjoy taking a switch to that swaying bottom of hers. He pulled his eyes away from the tantalizing sight she made crossing the room.

Reaching down, he strove to extract the wet shirt from his skin. He smelled like a brewery. As Beth Ann wiped the remains of the food from her face and dress, he shrugged his shoulders in apology. Swaying, he blinked in surprise. The liquor had caught up with him. How had he gotten so soused? If he didn't lie down now he'd fall down. Wrapping his arm around Beth Ann, who offered the nearest support, he headed toward the staircase. "Come on, sugar," he muttered, knowing Rivalree listened. "I do believe we have some unfinished business between us."

He stumbled as his feet skimmed over the wooden steps. By the time they reached the small bedroom he called his, there was no doubt in his mind he was roaring drunk.

"Oh, Jesus," he moaned, hitting the bed with a gut-wrenching jar.

Beth Ann shut the door, and the sound rattled around in

161

his head. "Braven Blackwood," she scolded with a shake of her head. "I don't believe I've ever seen you in such a mess. That girl has a real clutch on you, don't she?" She clucked her tongue.

"Bitches and whores," he mumbled. "All I seem to attract are bitches and whores." He wished at that moment he'd never laid eyes on Rivalree Richards or had tasted her honey lips. If he had it to do over again, he'd tell Judd to go to hell. He didn't want the responsibility of any ill-tempered, game-playing woman.

Rivalree wiped the last plate as if trying to erase the last few months of her life.

"It's not going to get any drier," Pat insisted, catching her swirling hand in his gnarled ones.

"No, I suppose not." She set the dish on the shelf and draped the damp cloth on a stove handle to dry.

"The boy made an ass of himself, to be sure. But I do think you'll find him sorry in the morning."

"Sorry for what?" She planted her fists on her hips. "Sorry for taking that woman upstairs to do God knows what? Sorry for being a black-hearted . . . Oh, damn him." She tossed her hands in the air. "I doubt he's been sorry for anything in his life—except marrying me."

Pat's Irish green eyes bore into her. He was doing it again, seeing right through her to the hidden recesses of her heart.

"Is there a reason you feel he should regret your marriage?"

Panic rose like floodwater inside her. She turned away attempting to hide her secrets. "Of course not."

"You know, Rivalree—you don't mind if I call you by your given name, do you?"

She smiled and shook her head. Her name sounded so musical when he spoke it.

162

"You remind me of my daughter, me own sweet Carrie, never satisfied with the way things are. You look nothin' like her, yet you could be sisters of the soul, except that her heart has turned bitter." He shook his head with sadness. "There's a sayin' we have back on the Emerald Isle. Things aren't what they always seem. Fear and hate, as well as courage and love, can cloud the truth. Don't go lookin' for problems where they don't exist."

She cocked her head to one side. What did he mean?

"Come on," he urged. "I know you must be tired. There's another room upstairs, Judd's old room. We'll make it yours until you and Braven work things out."

She shot him a doubtful look.

"Aye, and you will, colleen," he informed her with a chuckle, "as sure as I'm Patrick O'Grady. In your own time and your own way, but you two will solve your problems."

The stairs sagged under her feet as she followed his elfin steps. Her heart quickened as they neared the top. She could see two doors, both closed. Which one was Braven and Beth Ann behind? Her gaze jumped from door to door, but they were exactly the same, giving no clue to the answer to her question.

Pat swept past the first door. "The room hasn't been disturbed since Judd . . ." He trailed off apologetically.

The loud squeak of a bed drowned all thoughts from her mind. She blinked in shock. Braven was actually doing what he threatened to do. He and that woman were in there, together. Somehow she hadn't believed he would stoop so low. She had thought he was trying to make her jealous. He had meant it and was carrying out his intentions.

"Rivalree."

Her name spoken in the soft Irish lilt brought her head around with a snap. In horror she realized she stood in front of Braven's door, staring at the barrier, her hand poised to touch the handle. Pat must think her a naive child.

"I'm sorry. Must be the wrong door," she mumbled, jumping back.

The Irishman cleared his throat, embarrassed, as he opened the other door. "If there was anywhere else to put you, I would."

"Oh, no, Pat. This will be fine."

"Like I was sayin'. Judd's things are as he left them. I wanted to clear the room, but Braven made me promise not to disturb anything until he returned and had a chance to go through the boyo's possessions himself."

A loud moan filtered into the hallway from the other room. Pat reddened, the flush beginning at the tip of his ears and dropping. "Maybe it would be better if you took my room off the kitchen. There, at least, you won't be bothered by—"

"No," she answered briskly. "The room will be just fine." With a decisive step she entered. Smiling back at Pat, she closed the door with a soft thud.

With a deep breath she whirled to face the darkening room. Judd's domain. She had forgotten completely about him. Her self-centered coldheartedness sickened her. Judd had been the joy of her life not so long ago. Now she could forget his very existence with a snap of her fingers.

She stepped forward, guilt pushing her along. A stack of freshly laundered shirts graced the top of the pine dresser, each neatly folded. How like Judd. Everything had to be in its place. She fingered the top one, a pale blue cotton flannel she had stitched with her own hands. He had been so proud of it and had promised to save it for special occasions. It sported a patch at one shoulder by an inexperienced hand.

"Oh, Judd. Why did you leave me," she murmured into the fabric as she lifted the garment to her face, rubbing her cheek against its softness. A tear slipped from the corner of

164

her eye and settled on the flannel. "You would have never done what he's done. Humiliate me."

Beth Ann's voice shattered her silent tears. "Get off me, Braven Blackwood. Damn, but you're heavy."

Rivalree gasped. She had hoped she had misunderstood the sounds she'd heard earlier, but there was no denying what was taking place in the next room. While she stood there feeling sorry for herself, he was with that woman having the time of his life, not once thinking about how she felt.

"Oh, Christ, Braven. Look what you've done now." Beth Ann's whine rang clearly through the thin walls. "I'll have to clean us both up."

Wiping her face on Judd's shirt, Rivalree slammed it back down on the stack. "Damn you, Judd. Why did you have to go and pick a man like Braven Blackwood to be your partner? I can't let him get away with this. He has no right to shame us both this way."

A door slammed. Someone left the other room. Tiptoeing, she returned to peek out into the hallway. Beth Ann's swaying figure took the stairs in easy strides. Braven was alone. She would confront him with his disloyalty and demand an explanation.

Down the long corridor, she wavered momentarily. What if he misunderstood her reasons for entering his room? She scowled. He'd figure out soon enough what she wanted. An apology and admission of his guilt.

A low growl reverberated in the dark hall. Rivalree came to an abrupt halt. The sound ceased. As she lifted her foot to continue, the throaty noise began again. Zoey. She had forgotten about the damn dog. Glancing down at the floor, two illuminated eyes glared back at her, daring her to take one step closer.

"Damn you, dog, get out of my way."

Zoey answered by deepening the mencing sound.

"You can't protect him from me forever. Worship him,

you dumb animal. But you have a lot to learn. He's not so wonderful. He's a low-down, drunken scum. You and Beth Ann deserve him." With a flounce, she spun and returned to the solace of her room.

The words she had said to the dog came back to her. He was no better than anybody else. No better than she, Rivalree. He deserved everything that happened to him, including the fact he had married an impure woman.

Chapter Eleven

Rivalree leaned over the loft railing and surveyed the common room below. The long plank table was crowded with men, each eating in silence, a change in pace from the meal the evening before. The oil lamps cast eerie shadows across the raw wooden walls, like haunts from the night waiting for the darkness to return. She sighed as she descended the stairs.

Braven sat among his men. Hoping to avoid him this morning, she had stayed in her room until she thought the men would be gone to work in the mines. She frowned slightly. How did he expect to be successful getting such a late start?

Pat's head rose, and he saw her standing on the steps. "Colleen," he called, "join us."

She lifted the light blue cotton of her skirt and treaded softly down the stairs.

Beside the Irishman was an unused place setting; he hadn't forgotten her. She offered him a grateful look, which he acknowledged with a nod as he filled her plate with heavenly smelling pancakes. Accepting the small pitcher of molasses, she smothered the golden cakes until the dark liquid flowed down and over the small stack. Without thinking she wiped the drip from the pitcher's spout and brought her hand to her lips, sucking the sweetness from her finger.

Realizing what a childish thing she had done, she glanced up to find Braven glaring at her. "Good morning," she whispered sheepishly.

"Morning," he grumbled, and stared back down into his uneaten food.

She sliced through the thick stack of pancakes. "I thought you would be working already this morning. Do you always get such a late start?"

Braven's blue eyes shot back up to take her in. He reminded her of a cornered beast, hair mussed, eyes red, his mouth arched in a frown which flattened into a sneer. "Are you trying to put me on your schedule?"

She lifted an eyebrow. He looked terrible. No matter what his problem this morning, he had no right to take it out on her. Blinking, she swallowed the bite of food in her mouth. "Not at all, sir. I thought you would be eager to look for gold."

"Stop thinking, Rivalree. You'll be better off."

Her jaw dropped in surprise. "I don't think you have a right to talk to me that way."

"I have the right to do anything I want. I'm in charge here."

Mortified he would treat her so shabbily, she glanced around the table expecting to see smirks and grins on the other men's faces. Instead they either stared down into their plates or into space as if trying to pretend they didn't hear the horrible words he said to her.

Pat touched her arm and shook his head slightly, warning her not to argue. She riveted her eyes on the man across the table. Was this the real Braven Blackwood? Tyrant?

She licked her bottom lip. All right. She wouldn't bicker with him. She would make an effort to get along, even though she had every right to claw out his eyes for what he

168

had done last night.

"I was hoping to take a look around today." She forced a bright smile and tackled her food with gusto. "Could you give me a tour of the mine?" She mentally patted herself on the back for being so cleverly tolerant.

Braven rose and stepped away from the table in stony silence.

"Well," she challenged, "did you hear what I said?" How could he have not? Surely, he didn't mean to ignore her polite request.

"May I suggest you spend the day with Pat learning how to be the lady of the house." The word "lady" came out almost in a snarl.

Rivalree stood, ready to do battle, but Braven presented his back and thumped out the door, never once glancing in her direction.

Damn him! What a brute. Why did he treat her this way? Again Pat's hand came to rest on her arm and gently urged her to sit back down.

As if obeying a silent command, the men sprang to their feet to follow Braven's lead. One man stopped, his fingers kneading the heavy canvas of his pants. "It's all right, ma'am. Braven just had a bad night." He tipped his thumb up to his mouth in a drinking gesture. "He'll be to rights later this afternoon."

She couldn't believe what she heard. These men protected him, making excuses for his inexcusable behavior. She glared at the Irishman, and he nodded his head in agreement. Even Pat. They all treated Braven Blackwood as if he were a god. Just like the damnable dog trailing him out the door.

But she wouldn't. She'd show him. She'd tell him exactly what she thought of his domineering ways the first chance she got.

*　　*　　*

The rocker squeaked a soothing rhythm reminding Rivalree of home. Back and forth, back and forth. Like cymbals the fire crackled accenting the metronome beat the moving chair made beneath her. Her hands worked in time with the music, the needle pushing in and out of the fabric she held, a soft woolen shirt of Judd's she was scaling down to fit one of the men whom she had noticed wore clothes so old and patched she couldn't imagine what held them together. There was no sense in perfectly good clothes going to waste when there was an obvious need for them. Judd would have wanted it that way. In fact, he would have been angry if she did otherwise. Pat had thought hers a good idea as well. However, she must be honest with herself. What better way to make friends with the miners than to offer what she had, her talents as a seamstress? She needed friends here desperately, to serve as buffers between Braven and herself.

When Braven had so rudely dismissed her this morning, she had considered packing and leaving the mine to go back down the mountain. But even if she did manage to escape, where would she go? The thought of facing what waited for a woman alone in the wilds of the Sierra Madres frightened her more than dealing with Braven Blackwood. At least he had never physically harmed her, though his mental cruelties cut deeply. Circumstances could always change. That was one thing she had learned in her few short years. As long as she was healthy and alive, she could be ready to take advantage of whatever fate brought her. She would get out of this predicament. No matter what, she had to believe that, or she would lose her sanity.

The rocker stilled beneath her, and her hands came to rest in her lap with no rhythm to follow. She pushed back and continued the movement and her sewing with renewed determination.

Beside her a soft snore cut through the silence. Glancing at the Irishman sitting in the chair next to her, she smiled.

Pat's head nodded, the pipe he clenched between his teeth threatening to escape his slackened mouth. She giggled at the comical sight he made as she reached over to remove the churchwarden from his lips before it dropped hot ashes into his lap. His head jerked, and she feared he would awaken, but the soft rumble continued as he settled more comfortably in the chair.

She caught up her work, in a way contented, feeling much as her mother must have felt as she had worked mending clothes for her and her father. Until today, she had never understood how a woman could enjoy the ordinariness of her life, but now she craved to have what she had considered mundane not so long ago. She had dreamed of adventure all of her childhood. Experiencing it, she'd gladly trade it for security and the warmth of a loving family.

Her shoulders lifted in a deep breath. *Ma had been right. The grass is always greener.*

She eyed the ornate timepiece squatting on the mantel, amazed how out of place the clock was in the rustic cabin. Pat had told her Braven had brought it with him, a reminder of his home. She tried to conjure up a picture of the house to which it belonged, but her simple upbringing couldn't do justice to the image of the southern mansion with white columns across the front that insisted on invading her thoughts.

Glancing down, she concentrated on tying a final knot in the thread she stitched with. With clenched teeth, she bit off the strand, placing the finished shirt in her lap. The rocker stilled beneath her, and she scanned Pat's sleeping form. The men would work a few hours more to make up for their late start. She would let the Irishman sleep a while longer before waking him to prepare the evening meal—a dish he called poacher's rabbit, a recipe from his childhood in Ireland where a stolen hare had been a peasant's delight.

Laying her head back against the spindles of the chair, she closed her eyes, enjoying the silence interrupted only by the squeak of the rocker, the ticking of the clock, and the mumbles of the sleeping man beside her.

The front door crashed against the wall. Startled from her peaceful daydreaming, Rivalree flew from the rocker, the shirt clutched to her bosom. In her haste, she tripped over Pat's outstretched legs, and the little man jumped, as well, in sleep confusion.

Braven's imposing figure filled the threshold, a bucket of water in each hand. He glanced around the room taking in the domestic air, and the glint in his eyes softened for a moment.

"Braven," Pat mumbled, glancing at the clock. "Didn't expect you in so soon."

Braven set the buckets of water by the stove. "There was a small problem in the mine." He stepped into the light cast from the lone lamp on the table.

Rivalree gasped. He was covered with flecks of dirt and mud from head to foot. "Are you hurt?" she asked before she had a chance to think about what she said.

Braven glanced in her direction. "No," he answered. "Are you sorry?"

Her eyes narrowed. If he wanted a fight, then by darn she'd give him one.

Pat stepped between them, breaking their eye contact. "Let me heat that water for you, man. You look as if the mountain spewed its guts all over you."

A spurt of merriment burst from Rivalree's lips. What an accurate description of how he looked.

Braven's drew into a taut line, but her laughter intensified. She couldn't control the giggles if she wanted, but she didn't try. Why should she?

"You find it funny that I could have lost my life?"

She bit her tongue. "Oh, Braven, of course not. It's just that you look so comical."

He turned, ignoring her. "Thank you, Pat. I'll get the tub."

The tub? Her mouth clamped tight, the laughter dying in her throat.

Braven returned with a large, metal bath. He halted in the middle of the room, near the fireplace, and dropped the object, busying himself with setting the bottom on the uneven floorboards to his satisfaction. He planned to wash right here in the middle of the common room. Panic rose from the pit of her stomach. She must leave, but wasn't sure which way to go, out the front door or up the stairs. She swayed in indecision, her nostrils flared and quivered. With a swish of her skirt, she turned to gather up her sewing.

Behind her Braven emitted a loud groan as he sat heavily on a bench. With a plop one boot hit the floor, and her hands stilled, anticipating the sound of the other shoe joining its mate. He grunted, then cursed. She heard him strain to remove the boot, but to no avail as he swore under his breath again.

"Where the hell is the bootjack?" he demanded.

She ignored him, assuming Pat would answer his question, but silence greeted his words.

Whirling, she expected to find the Irishman at the stove. Instead, the kettle hissed over one burner, the room was empty except for her and Braven, who still struggled to remove his boot.

"It was filthy," she snapped. "I took it to the creek and cleaned it off. I imagine it's still drying outside on the porch." She gave him a look that dared him to comment on her actions.

"Then how in the hell do you expect me to get this damn boot off?" He rose from his bent position, his shirt unbuttoned to his waist. One sleeve had a large tear in it, and she noticed there were several buttons missing. Mesmerized by the strong expanse of chest muscles

173

rippling with each move he made, her face grew hot as she took him in, every vibrant inch of him.

Confused, she fumbled with her mending, dropping the shirt, and stepped toward the front door. She needed freedom, a place to catch her ragged breath. "I'll get it for you."

As she swept past him, his hand snaked out and grasped her arm. "Never mind, Rivalree. I'll manage without a bootjack."

"Will you?" she whispered, wishing she still had a reason to rush from the cabin. Again her eyes riveted to his bare chest where a light matting of golden hair peeked out. She pulled her gaze away and, covering the emotions raging through her mind, she offered, "If you leave me your shirt, I'll mend it and replace the missing buttons."

With a thud the cantankerous boot hit the floor. Before she could escape him, he removed his shirt and volunteered it to her. "I'd appreciate that."

His chest glistened in the faint lamplight. Her hand trembled as she reached to accept the garment from his fingers. Forgetting the dirt and mud covering the cloth, she crushed it to her breasts. How handsome and golden he looked standing before her. She swallowed, confused by her inability to turn away.

The kettle rattled on the stove behind her, beginning to boil. "Oh," she blurted, "the water will be too hot." Her eyes darted around hoping to find Pat back, but they remained alone—the air crackling with the tension pulling at her heart.

She dropped the shirt on top of the one she had tailored earlier and scurried to the stove, relief flooding her as she escaped the magnetic pull emitting from Braven. She should leave now before things went further, she told herself. Just as soon as she poured the water into the bath and started another batch to heat. Then she would go.

Her hands grasped the kettle; Braven's hand claimed

hers. "Let me," he offered. "It's much too heavy for you."

She stepped back, watching him pad in stockinged feet across the floor to pour the water into the tub, then mix in enough cold until the temperature reached his satisfaction.

"Perfect." His head raised, and he grinned at her. Adding more water to the kettle, he brought it back to the stove and set it on the burner. His eyes locked with hers, a mistiness clouding the lapis lazuli hue to a steel blue. Forgetting his original purpose, he placed the vessel on the stove corner as his hands rose to grip her shoulders. His clutch relaxed as he spidered his fingers up and down her arms causing chill bumps to rise wherever he touched her.

She tensed, her mind refusing to accept the thrilling shocks trailing his caress. His head tilted, and she held her breath, knowing what would follow. He would kiss her now. Lashes drifting down over her eyes, she waited, suspended, for the feel of his lips on hers.

Instead, the warm moistness of his mouth grazed her forehead. He dropped his hands and stepped back. Her eyes flew open, the disappointment eddying through her so strong it formed a knot between her breasts. Why hadn't he kissed her?

A curious glint in his eyes greeted her gaze. "What were you expecting Rivalree?"

She pulled back, the momentary desire he had stirred in her disappearing. "Nothing." She twisted away. "I should leave now."

"Why?"

"So you can bathe . . . in privacy."

"I'd prefer it if you stayed."

"Why?" she whispered, insecurity battering her insides.

His eyes danced, and his mouth lifted in an arrogant smile. "*Why*, woman? Why else? I need somebody to scrub my back." He turned presenting the broad, tanned expanse to her view, his hands releasing the belt buckle at his waist and working on the fasteners on the front of his denim pants.

Fascinated she regarded the play of shoulder muscles as he undressed. She must leave, but her eyes refused to tear themselves away.

"Do you know how long it's been since someone washed my back for me?" He chuckled. "Let me see. I can't remember."

Like wind in a wheat field the sinews jumped and rippled. Then like iron, they bunched and knotted. How beautiful he is, she thought. Her fingers ached to reclaim the living flesh. She buried her hands in the folds of her skirt to keep them under control.

With regret coursing through her, she averted her face as he bent to remove his pants. If she watched she would be lost—victim to the spell his maleness cast over her.

As he stepped into the water, his splashing made the clothes on her body feel as if she had been in them for a lifetime. The last time she had bathed was before they started up the mountainside from La Porte. Braven emitted a deep, satisfied sigh. She envied him. In fact, she'd give anything to change places with him. Almost anything. She wouldn't want him watching her the way her eyes had a tendency to wander to his unclad form.

"You can turn around now, Rivalree. It's safe."

She whirled, vowing to remain unaffected by the sight he made lounging in the water. He faced her, his arms draped over the tub rim, his eyes like the blue flame of a fire piercing through her, breaking down the barrier she'd struggled to erect in her mind.

"I can't decide if you're staring at me or the bath, or perhaps both. If it's me you want, I'm here for the asking. But if it's a bath, you'll have to earn it." He lifted a wet cloth from the steaming water and tossed it in her direction.

Catching the washcloth as it slammed into her chest

176

leaving a wet mark across her bodice, she narrowed her eyes at his arrogance. Earn a bath, indeed.

"There's soap in the cupboard by the stove." He waited, his shoulders propped against the sides of the tub.

Wadding the cloth in her hands, she was tempted to throw it back at him, but instead she met his challenge. "A bath is all I desire, thank you."

He chuckled, his stare insisting he knew she lied.

"If I wash your back will you prepare a fresh tub of water for me, and give me privacy to bathe?"

He leaned forward and peered into the buckets standing near the tub. "Not nearly enough for another bath. You want me to empty my water, carry more from the stream, then tote it from the stove. Seems like I'm getting the raw end of the deal. Especially since you won't allow me to watch you as you're watching me now. You drive a hard bargain, ma'am."

She offered a crooked smile. "Take it or leave it, sir, it's your choice."

"You'll wash to my satisfaction?"

"To your satisfaction." She wadded the cloth tighter in her fist and threw it at him. It cannonballed in the water splashing his face and hair.

"You minx," he exclaimed, and started to rise from the water.

"No, don't get up," she shrieked, covering her face with her hands. "I'll scrub your back, just don't stand up."

She circled him, warily, not sure if he would retaliate.

"You'd better be on your guard, lady. I plan on getting even. But for now soothe the savage beast." His hand stretched out and offered her the cloth. "Wash."

"Breast," she corrected.

"What?"

"Soothe the savage breast."

He looked up, grinning. "I know. I thought you might be embarrassed if I said the word breast." He stared

177

pointedly at the soft swells of her bosom.

Her face colored, realizing his implication. She took the cloth from his hand, warm and moist from the bath. Escaping his gaze, she hurried to the cabinet to retrieve the soap to circle around the table and approach him from the rear.

She froze when confronted with the bronze expanse of back and shoulders. *Pretend he's a small child, it's only skin and bone and muscle.* She swallowed, a task she found most difficult. By dipping the cloth in the bucket by the tub, she avoided touching him sooner than she was prepared. She soaped the rag until the suds ran down her arm. There was no reason to hesitate any longer. Expecting to be burned by the contact, she eased the cloth forward and wasn't disappointed. She skimmed over his back, dipped the cloth in the water, careful not to touch him except when she had to, and rinsed the soapsuds away. Leaning back, she started to rise, satisfied she had fulfilled her end of the bargain.

"Is that all?" He twisted to look at her. "You missed a spot." His arm arched around, and he pointed to a place on his lower spine. "There."

"I washed your back. Don't try to . . ."

"But not to my satisfaction. That was the agreement."

Kneeling, she gathered up the cloth and began scrubbing as if she wanted to take the flesh off.

"Ouch." He pulled away from her punishment. "What are you trying to do, skin me alive? Do it right, or I won't keep the agreement."

Her hand slowed, and her anger simmered. She washed and rinsed until she thought her arms would drop. Did he plan to keep her scrubbing all day?

His hand reached around his body and captured hers, guiding it around to his chest. Her palm rested in the soft mat of hair on his chest. As she tried to pull away, his fingers looped around her wrist, handcuffing it.

178

"Your back. The understanding was your back."

"So it was. But you owe me for throwing the washcloth. I told you I would get even." He pressed his shoulders against the tub, the soapy water hiding his nudity.

The faint outline of his hips and thighs tantalized her.

"Disappointed you can't see more? I'd be happy to stand for your inspection."

"No," she gasped, tearing her eyes away and pushing his shoulders down. She began washing his front, shoulders, and chest. His nipples puckered as her hand feathered across them. She reddened, and he glanced down to see what disturbed her.

Again that maddening, lopsided grin. "Can't help it. You have a nice touch."

His arm circled her shoulders, pulling her down. His lips brushed hers. She strained against the imprisoning arc, but he held her tight, and she relented, molding her form to his, not once considering the sudsy water staining the bodice of her dress a darker blue. Combing her fingers through the down on his chest, she reveled in the feel of his nipples hard against her palms. Her mind fought the swirling sensations threatening to drown her—to send her beyond the point of reason.

His mouth lifted, and his brow quirked upward. "About as nice as any woman I know."

Embarrassment flared to indignation at his words. She rose from the kneeling position beside the bath and grabbed the first thing she could reach, the bucket of cold stream water. "Nicer than Beth Ann's. After last night, this should cool your ardor."

Braven reacted, but not fast enough. The icy water hit him square in the face and chest, his look of surprise so comical, Rivalree dropped the bucket as she doubled with laughter.

Knowing he would never let her get away with what she had done, she glanced up in fear to find him standing in all his natural glory above her. She squealed and dodged to escape his revenge she knew would come quick and furious.

Scooping her up in his arms, he dangled her over the murky water. "If it's a bath you want, sugar, then it's a bath you'll get."

"Oh, no, Braven, please don't," she begged as she tried to still the laughter erupting from her lips. "Besides, I was paying you back for what you did last night."

"Last night?" His arms released her and down she plunged, the water engulfing her. She surfaced, sputtering in protest.

As her head reached the surface, the flat of his hand came to rest on the top of her sodden head, her hair tumbling down from its pins in wet tendrils. "Now, just what did I do last night that made me deserve such treatment." His hand threatened to dunk her again.

"No, Braven, stop," she pleaded.

"Tell me, or you'll go under."

"Don't try to act innocent with me, Braven Blackwood. I was in the room next to you and Beth Ann. I heard the disgusting things the two of you said and did."

He chuckled. "You were listening? What did you do, put your ear next to the wall?"

"No, I didn't have to. You two were so loud the whole camp could hear you." She closed her eyes expecting him to douse her again.

Instead, his hand lifted from her head. A glint of amusement sparkled in his blue eyes. "You are naive, aren't you? If you think heaving your guts up over a woman is anyone's idea of a good time . . ."

She stood, water running from her clothes, plastering them to her skin. "But I thought—"

"I know what you thought." His eyes skimmed over her form outlined in the wet material. "Jesus, Rivalree," he said, his voice catching in his throat as if his spoken words didn't reflect the thoughts swirling in his mind. "I was dead drunk. I don't remember much after falling facedown across the bed." His gaze continued to take in the roundness of her breasts and the curve of her thighs.

"Well, what you did and what you planned to do are two different things. Yours was a sin of the mind, just as wrong in the eyes of God."

His head flew back in laughter. "Oh, sugar. You're the only woman I know who would dare to stand there so provocatively, soaked to the skin, and moralize at me. I had no plans to take what Beth Ann so readily would have given. I was trying to bring that green-eyed glint back into your lovely, flashing eyes."

He scooped her up in his arms and held her over the bath, rivulets pouring from her garments back into the tub and onto the floor. "There's only one woman I want. You. Damn it. My heart wouldn't consider any other. Only you."

His mouth descended, catching her before she could respond to his confession. She was drowning in the happiness that swelled in her heart. She might die from lack of air, but she didn't care as long as his kisses were the reason.

Lips still locked to hers, he let her feet slip to the floor. Working swiftly, he removed the clothes clinging to her skin. She shivered in the cool, evening air, unashamed that she stood before him nude and vulnerable. His gaze traveled the length of her as his hand trailed a fiery path from her shoulder across to one soft, round breast. Rubbing his palm against her nipple, it sprang to life. "What you feel is no different than what I feel. See. You can't help the reaction any more than I could."

Taut and hard, there seemed to be an invisible string running from her aching breast to her belly, tugging, demanding something more. The rigidity of his manhood pressed against her stomach accentuating the sensation.

"Say you want me," he demanded so very gently.

Her arms circled his neck, and she pulled his face down to hers. She kissed him, passion rising to a peak with her boldness.

"No, Rivalree," he insisted, tearing away his mouth. "I know what your body wants. I want to hear the words from your sweet lips."

She strained toward him in silent communication, but he kept her inches away.

"Say it."

"I . . . want you."

"What do you want. Tell me."

"I want you to . . . make love to me."

His arm cupped the back of her legs, and he swung her up against his chest. As if they were nothing, he took the stairs in easy strides. From the loft balcony she stared down to the room below. "Oh, Braven." She eyed the watery mess they had left. "What will everyone think?"

"They'll think the truth. We're a man and woman who couldn't wait another minute to be together. Who the hell cares what they think."

The door to the bedroom clicked behind them, the only light a partial moon flooding through the open window. The chill of the breeze rippled across her bare dampness. She shivered, both from the cold and anticipation. Braven wanted her, only her.

He spun her around, and the silver beams of light accented the even whiteness of his teeth as he smiled down at her. The breath from his body feathered against her neck as, chuckling, he buried his face in the thick coil of golden hair cascading across one shoulder.

"There were times, my sweetness, I had doubts you would come to me willingly. Almost as if you hid some deep, dark past, as if you were so frightened I would never have the privilege of touching you, caressing you, making love to you whenever I wanted." His lips nibbled her ear.

Why did he have to remind her of what she so wanted to

182

forget—her sordid past? Memories of the first time he had taken her tumbled through her brain. What if the act of love hurt again? Braven swore it wouldn't. Did that mean there was something wrong with her? Had Silas Guntree injured her physically? But worst, what if she didn't feel pain? That meant she had left her home for unnecessary reasons. She could have remained in New Jersey and not come to this ungodly country—never to meet the man bending over her, forcing her to admit to feelings she hadn't known existed. The thought of not experiencing the wild excitement he stirred in her left her feeling empty and sad.

And confused, wanting to forget everything except this single moment and the way his touch sent shivers radiating from the very core of her being to the outer limits of her body.

What she felt was lust, she knew without a doubt, but it was more. Oh, so much more. She was content, and for the first time in her life, truly in love. The desire to please Braven in all ways possible transcended every facet of her life. She would give him what he most desired, a willing, wanton wife.

Balanced on tiptoes, she curled her arms about his neck, pressing her lips to every part of his body she could reach, the hollow at the base of his throat, the point behind his earlobe, then gently sucking the pendant of flesh into her mouth, teasing until he bent lower. Discovering the contours of his ear with her tongue, her heart soared when he shivered, goosebumps dotting his flesh. The heady feeling of control urged her to further boldness, and, lowering to her heels, she pressed her mouth to his hard nipple nested in a swirl of hair.

"Jesus, woman," he rasped, cradling her chin in his palms to bring her mouth to his. "You never cease to amaze me."

His kiss was hot and demanding, his tongue plundering

the moist inside of her mouth with such intensity she quivered, alarmed by the tempest she'd released in him. Had she gone too far with her brazen actions?

With one smooth motion, he swept her up and carried her to the bed where the silver moonlight mottled the coverlet. He towered above her, drinking in the sight she made, her hair draped like a river of molten gold across the star pattern of the quilt beneath her. "You are more beautiful than anything I've ever known."

He knelt on the floor beside her and buried his face between the twin peaks of her breasts. Moaning softly, he cupped them in his hands, kneading, molding them to line his palms as if he were a sculptor and her flesh the clay. His tongue curled around one nodule, and she cried out in undeniable pleasure as he drew the aureola into his mouth. How right it felt to express instead of suppress the need rocketing through her. Her fingers buried themselves into his hair urging him on.

Tracing the contour of her ribs, his hand drifted down the swell of her stomach, the muscles there jumping in response to his feather touch as he continued the oral assault of her bosom. He shifted his position until he bent above her, his fingers finding the button of feeling between her legs and his mouth worshipping the other breast.

Her lips parted, dragging in air that seemed as thin and unreplenishing as the atmosphere of the highest mountain, and his mouth covered hers drinking of their sweet nectar. Whimpering her concupiscence, her arms sought to pull him closer as she stroked the hard muscles of his back.

His probing fingers picked up speed and soon she sprawled mindless of anything but his hand as he played her body as if it were a fine-tuned instrument. Her hips rose against the pressure of his strumming only to find his shoulders pressed against the back of her knees, his mouth replacing his hands, which moved down to support her elevated buttocks and thighs between which he knelt. Nothing in life prepared her for the soul-wrenching ecstasy she experienced under his masterful ravishment of her being. She sobbed once, ethereal shudders washing over her, yet he continued until she pleaded for reprieve, her heart still roaring in her ears.

As if she were made of fragile china, he laid her against the bed, weaving his hard-corded torso between her legs until he pressed against her—thigh to thigh, breast to chest, mouth to mouth—taking her in one swift motion. His thrusts were powerful and unrestrained, and she met them with a driving strength she didn't know she possessed, craving the feel of him deep inside her. Their hips touched and parted in age-old rhythm until the crest of passion engulfed them both, drowning them in a splendor of epic proportions.

The rocking of their united bodies slowing, the harmony of their thundering hearts calming also, Braven drew the jut of her chin into his mouth, his teeth grazing her flesh. "Rivalree, Rivalree, my dearest love, how did I survive without you so long."

The emotion in his voice stirred a cord deep inside her, and joy took seed and sprouted.

He drew her into the circle of his arm as he rolled to his back, his fingers running through the damp silkiness of her hair. "Tomorrow we'll spend the day together. I'll show you everything. It's ours, Rivalree—yours and mine, always," he mumbled, sleep claiming him.

"Yes, my love," she vowed, her lips pressed to his temple. "Ours. But more important, *you* are mine."

Hours later the waning moonlight threw pale rays across his face. Fascinated she watched him sleep. The strong lines of his face softened giving him an air of vulnerability. How could she have seen anything in his beloved face to frighten her not so long ago?

She brushed a strand of flaxen hair from his forehead, touched her fingertips to her lips and transferred the kiss to his. Rolling to her back, she nestled under the coverlet, a secret smile on her face.

A soft but persistent scratching invaded her thoughts. She lifted her head to better listen, and the sound stopped. Seconds later, the noise resumed. Scratch, scratch. Scratch, scratch. A gentle whine followed.

Zoey. The dog was outside the door asking to be let in. She crossed her arms over her chest. The bitch didn't deserve admittance. Scratch, scratch. Yip.

Oh, damn. The animal would continue until she got what she wanted.

Rivalree rose from the bed and stepped to the door. She opened it wide enough to peer into the hallway. Zoey sat wiggling on the floor, her tail whipping back and forth. The roving eyes she had found so menacing before pleaded up at her for approval.

"Fickle female," she chided, and pushed the door open a little wider. "Come on in."

Zoey nosed by her and padded across the floor to stand at the foot of the bed. She crouched to leap, hesitated, then turned to stare at Rivalree, again respectful, askance on her face.

"Go on." She waggled a finger in the dog's direction. "Just don't forget. He may be your master, but he's my man, so you'd better get used to the idea of my being here."

Zoey leaped upon the quilt, circled once, and dropped in a curl beside Braven's foot. He mumbled, moving his leg to give her room, a gesture Rivalree decided was automatic from nights of doing the same. With a sigh, the dog laid her furry head on her paws and watched as Rivalree crossed the room to join Braven under the covers, never once uttering a protest.

Chapter Twelve

Braven canvassed the dark tunnel, the miner's light attached to his hat illuminating each spot he focused on. He shivered in the dank mine air, a feeling he wasn't alone gripping his insides.

As he turned to investigate, Zoey's warmth brushed against his pants offering assurance. She whined softly, her tail swishing the air beside his leg.

"Who's there, girl?" he whispered, reaching down to pat her head.

From a distance another light swung back and forth in the rhythm of the person approaching, closer and closer. Braven waited, eager to identify the intruder, knowing someone had witnessed his early-morning entrance into the mine and had come to investigate. What he had discovered in the few moments he'd been in the tunnel was disconcerting. He frowned, wanting more time alone to search the other shafts before anyone else became aware of the information. The mining cave-in yesterday was no accident.

He considered dousing the flame in the lantern on his hat, but decided if he'd seen the intruder's light, chances were they had seen his. Squatting down beside Zoey, he waited, wondering if he would be confronted with friend or foe.

Zoey's tail tapped the dirt in eager anticipation.

"I hope you're right, girl."

The approaching light cast a shadowy figure, but the face remained hidden behind its glare. "Braven, that you?" called a familiar Irish lilt.

The tension in his shoulders eased. "Yeah, Pat. Didn't expect to find you in here since your accident."

"Usually don't." The little man set the lantern down on a large boulder. "What are you doing in the mine so early?"

Braven studied him for a split second. "Seeing how much damage was done yesterday."

Pat lifted the light and peered around the cave. "What do you think?"

"It'll set us back a few days, nothing more."

"And was it an accident?"

Braven glared at the older man. How much did the Irishman know? How had he figured out the situation so quickly?

"Possibly," he evaded.

"But not likely," Pat finished.

"And how would you know?"

Pat chuckled. "Weren't my powers of the mind, me boy. Judd's death was no accident, either."

The words crashed in the pit of his stomach like a cannonball. "How do you know?"

Pat hunkered down beside Braven, his hand running over Zoey in an absentminded gesture. "When Judd died, you left right away for the city, to see his little colleen. I checked the beam that fell on him. It was weakened by a cut near the joint."

Braven felt as if his lungs had quit working; they refused to draw a cleansing breath. "I was the one working under that timber. I was the intended victim, wasn't I?" he asked, dazed. "Judd saw the beam falling and pushed me out of

188

the way. Then, yesterday somebody made certain that cave-in happened when it did. But why, Pat?" He looked up askance. "Who wants me dead?"

"Don't rightly know."

Braven ran his fingers through his hair. There were only two people who would have benefited from his death in May—his partners. Judd was not guilty of foul play. He had claimed his innocence with his life.

But the other, the jackal sitting in his lair in San Francisco, that bastard was capable of anything. John Masters would murder his mother for a few dollars.

Which meant at least one of the miners, if not more, had to be working for the gambler. The dirty slime had thought to get rid of him and take over, knowing Judd would never have been strong enough to keep him at bay. No wonder Masters had known of Judd's death. No wonder he had demanded to know what would happen to the boy's share of the gold. The share he had given to Rivalree.

He choked on that thought. Rivalree. Was she a part of this plot? She had been on the same ship with Masters, then had gone to him after discovering Judd's death. Was she really the girl Judd had sent for, or some woman Masters hired to masquerade in her place? She had been so determined to get to the mine, and she had known Judd's death was no accident.

He pressed his face into his hands, and Zoey nosed his cheek with concern. He hugged her to his chest, and shoved the destructive thoughts away. Memories of Rivalree's surrender to him last night flooded his mind. So sweet and innocent. How could he even think of her as guilty?

Feeling like a sewer rat, nowhere to turn, no one to trust, he glanced up to see understanding in Pat's eyes.

"Aye, me boyo, 'tis a pickle you're in. I'm not sure who ya should trust. Might be any one or more of the men involved."

"And Rivalree?"

Pat raised one bottlebrush brow.

"She's well acquainted with John Masters. She worked for him a while.

Pat scratched his head. "The girl isn't easy to read, though she's who she claims to be. But she's hidin' somethin'. Somethin' she don't want you to find out."

Braven released the dog and placed the heels of his palms on his forehead. "Then you do think she's involved."

"I didn't say that, Braven. She's a girl of passion and dreams, and I do believe she'll go to any extent to fulfill them. But a schemer or in cahoots with Masters, I honestly don't think so."

"What else could she be hiding from me?" His eyes bore into the other man's. Pat knew more than he was telling him.

"It's not my place to say. Don't misjudge or accuse her of things she's not guilty of. She could love you if you'd give her half a chance."

"I don't need love at the moment. I need answers." He rose and started toward the mine entrance. "Whoever is involved will pay—and pay dearly—for their part in this scheme. For me and for Judd. Especially for Judd."

Rivalree dipped to her knee and placed the handful of wildflowers she had picked on the unadorned mound of dirt. Judd. It was hard to believe the life-loving person of her past lay imprisoned beneath the brown earth. Ashes to ashes, dust to dust. A sob bubbled in her throat, and she pressed the heel of her hand into her mouth. *Forgive me, sweet Judd, if I betray you, but I have never experienced a love like the one I know with Braven. God help me, but I don't know what would have happened if you lived.* Guilt ressed hard against her heart.

The soft pad of feet echoed behind her bent figure. She turned, wiping her weeping eyes with the back of her hand. Braven worked his way up the path toward her, Zoey leading the way.

Relief flooded her. He understood the emotions tearing her apart and had come to express his sympathy. She rose to her feet and ran to meet him, her arms flung open in invitation.

He stopped in the faint path, his hands planted in the front pockets of his pants, his face closed, his body radiating feelings she had thought gone forever—since last night. Distrust and anger.

She halted her forward motion, unsure how she should react to his change of attitude. Zoey reached her, jumped up against her thighs, barking a greeting.

She pushed the happy animal down, the only creature she felt was truly glad to see her, and waited self-consciously for Braven to tell her what was on his mind. Something bothered him, but she couldn't fathom what.

He scowled at the dog. "Seems you gain trust quickly."

Was he talking to her or Zoey. She shrugged her shoulders in a noncommittal response. Her heart drum-rolled in her throat. Dear God, what had she done to anger him?

His eyes flicked once over her figure. She straightened to her full height, trying to deflect the barbs in his glare.

"Braven, I . . ." A sob crowded her voice. Not another word would squeak by.

His gaze softened, and his arms lifted from his sides, opening, beckoning to her.

The sob surfaced as she stumbled toward him, falling into his welcoming arms. Whatever had upset him was no longer a threat. She threw her arms around his neck and clung like a disobedient child who had been punished, then pulled into the circle of her parent's loving embrace.

"What is it? What have I done?" she asked, the word muffled against his shoulder.

"It's nothing, sugar. Nothing you need to be concerned about." His hand rested in her hair, stroking, soothing, caring. "I'm just surprised to see you up so early. Go back to the cabin and help Pat with breakfast, then we'll talk. In fact, we'll spend part of the day together, and I'll give you the grand tour."

She studied his face looking for clues to the answer to her questions. Was something wrong that he didn't tell her?

He turned then and started down the path, his arm still encircling her waist. No, everything was going so well now, it was only her imagination. She glanced up at him to find him staring out at nothing in particular, almost as if his innermost thoughts held his rapt attention.

His gaze swooped down, and he smiled, yet the gesture never quite reached his eyes.

With an experienced tug, Pat adjusted the cinch on the pack horse, then fixed his attention to the saddle on the other animal, giving it a final jerk to be sure it was sufficiently tight. Slipping the cinch strap through the flap on the saddle, he glanced over his shoulder at Rivalree.

"Are you sure you can handle things, colleen? I won't go if you're not."

She nodded stoically. "Of course, Pat."

"I'll be back late this evening, so don't be worryin' about me. Old man Tyler was down to his last scrap of jerky and beans the last time I saw him. He'll be glad for these supplies. I wouldn't go otherwise."

"What could happen in a few hours? The noon meal is planned, and I'll make something simple this evening. The men won't starve in one day, no matter how bad my cooking is." She grinned at him.

He nodded and led his mount to the front steps, using the edge of the porch to mount. Taking the reins of the pack horse from her hands, he dipped his head and pushed the animals into a trot, heading away from the house.

Rivalree rested her hands on her hips and watched the Irishman leave. The tiny seed of fear and uncertainty ballooned as he disappeared around a curve in the trail. It was easy to be brave vocally, but now that she was alone, that was a different matter. How foolish, she chided. Braven and the men were just inside the mine. If she called to them they would be at her side in minutes. Besides, Braven had promised they would spend time together today, touring the mine. Wiping the back of her hand over her forehead, she headed back to the cabin and the stack of breakfast plates waiting to be washed.

By the time the dishes were done and the cabin tidied from the morning meal, the sun had risen to its full glory, peeking between the trees, a herald of the splendid day ahead of her. She hummed as she went about her duties, a contentment she hadn't know in a long time settling around her.

Braven. She smiled as she shoved the benches under the long table. All their problems had been solved in one short, wondrous night.

Her mouth curved down in a perplexed frown remembering the way he had stared at her as she knelt by the grave. Had he been upset that she had felt the need to see Judd's resting place? Was he jealous of a dead man? Though he denied that something bothered him, she knew him well enough. She would insist on an explanation later, once they were together. Their marriage would work only if they kept no secrets.

Her busy hands stilled. Kept no secrets of the present, she particularized. The past was no longer important. She resumed her humming, sure she had done nothing wrong.

She would put her past—all of it—behind her where it belonged and look forward to sharing her future with the man she loved.

She halted on the stairs, her hand resting on the rough banister. The man she loved? The words came so easily to her mind. When had she fallen in love with Braven Blackwood? Considering their stormy relationship, she saw his actions and manners in a whole new light. She had pushed him relentlessly from the moment he spoke to her on the docks, yet he had maintained a patience with her that could only be described as phenomenal. No wonder she loved him. He was all she had dreamed of finding in a man. Having been blind so long, she had wasted precious time fighting him, but no more. She would love him, cherish him, and make him proud to call her his wife.

She skipped up the steps anxious to check her reflection in the shaving mirror he kept on the washstand. Now and always, she wanted to look her best. Her fingers worried the loose strands of hair falling from the ribbon at the nape of her neck.

In the bedroom, she paused in the doorway, taking in the rumpled mess of the bed and flushed, re-creating details of their nocturnal lovemaking. She wondered if Braven remembered also as he worked in the dark recesses of the mine. She straightened the bedclothes and pulled the patchwork quilt over the pillows, taking a few moments to caress the dent where Braven's head had lain a few short hours ago. She sighed, wishing the day over and the time for sleep to return. Blushing with her thoughts, she turned away from the bed.

The sun's warmth beckoned to her through the shuttered window. She crossed the room, throwing up the sash to allow the light and heat admittance into her world. Leaning out the window, she inhaled crisp mountain air and savored the feel of it in her lungs before letting it out. She was happy, so content. Feeling closer to God on top of this mountain than she had ever in her life, she prayed the bliss would last forever.

Her spine tingled, and she stilled her breathing, listening. Silence greeted her; no unusual sounds could be heard. Yet a feeling that all wasn't right pricked at her consciousness.

The trees towered unmoving, not one leaf rustling. How odd. And the birds. She strained her ears as hard as she could. Not one chirp or peep anywhere. The dead calm, that's what was wrong. It was as if the earth held its breath, as she did, waiting for some ominous event.

The only sound audible was her heartbeat accelerating with each passing moment. "What is it? What's wrong?" she whispered.

As if in answer to her questions, the mountain grumbled protesting the stillness. She leaned farther out the casement and surveyed all she could see. Nothing moved. Dear God, she must be losing her mind to think the ground spoke to her.

Far away a rumble began, growling closer by the seconds. In the distance a jay screamed its warning to any who would listen. From the corner of her eye she caught sight of the mine entrance, a yawning black hole in the mountain, a mouth from which the earth communicated.

She blinked several times in quick succession, and her tongue licked her lips dry from anxiety. In stunned amazement, she watched smoky dust billow from the mine.

"Braven," she gasped.

Again the chasm belched disaster.

"Braven," she screamed in a key as high-pitched as the screeching blue jay. "Oh, God, no, not Braven."

Her leaden feet fought their temporary paralysis. Lifting her skirts, she crossed the room and tore down the stairs.

"No, God, please," she groaned over and over as she

195

raced across the common room and out the front door.

The blinding sunlight struck her in the face. Birds chirped and the trees shimmied as if nothing unusual had happened. Rivalree's pounding heart and aching lungs told her different.

She halted before the black opening to the mine. *What am I going to do?* Alone on the outside, the mountain seemed to challenge her to combat. What could she, one lone woman, do if the earth had swallowed up the man whom she had built her dreams around?

Chapter Thirteen

Thrown from contentment into a state of wild fear, Rivalree experienced a confusion that, at first, was concealed in anger. Anger at the fact she had no idea what she should do, yet knowledge that every precious second she took making a decision might be fatal to the men in the tunnel—to Braven.

Lifting her skirts, she tore across the dirt yard to the mine's entrance. Dust and smoke still puffed out as if the hole in the earth was a living, breathing being, as if demanding no interference from her. Taking the hem of her dress she placed it over her mouth and rushed into the darkness of the gaping chasm. But a few feet inside, she was encompassed by total blackness, the dust thickening with each step she took. She would be of no help to anyone if she fell or got lost.

Vague images of the funny-looking miner's hat she had seen on the table as she hurried from the cabin sawed at the edges of her thoughts as she felt her way back into the bright morning air. Bounding unladylike, her skirts hiked around her knees, she hurried back to the house. She prayed her memory served her right and the hat was where she remembered.

The headgear sat casually tossed on the edge of the table,

its candle no more than a stub. Perhaps that was why it had been discarded, but it was all she had, and she'd have to make do. Gathering a matchbox from the top of the stove, she crammed the hat on her head to find it fit like shoes three sizes too large, rocking from side to side as she ran outside.

With shaking hands she struck a match, which flared brightly in the shadow of the mine entrance. Just as quickly it died to a black, smoldering tip.

"Damn," she muttered, angling her body to keep the draft from blowing out the next one. The second match trembled in her fingers, but she managed to ignite the thin stub of wick before it became too hot to handle.

The faint light the reflector on the hat cast barely lit a few feet ahead of her as she entered the darkness of the mine. She was scared, there was no denying the fact, but she pushed her fears to the side declaring them unfounded.

A dozen yards ahead of her halo of light, a pair of glimmering eyes blinked at her. She gasped, a sound repeating several times in the hollowness of the tunnel, as she held the light at arm's length hoping to glimpse their owner.

Zoey barked, and she welcomed the greeting. The dog pressed against her outstretched hand as Rivalree knelt to pat her head.

"Oh, Zoey," she murmured, wrapping her arms around the dog as much in comfort as in relief. "Where are they?"

As if the animal understood her question, Zoey darted out of her line of vision.

"No, wait, girl. Don't lose me." She stumbled over the hard-packed dirt of the mine floor, praying the dog would respond. The candle flickered, threatening to blow out, and she cupped her palm around it in protection.

Above her the spine work of timbers creaked and groaned reminding her of the spars in the wind on board the ship she had taken to California. Then, the sounds had been natural and comforting like the creaking of an old, familiar house settling in the cool of the night. Now, the noises were threatening, unnerving, and her heart jumped with each ghostly moan. Would the beams hold, or would they fall crushing her beneath their mighty weight? No time to think of that now. She must concentrate on reaching the trapped men.

With no idea how deep in the bowels of the mountain the tunnel ran, she focused on each step she took, not on how many. Zoey raced ahead of her, now and then returning to her side to urge her to go faster.

A feeling worse than fear crept up and down her spine. Panic. A sensation that the earth had swallowed her up and would never let her escape from its clammy depths. She rubbed her arm with her free hand to erase the chill bumps peppering her skin as she forced her feet forward. "I'm not afraid," she whispered.

Ahead a rafter snapped, and the earth grumbled sending a fresh wave of dust billowing around her.

"Oh, God," she choked, pulling her skirt back up to her mouth, afraid her very words might cause the mountain to close around her.

Zoey's wet nose touched the side of her exposed leg in comfort and encouragement.

The beam of light bounced and split, revealing a "Y" in the tunnel. Two yawning holes of darkness beckoned her. Which one? Which way did she go?

The dog lowered her ever-seeking nose and sniffed, tilted her head to glance at Rivalree, then, without further hesitation, started down the path to the left.

Rivalree hesitated. Zoey led her in the right direction, didn't she? The dog did understand what she wanted? Would she take her to Braven or down some endless tunnel to die in the depths of the earth? Zoey's insistent bark demanded attention. She had to follow the dog's lead. There was no other choice. Braven's life could very well be lost as she stood here debating.

Dust filled her lungs in spite of the doubled fabric of her skirt she pressed to her nose and mouth. She coughed and choked, her body fighting the strange invasion. The light caught and illuminated the individual dust particles swirling around her to thicken with each step she took. This had to be the right way.

The hard-packed dirt beneath her feet became uneven with large rocks strewn across the ground. Sure that she must have stumbled over every one of them, her feet grew numb and insensitive to the pain, but she refused to give up the demanding pace she set in order to keep up with Zoey. The thick air blocked the light, and she couldn't see a foot ahead of her. The dog's barking intensified.

Sensing she couldn't be far from the cave-in, she pressed on, fear and panic increasing when nothing but her running feet and racing heart could be heard. Where were the men? Please let them still be alive.

As if a steel band tightened around her chest, her lungs refused to draw another breath. She stopped, wheezing loudly, her hand outstretched in an attempt to feel her way.

A wet nose touched her leg, and she skittered to one side. Had she not caught her breath in that moment of fright, she might have missed the soft groan, a human moan, so close yet so far away. She strained, listening as hard as she could, fearing what she'd heard had been her imagination. The sound whispered again. Yes, she was sure she heard it now.

"Braven," she called hoarsely.

A scatter of stones pinged close by. Setting down the useless lamp, she yanked at the hem of her dress still pressed to her mouth, attempting to tear a strip from it to tie around her face to free her other hand. But the skirt was new and the seams tight, and the fabric wouldn't yield to her frantic tugging. "Oh, please," she grumbled. "Give."

Zoey's tail swished against her leg, and she remembered the red bandanna tied around the dog's neck. Catching a deep breath, she dropped her skirt and bent, fumbling with the knot at the animal's throat.

"Keep still," she hissed between clenched teeth as Zoey attempted to wriggle away.

The knot released, and, without considering where that handkerchief had been, she wrapped it around her mouth and nose, securing it behind her head.

Feeling her way along the pickax-eaten wall, she discovered a barrier of softer dirt. Without thinking she began to dig with her bare hands, the need to remove what stood between her and Braven stronger than the pain as her fingernails were ripped and torn at the quick.

"Braven."

Zoey echoed the panic in her voice, yipping and barking to her master.

"Rivalree?"

"Yes," she answered, deep sobs ripping from her raw throat. Braven was alive. He had spoken to her. With renewed vigor, she clawed at the sharp rocks. "I'm here, my darling. I'm here."

"Rivalree," Braven sputtered. He coughed, a deep hacking sound, over and over. "Listen. The tools. On your side."

She blinked in the hazy light trying to decipher what he meant.

"On the wall to your right."

Feeling her way along the cave out of the halo of light, her hands struck hard virgin earth. She continued inching her way, Braven's words giving her confidence. He said the tools were here, and they would be. She would find them. Her fingers curled around the smooth roundness of a handle. Setting off a chain reaction, the stack of tools clattered to the floor, the sound echoing through the tunnel. The earth grumbled in protest above her head. A scream ripped from her throat.

"Rivalree," Braven called, the fear so strong in his voice that unbidden tears welled in her raw throat.

"I'm all right."

"Thank God."

His voice was so close, so comforting. Her head snapped up. Why could she hear him so clearly if there was a wall of dirt and rock between them?

"Braven, I can hear you," she exclaimed.

"Ssh, don't waste words and breath. Grab a shovel and Zoey's collar. Follow her. She'll lead you to the opening."

The shovel in one hand and the scruff of fur at the dog's neck in the other, she obeyed.

"Come on, Zoey," Braven called softly. "Here, girl."

Led by scent and sound, the dog scaled the crumbling barrier to a point above Rivalree's head. With a tug, Zoey slipped from her grasping fingers, disappearing. Excited, she lifted the shovel and scraped at the small opening.

"No, Rivalree," Braven said. "Push the shovel through to me and go back to get more. We'll widen it from this side."

Turning the shovel handle first, she guided the tool into the fissure. Not until there was little to grip did hands retrieve it on the other side. So much dirt between them. Would Braven be able to dig his way out? She shivered in fear.

Trying to memorize where the small opening was located, she squinted, studying it. She would never find it again in the dimness. Casting her eyes about, her gaze settled on the miner's hat. She retrieved the light and placed it on the ground below the hole, praying it would give her guidance.

After several arduous trips, she managed to drag the remaining tools to the opening. Each time Braven accepted a shovel or pick from her, she wanted to call out to him, tell him how much she loved him. But there wasn't time, and this wasn't the place. She would tell him, though, the moment they were together and alone. *I love you*, her heart sang, making the work go easier.

Once the chore was completed, Rivalree huddled down beside the candle stub, watching the dust settle against the flickering shadows on the tunnel walls and ceiling. In her idleness, she concentrated on the scraping sounds wafting through the opening from the other side. Realization of where she was and the feat she had accomplished rocketed through her until she shook with the fear she had denied for so long. How alone she felt in the darkness of the tunnel.

She welcomed Zoey, who scrambled through the widening hole to join her. Had Braven sent the dog to her, knowing she would be apprehensive? Hugging the animal to her chest, she waited, Zoey displaying more patience than she. She found the quiescent suspense harder to bear than the initial panic when she'd discovered the cave-in.

The bit of candle on the hat at her feet dimmed, then began to pulsate. Anticipating the light wouldn't last much longer, she laid her head against Zoey's soft fur. The light winked, then sputtered, leaving her in a total darkness she was unprepared for. She clutched the dog close to her heart, and Zoey accepted the crush of her arms as if she understood.

The seconds pounded by with the beat of her pulse. The scraping of the shovels stilled, and she rose, fingers guiding her upward to the spot where the hole should be. Where once had been a gap barely wide enough to pass a shovel through, there was now an opening large enough for a man.

"Braven," she called, anxious to hear another human voice.

His hand reached out and brushed hers. "Don't you have a light?"

"The candle burned out. I didn't have time to . . ."

"Here," he interrupted. Illuminated warmth touched her face as he handed her one of the miner's hats from his side. "Stand back, the men will be coming through."

Clutching the hat to her chest, she stepped to one side. The relief that should have washed over her didn't come. The crisis was over, Braven was safe, yet her heart hammered against her ribs, and she watched the gap anxiously. One by one the men pulled their way out, until four joined her. Then the flow stopped.

"Where are the rest of the men?"

Politely the miners sidestepped her, and, reaching through the opening, they eased a fifth man through, limp and unconscious.

"Oh," she gasped, shaken by the ashen face. She raised her light and indicated a cleared spot on the floor. The miners laid the injured man down and turned to help their other companions to safety.

Each face emerging she studied, looking for Braven. Why didn't he come through? She knew the answer in her heart. He would see to the safety of his men over his own. The timbers above them trembled and creaked.

She turned, pointing at the unconscious man on the ground. "Get him out of here now."

Two of the men lifted the inert body and started out the tunnel.

"Excuse me, ma'am. Why don't you go with them. It would be better if you did."

"No," she insisted. "Not until my husband is with me."

The speaker nodded, understanding, respect glistening from his eyes. He pivoted, giving his attention to the escaping men.

Braven's blond hair, barely recognizable from the dirt and filth encrusting it, finally presented itself through the hole. Rivalree rushed forward, hands outstretched, the need to feel his arms about her so strong, she didn't care

204

what the men thought.

"Thank God, my darling," she breathed as she pressed her body against his, uncaring of the dirt on his clothing.

She lifted her face, still encompassed in Zoey's handkerchief, to his for assurance. Instead she found the enemy staring down at her, not the cool, distant southerner she had first known, but a hard, spiteful man.

"Braven, what's wrong?"

His fingers hooked in the bandanna and pulled it down, the calm on his face unforgiving. He held his arms straight and stiff at his side. His mouth lifted in a sneer. "Don't play games with me, Rivalree. Spare me your loving wife act, all right?"

Her empty, aching arms dropped to her sides. Confusion swirled through her brain. What had she done wrong?

"If you need to ease your guilty conscience, come with me." He handcuffed her arm in an ungentlemanly fashion. "Buckley's leg is broken, and God knows what else. I want you to see his pain."

Indignation rose from her middle. Guilt? She had nothing to be guilty for, unless it was the undignified way she'd thrown herself at him. How dare he trample her exposed affections. What did he expect of her? She had just risked her life to save his. She was not some simpering southern belle on a pedestal. She was earthy, honest Rivalree Blackwood, his wife—nothing more, nothing less.

She straightened her shoulders and twisted from his crushing grip, walking a few paces ahead. He would be sorry he had treated her so insensitively.

The agonizing screams of the man lying on the table ripped through Rivalree.

"Goddam it, hold him still," Braven barked. "And

you," he ordered, whipping his head in the direction of the man standing at Buckley's head, "get some more of that whiskey down his throat. He's in agony. There's not a damn thing we can do about it except get him so drunk he can't feel anything."

Rivalree swallowed hard. She had seen livestock treated more humanely than the man screaming on the table.

"Braven, I think we should . . ."

"What, Rivalree?" he snapped. 'If you don't have the stomach to do what has to be done, then get the hell out of here."

She whirled, hiding the angry flush of her face. Now was not the time to air their differences.

"On second thought, you stay. See what you've done and remember."

Her head whipped back around. "What *I've* done? *I* risked my own life to save yours and every other man's in this room."

The electrifying silence rankled the hairs on her arm.

Braven's gaze hardened, but he said nothing. Buckley whimpered drunkenly.

"We've got to get this bone back in place, or he'll never walk again. We'll discuss our personal differences later. Just help me now," Braven muttered.

Their eyes locked and held for an eternal moment. She glanced away first, staring down at the gaping wound on Buckley's leg, the edge of the bone thrusting out of the torn flesh. Bile rushed to her throat.

"Pull it a little more, Braven." Without asking, she seized the bottle of whiskey from the hand of the man beside her, liberally pouring the liquid over the wound. Buckley moaned and twitched. She pressed clean bandages against the leg, bound them tight, before placing the makeshift case, two long boards, against the broken leg.

Using bits of heavy twine, together they managed to bound cast and all securely.

Braven glanced around. "Take apart Judd's old bed and reassemble it down here. I want Buckley where he can be observed day and night."

Three men jumped to do his bidding.

Rivalree watched with a sinking heart. Her only means of escaping the confines of the bedroom she shared with Braven was carried down the stairs and set up before the hearth. Without access to Judd's bed, she would have to confront her husband. She scanned his closed face trying to penetrate his thought, his reasons for the way he treated her.

As if he sensed her scrutiny, his gaze clashed with hers, his mouth turned down at the corners, and his eyes iced. She had seen many emotions radiating from his countenance in the last weeks—irritation, exasperation, frustration—but until this morning never the cold, hard hatred that shone from them now. Her hand ached to reach up and brush the look from his features, but she dared not. She sensed the violence under the calm he presented.

"Braven," she pleaded softly, hoping beyond reason for the adoration to return.

His look never faltered.

"I'm sorry. Whatever it is I've done, I'm truly sorry."

Doubt flicked in his lapis lazuli eyes, only to fade. "Tell Buckley that when he comes around." He whirled and headed for the front door.

She couldn't allow him to leave like this, not knowing what it was that upset him so. She rushed after his retreating figure, her hand claiming his arm. Her touch was firm but gentle, and he could easily tear from her grip. She waited, breath held deep in her lungs, and though his muscles beneath his fingers remained rigid, he stopped.

"Please, Braven. I have a right to know what I've done."

His biceps twitched once. He turned, facing her, the emotions battling inside him bubbling forth. As if she'd known him all her life, she read each and every one of them—pain, confusion, betrayal, and anger. His jaws sawed back and forth as he formed his answer.

"The cave-in was no accident, just like the one the other day. But you knew that, didn't you."

Her mouth opened in protest.

"You were right about Judd, too. His death was no accident, either. You were aware of the fact long before I was. How?"

Her slackened jaw refused to work. In shock, her head shook, denying his implications. Her hand released his shirt to press against her mouth.

"Since you've been here, there have been more 'chance disasters' than most mines see in a lifetime. Why, Rivalree? Did John Masters set you up? Did he send you up here to do what he's not been able to do on his own? Does the money mean so much to you? Or is it revenge?"

Her head swung in denial to each accusation he flung at her.

"Tomorrow I'm sending you down the mountain and back to your accomplice. This marriage was a mistake from the beginning." Pulling his arm from her frozen grip, he strode out the door leaving Rivalree stunned with disbelief at his revelations.

Chapter Fourteen

Rivalree lifted sleep-laden lashes to the bright sun pouring through the open window. Glancing at the other side of the bed, hoping to discover Braven beside her, she found instead the pillow stiff and the coverlet smooth from disuse. He had failed to return last night after his harsh words, though she had lain awake for hours praying he would come to bed and give her a chance to refute the angry accusations he had slung at her.

Pat had returned at dusk and listened to her sob-broken story with a sympathetic ear. Shaking his head, he'd promised to talk some sense into Braven's bullheadedness and had left her in charge of Buckley, going back into the twilight to locate him.

Several hours later, the night firmly settled, the Irishman had returned, informing her the men were in the mine clearing away the debris from the cave-in. Braven was working his anger away with a shovel and pickax, and the best thing she could do was give him time to cool off and think. The best thing for whom? she wondered. Not her.

Reluctantly she had agreed, though her first impulse was to dash back into the black depths of the tunnels, demanding he listen to her. She would not leave the

Louisiana Mine, no matter what. He would have to drag her kicking and screaming down the mountain, and the moment he left her, she would find a way to return even if she had to walk.

She sighed. How ironic. Only a few days ago she had felt as strongly about wanting to leave. How had she changed in so short a time? By admitting to love.

The thought of trying to find her way up the mountain on her own wasn't one she relished. She swallowed hard, hoping Braven would relent now that he'd had time to reconsider.

Excited voices filtered through her open window, laughter and the sounds of camaraderie among the men. She rose and padded across the room. From the dormer she caught a glimpse of a makeshift baseball game in progress, an unusual sight especially so early in the morning. Why weren't the men working?

Ticking the days off in her head, she calculated it was Sunday, the miner's day of rest. Her heart skipped a beat as she studied each of the men below. Braven wasn't among them. Had he truly meant it when he said he was taking her away today? Did he wait downstairs for her?

She must talk to him and convince him she wasn't responsible for the cave-in. The shock that Judd had been murdered and that someone attempted to take Braven's life as well had left her speechless last night. Now her head was cool, and with calm, mature logic, she would prove her innocence.

Tossing on a simple skirt and blouse which complemented her tiny waist and full bosom, she brushed the tangles from her golden tresses. She tied her hair back with a ribbon thinking it gave her an air of vulnerability. If it took standing on her head or doing cartwheels down the stairs to make Braven listen to what she had to say, she wouldn't hesitate. At the moment, her pride meant nothing. The need to feel the protecting warmth of her

210

husband's arms around her was all she could think of. He couldn't send her away without giving her a chance to defend herself.

As ready as she would ever be, she thumped the brush down on the dresser and headed below.

The common room was empty. Heading out the front door, she searched everywhere for Braven, starting with the outbuildings and storage sheds. As she passed the men, some playing and others praying in a small gathering under a tree, they greeted her with warmth, each remembering her part in the rescue the day before. Their kindness and friendliness was welcome and served to strengthen her determination to halt the misunderstanding between her and Braven.

Thirty minutes later, she found him by the creek, a pile of clothes at his side. Zoey sprawled faithfully at his heels watching every move he made.

Rivalree paused, aware he had no idea she observed him. Even bent doing a menial task like washing clothes, she found him strong and exciting. How she wanted to rush to him and press herself against the warm hardness of his chest.

Zoey looked in her direction, and in greeting her long tail began to sweep clean the rock on which she laid. Braven glanced over his shoulder, a shield of distrust hooding his eyes the moment he saw her.

Her resolve turned to mush in the harshness of his glare. Then, crossing her arms over her bosom where his gaze lingered, she followed the well-worn path to the creek's edge until she stood a few feet from him. He rose, twisting a well-pounded shirt of its excess moisture, his eyes never leaving her slim figure as she approached.

Without a word, she reached out and took the garment from his hands, raised her lips in a gentle smile, and bent to place it beside two others he had washed.

"What do you think you're doing?" he demanded.

"I'm your wife, Braven. I'll wash your clothes." Selecting a pair of filthy jeans, she began the laborious task of beating the dirt from them. She glanced around, searching for a bar of soap, but couldn't find one, although fat, healthy suds floated in the creek.

With his boot toe he pushed a strange, onion-shaped root toward where she knelt. "California soap," he informed her. "Doesn't look like much, but it's effective."

Fingering the odd object, she studied it for a moment before pressing it against the denim material and working up a surprisingly easy lather. The toe of his boot, so close to her now, began tapping out a soft rhythm. She could sense he was making a decision, a crucial judgment about her future. Though she held her breath, her hands never ceased scrubbing the laundry.

The boot stilled, and her hands stopped on their own accord as she waited for him to speak.

"This doesn't change anything, Rivalree."

She dipped the jeans into the water and raised them, resuming her attack on several stubborn stains. "I didn't expect it to."

Dropping the clothing and her meek facade, she stood to face him. "All I ask is a chance to speak, to prove you're wrong about me." Her eyes pleaded with him for understanding.

His unyielding gaze was like a slap in the face and panic rose inside her. He wasn't going to listen, no matter what she said. Finding her guilty of betrayal, his heart had turned against her.

Staring up into the blue granite depths of his eyes, she clung to his arm. "At least let me have a few moments before you send me away. I've done nothing against you. I swear on my dead mother's soul, I know nothing of this plot you so wrongly accuse me of."

The muscles in his arm tensed, and he pulled away.

"If I was trying to kill you, why would I risk my life to

212

go into the mine to rescue you?"

"Like a vulture, you came to pick over the bones."

She couldn't believe the venom in his voice. "Braven, no," she cried, her resolve to keep cool and logical dissipating. "I first met John Masters on the ship to San Francisco. I wasn't aware he knew you or Judd until yesterday."

Braven began walking away, but she clamped his arm, refusing to let go. He must listen. He had to believe her.

"I cared for Judd. I would never do anything to hurt him," she shrilled.

"You loved him so much, you married me?" His brow quirked in skepticism.

Her hand drifted down, and she straightened until her stiffened spine threatened to snap. "Judd was dear to me. A friend for as long as I can remember. We grew up together, played house since we were five. His loyalties were, and still are, mine." Her fingers tangled in the fabric of her skirt. About to open her soul to Braven Blackwood, she prayed he wouldn't trample her heart under uncaring feet. "What I feel for you is something different. From the first moment I saw you, so tall and rugged on the docks, you were like a turbulent storm sweeping into my life. God help me I tried, but I can no longer oppose the strength of your prevailing winds." She lifted her chin and stared proudly at him. "I love you, Braven. With every misconceived bone in my body, I would give my life for you." A sob ripped through her, and she shook with the violence of the emotions inside her. A look she couldn't decipher clouded his face. "If you send me away, I'll go, but my heart will remain here, with you, always."

There, she had said it. Now she had to get away before he destroyed her completely. Tears blurred her vision. She dropped the wash and stumbled, trying to ascend the rocky bank of the creek.

"Rivalree," Braven called, his voice crackling with

emotion. "What a fool I am." His hand so hard and frightening moments before, softly caressed her arm.

Was he saying he believed her? She turned, the sun-heated rocks pressing against her back, the passion-heated strength of his body crushing against her heart.

"I've waited what seems a lifetime for you to say those words to me," he murmured as his mouth crushed down on hers.

Melting against him, she kissed him with all the fervor she possessed.

His lips moved across her cheek to capture her earlobe. "I don't want you to go," he whispered huskily. "I never did. I fight the demons of fear like any other man, you know. It was easy to blame you. I can battle my enemy as long as it's tangible." His hand reached up and pushed stray hairs from her forehead. "I'm sorry, Rivalree."

Again his mouth descended trapping her in a kiss. Forgiveness engulfed her, and her arms circled his neck pulling him as close as she could.

"Just love me, my darling," she beseeched, "and together we'll conquer the enemies, both yours and mine."

Braven tilted his head, his eyes lit with a passion she'd learned to recognize. Clasping her fingers in his, he urged her to follow. "Come, there's a place I want to show you, to share with you. Until now it's been special only to me."

A shyness overcame her, and she found it hard to look at him. Sensing what was soon to happen between them, she was unsure, yet, at the same time, the tingle of brazen anticipation sent shivers up and down her spine. For a moment, she resisted. "Braven, I don't think we should . . ."

Drawing her to him, he stilled her halfhearted protest with a kiss. "Don't think, Rivalree, just feel. I promise no one will find us. We'll be like Adam and Eve, alone in the wilds."

How she wanted to believe him. The thought of him

making love to her in the bright morning light sent a thrill coursing through her insides. To see him and touch him and glory in his virile manliness would be a dream come true. She smiled, her shyness slipping away, as she followed him with eagerness.

The creek twisted and tumbled over rocks and ledges, yet he continued guiding her along. Minutes later, both out of breath from scaling the banks of the stream, he led her up a high rise and stopped.

Rivalree's breath caught in her lungs. Below them the water rushed over a fall twelve feet high to an emerald-green pool of enormous size.

"Oh, Braven. It's beautiful."

He chuckled as he led her down a faint, fern-covered path to the water's edge. "I thought you'd like it," he said, sitting on moss-encrusted rocks to remove his boots and stockings.

In total fascination, she watched as he drew off his shirt. How truly magnificent he was. The crisply curled pelt on his chest was as pale as the hair on his head. As the garment left his shoulders, she marveled at the way his muscles flexed and jumped, more beautiful and manly than any statue of a Greek god she'd ever seen. He grinned at her as if sensing her approval, one eyebrow lifting devilishly, knowingly.

"Do you plan to watch, or are you going to join me?" His fingers began working the buttons on the front of his denims.

She sucked a deep breath into her lungs, conscious she had ogled him. Her heart thundered louder than the water cascading over the falls.

"Oh, of course." A blush spread across her face and neck. The thought of removing her clothing with him waiting deepened the flush. Would he make similar comparisons? Would she meet his expectations? The other evening under the cloak of darkness it had been easier to unveil herself. Somehow that had been spontaneous and natural. Her fingers hooked the button at her throat. His eyes glistened with undeniable desire. She couldn't display herself for his inspection like horseflesh at an auction.

Her hand stilled, and she spun to leave. Mumbling a curse when his tender feet contacted with sharp stones, he dogged her heels. The warmth of his flesh closed over her arm. Spinning her around he demanded, "Where do you think you're going?"

"Braven, I can't. Not like this." Her chin quivered slightly as she leveled her eyes with his. "You must understand," she pleaded. "I can't strip before you, waiting for your approval." Her gaze dropped, and he drew her face to rest against the soft down of his chest.

"Don't you understand yet? You're my wife. You please me, Rivalree, in more ways than you know." His hand fondled her earlobe, then followed a fiery path down her neck to the button at her throat. "I desire you, woman. I won't deny that. And when I see the flash of want in your eyes, it flames my need even higher."

The button slipped from the loop, and she didn't stop him. Instead, she leaned into the warmth of his palm, closed her eyes, and listened to the soothing rhythm of his heart thumping against her ear. "I love you," it said over and over, and she believed what his body told her.

Sensing her surrender, his fingers worked down the front of her blouse and brushed the fabric from her shoulders. Her chest rose and fell in nervous anticipation. Without asking he pushed down the soft fabric of her chemise, her quick breaths sending tiny quivers through the flesh of her bosom like leaves in a gentle spring breeze. Touching her breasts, he knelt before her and savored the warmth and taste of them. She molded against his seeking mouth until she thought her spine would break, her head thrown back in wild abandon. Each time his mouth left

216

her flesh, her hands tangled in his hair and pulled him back, and he offered no resistance.

Aware of nothing but the pleasure of his oral assault, it wasn't until the summer wind caressed her bare legs and thighs that she realized he had removed the rest of her clothing. How free she felt with the gentle warmth of the Sierra sun kissing her skin. How unrestrained and alive.

His tongue moved between her breasts, tracing a line to the hollow at the base of her throat, not stopping until he possessed her willing mouth. The evidence of his arousal pressed urgently against her bare stomach. And though she ached to accept him in the cradle of her womanhood, she didn't want to rush the exquisite feelings his eager stimulation sent crashing over her. Her knees turned to jelly, and she leaned against him until she thought the heat of their bodies would fuse them together.

Sweeping her up into his arms, he carried her down the pathway to a mossy ledge near the water's edge. Behind them, in the guise of their carelessly tossed clothing, lay civilization, and they became like the first man and woman surrounded by the bountiful gifts of God. As Braven marveled in the beauty of her body, she experienced the tingle of excitement his worshiping gaze created. The world around them came to a crashing halt, as if only the two of them existed. The thundering falls so close that a light mist rained down on them couldn't compare with the undulating tide of pleasure he created as he touched and kissed every crevice of her body, including the secret hollow between her thighs. Not until she begged him, did he take the final steps to consummate their love.

Like the tiniest flower offering up its sweet nectar to the hovering bee, they joined together as man and woman in the most intimate of rituals. Their bodies met in glistening glory, the tempo building until she thought her essences would fragment into a thousand slivers and remain scattered across the universe for all eternity. Yet as reality came crashing down against her, she discovered a fulfillment she never thought possible until this moment, a completeness Braven had given to her. No, shared with her. She sighed, a harmonic duet with the summer breeze, as he rolled to his side tucking her in the contour of his shoulder.

"Braven?" she asked, toying with the damp curls on his chest.

"Ummm?"

Her lips curved in a secret smile. He felt as rapturous as she. "Is it always like that between a man and woman?"

His head lifted from its pillow of greenery, an amused sparkle in his eyes. "Depends on what you mean. There are many variations, but the basic mechanics are generally the same."

She glanced down, embarrassed at the boldness of her question. "No, I don't mean that. Is it always so breathtaking and . . ." She paused. There were no words to describe how she felt.

He pulled her as close as he could. "I do believe you're paying me the ultimate compliment." A light grin played across his face.

She smiled shyly, then her mouth relaxed, a seriousness touching her countenance.

Responding to her mood, he sat up bringing her with him. "Oh, my little innocent, your question is an earnest one, isn't it?" His fingers curled around her uplifted chin. "The answer is no."

Her expression dropped in disappointment.

"What a greedy little urchin you are," he teased as his finger traced her solemn mouth. "But I'm glad you are. Desire is a marvelous feeling, but when love is added, it's electrifying. When lovers join in body and mind, it's miraculous. I pray it's always that way between us. It will be if that is what we want. I love you, Rivalree. No matter what happens, remember that. Love is not an emotion you can turn on and off at will, at least not for me." His arm tightened around her.

She nuzzled against him, pleased with his confession.

"But now, I think a nice swim in the cold stream will do us both wonders." He imprisoned her in a bear hug, and with a twist, he pulled her with him into the icy creek.

The breath in her lungs whooshed from her body as she hit the freezing water. She squeaked in protest as her head went under. Sputtering as she surfaced, she discovered Braven grinning at her, dry from the waist up.

She lunged determined to dunk him as he had her, but his long arms spanned the distance and pushed her head under again. Learning caution, she bobbed up a safe distance away.

"You won't get away with that again," she threatened, circling him warily as she sought an opening in his defense.

"Braven," came the far away lilt of Pat's voice.

Rivalree gasped and submerged herself. Braven's strong hands clasped her under the arm. She could feel the rumble of his laughter before she could hear it as he lifted her through the water.

"You're too easy," he bantered, cradling her next to his heart.

"Braven, are you down here?" queried the Irishman much closer.

She stiffened in his arms, and he reluctantly released her.

"Yes, Pat. I'm down in the creek." He waded to the shore and rose, dripping water. From the shelter of a jutting ledge she watched him dry off with his shirt and slip on his pants.

"The little colleen with you?"

"She's here," Braven answered, the tone in his voice announcing his displeasure at the interruption.

Pat chuckled. "Good. Then I won't come any closer."

Relief flooded through Rivalree. At least she would be spared the embarrassment of being seen.

"I wouldn't've disturbed you if it wasn't important. I've discovered something at the cabin I think you need to see."

Braven sighed and brushed the wet hair from his eyes. He glanced at Rivalree where she huddled. "Don't you move. I won't be long." He grinned. "I'm not quite done with you."

She lifted her hand in a wave and watched him wind his way up the embankment. What had Pat found that was so important that he felt it necessary to call Braven away?

Chapter Fifteen

Braven followed the silent Irishman past the spot where his freshly washed clothes lay neglected on the ground, his thoughts slipping back to the woman he had left moments before. He marveled how he had found such a pure and lovely woman in this cesspit of humanity called California.

"Things seem better between the two of you," Pat commented as they edged their way up the embankment toward the cabin.

Braven chuckled. "I'd say a blind toad could've figured that out. What's so damned important that you felt the need to interrupt?"

"Sorry about that, but what I discovered will no doubt interest you."

They skirted the groups of men enjoying their day of leisure. Pat led him around to the side of the cabin to a spot beneath Braven's bedroom window. He stopped and pointed upward. Braven's eyes followed his finger to a place under the ledge. Hastily packed were several cartridges of black powder with a long fuse leading downward about eye level with a man.

"Jesus God," Braven hissed as the implications of what the other man had found rammed home. There was enough explosives attached to the window ledge to blow the entire upstairs of the building to rubble. The destruction was meant for him. Whoever wanted him dead was no longer fooling around. Braven studied the fuse and the still drying mud used to hold the explosive in place. It hadn't been there long. He glanced at the Irishman. If it hadn't been for Pat's alertness, today might have been his, and Rivalree's, last day on this earth. "Which one of the men did this?"

"Well, you know it wasn't you, or me, or Rivalree . . ."

Braven nodded.

"I'm glad to hear you agree with me about the colleen. And Buckley is in no shape to do anybody harm. So that leaves a dozen men, give or take a few," Pat offered with a snort of disgust.

The image of each man who worked for him crossed Braven's mind. Not one face stood out as the obvious culprit, yet it had to be one of them, at least. Which one? Who would be willing to destroy an innocent woman for the sake of revenge, a woman who had risked her life to save his. And it was revenge. John Masters was somehow involved in this plot.

Pat reached up to jerk the fuse and cartridges from their resting place.

Braven placed a restraining hand on his rounded shoulder. "Leave it. I plan on catching the bastard tonight when he comes to set it off."

Pat frowned slightly. "Are you sure, Braven? You're taking a mighty big risk."

"Perhaps. But I'm tired of this cat-and-mouse game. The son of a bitch is going to pay for everything he's done, but mostly for Judd."

Pat nodded, his mouth a solemn slash across his face as he stepped back, the fuse swaying in the gentle breeze.

"Thank you, Pat. You're a true friend. Judd and I were lucky the day you showed up."

The Irishman smiled crookedly and turned away with a dip of his head to acknowledge Braven's words.

Rivalree fastened the last button on the front of her blouse, then tried to smooth her damp hair back in some semblance of order. Following the path Braven had led her along as best as her memory could serve, she was relieved when she reached the spot where they had left his wet clothes tossed on the ledge by the creek. She began to hum as she spread them out on every available bush and shrub to dry as wrinkle-free as possible.

What she needed was a clothesline. This afternoon she would ask Braven to construct one for her. She chuckled softly as she thought of Braven doing something so domestic. For her there was a deep-seated satisfaction in doing simple, wifely chores for her husband, and she savored the feeling as she meticulously pressed the drying shirts and pants with her hands. At the sound of returning footsteps she swirled, pushing back drying wisps of hair from her face.

Braven approached her, a set look on his face. Something was wrong, dreadfully wrong. She offered up a tiny encouraging smile hoping to erase the deep furrow between his brows. Their eyes touched and held as he returned the smile, but the frown returned several heartbeats later.

"What is it, Braven," she inquired.

His mouth clamped over his even white teeth, and the thumpity-thump of her heart roared in her ears before he answered.

"Nothing you need to worry about." He grinned, but it was an act on his part strictly for her, as the merriment never reached his eyes. "I'd hope to find you sunning your sweet, bare bottom, not being a washerwoman."

"Washerwomen can be appealing, too, you know." She

batted her lashes at him. She found it hard to banter with him when all she wanted to do was demand to know what was going on. She presented her backside to him, and the smile slipped away.

Why was he shutting her out? Did he still not trust her? She finished spreading out the last shirt, dusted her hand of imaginary dirt, then planted her fists on her hips, surveying her handiwork.

"If you're through admiring my wardrobe," he said so close his breath tickled her neck, "then I thought you might want to learn how to earn your keep."

"I earn my keep very well, thank you." She turned, ready to spar. The smile lit his lapis lazuli eyes. In his hand he held a large tin pan that reminded her of a pie plate, but twice as big as any pastry crust she'd ever seen. "What am I supposed to do, bake pies?"

He threw his head back in honest laughter, and the sound made her heart swell with joy.

"Well, then, if you don't want to learn how to pan for gold, I guess I won't teach you." He spun as if to leave.

Like an eager child her hands circled his arm. "Do you mean it? Will you really teach me how?"

"You'll have to do something about your skirts."

She hesitated. She didn't dare remove the cumbersome garment. Remembering how her mother would pull the back of her dress up between her legs and tuck it in her waist when it hindered her and she thought no one was looking, the corners of her mouth lifted wickedly as she bent, grabbed her skirt, and stuffed it in her waistband, pulling the material up and over her knees. "Is that good enough?"

His eyebrow lifted in mock disapproval. "You are one lady who never fails to amaze me."

"And why is that, sir?" she asked in her best imitation of a southern accent. "Is it because I don't sit upon my lily white hands, discussin' my wardrobe and waitin' for another all important invitation to a ball?'' Pretending to raise an imaginary fan to her face, she fluttered it and peered coyly over its rim.

Braven's laughter rang down the canyon. "I do believe, sugar, you do that better than any belle I know, even with your skirts hiked up like a common field hand." He sat on the bank and rolled up his pants legs, then joined her in the swirling water. "Come here, you little imp," he demanded.

With a giggle, she moved closer and watched fascinated as he bent scooping up river bottom into the pan from a spot between two boulders. Swirling the contents round and round with an experienced hand, he allowed the water to roll over the sides. He made it look so easy as the silt in the bottom slowly disappeared and he dipped the pan back into the creek to add more liquid. She held her breath, not sure what to expect, and didn't give in to the need to breathe until her lungs demanded she do so. Still he continued to swirl the water.

Finally he stopped and tipped the tin so she could see the bottom. Three golden lumps shone up at her. Her mouth formed a silent "o." Gold. She glanced at him to confirm what she saw. He nodded and tilted the pan further, pouring the nuggets into her open palm.

"That was so simple," she breathed. She glanced up at him again. "How much do you think they're worth?" Her voice broke with excitement.

"Why, Mrs. Blackwood, I do believe you've been struck with gold fever. I didn't know women were susceptible to the disease, too." He stuck out his hand, and after she dropped the gold into it, he placed it in his shirt pocket.

Her eyes questioned him. "If it's such a cinch to take it from the creek, why go to all of the trouble to dig for it?" She pointed toward the mine entrance.

"If you think it's so effortless, here." He handed her the tin pan. "Why don't you try?"

She clamped her fingers around the rim and bent to dip it into the swirling water. Her first attempt to wash the silt ended in quick disaster, and everything went flying out as she shook the pan. She stooped again, determined to prove she could do it, and lifted the receptacle. This bout she took more care with. By the time she had filtered out most of the trash, her wrists ached, but nothing glimmered. Frustrated, she scooped up another panful. Swishing the water, she washed away the grit, and a multitude of tiny flakes shined up at her. Her gold. She had found it. She tipped the pan, the sparkling chips filtering into her open palm.

Straightening her back, the muscles rebelled sending a sharp pain up her spine. The gold might be hers, but she had worked hard to earn it. She didn't think it so easy any longer. She thrust the empty container at Braven, ignoring the I-told-you-so look on his face.

Her gaze followed the line of the creek to the odd contraption she had noticed several times before. The equipment reminded her of several ladders fitted together but with a solid bottom beneath the rungs. The long trough ran at least twenty-five feet from a high ledge at the river's edge to a small pool below, allowing the flow of the water to run down it. Braven's eyes traveled with hers.

"That's the sluice box," he answered her silent question. "Much easier on the back than panning. All the dirt we haul from the mine is run through the sluice. Most of the gold we find comes from the sluice, unfortunately."

Rivalree shot him a surprised look. "Why, I thought you would be digging big chunks of gold out of the mountain."

"I wish to God we were. We wouldn't be scraping a living up here in this crude cabin with a handful of rough miners. We'd be living it up somewhere civilized, maybe New York, or better yet, how about Paris or London?" His eyes crinkled with amusement at her innocent ignorance.

"Then why do you do this?" she pressed softly, remembering what she'd learned from Janet Longstreet in Marysville. "Your family is wealthy enough for you to live the lifestyle you dream about." As soon as the words were out of her mouth she wished she could stuff them back where they came from.

Braven's face tightened, and his brilliant blue eyes turned a turbulent shade of granite. "I'll not live off money made from the blood of another human being. I'll make my way like any other man." He spun, presenting his rigid back, and stepped toward the bank.

Rivalree's mouth fell slack in awe. She had never considered his conviction. A man of the South who venomously denied his right to own slaves? Her heart swelled with newfound pride for the man she called husband.

"Braven, wait." Her leaden feet tried to hurry through the eddying water. Like a dancing shore bird, her long legs lifted high to enable her to reach him before he escaped.

Reaching the shore several yards behind him, she whipped her skirts from their fetter and let them fall into their proper place. "I didn't mean to pry," she offered breathlessly, racing after his retreating figure.

Though still guarded, he paused, waiting for her to catch up.

"Please, I was so enjoying learning about gold mining. I didn't mean to ruin everything with my stupid questions."

"Then, come on," he said, waving her forward with his hand. "I've saved the best for last." His eyes lit with a glowing fervor. "I want to give you a proper tour of the mine."

She held back. The mine? She didn't relish the idea of reentering the place that had so filled her with terror a few days ago. As if he sensed her reluctance, his hand touched her elbow, caressing softly, to guide her forward. "There's nothing for you to fear. I've checked the tunnels over thoroughly. There will be no more accidents," he said with conviction.

There would be no more accidents. Braven had no doubt that the mine itself was about the safest place he could be. Whoever was determined to kill him had decided to stop being indirect. But he didn't want to dwell on those thoughts now.

He glanced down at the woman at his side. Rivalree was like an unlearned child soaking up his words. She was a strong, intelligent woman, even though her willfulness exasperated him at times. His ego swelled like a croaking frog's throat whenever she looked at him with the reverence she did at that moment. He liked being loved and being *in* love. Grinning down at her upturned face so full of trusting hesitancy, he wrapped his arm around her shoulder in reassurance as they entered the dark, gaping mouth of the mine.

How had she learned so much about his past? Who had told her? Pat, perhaps, but more likely the never quiet Janet Longstreet.

The placid coolness of the cavern washed over him, and even though he understood why the tunnels held such fear for Rivalree, he felt nothing but peace and security. It was as if he could communicate with the soul of this untamed mountain. Soon, with enough patience, the docile giant would offer up its riches to him.

As the pathway narrowed, he stepped into the lead urging Rivalree to follow as he squeezed her hand. The light of the new candle in the holder on his hat lit the way extraordinarily well.

"It all seems so different," she commented. "The light I held the day of the cave-in was so dim compared with yours."

"Because the reflector was tarnished. That's why I left it on the table."

"Oh," she replied, a bit embarrassed at her ignorance. "I don't think I've thanked you for coming to my rescue, have I?"

Her silence baffled him, but he continued on ahead. He had been such a fool to think her involved in a plot against him. It was like accusing Pat O'Grady. How close he had come to losing her, and that thought sent a rush of despair spearing through his heart. She was in his blood, a golden fervor as strong as the gold fever that had pushed him for the last five years to hit a bonanza. He could no more give up the yearning for her than the need to strike it rich.

Maybe she was right. He should gather up his few belongings and what was left of his pride and dignity and head home with his new wife to take what was rightfully his. No, damn it. His brother's smirking face smiled at him in his mind just as it had that day so long ago. Brent had said he'd be back with his tail tucked between his legs like a starving cur. No, he'd go back successful, with the ability to carry through with his dream, or he'd not return at all.

Braven came to a halt in the tunnel, his thoughts spinning back to the present.

"Oh, my," Rivalree whispered behind him. "It's so large."

Pulling her into the circle of his arm, he was relieved to hear the fear fading from her voice. It was important she not spend the time he worked in the mine worrying about his safety. That was the point of bringing her back here. Like falling off a horse, one had to get right back in the saddle to conquer one's fear.

"Actually it's rather cozy. In the summer it's cool, and in the dead of winter we should be as warm as if we were sitting before a fire." He watched, fascinated. She

229

cautiously scouted the cavern, picking up tools, then peered down into the ore cart they used to carry out the dirt as they tunneled farther into the side of the hill, hopefully closer to the vein of gold he knew existed. Time, just a matter of time.

"I don't see anything that looks like gold. Why dig in this particular spot?" she queried.

Encouraged by the sincere interest she showed, he formulated his answer. "Several reasons. The lay of the land, for one, and the angle of the rock formations pointing toward the creek. About a hundred yards back we ran into a large deposit of quartz."

"Is that good?"

"Promising. Two days ago we hit a pocket of iron pyrite that for a moment had me fooled."

"Iron pyrite? What is that?"

"Fool's gold." He smiled indulgently. "There's been many a man who has lost his sanity or his life over worthless fool's gold." He turned and sifted through the dirt in the miner's cart. "Here," he offered, placing a small chunk of shiny metal in her hand.

"But, Braven, this looks like the gold we took from the creek," she insisted.

"Think so? Examine it closely, Rivalree." He lifted the piece of metal between his thumb and forefinger, rolling it about. "Notice how cubical shaped it is?"

She nodded.

"Gold never has this squareness about it. Besides," he pointed out, taking the gold nuggets they had found in the river from his pocket, "see the difference in color. The pyrite has a brassy hue to it."

Side by side, the differences were obvious. He slipped the gold back in his pocket and casually tossed the pyrite on the ground.

"Then this digging sight is a false trail. There's no gold, just that worthless iron." She kicked the cube with her toe.

"Not at all. Where there's gold, iron pyrite is almost always abundant. This is a good sign, not a bad."

She placed her small, delicately made hands on the wall and feathered her fingers over the crevices and ridges the picks had made the previous day. She glanced up eagerly at him. "So, what do you do? Dig away the dirt and rocks and carry the debris out in that?" She pointed at the miner's cart.

"Pretty basic," he answered with a chuckle, "but most accurate. We try to follow the angle toward the core of the mountain." Lifting a pickax, he began the ritual of swinging and embedding the sharp point into the wall before them.

Her eyes watched his every move. Up and over his shoulder, down until the point thudded into the earth to crumble the dirt. He felt the eagerness radiating from her.

"Here." He offered her the tool. "Would you like to give it a try?"

She grasped the implement's handle, and the weight of the pickax threw her off balance. "I didn't think it would be this heavy."

As she struggled to raise the tool and embedded it in the wall of dirt, he studied her fragile physique, so like his mother's Dresden figurines sitting on the mantel back home. Remembering how rough he had been on her time after time, he praised her ability to maintain the strength of mind to survive each encounter with grace and dignity. Perhaps that was what he loved about her best, her capacity to survive hardship without being tainted.

Her groans of determination, as she swung the heavy tool, brought a smile to his lips. Amazingly, she had managed to scrape away a considerable amount of debris. The evidence lay at her feet, a mound growing higher with each rotation of her arms. Squelching the desire to bring her struggle to an end, he empathized with the emotions gleaming in her amber eyes. That overpowering need to strike it rich had stuck its long claws in her. Crossing his arms over the wide expanse of chest, he waited patiently for her physical endurance to lose the battle. He knew the feeling well, as he had combated it himself for the last five years, until, at times, his body had reached the point where it refused to go on.

His heart contracted as her breath came in short, spasmodic gasps. He hadn't meant to bring her to this level, to infect her with the mental disease more fatal than any of the body.

The pick dropped from her hands as she leaned heavily against the wall, the words she tried to speak coming out in breathless pants. Giving up the attempt to communicate, her fingers scraped at the barrier of dirt and rock.

"Good God, Rivalree, slow down." He stepped toward her. Never had he seen anyone so crazed by the gold fever. "There's no need to try and dig through the mountain in one day." His hands captured hers, and a golden glint caught the corner of his eye. He froze in disbelief. Rivalree slumped against his chest, relieved he understood what she tried to say.

Gold. A vein as thick as his wrist and God only knew how deep. He couldn't imagine that the cave of the forty thieves discovered by Ali Baba could have glistened more.

"Jesus Christ," he whispered in awe. "You've the luck of the beginner. I think you've struck the mother lode."

She began to tremble as she turned in his arms and tilted her head in order to see him better. "Is it really gold?"

Her excitement made it difficult for him to keep his head. Now more than ever, he had to catch the man determined to kill him. If John Masters got wind of their discovery, his life would be worthless. Remembering the little ditty so popular in the mining camps, he prayed inwardly, "But most of all I do plea, protect me from partner treachery."

*　　*　　*

Squatting in the shadows behind the large boulder, Braven waited, his patience running thin, but he dared not move or he might reveal himself. Why didn't the bastard who planted the explosives show up? What was he waiting for?

His gaze moved up to the drawn shade of the upstairs window—the bedroom he shared with Rivalree. The shadowy image of the woman as she prepared for bed held his attention, so suggestive as she moved in and out of view. He would cover that damned window in the morning with something more substantial. The idea that others might have enjoyed the tempting display he witnessed was intolerable.

The open window gave vent to her voice, so soft and lyrical as she hummed an unrecognizable tune. God, he loved her.

Brush rustled to his left, and he ducked down. At last he would know who was behind the attempts on his life. He waited, breath held, as shuffling footsteps neared. The pistol he held weighed like icy death in his palm. He would give the man long enough to reveal himself, no more, then he would dispose of him quickly. That was the justice of the land. Never give a thieving back-stabber a second chance.

With the instincts of a predator, he waited, leg muscles taut and ready to spring at the precise moment.

The scuttle halted as Rivalree's voice came to a trilling crescendo. Braven raised the pistol to eye level, cocked it, and aimed in the general direction, prepared to follow through with his plans.

"Braven," called a lilting Irish voice.

What in the hell was Pat doing here now? Braven sighed and disengaged the hammer of the gun, dropping it to his side as he rose from his hiding place. Anyone else lurking about would have been alarmed by now. "Over here, Pat," he answered.

The Irishman stepped forward into the thin moonlight.

"Thought I'd rescue you from your fruitless vigilance."

"How did you know no one has shown?"

"Jacobs came around a few moments ago to let you know Jack Quincy done up and disappeared sometimes today. Says he left most of his things."

"Did Quincy talk to anybody before he went?"

Pat shook his head. "Seems he departed in rather a hurry."

"Because he left mysteriously, you think he's the one behind all this?" With a sweep of his arm he indicated the explosives.

"He had pay comin', Braven. Why else would a man leave so quickly unless he was afraid of gettin' caught?"

What Pat said made sense. With a sense of relief, he stepped over to the dangling fuse line and gave it a mighty jerk. Death's instrument tumbled to the ground. Maybe it was best this way. Now that they had struck a rich vein, he trusted no one, not even himself, to leave the camp. One slip of the tongue around outsiders, even in innocence, could bring a stampede of the Louisiana Mine the likes of which hadn't been seen in years, since the rush of forty-nine.

Chapter Sixteen

August 29, 1851

The creak of the leather harness, the gentle blowing sounds the horses made as they fidgeted in their place, but most of all the shrill mimic of the mockingbird high in the pine above her sent thrills racing down Rivalree's spine. She had been at the Louisiana Mine almost a month, never once going more than a few hundred yards away from the cabin. The thought of going to Poker Flat, even though it was such a small community, was intoxicating. Like a farm girl fresh out of the hayloft she giggled. She was going to town.

"Get down, Rivalree."

Her head revolved on the column of her neck, her attention snapping down to the man, her husband, standing beside the wagon. She had been so caught up in her own excitement, she hadn't noticed his approach.

A smile so tremendous that she thought her face would shatter lit her mouth. "It's okay. Pat said I could go in his place today."

The frown on Braven's face deepened.

"He gave me an exact list," she further explained. "I won't have any problem getting the few supplies we need.''

"I said, get down out of that wagon.''

Rivalree blinked in confusion, her lower jaw dropping in surprise at the irritation in his voice. Didn't he understand what she'd said? The tight look on his face suggested he didn't.

She glanced at Mace Lockman on the seat beside her, but the man lifted his shoulders in a noncommittal shrug. Damn it. Didn't anybody on this mountain stand up to Braven Blackwood? She twisted to face her domineering husband, her chin lifted in defiance. "No. I don't have to.''

Before the words cleared her mouth, his hand shot out and captured her wrist. Their gazes locked like rapiers, parry and thrust, waiting for the other to show a moment of weakness.

Everything had been going so well between them during the last few weeks. The vein of gold they had discovered that Sunday had proven true, like an endless river weaving deeper and deeper into the side of the mountain. Why then did he look at her now as if she were a wayward child? She owned as much of this mine as he did. She didn't need him telling her what to do.

Twisting her wrist, she wrenched from his grip at the point where his fingers and thumb met.

His jaws clamped down so hard she heard his teeth grind together as the wagon springs squeaked when he stepped upon the footboard in order to grasp her upper arm. "Don't argue with me. Do as I say. Mace.'' His eyes shot up at the man holding the reins. "Put the wagon away. No one is going to town today or any other day unless I give specific instructions. Understood?''

Mace nodded mutely, getting down on the other side to do Braven's bidding.

Her temper simmered, threatening to spill forth as he swung her down from the seat and started back to the cabin, never once releasing the manacle grip on her arm. What was wrong with him? There was something more than anger with her for going in Pat's place.

At the foot of the porch, she struggled to escape his hand. He released her with maddening easiness, stepping up on the landing, leaving her in the position of staring up at him from the ground.

"Why, Braven," she demanded, unable to keep the high-pitched anger from invading her voice.

"Because that's the way it's going to be."

Lifting the packet of letters she clutched, she waved them under his nose. "We were only going to get a few supplies we're running low on and to mail these . . . letters to family back home from most of your miners."

"I bet every one of them talks about how we've hit it big and how they're coming home soon rich men."

She stepped back, his words hitting home. That was exactly what her letter to Prudence Bankhurst said. They had struck it rich.

"I even bet a few of those missives are to sweethearts in San Francisco," he continued. "If you can call the whores most of these men take up with anybody's sweetheart. Just how long do you think it would be before this mountain would be swamped with claim jumpers and riffraff? My God, woman, all you or Mace had to do was let it slip out in Poker Flat, and every tenderfoot in a hundred mile radius would converge on us."

"Don't you think I'm smart enough to keep my mouth shut?"

"Tell me, sugar, how did you plan to pay for the supplies you were going to get?"

"Pat gave me plenty of gold to cover anything we needed," she answered smugly, offering up the leather pouch for his inspection.

"That's all we need. You running around Poker Flat flaunting gold nuggets." He tore the pouch from her hand. "I can understand you making a stupid mistake like that, but not Pat." He whirled, storming into the house.

"I wouldn't have flaunted it, damn you," she insisted to his retreating figure. "You could have trusted me to be discreet."

Just before entering the door, he stopped but didn't turn around. "Don't you understand the seriousness of our situation? I don't trust anybody—not even myself—with news like this." He pressed forward again.

"What about the supplies we need?"

"They can wait. Learn to make do with what we have. You'll have to this winter," he offered matter-of-factly.

Rivalree's mind spun in confusion as he disappeared into the dark cavern of the cabin door. This winter? she questioned herself. What did he mean by that? It was understood you go down off the mountain when the bad weather sets in. She gazed, openmouthed, at the empty doorway. She could hear him calling Pat's name in the same irritated voice he had used with her. Surely he didn't mean for them to stay up here in this godforsaken country all winter. They would starve to death. She wouldn't risk her life just to keep his precious secret. She would leave the first chance she got.

Stumbling down the step, she rushed from the house. She must think this through.

Outside the chicken pen she picked up the bucket of mash and, lifting the latch on the gate, entered the peaceful confines of the coop. She had to do something with her hands while she worked on a solution to her problem. With expertise, she began the age-old task of broadcasting the grain on the ground.

"Here, chick, chick, chick," she called to the pecking fowl.

She sighed. In a matter of moments the fragile relationship beginning to build between her and Braven had been scattered like the seed around her feet. Unknowingly, he had spoken the truth that Sunday by the river.

She, as a woman, wasn't infected with the gold fever like he was. Their lives were not worth the risk they would take staying here, high in the Sierras, all winter. What good would all the gold in California do them if they were dead? He was so pigheaded!

"I've already fed them, colleen."

Rivalree glanced up at Pat leaning on the outside of the yard fencing.

"I thought you were headed into town?"

"Plans changed," she muttered, grasping a handful of grain and tossing it as hard as she could to the ground. Squawking chickens fled from her onslaught to the corners of the coop.

Damn him for being so arrogant, she thought, tossing the empty bucket at the enclosure wall.

Pat chuckled. "Braven have a burr in his britches again?"

She glared at his amused face. "He's mad as a hornet, and he's looking for you."

The Irishman guffawed as he pushed away from the coop and headed toward the cabin. "Didn't think we'd get away with a trip to town, but it was worth a try."

Rivalree blinked in disbelief. The Irishman had known Braven would disapprove all along. Then why had he sent her, unsuspecting, on her way? Her eyes narrowed. She didn't like being a pawn in a game, especially one involving Braven Blackwood.

The tension in the common room was thick as freshly churned butter, the only sounds those of an occasional click of flatware against plates. Even Zoey lay quietly in one corner, not at her usual spot at Braven's knee waiting for a tidbit.

⸻ree sat down in silence beside him. His eyes ⸻n circled the table analyzing each sullen face his gaze touched. No doubt word was out Braven was allowing no one, not even his wife, liberty to leave the mining camp.

Pat joined the table, sitting opposite Braven. Silent communication passed between the two men as the Irishman lifted his fork to his mouth. "I think it's time to explain the situation to them, Braven, me boyo."

With a sigh, Braven dropped his utensil onto his plate and rose in place, again taking in each person at the table. When his eyes met Rivalree's, he hesitated for a moment before passing on to the man sitting beside her. Lifting his foot, he placed it on the bench, resting his arm across his knee in what Rivalree knew was a deceptive pose of tranquility. What he was about to say would change every life in the room, especially hers.

"With luck," he began, "we have a little over four weeks until winter sets in. Four weeks of hard work."

The men nodded in agreement, curiosity piquing their faces.

"If we leave and head to Marysville to wait out the weather, how long do you think it will be until words gets around we struck a bonanza up here?"

Grumbles of protest tinged the room.

"I'd never say a word," one man insisted.

"Jesus Christ, Braven, who'd be stupid enough to talk?"

Braven raised his hand. "That's a good question, Mace. I'm not that ignorant, and you aren't either. Unless I've had too much to drink." He grinned. "Or there's a pretty little miss sitting on my knee asking questions."

Laughter circled the table.

"But what about the person next to you? Or the one across the table?"

Eyes studied each other around the knot of miners.

"Can you be sure of him? Or her?" Braven nodded at Rivalree. Her back stiffened as he singled her out.

The murmur of voices began to eleva

Braven lifted his hand for silence. "Each one of you has a personal stake in the proceeds from this mine—a percentage of the take."

Rivalree's head shot up. What was he saying? She thought the men were paid wages. How much was he giving them?

"With time we can pull enough gold out of this mountain to make each of us rich for the rest of our lives. It's there, and we all know it." He paused and demanded each person to look him in the eye. "Unless we have to spend next spring fighting off claim jumpers. By that time we could be rich enough for all of us to go home. If we stay through the winter."

"But won't we have problems with claim jumping anyway? When we don't come down the mountain, won't people suspect we found something?" one of the men asked.

Braven smiled. "By the time flatlanders realize we have no intentions of leaving, it won't matter. No one will be able to get past the snows. In seven months we'll dig enough gold so we can sell this damn mine to some other gold-crazed sucker."

Rivalree began to panic. If everyone agreed to stay with Braven how would she ever get away? "But what about the monthly trips into town? Won't people get suspicious when no one shows up as usual to replenish supplies?"

Braven's eyes narrowed slightly at her. "I don't think so. The townspeople will assume we're preparing to return and are using up what food we have."

"But the cold," one man piped up. "We're sleeping in a tent now. How will we manage to combat the weather?"

"As soon as the weather deems it necessary, each man will bring his cot here to the common room near the fireplace."

"When the snows come," another man asked, "and the drifts are higher than the doors, how will we reach the mine?"

"I've thought about that, too, Dan. What if we build a covered walkway from the porch to the mine entrance? Then we wouldn't have to go outside all winter."

"Will it work?" Dan asked.

"Of course it will," Mace shouted, slapping the other man on the back with enthusiasm.

Rivalree's gaze darted from one face to another. These men were falling under Braven's carefully cast spell. She didn't want to stay here. "But what about supplies?" she demanded in one last desperate attempt to squelch the approval buzzing about the room.

"I'll make one final run down the mountain to get what we need."

"Why you?" she pressed.

A frown furrowed his brows. "Because that is what I've decided."

They could have been all alone in the room, for the men were laughing and pounding each other's backs with such excitement they were unaware of the tension snapping like dry twigs between husband and wife.

"But what about those who don't want to stay?" she choked amid the confusing den.

Braven glanced around the room. One eyebrow cocked at her in amused triumph before his gaze hardened into a glare that seemed to say, "If that's the way you want it." He banged his knife handle against the table to gain the men's attention. "It appears we're not all in total agreement."

The men glanced around the room to see who wasn't with them. Rivalree held her defiant chin high.

"There's only one way to be fair to all. We'll take a vote. Majority wins. Either we all stay or we all leave. Agreed?"

In unison the men shouted, "Agreed."

Braven smiled down at her. He had won, and there was nothing she could do or say to stop the madness prancing around the room like an outbreak of smallpox. She had no choice except to stay, but the day would come when she would tell Braven Blackwood to go to hell.

Braven watched as Rivalree ran the boar-bristle brush through her golden tresses with a maddening slowness. Catching glimpses of her unsmiling face in the mirror before which she sat, he tried to capture her eye, but she refused to acknowledge his presence behind her. Propped upon the bed, his stockinged feet draped across the coverlet, his bare shoulders and back pressed against the pillow that normally cushioned Rivalree's head, his hands splayed behind his head, he studied her intently, awed by her beauty seeming to glow brighter with each passing day. God, he loved her, so much sometimes it twisted his insides into an unbearable knot. Even now, with anger mantling her shoulders, he desired her and wanted her to turn to him with a need of her own.

He sighed, knowing full well she wouldn't come to him, not until the misunderstanding between them was cleared up, not until he was willing to open his heart, the cache holding his many secrets and dreams, to her perusal.

But how could he explain what drove him to do the things he did? Would she understand the nature of his pride? He pushed up from his sprawl on the bed and approached her where she sat. He would lay bare his soul to her inspection if he must. Something he had found impossible to do with anyone, until now.

Her shoulders stiffened with each stride he took in her direction. He tried to decipher the emotions mirrored in her reflection: anger, mistrust, hurt, confusion. But she looked down, hiding her face, her hands fumbling with the brush.

Cupping her elbows in his palms, he bent low, pressing his lips to the top of her shiny head, and, staring into the mirror, he willed her gaze to lift to his. Their eyes locked for a breath-held moment before he reached down removing the brush from her hands and placing it on the dresser.

The tenseness of her body gushed away as she dropped her head back against his torso, her lashes lowering over the amber pools. "Why, Braven? Why are you so determined to destroy us, body and soul? How will we ever survive a long winter here?"

He whirled her around, bringing her to her feet to tuck her in the protective circle of his arms. "Destroy? No, never. I wouldn't allow you to stay if I didn't feel you would be safe. Can't you trust me, Rivalree? Believe in my judgment and my ability to take care of both of us."

She examined him, her stare burning into his brain. "I believe you are driven," she offered, her hand coming up to knead the furrows between his brows, "but don't ask me to follow blindly. I pray there is more behind this . . . insanity than the need to become rich, more than the driving fever to possess gold."

Her probing words took him aback. He released her, shrugging her away, as he strolled across the room, somehow requiring distance between them. He sat on the bed and buried his face in his hands, torn in his commitment to reveal his secrets to her and his need to maintain the privacy of his thoughts.

"Tell me, my love," she urged in a whisper, kneeling between his thighs, her chin lifted and her eyes pleading. "I promise I'll try to understand."

Could he ask for more? His fingers plowed a path through his cornsilk-colored hair then moved down to entwine with hers. "Where do I begin?"

Disjoined images of his childhood swirled in his mind: the beating he had suffered on his tenth birthday when he had freed Carter, his childhood playmate; the ridicule he had received from his older brother Brent, when he spoke of his desire to see all slaves free; the tearful pleading of his mother when he'd refused to recant the vow his father had declared blasphemous; the coldness in his father's eyes as he had set out for California, and the smirk on Brent's face as he had swore he would return to prove his theory that the South could survive without slavery.

The story spilled from his mouth. Rivalree's face softened with each word he spoke as respectful comprehension inflamed her gaze. "But the money, I don't understand. Why is the gold so important?"

"I'll purchase one of several failing plantations in the parish, free the slaves, then hire them on for wages, or like I'm doing here, for a share of the profits. I know my plan will work."

"I'm sure it will, too." Rivalree rested her cheek on his knee. There was a hesitancy in her voice he couldn't fail to hear.

He brought her up and placed her across his leg. "Can't you see it now? We'll go home, triumphant, you and I. We'll show them, sugar. We'll show them all."

His mouth descended, trapping the response he sensed struggled to escape, the answer he hoped agreed with his confession. But more important was the way her lips molded to his, begging him to make her believe.

His arms drew her closer, pressing the roundness of her breast encased in the thin chemise against his chest. With her at his side he could accomplish anything including miracles. And it would take just that, a miracle, for them to reach the safe haven of home once the gold was in their possession. Blocking the stark reality from his mind, he immersed himself in the feel of her warm body straining against his, the touch of her dancing tongue in his mouth, and tingle of her fingers massaging the hard sinew of his back and shoulders.

Locating the fasteners on the front of the thin garment she wore, he freed the swelling flesh of her bosom. Their beauty never failed to amaze him as the round globes nestled in the cradle created by her arms. The nipples, blushing pink, beckoned, and unable to resist their bidding, he dipped his head and drew one rosy tip into his mouth.

Her back arched, thrusting the pursed aureola closer as her fingers burrowed in his hair holding him near. Losing himself in her warm, willing flesh, he allowed her to direct him from one breast to the other until a deep moan of soaring passion rose from her throat.

With confident movements he took the lead, gliding her from his lap to lie across the bed. Her head was thrown back, her golden hair fanned over the coverlet, her quivering breasts tempting him to forget the finesse of making love to plunder her willing body. Perhaps if she had been any other female he would have, but not the woman who dominated his heart and soul, his partner in life.

"Rivalree," he called softly. "Look at me."

Her lashes lifted revealing liquid desire. With one swift motion he stripped the unbuttoned chemise from her body, exposing the perfect hills and valleys he had come to revere. Unashamed, she raised her arms in welcome, and he wasted no time removing his clothing and tossing them on the floor.

Kneeling between her open thighs, his gaze traveled from glistening lips to the dark triangle of her womanhood. Then, when her fingers clasped his rigid shaft, stroking until he thought his being would shatter, he succumbed to the demands of his body and hers. Plunging into her heavenly depths he nearly lost control as her torso rose to meet him halfway. He grasped her undulating hips, holding them still, until he mastered the waves of passion threatening to wash away the last vestiges of restraint.

"Easy, my love," he groaned, guiding her into a rhythm that would give them both what they desired—

mutual satisfaction.

With a tiny sob, she accepted his authority, meeting his powerful thrust with equal fervor until the tempo built to a natural crescendo. She cried out her fulfillment, and only then did he focus on his own release which crested before the echo of hers had died away.

Spent and joyous, he fell across her with one final shudder as she welcomed his weight. He was a man with a purpose, with a dream to attain, and a woman to stand by his side in support. What more could he want?

Rivalree traced the line of Braven's brow, relaxed in slumber. *Men and their grand dreams,* she thought with a silent sigh. *Why do they always wish to change the world?* Brushing away a lock of wayward hair from his forehead, her hand drifted down to rest on his chest, rising and falling with the shallow breaths of untroubled sleep.

The lovemaking that had transpired between them hours before had been an attempt on her part to erase the mad yearning from his mind. Her ploy had worked for the moment, but she had no illusion that in the morning he would still expect them to stay here in this cabin, struggle to survive the harshness of the winter, all in the name of righteousness. She knew deep in her heart she would never mean more to him than his personal goals. Why else would he insist she stay against her will? The thought rankled, leaving her empty and lost, and feeling bitter.

Judd had been a dreamer, too, but his plans for improving the future had centered around her. If Judd had lived, how simple her life would have been. His love had been giving, considerate, not consuming and overpowering like the emotions she felt for Braven.

Confusion rocketed through her. How could she be doing this, comparing one man with the other? It was wrong to think about what might have been; wronger still

247

to consider any man in her life except her husband. Almost as if in her mind she were contemplating adultery.

"No," she hissed in the darkness.

Braven stirred, pulling her into the crook of his shoulder, his lips brushing the top of her head. "Sweet Rivalree," he murmured into her hair.

Rivalree lay as still as she could, a whimper of guilty despair lodging in her throat.

Forgive me for my selfishness, she prayed, *but I don't know if I can survive what Braven asks me to bear. I'll remain imprisoned on this mountain only because I don't know what else I can do.*

Chapter Seventeen

The sounds of hammers and saws invaded Rivalree's tired brain. She had lain awake most of the night worrying about her situation, accomplishing no more than a puppy gnawing at an old shoe, its tiny milk teeth barely penetrating the tough leather.

She rose from the bed, weary to the bone, and pattered to the window. Just as she suspected. From her vantage point she could see Braven directing a crew of men pulling logs from the woods to begin the construction of the walkway from the cabin door to the mine entrance. The nightmare had begun, and there was nothing she could do to stop it short of mass murder and matricide.

The men were jovial, much like untried soldiers marching to first battle. And Braven. He whistled a contented tune, the sound setting her nerves on edge. Didn't they realize what they would face in the next few months? Was she the only one not infected with the insanity of this place?

With hands on hips, she turned away from the window, dressed, and headed down the stairs. The common room was empty, freshly washed dishes propped in the dry sink, a plate of biscuits left warming on the stove. Even Pat was caught up in the excitement and had deserted his post to participate in Braven's wild scheme.

Popping one of the biscuits in her mouth, she stepped out the front door, glancing around. So much activity. Already a skeleton framework arched from the porch steps to the mine. Braven hunched over a stack of tree trunk yet devoid of limbs and branches, a schoolroom slate in his hands as he jotted figures on it. She wondered where the slate had come from, a strange object to be found among a group of grown men. Easing around the growing structure, she chewed the remainder of the biscuit and dusted her hands on her skirt.

Braven's gaze climbed, touching her, and he smiled, a broad, beaming gesture of welcome. "Thought you'd never get up, sleepyhead. I tried to wake you earlier, but you just wouldn't budge." His arm lifted, and he scooped her to his side and held her, draping his wrist over her shoulder to continue writing.

"I didn't think you would begin so soon?"

"Not much time till winter arrives. Only a few weeks at the most." He looked away, his arm drifting to his side, releasing her. "Mace," he called. "We'll need more logs. Keep 'em coming."

The other man nodded, grabbed the reins of one of the wagon horses in harness and led the animal into the woods. Zoey followed the placid dray, nipping at its heels, as if sensing her master's urgency.

Rivalree turned her head, a deep frown on her face, and studied the man beside her. He looked once at her, giving her a flashing grin, then ambled away.

Couldn't he see how unhappy she was? Didn't he care? Judd would have noticed how she felt. There she went again, comparing. She must stop doing that. But, damn, it was true. Braven Blackwood was nothing more than an insensitive boor.

She spun and fled the scene of activity, treading her way to the stream. There she let loose of her emotions, tears

250

brimming her lashes and spilling over on her cheeks. How could she love and despise a man all in the same breath? Oh, Judd, Judd, why had he led her to this soul-rending fate?

Braven watched her departure. He saw the tear-brimmed lashes and the trembling bottom lip. His heart bucked in the cage of his ribs demanding he go after her. But he couldn't. Not now. She would only reject him.

What was she so afraid of? She had grown up in country where winters were cold and snowbound. She knew the hardships were tedious but not permanent. There was more to this than the fear of foul weather.

He shook his head in confusion. He knew the risk they took, but with proper supplies and protection from the numbing snows, there was nothing to fear.

Thinking back, he remembered the words Pat had spoken about her. "She's hiding something from you," the Irishman had stated. Her secrets had bearing on her overreaction.

He clamped his jaws tight. Last night he had bared his soul, offering up the emotional scars of his youth to her inspection. He had every right to know what events in her past had made her the woman she was today. He had no doubt demons drove her. Why else would a lone woman come to this forsaken country and then refuse to go home, unless something kept her from returning? Never did she mention her life before him, almost as if she buried her past in a deep, dark hole.

"Braven?"

He spun around at the call of his name. "Yeah, what do you want?" he snapped.

Buckley blinked at him, taken aback at the sharpness in his voice. "Just wanted to know if you were ready to start on the walkway walls." The man limped away, a reminder of the near fatality not so long ago that had nearly cost him a leg.

Braven's jaw worked in indecision. No matter what, the walkway must be completed. There would be time later for dealing with his wife. More than she depended on him to see them safely through this coming winter. There were a lot of preparations to be made if they were going to be ready when the snows hit.

Damn it all, why did there have to be this thread of mistrust between them? This seesaw of misunderstanding that never seemed to find an end? He had grown up believing love was a solution to problems. Instead, the need of another person seemed to be creating more difficulties than it eliminated.

With a decisive snort, he turned his back on her fleeing figure. There would be time later to make things right between them. One final trip down the mountain for supplies still had to be made. By taking her with him on the ride, maybe they would have a chance, a private moment, to talk their problems out. That plan had worked once; he would make it serve again. Besides, her presence in town should give the very excuse needed, a reason why they would prefer to remain secluded in the mountains over the long, arduous winter.

At the bottom of the last steep grade Braven pulled the team to a halt. A deep breath of relief puffed from Rivalree's cheeks, twofold in reason. At last the terror-fraught trek to La Porte was at an end, and the two long days of strained silence between her and Braven would be broken.

The old Braven Blackwood was back. The man who had met her on the docks and pursued her through the streets of San Francisco sat beside her on the seat. Polite and

252

distant, it was as if she no longer knew him, had never shared an intimate moment with him, was unaware that the feathery touch of her lips against the hollow at the base of his throat could make him shiver in delight. As he revolved on the seat to face her after tying the reins to the brake handle, she studied that very spot intently, wishing she possessed the courage to end the tension crackling between them since that night they had made wild love in the wake of his personal revelations. But her hand refused to obey the command of her heart, and her tongue lay thick and useless in her mouth when her eyes locked with his.

His gaze burned like a redhot branding iron, then it slid away. Her heart lurched. Had he been about to say something to her? Clutched at her sides, her arms ached to reach out to him, to beg him for forgiveness. Absolution for what? For trying to make him see the foolishness of his ways? She straightened, tearing her eyes away as he descended from the seat.

With a regal air she watched him move to the rear of the wagon bed. Nelly and Clementine stood placidly at the ends of their tethers, chewing cud. The cow's liquid eyes and the goat's buglike stare followed Braven's actions as well, as he unleashed the heavy stone weights from the back wheels, rolling the rocks to the side of the road to a large pile that had grown from the many trips to town.

At the start of their journey, she had questioned him incessantly as to why he had secured the large boulders to the rear wagon wheels. He had explained they were necessary to keep the wagon from overrunning the team on the steep trail down the mountain.

Braven straightened from his task, and Rivalree twisted in her seat, not wanting him to catch her observing his actions. The vehicle bobbled as he settled back in the seat beside her, and only then did she allow her glance to dart in his direction. The lapis lazuli orbs bore into her. She gulped, knowing confrontation was at hand.

"I allowed you to come with me on this trip for several reasons."

Her chin tilted. Praying he would voice regret for the way things had been between them, she waited for him to complete his thoughts.

"Keep your mouth shut, and don't act surprised no matter what I or anyone else says."

Her mouth that had softened in expectation drew into a taut line on her face. What had made her hope for more? She dipped her head in acquiescence.

"Good." His gaze lingered, almost caressing, then swept to the task at hand, as he took the reins and snapped them over the backs of the horses.

They entered the edge of La Porte. The small, quiet town she remembered no longer existed. Where once there had been empty streets, a dust cloud alive with men and horses now resided.

Rivalree held her chin high and her gaze riveted to a point above the team's heads, though Braven nodded several times to men who were strangers to her, even as a crowd pressed against the wagon like magnets as they plodded their way down the thoroughfare.

"It's her, it has to be," one observer said to another.

The harnesses jingled and Clementine "baaed" as a cur unfurled itself on a porch and began barking.

Braven brought the wagon to a halt in front of Jackson's General Store, the knot of men following them down the street stopping as well. The once peaceful building seemed to groan in protest as miners hustled in and out its door, entering with picks and pans and exiting jamming money in their pockets.

"Braven," she asked, clutching his arm, not caring what he thought of her. "What's going on?"

"Just what I hoped would happen. The Sierra Angel. Remember? It appears your reputation has grown since

254

you last were here."

"The Sierra Angel? Braven, that was just a hoax. I'm not what they think I am?"

His mouth curved upward. "Aren't you. My pockets will soon be bulging with gold," he whispered in her ear.

"About time you came down off that mountain, Blackwood."

Braven whipped around, confronting Eloy Jackson, the shopkeeper's beefy hands crossed over his barrel chest. "Howdy, ma'am," the man said with a nod in her direction.

Bewildered, she glanced about, unsure what to expect from the rapt crowd. Braven gripped her elbow, squeezed once, summoning her attention. "Don't disappoint me," his look demanded.

"Eloy," he called. "Good to see you again. I brought Nelly and Clementine as usual. Hoped you take care of them for me again."

"Put them back in the shed. I figured you would," the other man answered with a grin. "They kinda keep the winter from gittin' too borin'."

Helpful hands steadied the horses as Braven leapt from the seat. Others offered Rivalree a hand down, eager to be the first to touch her. She hesitated, feeling safer perched above her admirers.

"Wait in the wagon for me, sugar," Braven ordered. For once she was glad to do his bidding.

The men backed off, disappointed, but respectful of her husband's authority, their eyes turned upward, waiting.

Keep your mouth shut, Braven had told her earlier, but how could she just sit here staring back at all those expectant faces? Damn Braven Blackwood for leaving her like this. Judd would have stuck by her side to protect her. Judd. Judd. Judd. She had to stop comparing him with Braven. Right now, she must say something to the throng below her.

"Gentlemen," she acknowledged.

A roar of excitement swept through the crowd. "Sierra Angel," the voices cried. "Bless me."

She reached out tapping the outstretched fingers, most worn and grubby, but willing to make room for other anxious seekers.

A heady feeling washed over her. Like a goddess before her worshipers, she soon found herself playing her part to the hilt.

"Good luck to you. God bless you," she stated over and over.

Braven stood poised in the shade of the store porch, every muscle in his body tense and ready to spring forward in Rivalree's defense. Damn her, why hadn't she done what he instructed her to do, keep silent.

"You plan to do what?" Eloy Jackson demanded.

"The missus and I are going to winter up in the cabin." Braven let his breath ease out as she bent forward, bestowing a blessing to outstretched hands. Hell, if he hadn't created the story of the Sierra Angel himself, he might believe her little charade.

"Man, have you lost your senses?"

"You tell me. If I don't, I'll have to share her with every man waiting the winter out in Marysville."

"Are you sure there isn't more to this than husband's jealousy," Jackson asked, skepticism tainting his tone. "I've yet to notice any of your men in town. You sure you're not hidin' the mother lode from your fellow miners?"

Braven stiffened. If he could keep Jackson's bloodhound keen senses from discovering the truth, the Louisiana Mine would be safe from claim jumpers. Men from all over took the storekeeper's word as fact and wouldn't question his decision to remain on the mountain as long as Jackson believed his story. At least not until it would be too late to investigate any growing suspicions.

"With the town so crowded you might not have noticed my boys. They have money in their pockets and nothing to sell," he explained with a lift of his shoulders that conveyed nonconcern. Inside the strain clawed at his guts. From the corner of his eyes he watched Jackson, who in turn scrutinized him, looking for signs of uneasiness.

"Well, can't say as I blame ya." The burly man's expression softened as he eyed Rivalree. "If she were mine, I'd want to be alone with her every minute I could. I imagine you'll be needin' supplies. Come around late tonight, after the streets empty, we'll load you up and get you back on the trail. That way none of these good-for-nothin' jackasses will follow you home."

Braven let his chin drop in relief, a great rush of air whistling from his lungs. "Thanks, Eloy. I won't forget the favor."

"What about your horses. What do you plan to do with them?"

"I was hoping to leave them here, and take your team. Those two big bays are like homing pigeons. I could turn them loose and they'll come back to you."

Eloy nodded. "Suspect you got it all worked out. You want me to come get you in the spring?"

"I'd be much obliged if you would."

"Consider it done."

"Thanks, my friend, you won't be sorry." Braven smiled to himself. Jackson wouldn't regret his help. He planned to give the big man first chance at buying the mine when he showed in the spring. If anyone could handle claim jumpers, Eloy Jackson could.

He eyed Rivalree's fragile form. Now they were committed. Once they got back to the mine and turned Jackson's horses loose, there would be no way of coming back down the mountain. Not until the big man showed in spring. He prayed he wasn't making a mistake. The thought that the woman who owned his heart and soul could possibly suffer because of his need to prove something to his father and brother sent a shiver bolting through him. Her life meant more to him than anything else, and he would make sure she was aware of his feelings.

A chilling wind traced icy streamers across Rivalree's cheeks leaving them numb and ruddy. The weather had turned cold and turbulent in a matter of days. She shuddered as if infected by Saint Vitus' dance, her arms wrapped around her shoulders, her heart trembling with undisguised fear, knowing what was in store. From where she stood at the bedroom window she could survey the camp yard: the empty pasture, the horses long returned to the storekeeper; the deserted chicken coop where the unscratched ground sported a layer of frost, its occupants now hanging in the storeroom, food for the winter; the summer garden deep in dead vines and weeds from neglect; the near completed walkway from the cabin to the mine, a roughhewn monster out of place in its setting; and off to to the far left, Judd's grave blanketed in an array of multicolored leaves, protection against the cold weather, the one thing he had always despised.

As she watched, winter's first flakes of snow drifted downward, only to be lifted by the dancing wind like kites, to come to rest on the tips of her outstretched fingers. The fragile piece of frozen lace melted, leaving a teardrop of moisture in its stead. How could something so transient strike such fear in her heart? She licked the wetness from her finger bringing its life to an end.

From her perch, she could see Braven and the men hurrying to complete the walkway. He glanced up once, studying the skies and the mounding flakes of white beginning to accumulate on the blades of brown grass and black tree limbs reminding Rivalree of icing on chocolate cake.

Rising, unable to bear the frosty breath of winter one minute more, she pushed the hide-covered casement closed. Just as the two wooden frames were about to meet, she caught a glimpse of Braven, lifting his face in interest as Buckley pointed his finger down the road leading to Poker Flat. Curiosity piqued, she reopened the window and leaned forward, but the road was out of view. What did Buckley see?

Braven handed the other man the mallet he'd been using, turned the collar of his coat up against his neck, and stepped forward almost from Rivalree's view. An inner voice whispered, a nagging, ill-boding sound. It was from this same vantage point she had witnessed the cave-in that had nearly taken Braven's life. Her heart fluttered, weak with dread for what came up the road.

Zoey barked, the deep-throated sound accenting the word marching through Rivalree's mind. Death, death, death. The end of what she clung to. But what it was she held so dear, she wasn't sure.

When finally the foe did arrive, it didn't come in the guise Rivalree expected. The young girl sat upon the burro, her chin lifted, the coarse woolen wrap she clutched covering her head and shoulders reminding Rivalree of the pictures she had seen as a child of the Virgin Mary on her way to Bethlehem. As the shawl fell away from the girl's arms she wasn't surprised to see the mountainous swell of her belly as if the child within demanded release at any moment.

Rivalree's hand flew to her open mouth. A child? Whose was it? The way Braven lifted the fatigued girl in his arms and rushed her toward the cabin could only mean one thing. The babe must be his.

Chapter Eighteen

Braven cradled his burden in stunned silence. The girl's pale face was young, not more than seventeen, yet lines of worry etched their way around the closed eyes and puckered mouth. Snowflakes cleaved to the thin, dark lashes. He had seen this girl before, but where? He couldn't quite remember.

The words that had tumbled from her lips as she had fallen from the donkey left him bewildered. She had come seeking the father of her baby. One of his men had sired this girl's child, and as soon as he possessed the name, he would have the culprit's head on a platter.

He glanced up at the gray skies. By morning the ground would be covered with snow, the road impassable. What was he going to do with a female ready to drop an infant any moment?

Pressing open the cabin door, he came face-to-face with his wife. He inhaled a deep breath of relief. At least there was another woman to handle a birthing. Shifting the weight in his arms, he looked perplexed at Rivalree's frowning countenance. Almost as if she stared down her nose at him, condemning. Accusing him of what? My God, the girl was pregnant! Did she really think he was so lecherous that he would show unnatural interest in a

261

brooding woman?

The girl moaned softly, her head rolling back. He glanced down, concerned, and eased the lolling chin against his chest, determined to ignore the absurdity of Rivalree's verdict and sentencing in one glare.

Elbowing his way past the barricade she presented, he laid the unconscious girl on Judd's bed, still in the common room after Buckley's recovering.

"How dare you bring that . . . person here," Rivalree hissed.

Braven whirled, aware of the crowd of men sandwiched in the doorway watching. "Control yourself, woman," he demanded, standing between the helpless stranger and his wife. "I didn't bring her here, she showed up on her own."

"You have humiliated me for the last time, Braven. First your whores, then your demands we die for the sake of your gold, and now . . . *this*." She pointed an accusing finger toward the bed. "I won't allow that woman and your brat to come here."

"You won't allow. Just who do you think you are?" The meaning of her words peppered through the angry haze clouding his control. His child? He stopped, fury-ladened words suspended on his tongue. She thought the girl carried his baby. He stepped forward, taking her arm in an attempt to make her see reason. "You have it all wrong, sugar. I'm not the . . ."

"Why didn't you die in Judd's place? He would never have done these awful things to me." The words spewed from her mouth with the force of a volcano. With a gurgling sob, she tore from his grip, horror clouding her face.

Her words stung like a swarm of hornets, stilling the explanation in his throat. But worse were the feelings of guilt. Had he wounded her so deeply that she was driven to say such terrible things? Maybe she was right, everyone would be better off if he'd died instead of Judd, just as it was supposed to have happened.

"Judd," the girl whispered. "Where is he? Please tell him Joleen is here." Her gaze latched on to Rivalree, the only other woman in the room, seeking understanding. "I wouldn't have come if I'd had anyplace else to go. Tell him I'm going to have his baby."

The confession riddled through Rivalree, leaving a look of stark disbelief in its wake. Trembling, she fell to her knees beside the girl's prone figure. "Judd Baker, are you sure?" she asked incredulously. "You must be mistaken."

"Judd Baker." Joleen's lips formed the name, and her features relaxed. "Thank God, I've found him at last."

"But that's impossible." Rivalree's gaze skittered around the room, searching for denial on the sea of faces surrounding her, to settle on Braven. "Judd's child? It can't be."

The confusion in her voice pleaded with Braven to make it not so.

"That would mean while I was on my way here to join him, he was with her, saying and doing those things that belonged to me. Dear God, I've . . ."

She rose, horror and shame swimming in her eyes. Darting like an injured child, she elbowed her way through the front door and out through a break in the uncompleted walkway.

Braven whipped around, pointing a commanding finger at Pat. "You take care of the girl." He swiveled to face the crowd of men at the door that had swallowed up Rivalree's fleeing figure. "And you, see to it your personal gear is brought inside the cabin and the tent is struck. Winter is here to stay. As soon as I return, we'll finish the walkway." He raced after her, following faint footprints in the thin layer of snow. This time he must confront her, make her see reason.

His temper cooled in the freezing air, leaving only pain and pity. Now he remembered where he had seen Joleen—

with Judd in Downieville last winter, a frightened girl seeking a means to escape an abusive father.

The sight of Rivalree's huddled figure headed toward the stump used to split firewood, no coat or hat to protect her from the cold, tore at his heart. God, he loved her but didn't know how to get through to her, to make her realize how much he cared about her.

How could Judd have done this to her? As she walked, the accumulated snow under her shoes crunched with the humiliation in her steps. Lowering herself down on the hatchet-marked stump, she hunched her shoulders to the wind beginning to pick up speed.

Judd had been the one shining light in her life, an aide to help her survive the muddle of her existence, but he had betrayed her trust.

She pressed her bloodless fingers to her temples. Then there were the horrible accusations she had flung at Braven. Dear God, would he ever forgive her? She couldn't blame him if he didn't.

She stood, determined to return to the cabin and face her husband, willing to plead for his forgiveness if she must, ready to . . .

Her breath caught in her lungs. How handsome Braven was, waiting at the bottom of the hill, his collar angled to shield the snow from his neck, his hands so large and powerful lying at his sides, his eyes watching her, reading the apology radiating from the depths of her soul. Did he offer acceptance or rejection? She hung suspended for an eternal moment, a prayer whisking through her mind.

A shiver set her teeth to chattering, ushering in the realization her hands and feet had no feeling. She was freezing. What had possessed her to flee the warmth of the cabin? Shame and humiliation, she reminded herself.

She rubbed her bare arms with numb fingers. When had

it turned so cold? It was as if the world presented an icy shoulder of disapproval to her.

Unflinching, Braven held his ground, expectant. She must say something. If she didn't, he would forsake her, too.

"I'm sorry," she offered from behind the muffle of hands covering her face in disgrace, knowing the words inadequate but unable to think of any others.

Braven's face clouded, an unreadable expression wrenching his mouth into a taut line.

I have lost him, she decided, her chin elevating, determined to maintain her pride in the face of losing all else. *I will not crumble to defeat.*

His eyes narrowed at her haughty gesture, and he sighed, a sad, defeated sound. "Come, Rivalree," he bade, stripping the coat from his body. "There's no sense in us both freezing to death." He placed the warm fur garment about her shoulders and urged her toward the cabin. "We have a long winter ahead of us, and there's not much we can do about it now."

Her feet shuffled to a halt. "The girl? Joleen?" The name left ashes in her mouth. "What will we do?"

"Not much we can do except allow her to stay. To send her away would be to condemn her and her child to death." He gently pressed the hill of his hand against her back.

"I wouldn't think of refusing her shelter. I meant, what will I say to her?" She pushed frozen tendrils of hair from her eyes.

"About what?" A frown furrowed between his powdered brows.

"How will I explain about Judd?"

"The truth would probably be best. Don't worry. Pat has more than likely told her he is dead. I don't believe Joleen came in search of love but for protection from a father who's a tyrant. I met him once."

"But what about Judd and me . . . ?"

"What is there to explain?" He threw his hands up in what she interpreted as frustration. "You are *my* wife, Rivalree. Not Judd's. When will you accept that fact?" His hand descended, catching her arm in a frosty grip. "Until you do, both of us will live in misery. Sometimes I think you're contented shrouded in gloom. Is that it, woman? Are you happy when you're miserable?"

She choked on the denial crowding her throat. Without resistance, she allowed him to push her up the path, back to the cabin, a winter prison of stark reality with no means of escape.

Sepia eyes, reminding Rivalree of the color of the few daguerreotypes she had seen, stared up at her, doelike and seeking approval. "What shall I do?" Joleen asked.

Rivalree sighed, the sound so soft the girl probably didn't hear it. How could she feel anything but pity for Joleen? Like so many women before her, she had fallen victim to a man's knowing ways and had trusted him. Had trusted Judd, just as Rivalree did once. But the Judd she knew had been an untried youth, one who had never demanded more than a chaste peck of a kiss from her. Yet Joleen sat before her, evidence that he had changed. This wild, unbroken country had done that to him, just as it had molded her, Rivalree, into a woman in order to survive. Something Judd had been unable to accomplish.

She reached out, patting the pregnancy-swollen hands, a smile parting her lips. "You'll stay here, of course. Judd would have wanted it that way, I'm sure." The tactfully couched lie tasted bitter. What Judd Baker desired was no longer important. He had wrecked more than one life this day. "Now you lie down and rest. You mustn't worry anymore. There's the baby to consider." She pressed Joleen's frail shoulders toward the mattress and covered her with a blanket.

"But there's so much I need to know," the girl objected, yet she didn't resist the pressure urging her down.

"We'll have plenty of time for talking. Later. There's the entire winter ahead of us."

Joleen's pale lids flicked as she closed her eyes with a weary rush of air. "Thank you kindly, Miz Blackwood. You're as saintly as they say."

Saintly. A sob of wretchedness clogged her throat. How could anyone think of her in that way? She had lied, cheated, and accused others of the most horrible of crimes. There was no saintliness in her, only sinfulness. "Please," she whispered, "call me Rivalree. Mrs. Blackwood makes me seem so ancient . . ."

"Rivalree," Joleen savored the name. "How unusual. How did you come by such a name?"

Taken aback, Rivalree studied the girl's earnest face. Was she really interested to know her history? Not sure, she decided the rhythm of her voice telling a story might help the girl sleep. "The name is an old one, in my family for many generations. My mother's ancestors were from France, a far-reaching line of lords and ladies. The first Rivalree was a long-awaited babe. She was to have been a boy, a child to unite warring houses. In those days of knights and ladies, quite often offspring were pledged among the nobility, daughters to sons."

Rivalree closed her eyes, spinning the tale her mother had woven so many times before a winter fire. "At her birth, her father flew into a rage, condemning her mother for her inability to produce the needed son. The rivalry between houses went unchecked, and in penance for her sin, the lady named the child Rivalree."

"How sad for the child and for you," Joleen murmured.

"Not really. The name is coveted, the firstborn girl in each generation claiming the honor. You see, each namesake has gone on to do something heroic. The first

Rivalree, upon reaching the age of fifteen, threw herself at the feet of the rival lord upon the death of his first wife. They married and the families united and continued strong until the bloody revolution. The Rivalree of that generation managed to secure her family on a ship to America in order to escape the guillotine. That was my grandmother."

"And you, you have followed in their footsteps. The Sierra Angel."

Rivalree frowned. What a fraudulent claim to legendry. She was no heroine, just a woman whose life was based on lies and deceit.

She glanced away from Joleen's eyes, wide with adoration, to discover Braven standing in the doorway, a look of perplexity slashed across his face. With a nod, he turned away, closing the front door softly behind his back.

How much had he heard? Was that disdain she had witnessed in his eyes before the barrier had separated them? God help her, she loved him but wasn't sure she could humble herself before him in order to receive his acceptance.

Braven spun away from the scene of his blue-blooded wife, grateful for the partition between them, concentrating instead on the unchinked walls of the walkway, but their footprints, still visible in the snow, jumped out at him between the spaces in the logs, his large and deep, hers dainty and light, reminding him of her presence so near and yet so far away. He understood her need for a person of strength to look up to, but why, why couldn't that someone be him? Why Judd Baker?

He felt the anger and wrath inside him transform into something much stronger, a need to make the woman who had stolen his heart understand the nature of a man, especially one alone and drowning in self-made pity, the man Judd had been the winter before his death.

Damn Judd for being the weakling that he was. No man in his right mind would have anything to do with an innocent girl like Joleen, knowing a woman like Rivalree was on her way to join him.

Remembering clearly Joleen's identity, he drew his mouth into a tight line. The blacksmith's daughter in Downieville, the settlement on the other side of the mountain, where they had waited out the winter. The smithy had been a violent man, and he had seen Joleen shrink from her father on at least one occasion. Turning to Judd, she'd sought a means to escape. There had been no love, just need between the two of them. That March before they had returned to the mine, he'd pressed the younger man, demanding to know the nature of the relationship, but Judd had sworn he'd never touched the girl. The evidence of his lie flowered before them, a child to be born in the wilds of the winter Sierras. Not at all a fitting place for such an event. He calculated the months quickly in his mind. The baby would arrive by the end of the year. He could smell the trouble brewing long before it occurred, but he wasn't sure of its nature.

Picking up a trowel, he began working filler between the gaps in the log walls, his thoughts trailing back to Rivalree. The woman was like the wild poison ivy vines, so beautiful and alive, invading the pecan trees back home. They took hold, twisting, choking, ingraining themselves in the bark of even the strongest one, until, with time, the tree and the vine were indistinguishable. Yet, always, if left untended, the ivy claimed victory at the expense of the tree's life, its strangling runners resembling branches in strength and texture. He mustn't allow that to happen to him. The demons that drove Rivalree pressed hard to swallow them both up. Only by remaining stronger than they could he help her defeat them. But how could he tell her he understood? She was an easy woman to love, yet hard to decipher. She would never accept his intrusion into her private world.

Winter would be long and cold unless they came to an understanding. He loved her with all his heart, but he could not sacrifice his dreams because she demanded it.

Hours later, perspiration trickled between his shoulder blades, regardless of the raging storm pounding at the newly mortared walls of the walkway. Slipping off his coat, he wiped the sweat beading his temples with the flannel of his shirt-sleeve as he surveyed the completed structure. There was no going back now; they were firmly committed to seeing the winter through no matter what other disasters struck.

Rivalree shivered, the cold lapping against the covers washing over her as if she lay naked to its tidal wave. She could remember chilly evenings in New Jersey, but nothing compared to the bitterness she'd experienced for the last three nights.

The warmth of Braven's body radiated from the other side of the bed, and more than anything, she yearned to curl around him, her breasts pressed to the slope of his broad back, her thighs hugging the curve of his firm buttocks. But if she touched him, she would be lost. She would never be able to mold against him and not explore the fur of his chest. And that would lead to other things she didn't want to think about.

Rolling to her side, away from the temptation, she was sorry she had moved the moment she did so. Lost was the little bit of warmth she had squirreled away in the hollow of her mattress. Spasmodic chills raced through her veins, and her teeth clattered so loud she feared she would wake Braven though she tried to compress her lips together.

"Come here, you proud little wench," he demanded softly. "I'm cold, too, if that makes you feel better."

She melted in the circle of his arms, his downlike chest hair tickling her spine as he pulled her closer. One hand came to rest on her breast covered by a woolen gown, warming her flesh until her nipple softened against his heated palm. Then as he kneaded the round globe, it grew hard and taut again, but not from the cold.

"Braven, I think we shouldn't." She clasped his roving fingers and stilled their resolve-destroying stroking.

"How long do you plan to punish me for not doing something wrong?"

Her heart clattered like an unoiled machine against the casing of her ribs. "Punish *you*? But I assumed . . ." Her hand released his, and he resumed the gentle exploration of her body.

The warmth of his lips nibbled her ear, erasing the chill residing there. "Haven't you learned yet, you get in more trouble by assuming?"

She revolved in the circle of his arms to face him. "But I said such terrible things, unforgivable words. I wouldn't blame you if you never . . ."

His finger stilled her mouth, trapping the apology in her throat. "We all say things we later regret. I know you didn't mean those accusations."

Peccancy pricked at her conscience like slivers of broken glass. She had meant what she'd said when she'd voiced it, and only the realization of Judd's betrayal had brought a halt to the condemning words she had hurled at him. Now she was truly sorry, but was it because she cared for Braven or because she no longer required Judd's approval and support? She wanted to believe it was because she loved the man she'd married, but in all honesty she couldn't be sure.

She cheated them both, by accepting this easy way out, by allowing Braven's well-meaning words to sugarcoat reality, but she didn't have the courage to reject his leniency. She needed him, this man of unfaltering strength, to help her find her way through the dense forest of self-doubt crowding in around her.

With a sound of defeat, she lifted her face to his. His mouth captured hers in the gentlest of kisses, as if he asked permission to unleash the passion she knew pounded in his blood. The wild pulsating in his neck and at his temples gave evidence to his suspicion, and she lifted a finger tracing the jumping vein below his ear as if discovering it for the first time. And, indeed, the feel of it left her breathless with wonder that she could stir such fervor within him.

He drew her nearer as the band of his arms tightened, and, for the first time in days, she was warm, heated to her very core by the passion rising up to claim her being. The shiver racing through her was one of anticipation as he rolled her to her back, lowering his body until his mouth encompassed one breast and then moved to the other, exposing the first to the cold air that iced the wetness his caress left behind.

Her hand drew the covers up over the exposed flesh, but the warmth wasn't the same, somehow lacking. Emerging from the tunnel the pile of quilts made over him, Braven laid his length against hers, the heat of his manhood seeking entrance to the cradle between her parted thighs.

Forgetting all except the molten lava of desire traveling through her limbs, she released the covers, allowing Braven to take their place, a heated barrier between her and the world beyond. With a welcoming sigh, she encased him in her womanly sheath, then held her breath as he drew back to plunge again and again until she became a willing vassal beneath his rhythm, wishing only that he take her with him to the higher planes of culmination.

If only they could stay wrapped in the shelter of desire, she knew she could survive the winter facing them. Yet she yearned to be sure he wanted her for who she was, not because there was no one better to satisfy his needs. Or, just as important, did she turn to him in desperation or honest love?

The ebb and flow of his hips erased the eddied thoughts from her mind, leaving only the surging passion he triggered climbing toward the zenith as their shared momentum increased. Drowning in the thundering waves of pleasure, she clung to him, trusting him to carry her over the crest and back down into the trough of reality. Yet when she reached that heart-stopping point, she struggled to remain there, oblivious to the troubled world she knew. Too soon she plunged into the calm waters of aftermath, her heart pounding painfully, her breath coming in little whimpers of despair that the moment of escape had passed before she was ready to give it up.

"My love," he declared, the huskiness of rapture coloring his voice. His heart met hers beat for erratic beat as he kissed her closed eyes, her parted lips, her damp forehead, her quivering chin, the touch of his mouth soothing her, telling her how pleased, how overwhelmed with love he was.

Lashes lifting, she met his gaze with wonder, a tiny sob bubbling in her chest as she read the commitment shining in his eyes. He loved her, trusted her, yet demanded nothing from her except honesty, the one thing she had never given him. The only thing she feared she couldn't offer. Her heart, her life, her dreams she'd give him willingly. But honesty? How could she give him what she couldn't give herself?

Rivalree opened her eyes to find Braven shuffling around the room, one of the quilts wrapped serape-style around his shoulders. The morning sun threw yellow streaks through the skin-colored window announcing its presence, yet the heat that usually accompanied it was missing. Winter glazed the earth with its icy breath without reprieve.

He lifted the pitcher of water from the basin and instantly set it back down. "Damn it," he cursed. "This is ridiculous."

Spinning, he faced her, his hands cupped about his mouth as he blew his warm breath into them to thaw his fingers. She waited for him to tell her what annoyed him, as if she didn't know. The room was cold, so cold the water in the pitcher was more than likely frozen.

"Don't you think it's time to accept the inevitable?"

Rivalree pressed her lips together in stubbornness. They had had this conversation over and over, always with the same results. She refused to sleep below with the miners. She'd not give up her privacy, even if it meant restless nights from the cold. "I will not sleep in a community bedroom."

"This is not the St. Francis Hotel. There's a need to be practical."

"I'd rather be uncomfortable than share my sleeping habits with a roomful of men."

"That's easy to say, sugar, from the protection of your bed. Let's see how you feel out here with me." He jerked the cocoon of quilts from her body, exposing her to the icy air.

With a squeal she lunged for the covers as they trailed across her legs. "Braven Blackwood, you're impossible."

Her feet slapped the bare wooden floor. As if she stood on ice blocks, she shifted her weight from foot to foot.

Beneath her woolen gown, she shivered. He was right, this was ludicrous. Her fingers and toes were already numb. Huddling in the tent of her nightgown, she batted her alternatives back and forth. Glancing up at him as he waited for an answer, the bundle of covers bunched under his arm, she knew she had no choice. They would move their bed down to the common room and deprive her of the one last pleasure she had, those private moments with Braven, those times she could forget the world beyond their door.

Misery wove its silent web about her. She would never survive the winter crowded in one room, no place to escape, no change of scenery, day in and day out. She looked up at him, hoping to find another option in his gaze. He offered none.

Damn him! So pragmatic and reasonable. Always right.

She turned her back and began drawing on her clothes, wondering how she would manage to get dressed tomorrow morning with a roomful of curious eyes. She couldn't imagine anything worse that could happen to her.

Chapter Nineteen

"What do you think, Rivalree?"

Rivalree's head snapped around, guilt chiseled on her face, to stare at Joleen. The girl held up a tiny, woolen gown fashioned from a volunteered shirt from one of the men. Her eyes radiated contentment and joy, something Rivalree had trouble understanding. How could Joleen be happy—a misbegotten bantling distorting her body, no family, no future, nothing but the ugly truth to keep her company?

Her gaze flicked over the picture the girl presented as that familiar feeling of guilt crept into her heart. Joleen deserved better. At least the girl faced her future squarely and with open arms. Something Rivalree found impossible to do.

"I think it's lovely. You have such a way with a needle." She glanced down at the forgotten sewing in her lap, then angled her eyes to the clock above the mantel. Hours yet to go before the men ended their day. Long hours of boredom. Time that would be impossible to face if not for Joleen.

One day had melted into another, creating weeks—now November peeked around the corner. The days began early as the men rose, ate a silent meal of corn pone and coffee and shuffled their way through the walkway to begin the day's work. Even Pat had begun joining them occasionally, a way to break the feeling that the walls were closing in on him. She envied the Irishman and the others. What she wouldn't give for a break in the doldrums.

Joleen stood and stretched, one hand placed in the small of her back, and the burgeoning child thrust forward by her gesture. "I think I'll start another one. There's time." Her head swiveled, a smile parting her lips. "Babies never have enough clothes."

Rivalree tossed down her mending, miffed at the other woman's unflinching cheer, and abandoned her chair. "I think I'll lie down a while," she mumbled as she stepped over Zoey's sleeping form and pushed back the blanket serving as a partition around the corner of the room where Braven had placed their bed. Thank God she had that little bit of privacy, something he had devised that first awkward morning they had moved downstairs.

Joleen's bed had the same curtaining, but she rarely used it unless she was dressing. Rivalree felt the need to retreat behind the barrier often, as inane as it might seem—a place to sort her thoughts and regroup in order to face the boredom of her life.

Only there did she feel alive, especially at night, lying in the arms of her husband. And though he never offered more than a chaste peck of a kiss, she clung to those moments as if they were the most tender of encounters, fervidly wishing for more, yet never daring to suggest it even as the men slept soundly late into the night.

A small sound penetrated her brooding, a rattling noise. She sat up on the bed, her ear cocked in the general direction, waiting. Nothing. Had the noise been only in her imagination?

"Joleen, did you hear that?" she called, pushing back the partition.

The girl stilled the rocking of her chair, turned her head,

then lifted her shoulders. "What?"

Scrap. Scrap. Rattle. Rattle.

Zoey rose from a dead sleep, a growl quivering in her throat.

"There," Rivalree whispered, eyeing the dog.

"Probably nothing more than the wind," Joleen offered, continuing her stitching and rocking.

"I don't think so."

Stiff-legged the dog edged toward the door leading to Pat's old room, now used as a storage place for all their supplies.

Rivalree bolted upward. "Somebody's in that room."

"Impossible," Joleen assured, snapping her fingers in irritation at Zoey. "How could anyone get in there? Nothing but miles of snow surround us outside. It's only the wind," she repeated.

An odd feeling of familiarity wormed its way into Rivalree's heart. She glanced around the room, seeking what?

A gun. Something to defend them from whatever prowled behind that door. Sweat beaded the fine hair at her temples as her gaze skipped from object to object. Propped against the mantel stood Braven's rifle, forgotten in the knowledge that a cocoon of snow separated them from the rest of the world.

Zoey waited at the door, whining, the fur on her back bristled. She looked over her shoulder at the two women asking for a command.

Scratch. Rattle. Crash.

Rivalree edged her way around the room, never once taking her eyes off the storeroom door. Her fingers found the rifle as if they had honed-in antennae, and, lifting the weapon to her chest, she checked to see if it was loaded. She breathed relief to find it primed and ready.

What should she do now? Open the door or wait for whomever was behind it to do so? Zoey pressed her nose against the barrier and released a growling bark of alarm.

Joleen stood, at last acknowledging the danger. "Rivalree, what are we going to do?" she whispered. The swell of the unborn baby rose and fell with her frightened breath.

"Go get Braven and the men," she replied. There was nothing the girl could do, she reasoned. It would be better if she was out of danger's way.

"But, Rivalree. I can't leave you."

"Go. Bring the men as quick as you can."

With an unsure nod, Joleen skirted the chair and bumped her way to the front door and out it without another word.

Fear crept with stealth to permeate the room until Rivalree swore she could smell its presence. At last realizing she was alone, no one else to depend on, no one else to protect, sent chills of terror tingling down her spine. Bending low over the weapon, she stepped toward the storeroom, still not sure what approach to take, attack or defend.

Zoey had no doubts. She hit the door with the force of her compact body demanding a confrontation there and then. The intruder slammed against the door from the other side, setting the hinges to rattling and the latch to groaning.

Rivalree brought the rifle to her shoulder, ready to face hell's demons. She wouldn't hesitate to shoot this time. Whatever was on the other side of the door would die the moment it entered the room.

Easy, she told herself. *Don't fire too soon.* Her finger ached to pull the trigger, her feet begged to turn and run, but she held her ground and grip steady. Waiting.

Again, Zoey threw her weight against the obstacle. The invader reciprocated with a similar action. Why didn't he just open the door? Her nerves frayed like overstretched rope, and snapped. Her hands began to shake, and the bead she held on the door wavered.

With a mighty crash and roar the door seemed to bow as it sprang from its frame. Now, her brain commanded, and her trigger finger responded.

Cr-r-rack!

The well-remembered sound echoed around her as the gun slammed into her shoulder with frightening familiarity. Blood spewed, speckling the nearby walls. The intruder, a huge, black blur of fur, roared in protest.

Rivalree lowered the empty weapon, a scream scraping her throat raw. A bear. Dear God, it was so immense, and though blood spurted from the bullet hole in its chest, the crazed animal came toward her swinging its mighty paws, its eyes red with fury, its nostrils flaring in pain.

Knuckles clamped between her teeth, she stumbled backward. She was going to die, ripped to shreds by the gleaming claws red with the monster's own blood.

Raising the rifle, she threw it as hard as she could at the bear. *What a senseless thing to do*, she thought as the stock left her fingers to go hurtling end over end to slam into the monster's chest. It bellowed in fury, continuing its lumbering attack on the one object it focused on—Rivalree.

Forgotten in the melee, Zoey scrambled to her feet. Without fear, the dog threw herself upon the bear, her bared fangs ripping at the unprotected stomach.

"Zoey," Rivalree screamed as one spayed paw sent the dog flying to smash against the bloodstained wall. Her yelp of pain was short and piercing, and Rivalree knew as she glanced at the twisted mound of fur, the dog was dead. She had given her life to save her mistress, but to no avail. The bear riveted pain-glazed eyes on the one living object in the room.

Backed against the stove, she could retreat no farther. Her hands fumbled behind her locating an iron skillet. She slung it across the room, and it glanced off the bear's snout then bounced across the floor with a dull thud

Knives, forks, and a canister of sugar followed, but nothing stopped the stalking beast.

With only a bench between them, Rivalree closed her eyes as the glistening claws bore down on her. How would it feel to have the flesh of her body torn from the bone? Liquid fire burned down one shoulder and arm. A scream pierced her consciousness. Had the sound come from her own lips? She couldn't be sure.

"Rivalree!" A voice offering safety called so near and yet so far away.

The hot, fetid breath above her turned away. The pain in her shoulder flared, sending sparks shooting through her chest. Her last thoughts were of Zoey, crumbled against the far wall, her fur, once so shiny and soft, soaked in blood.

Her heart wrenched in sorrow. *Oh, Braven, I'm sorry. I didn't mean for this to happen. All I wanted was relief from the monotony.* Blackness overtook her, and the pain and guilt melted into nothingness.

Braven placed Rivalree's slight figure down on the bed. Dear God, how close she'd come to being killed. Brushing back sweat-damp tendrils from her face, he knew he'd experienced love-sparked devotion, a willingness to die to save a life more precious than his own existence.

That moment when he'd walked through the front door and found Rivalree at the mercy of the raging bear, he'd had no thoughts except to aid her and had thrown himself at the animal. Fortunately the well-placed bullet in its chest had finally done its job, and the beast had collapsed under his weight, its lifeblood oozing from the wound.

With gentle fingers Braven peeled back the shredded fabric of her dress from her shoulder. The claw marks were deep but clean, and there didn't seem to be signs of permanent damage. Accepting the bowl of steaming water from Pat's hands, he washed the wounds and inspected each one. One appeared to need further attention.

"A needle, Joleen," he requested. "Thread it with the strongest twine you have, then put it in the boiling water to sterilize."

The girl hesitated for a moment, then turned to do his bidding. "Would you like me to make the stitches for you?" Her bottom lip quivered in dread.

"No, I will do this. Thank God, she's unconscious."

The moments crept by as he waited for the needle, Rivalree's shallow breathing causing creases of concern to furrow between his brows. How pale she looked lying there. Where had those dark circles under her eyes come from? He'd never noticed them before. His eyes darted down, taking in the lines of her body. She was so thin. The translucent skin across her cheeks spoke of unhappiness. How could he have been so blind? His finger traced the curve of her cheekbone and around her strong little chin.

How frightened she must have been, alone with the creature, sure she would die before help arrived.

"I'll be as tidy as I can," he murmured to her sleeping form. The thought of leaving scars on the lovely shoulder distressed him.

The needle moved in and out, resisting each stitch as he forced it through her skin. Once she moaned, and her shoulder twitched, but without a word Pat and Joleen grasped her arm and held her still. At last, the chore done, Braven released his pent-up breath and took the clean bandaging the Irishman offered.

Rivalree settled, and sleeping fitfully at best he turned to survey the room. His gaze inspected the bloodstained spot where the bear had fallen. Leaving a black, dried blood trail, the carcass had been moved into the walkway where several of the men welded, knives removing the fur for further use and the meat to be hung in the storeroom for later consumption. The storeroom. God only knew what havoc had been wrought in there.

Glancing one last time at Rivalree, he rose to inspect the damage. Mace Lockman grasped his arm to stand between him and his destination.

"Zoey," Mace said, the one word pronouncing doom. "Is she dead?"

The other man nodded once.

Something in Braven twisted. She was only a dog, he told himself, but the feeling he had lost a friend refused to dissipate. Pushing past Mace, he knelt beside her broken body.

"Oh, Zoey," he admitted, "you were the best damn dog I ever had." He placed his hand on her head, stroking the fur. With an abrupt movement he rose, knowing if he stayed his emotions might undo him. She was only a dog. But the words didn't ease the pain in his gut.

"I'll bury her," Mace offered. "There's a spot at the mine entrance . . . if you want."

Braven dipped his head, thankful for the other man's assistance and for the fact Rivalree wasn't the one to give her life.

Stepping past the storeroom door, which hung on one hinge, his heart plummeted even further. Flour and cornmeal sacks were slashed and their precious contents scattered about the room. The chickens they had slaughtered were missing, the barrels of salted and dried meat on their sides and broken, much of their content destroyed. He estimated that half of their remaining supplies were gone or damaged beyond use. Damn! Everything had been going so smoothly. How had the bear gotten in?

He glanced toward the only other way into the room, a small window high on the wall. The boarding that had been secured over it was down, the frame broken, the freezing north air rushing in on icy feet. Baffled, he raised one eyebrow. The window was much too high for anything to get in. Pulling a crate underneath the outlet, he pushed himself upon it and stuck his head out. Snow had drifted almost level with the window. With a groan of despair he slapped his thigh. How could he have been so stupid?

"So what's the verdict to be?" asked Pat in his lilting voice.

Braven swung around to face him and jumped down from his perch. "Not good. I'd estimate we lost half our supplies."

"So what do we do now?"

"Do we have a choice? We'll tighten our belts and make do."

"It won't be easy, you know. Hungry bellies make for unrest."

"We'll make do," Braven declared, frustrated with the older man. "Right now we need to secure this room to keep further intruders and the weather out. Buckley," he called over the Irishman's head, maintaining a frown of disapproval on his face.

Buckley limped in.

"Fix this damn window and do it right, then rehang the door."

Without comment the other man turned to get the supplies and tools he needed to follow orders.

Braven watched him walk away, studying the tension of his shoulders. How long would he keep this band of independent men in line? When would they decide he was the cause of their discomforts? Would it then be necessary to use force to get them all safely through the winter?

Frustration and worry jagged his brows at an angry crook. He would do whatever he had to do to maintain order.

Rivalree's eyes fluttered open, the pain in her shoulder

and arm so strong she knew without a doubt she must be alive. Images of the bear's paw, its gleaming claws as large as a man's fingers, invaded her memory with such clarity she jerked her head around expecting to find the beast standing over her. Instead she saw Mace Lockman carrying out the limp, bloody form that had once been Zoey, once so full of life and loyalty.

"Mace," she called in a voice choked with pain and grief.

The man turned, surprise etching his face. Zoey's glazed eyes stared at her, and her wish-filled question was answered.

"Ma'am?" he responded.

Emotion clogged her throat, but she managed to speak. "What are you going to do with her?"

"Braven says I'm to bury her at the main entrance."

"Of course. Thank you." She angled her face away to hide the tears pooling in her eyes. How would she ever explain the dog's death to Braven? He set such store by her. Rotating her eyes back toward the room, she saw Mace close the cabin door behind his back.

As if her thoughts were magnets, Braven stepped through the storeroom entrance, his gaze riveting her way. Anger curved his mouth downward. Was he mad at her? Who else could he be irritated with? His eyes cut away before she had a chance to say something, and her heart shattered into uncountable pieces at his rejection.

Trying to rise, the pain shot through her arm with paralyzing force. She caught her lip between her teeth to squelch the moan forming in her throat. She didn't want him turning to her in sympathy.

Gentle pressure held her good arm down. "There's no need to get up, Rivalree." Joleen smiled down at her. "Pat and I can take care of things until you heal."

"I must. I need to speak with my . . ."

"Not now. Mr. Blackwood says you are to stay in bed

and rest."

The front door slammed, swallowing up Braven's figure. Without further resistance Rivalree lay back against the pillow. He didn't want to speak with her, and by forcing her to remain immobile he could easily avoid contact with her.

How could he be so cruel? The last thing she wanted was for Zoey to die. She loved the dog as much as he, if not more. Since their bitter confrontation at her arrival, they had learned to tolerate each other, and then when they'd combined their energy to save Braven from the cave-in, a bond so strong nothing could sever it had grown between them. She would miss Zoey with all her heart.

She closed her eyes with a weary sigh. The squeak of a rocker invaded the pain-filled haze of her mind. Back and forth. Back and forth. Joleen's voice wafted toward her, humming a soft lullaby, a song to soothe the ears it fell upon. But to Rivalree it was a source of irritation, something to accent the losses she had suffered this day. The one thing she had to look forward to had been swept aside. Braven's companionship.

A small spark of hope flicked. When he came to bed later she would talk to him, explain how sorry she was. She waited, her eye darting up every few, maddeningly slow minutes at the mantel clock.

She used every device she could think of to make the time go faster. She squeezed her eyes closed conjuring up images of every object in the room trying to remember them all. Then she began making up rhyming words for each of those items until her brain could no longer function.

She peeked at the stoic face of the clock to find that only an hour had passed. Weary and hurting, sooty lashes drifted down over her amber eyes and a healing sleep encompassed her.

Frustrating dreams haunted her mind. She was running, but what to or what from? She couldn't decide. All she knew was that her feet kept slipping, keeping her stationary.

"Braven," she cried. "Please don't forsake me."

A cool hand pressed against her forehead, and she gripped it with all her strength, her lids popping open.

The room was dark, only the glow of the fireplace lit the space around her.

"Braven," she murmured, clutching the soothing hand.

"Hush now, Rivalree." Joleen's voice, peppered with sleep, sliced through the blackness.

"Where's Braven," she pleaded.

"You mustn't worry none. He's in the storeroom. He and Pat are taking inventory."

"But why now?"

"It's not my place to wonder or ask questions. Go back to sleep. That's the best thing you can do."

The best thing she could do. He wasn't going to give her a chance to explain or apologize. He was shoving her aside without a thought. But did she deserve better? Because of her selfishness and deceit, his life was a shambles.

Tears rolled down her face leaving a trail of regret in their wake. *I've lost him for good this time, and nothing will bring him back to me.*

Chapter Twenty

December 5, 1851

Braven lifted the pickax with resigned regularity and buried it in the wall of earth before him, knocking another large nugget of gold to the floor. The vein they had discovered those many months ago was not the mother lode, but rich enough to send them all home with more than enough money jingling in their pockets to live comfortable for the rest of their lives and for him to see his lifelong dream come true.

Setting the tool down, he retrieved the lump of metal without once feeling that surge of excitement he used to experience each time he held the precious substance in his hand. The fever had abandoned him. If it wasn't for the fact there was no way to leave until spring came, he would gladly turn his back on the Louisiana Mine and go home. But as long as they were forced to remain there, they might as well take as much gold as possible even though the vein of pure gold was petering out fast.

He tossed the nugget he'd unearthed into the cart set aside for that purpose, then raised his hand to halt the crew for a much deserved rest.

He studied the faces around him. Each man had worked

hard and earned his share, even Pat, who most days joined them, leaving the women to cook and clean. How many of his crew would take their cut and use it wisely? Buckley, probably. His game leg had left him wanting nothing more than a chance to return to Indiana and his wife and seven kids. Mace Lockman. Braven scrutinized him long and hard. Chances are the kid would blow most of his money on women and drink. He'd be back in the fields by the following year, Braven had no doubt. He shook his head. What a waste. Dan Butler had already stated he was going back to New York and the family farm. Gold-mining was harder work than plowing. Braven agreed with the other man's opinion. Mining was one hell of a way to make a living. The rest of his men, he couldn't be sure about, including Pat. The old Irishman never said a word about his future. But every evening before they quit, he weighed their take, his eyes gleaming with satisfaction. What was the little man up to, and why was he so determined to know exactly how much gold they had?

"Thinking maybe we should get back to work, me boyo?"

His head snapped around to find the Irishman beside him, that driving gleam residing in his Erin-green eyes. The urge to ask Pat what was on his mind, what drove him so hard, dominated Braven's thoughts, but he held his tongue in check, chastising his moment of distrust for the one person who had always supported him in his decisions.

Pat raised a brow in question. Braven glanced away. Had the old man read his mind again?

"I suppose so," he answered, his voice devoid of enthusiasm. He stood, and the men rose in silence with him. Back to work and back to the haunting thoughts that nagged at his conscience without relief. Though the gold fever had deserted him, the golden fervor for the woman who had stolen his heart grew stronger each day.

Rivalree's wounds had healed nicely, but Braven still made it a point to keep his distance. He ached for her, but the thought of lying close at night without the ability to revel in her warm flesh was more than any mortal man could bear. At first he had used her injury as an excuse; now he had none. If he didn't have time alone with his wife soon, he would go crazy. But there was no way. Even if he told the men to keep away for a few hours, there was still Joleen. He couldn't very well send the pregnant girl into the mine as well. Just best to keep to himself and turn his mind to other less disturbing thoughts.

Like the toboggan he was building for Rivalree, a Christmas gift. Since the day she was attacked by the bear he had been acutely aware of her haunting unrest, and he had concocted the idea of constructing the sled to relieve the winter tedium. Realizing the snowdrifts would continue to pile against the cabin, in time the frozen white would stretch to the upper portions of the building, and they should be able to escape through a window to the outside. The pasture sported a perfect, cleared slope and would make a fine place for tobogganing. He hoped Rivalree liked his offering.

With a resigned lift of his shoulders, he resumed his task, cleaving his way toward the center of the mountain to take all nature sacrificed to the miners' pickaxes and shovels.

A nubbin of a plan began formulating in his mind. If he couldn't send the men and Joleen out of the cabin into the mine so he could be alone with his wife, maybe they could escape to the solitude the tunnels offered. Would Rivalree be receptive or insulted by such a suggestion? Could he risk things getting worse between them? He must try. All he knew was that she was a vital part of him. He needed to feel her warm arms about him, required the strength of her love that flamed his flagging spirits each time she opened herself to his intimate exploration. The winter had been long and miserable and stretched unendingly before him. He needed her to help him make it through to spring.

Rivalree paced back and forth before the fireplace, her fingers twisting the faded calico of her dress. Harsh conditions and crude washing circumstances had ruined most of her clothing, not that she'd had much to begin with or that she cared about her appearance anymore.

Since her confrontation with the bear, Braven had made it a point to keep his distance, sleeping instead on a spare cot before the fire, leaving her alone in the solitude of their big, four-poster bed.

Why had he deserted her? The question had plagued her for weeks. At first she had accepted his excuse that he didn't want to aggravate her injury, but her wounds had healed and he still didn't join her at night. She rubbed the aching twinge in her arm, a pain that stubbornly refused to leave, and knew the answer to her question. The scar running down her shoulder almost to her elbow, a grim reminder of her near-fatal encounter with death, Braven found it distasteful. The thought slashed at her heart. She would never reject him for such a surface reason. Blind, lame, or limbless she would remain loyal to him, her love undaunted by a blemish of the flesh.

Joleen rose from her habitual place in the rocker with a groan that could only be described as maternal, the unique sound of a woman large with child making an effort to stand. Rivalree sympathized with her plight, but at the same time she envied the other woman. Soon Joleen would have a baby to hold and love, a child who would look up to and need her whether she was scarred or perfect.

Her feet stilled their insistent shuffling. When had this yearning for her own child captured her heart? Not so long ago she had pitied Joleen her condition, but sometime over the weeks of convalescence she had watched the younger woman press her hand possessively to her middle as the fetus had kicked and wriggled within her. Once she had even taken Rivalree's hand and placed it against her stomach that had bounced like a sacked kitten against her palm. Yes, that had been the fatal moment when the need to create an infant had taken a firm grip on her.

But how could she make a baby without the loving nurture of her husband? How indeed? Even if he wanted her, they never had a single moment alone, a chance to kiss or make love, or an opportunity to talk quietly between themselves. Maybe if they had a few minutes without others about, they could work out their problems. She sighed. Wishful thinking would not make a miracle. There was no possible way for them to be alone, even if Braven wanted to be with her. Which obviously he didn't.

With her thoughts circling back to where she'd begun, the solution to her problem no closer at hand, she returned to her pacing, stepping around Joleen's rotund figure as the girl warmed her icy hands at the fire.

"You'll soon wear a path, if you don't stop that traipsing," Joleen warned, her eyes following as Rivalree moved.

Rivalree held her resentful retort in check, caring too much for Joleen to hurt her feelings. Without a word, she angled her steps back to her chair, took up the handmade knitting needles Mace Lockman had fashioned with his whittling knife especially for her, and sat down resuming her work on a sweater she was making for Braven as a Christmas present. She had salvaged the yarn from a woolen shawl she'd brought with her. She glanced sideways as Joleen returned to her seat. Hopefully there would be enough spun wool to make Joleen a pair of leggins, as well. Constantly the other woman rose to place her palms toward the warmth of the flames.

"Are your toes cold, too?" Rivalree queried, eyeing the way Joleen kept stomping her feet.

"Aren't they always?"

Rivalree set down her knitting, vacated her chair, and headed toward the stove. Stoking the fire, she set a kettle of water to boil. She didn't envy Joleen's poor circulation. At least thrice a day she heated water so the girl could thaw her frozen feet by soaking them.

"Thank you, Rivalree," Joleen groaned. "You are such a saint to take care of me like this."

"I suspect you'd do the same for me."

Joleen watched her under lowered lashes. "I would like to think I would be as kind if the situation was reversed."

She shot the younger woman a bewildered look. Whatever did Joleen mean by that remark? As the kettle began to chirp, she poured water into a basin and carried the container back to Joleen, setting it by her chair. Kneeling, she stripped the shoes and double layer of socks from her feet, then guided the icy appendages into the water.

"Thank you, Rivalree," the girl sobbed. "I'm just so useless. Lord, I can't even see my toes, I'm so fat."

"Not fat, *pregnant*. A lot of women would envy you your condition."

Joleen placed a hand on her golden head. "I'm so sorry, Rivalree. I know I'm in the way. If I wasn't here, you and Mr. Blackwood could be together, like a husband and wife should."

The girl's statement struck a guilty cord. Rivalree shook her head in venomous denial. Her chin lifted, a frown tilting her lips downward. "Not so, Joleen. If Mr. Blackwood wished to be with me, he'd find a way. You don't know him like I do. Nothing stops him when he sets his mind on something, not you or me or the Creator himself. Our problems have nothing to do with you."

Joleen smiled weakly, belief not quite reaching her gaze. Looking away, Rivalree dried the now warm feet and slipped them back into their socks and shoes.

"Now, you just rest while I check out the storeroom.

Maybe I can come up with something different to stir your appetite."

Something different? There was nothing left in the storeroom but dried beans and flour, a half barrel of salted pork, and a few onions. How could anyone be creative with so little to work with? A sob of frustration slipped past Rivalree's tight lips.

Thinking back she remembered that first meal she had made for Braven on the trail. That evening she had reveled in her ability to cook with beans and not much else, but that night had been special beyond all others, the first time he had made love to her. How clear the emotions she had felt then were to her now. If she had only told him the truth of her past from the beginning maybe things would be different between them today.

Shoving away the unwanted chastisements, she focused on the problems at hand. With only the meager supplies they had, they would be lucky to have sufficient food to last them through the winter. Then there was the possibility of scurvy, the dreaded disease of sailors. On the trip to California from the East Coast she remembered clearly the captain's concern that every passenger and crew member consume a daily portion of fresh fruit or vegetable. Was it possible that they would get the illness confined to the mountains without a source of fresh provisions? Her tongue skimmed over her teeth and gums, looking for telltale signs of damage. She found none, but that fact didn't relieve her fears.

Kneeling, she scooped up a portion from the beans and a measure of flour, tucking one of the precious onions in her palm. Beans and dumplings. Didn't sound very appetizing.

"Is it as bad as it seems?" Joleen asked from the doorway.

"Joleen!" Rivalree turned, alarmed. "You shouldn't be

here. Your feet will only get cold again."

"I know," she said, hanging her head, her doelike eyes radiating guilt. "I don't mean to put you out," she answered with a rush of plaintive air. "But I heard your sounds of distress. We're running out of food, aren't we? It's all my fault. If I'd not come here, there would be plenty . . ."

Rivalree jumped to her feet and put a consoling arm around the other woman. "Not so, Joleen. There's plenty of food, and the little bit you eat each day has not made a difference one way or the other. Please don't cry. This isn't like you. Usually you're so cheerful and encouraging."

"I'm sorry. I don't know what's wrong with me."

The baby, Rivalree thought. Joleen was drawing close to her time. She ran comforting fingers through the girl's lusterless hair. The baby. Would she be able to handle a birthing? Without a doubt, Braven expected her to take charge and see that all went well. Picking up her supplies, she guided the distraught girl back into the relative warmth of the common room and eased her rounded body back into the rocker.

Things could be worse, she told herself as she drifted toward the stove with her foodstuffs to begin the evening meal. She could have no one. Silently she thanked God for sending Joleen to her.

As she molded dumplings, she came to the following conclusion. The only way to survive was to take the days one at a time and not worry about tomorrow until it came. Let each day take care of itself.

Braven opened the front door and spied Rivalree standing at the stove dropping dumplings into a big pot he knew must contain not much more than beans. His stomach roiled in distaste. If he ate more beans and salt pork, he'd be sick. But it wasn't food he came in search of—at least not of the body—but nourishment for his soul.

The men had agreed to his plan, and if Joleen was willing to watch the meal . . .

He grinned with self-satisfaction as he stepped behind his unaware wife and circled her shoulders with his arms.

Rivalree jumped, a lump of dough dropping from her startled hand to land on the floor.

"No wonder we're running out of food. Are you always this wasteful?" he said, blowing softly in her ear.

"Braven," she stuttered, his name popping out of her mouth with the staccato of rain on a tin roof. "What are you doing here now?"

"Remember, I live here." His tongue traced the shell of her ear.

She flinched as if she'd been branded. "What are you doing?" With suspicious eyes, she studied him as if he'd lost his mind.

"Something I've needed to do for a long time. I'm going to spend some time alone with my wife."

"You can't ask Joleen to leave the room. She's . . ."

"I'm not asking her, but you."

Rivalree narrowed her eyes, confused. Was she about to refuse him? Standing on tiptoes, she glanced over his shoulder at the other woman. Then she giggled. "But how?" she mouthed.

"I have it all worked out," he whispered back. "If you're interested."

She nodded, blushing.

He smiled, the grin splitting his face like a boy who'd gotten away with taking his first drink behind the barn. His mood infected her, and she giggled again. The sound was fresh and freeing, and he decided he loved her best this way, a little wayward and daring, willing to trust him.

"Good," he declared, and captured her flour-dusted hands in his and led her toward the front door, stopping only long enough to gather up fresh tapers, a couple o

297

blankets, and Rivalree's jacket.

Joleen struggled to stand, and managed to teeter like an unbalanced top beside her chair.

"Watch dinner, will you?" Braven indicated the pot of beans and lump of unfinished dumplings.

The girl nodded dumbly, her mouth dropping open as he led Rivalree out the door.

"Oh, Braven, what must she think?" she asked as the door closed behind them.

"I'd say by looking at her, she'll figure it out."

She slapped him on the arm, her hand leaving a perfect print on his coat sleeve. "What a terrible thing to say."

"Think so? I can come up with worse statements, like . . ."

She covered his mouth with her palm, again leaving an imprint of her hand on his face.

The shuffle of feet behind him brought him whirling about. The men stepped by them, some grinning, many glancing away as if they didn't exist. Regardless, he noticed the red tint creeping up Rivalree's neck to stain her face.

Pat was the last man in the string of bodies headed toward the cabin. He stopped and eyed the couple. "Shall we wait dinner for the two of ya?"

Rivalree's blush turned beet red. Braven held her in the protection of his arm. "No need. We might be awhile. If we're hungry, we'll eat later."

The Irishman nodded a look of regret passing over his features as he spun about and followed the other miners down the walkway.

Braven frowned, the creases in his forehead faint. The confinement was getting to Pat as well, he concluded, a bit shaken by the realization that the old man's spirit could flag like everyone else's.

After the last footfall faded and the door to the cabin shut the rest of the world away from them, he turned her in the circle of his arms and drew her close. He tugged her jacket tighter around her shoulders and urged her toward the mine entrance, a lit candle in his hand guiding the way. At last they were alone together, the entire evening stretching before them. He would make the time special for both of them, a night they would never forget.

Together at last, secluded from curious stares. Rivalree's heart thumped like a well-stretched drum, the sound full and exciting, compelling her to take Braven's hand and lead the way. He wanted her, its rhythm announced with a joyous tempo. He didn't find her repulsive, her racing blood babbled happily. He loved her, her tingling fingers confirmed as he squeezed her hand in response to her bold action. She wanted to laugh aloud and shout her discoveries to the world. But no one would hear. Not that it mattered; the only important thing was the light shimmering in his adoring eyes.

She slowed her pace allowing him to catch up. As they entered the dark confines of the tunnels, he lifted the candle he held, selecting a far, dry corner of the entrance where the floor was relatively smooth. Handing her the taper, he spread the blankets one on top of the other, until not a crease was visible. The candle he placed in a crack between two boulders high above their heads, an ethereal light showering down on them highlighting his lapis lazuli eyes and haloing the blondness of his hair.

The undying love she felt for him swelled until she thought her heart would burst. Lifting her hand, she traced the angles of his face, more prominent in the last few weeks, a sign he had suffered, too, while she had recovered from her injury. Why hadn't she noticed how thin he'd become? Thinner, perhaps, she thought running her hand across his shoulder and over his chest the sinew outlined more, but still hard and overpowering

Without words, he skimmed the buttons on the front of her dress with his fingers. She considered the way she must look, her hair a disheveled mane of curls, her hands covered with flour, and, glancing down in dismay, her dress dusted white as well. How could he think her attractive?

The buttons slipped with deceptive ease from their fasteners to reveal the swell of her bosom beneath her chemise. As Braven pushed the faded material away from her shoulders, a rush of stark fear tore through her. The scar. Would he find it offensive? Her hands lifted, stilling the activity of his, her eyes questioning him.

"What is it, my love," he demanded, the frown she'd noticed earlier returning to mar the perfection of his face.

She dropped her chin, unable to answer. Instead, her fingers spoke for her as they spayed across the white expanse of exposed flesh her open garment revealed. She swayed, trying to interpret his silence. *Please, don't let me find disgust in his eyes*, she prayed as she lifted her gaze.

What she discovered set her heart to pounding. With gentle pressure, he pushed her hand aside to trace the puckered flesh on her shoulder.

"Did you think your scar would bother me?"

She responded with a proud dip of her head.

"Silly girl." He tipped her chin higher, his lips seeking hers in the gentlest of kisses. "That scar is of my doing. Had I wielded a surer needle, it might not have been so bad. Can you forgive me for my inability?"

"Forgive you? You saved my life. Had you not arrived when you did . . ."

"Not true, Rivalree. Your level head and accuracy with a bullet saved you, not me."

"And you don't find the scar ugly and repulsive?"

"How could I? Anything that is a part of you I can only love." Bending low, he eased the bodice of her dress off her arms and placed tender kisses on her shoulder and down

300

her limb following the trail of the wound.

Her other arm curled about his neck, a support to keep her from falling. For one wild moment she considered telling him the truth of her past, his vow to love her no matter what still ringing in her ears, but as his mouth molded to one taut breast, the ability to reason escaped her. All she could think about was the way his tongue circled her nipple, teasing, demanding, seeking the response she so willingly gave.

With the grace of a dancer, he lowered her onto the blankets, the love nest he had created for them. Stretching out beside her, he removed the remainder of her clothes from her body, and, taking the top blanket, covered her the regret that he could no longer drink in the beauty of her form shining in his eyes.

Gazes locked, he tossed his jacket to the side, then guided his shirt off his chest, finally to strip his pants from his hips. Mesmerized, Rivalree marveled at the beauty of his torso, her fingers aching to comb through the fur of his chest, to trace the sculpturesque lines of his broad shoulders and back. She beckoned him with arms raised in welcome, the covers pushed to one side.

He joined her in the woolen cocoon, his warmth adding to the radiance she experienced. How whole she felt, his mouth heating her flesh wherever it touched, his hand igniting fire in her loins as it skimmed along her inner thighs to possess the womanly charms nestled there. Without inhibitions, she opened to his exploration, eager to reciprocate, her hand moving down to mirror his as she stroked his rigid manhood.

Too long they had been apart, separated by the whims of nature, to continue the caressing torture they wreaked upon each other. By mutual consent, he rolled, scooping her beneath him, and she urged him to unite their bodies.

The sizzle of lightning flashed across her closed eyelids and she soughed in distress as he refused to rush the oining. His strokes were slow, rising on a pause that tore a sob from her throat each time he stopped. Yet, with each plunge she eagerly met him halfway, her fingers grasping the taut muscles of his backside.

He paced his rhythm even though she cried for him to hurry. Soon the rising passion built with such tension, she was glad he had not listened to her demands, and she followed his quickening tempo with undaunted zeal.

The blinding rush of fulfillment crashed over her, washing away the troubles and anxieties haunting her for weeks. She knew without a doubt they would survive the winter trials, together, undivided.

His cry of release was like a balm to her spirit. She had gifted him with what he had given her. Drawing his head down to rest upon her rising and falling breast, she knew nothing could ever drive them apart again. Nothing less than an act of God.

Chapter Twenty-One

December 23, 1851

Flatware clicked without enthusiasm around the table Salt pork and beans, beans and salt pork, the fare neve changed. Braven eyed the meal before him with disgust How was a man suppose to maintain his sanity eating th same thing day in and day out?

With a snort of defiance, he tossed down his fork, th sound demanding silence from the other occupants of th room. The crowded table of diners complied almos willingly, expectant looks pivoting his way.

Damn! Two days before Christmas, and he had neve seen such bleak faces. They were all wealthy, but thei money couldn't acquire one decent meal. He stood pushed back his plate in a symbolic challenge, and stepped away from the table.

No one moved. Except Rivalree. She rose, her chin lifted, prepared, no doubt, for the tirade that crowded the back of his throat demanding release.

How proud she stood, an unbending oak waiting for the storm to strike. His words of frustration chameleonized, angry red to contrite gray, as their eyes locked, each struggling to understand how the other felt.

"By damn, there'll be fresh meat on this table for Christmas, if it's the last thing I do." He slammed his fist down against the newel post at the beginning of the stairs.

Her crystalline gaze clouded, uncertainly touching her face with a frown.

He hesitated for a moment, deciphering the anxiety in her eyes, before he spun about seeking his rifle.

"Braven, what are you going to do?" Rivalree's voice traveled with fear.

Other faces had the same question written across them.

"I'm going hunting," he stated matter-of-factly as he checked the gun with an expert hand. "Anyone care to join me?"

The sound of volunteering cracked through the air.

Braven glanced up. All of the men stood before their partially eaten meals, each eager to go with him.

Rivalree lowered back onto the bench, Joleen beside her, the only two remaining seated.

"I don't think that's such a wise idea," she objected, her hands squeezed white as they gripped the edge of the table.

"And why not?" he countered, slipping on his heavy coat, taking gloves from the pocket. Damn it! Why did women always have to look at everything with a negative eye? Pointing at four of the other men, he ordered, "You come with me. The rest stay here."

"Braven," she blurted, shooting up, her hands fanned across the table for support. "The weather. You could be injured or worse . . ."

"The snow's deep, but the sun's shining. I'll be fine. We'll be back by dark." He turned, gathered up a canvas bag, and shoved supplies into it. He could feel Rivalree's eyes following him.

Crossing over to the table, he dumped the tin of remaining biscuits from the noon meal into the backpack. Her gaze dogged his every move.

"What do I do, if you don't return?" she pressed, her

304

right hand coming up to rest on the swell of her breast over her heart.

He understood what she asked; he could hear the genuine concern in her voice. Yet something inside him clicked at her lack of confidence in his ability to take care of himself. "Why, nothing Mrs. Blackwood. You needn't do a thing. If I fail to come back, you'll be a wealthy woman."

Her gasp of surprise followed him up the loft stairs, and he heard the shuffle of her shod feet crossing the room. He stopped halfway up the steps, his back held rigid, fully expecting her to continue her badgering.

The banister trembled beneath his hand as her fingers grasped it far below; still she said nothing. With a great intake of air, he flexed his shoulder muscles, then turned to stare down at her where she stood on the bottom landing.

"Don't worry, sugar. Have faith in me. I'll be back."

She nodded, the fear lodged in her heart shining in her eyes.

Lifting his arm, he beckoned to her, and she glided up the stairs to take the final steps in unison with him. The rest of the hunting party followed silently behind them.

"Braven?" she asked. "If you're going hunting, why are we going upstairs?" Her tone indicated she feared at last he had come unglued.

His laughter reverberated around the cabin. "Don't be concerned, sugar. I haven't lost my mind. Wait and you'll see."

On the upper landing he spun her about, pulling the loose shawl around her shoulders tighter. "You should have a coat on up here. It's cold."

She shook her head in denial, but clutched the covering about her.

Pushing through the bedroom door, he headed toward the lone window in the room. If his calculation were accurate, the drift level of snow should be just about right.

The healing touch of the cold north sun burst upon them as he swung the casement wide. Blinking like an owl, he glanced down the outside of the cabin to find exactly what he wanted. Snow banked up the sides less than two feet below the window. "Perfect," he stated, swinging about to face his men. "The going will be slow in the high drifts, but we'll manage."

Eager faces jutted toward the window, including Rivalree. As the sunlight caressed her pale cheeks he read the near-envy resting in her gaze.

"I'm sorry, Rivalree. You'll be better off here. I promise, if the weather holds, we'll go on a hike out of doors together." His fingers curled lovingly around her chin.

"Wait," called Pat as he entered the bedroom, huffing as he struggled with his burden. "I think these will be helpful." In his wrinkled hands he held five pairs of snowshoes.

"Pat," Braven inquired wondrously. "Where did these come from?"

"Intuition, me boyo. I made them knowing the time would come when you'd need them. And while you're out there, gather some spruce needles."

"Spruce needles?"

"Aye and be so. We can make a tea, a bit bitter perhaps, but a good preventive against scurvy."

Braven nodded and smiled in gratitude, a guilty rush of relief spreading through him. He could trust the old Irishman, as sure as he could trust that spring would eventually find them in this frozen corner of the world.

Rivalree leaned out the casement watching the line of men tramp their way through the snow and out of view. The strange contraptions on their feet caught her attention. The wooden frames were strung with thongs over two crosspieces. But they seemed to work as the men walked across the white expanse of land barely sinking in the snow.

She glanced over her shoulder at Pat, grateful he had produced them as well as the idea of bringing back spruce needles to prevent scurvy.

"Thank you, Pat. You take such care of us. What would we do without you?"

The old man's eyes narrowed, and a frown crinkled his weathered face even more. Then the look passed, and Rivalree wasn't sure she'd ever seen it at all.

He grinned and lifted his shoulders in a shrug. "You needn't thank me, colleen."

"Do you think they'll be successful?"

"Would be nice, I'd be thinking."

She began pacing the room. So many things could go wrong. What if they ran into another bear? And avalanches. She had heard of people being buried alive by a wall of snow and rock. Her fingers twisted in the knit of her shawl, her cold breath puffing out in steamy, nervous whiffs. What if the weather should change, the men could easily be lost and . . . ?

"Calm down, colleen. I've never seen anyone have such a case of peedoodles."

"But, Pat!"

"Take it easy, girl. Let's go downstairs. There's nothing more we can do here. The waiting will be warmer below."

She nodded, seeing the reason of his words. But it was hard, oh, so hard, to turn her back on the window as Pat pulled the frames closed and urged her toward the stairway.

The firelight glimmered on the sea of faces arched around the hearth. How strange it felt having the men in the cabin instead of working in the mine this early in the

307

day. Rivalree fidgeted in her chair, wanting to run back up the stairs and search for the hunting party, but she'd checked only moments before, and it was too soon to look again. Folding her hands in her lap with deceptive calm, she tried to listen to the stories the miners bantered back and forth among themselves.

The men laughed in audience unison, as Pat slapped his thigh, pleased with the anecdote he'd told.

Buckley held up his hands, calling for quiet as he stated, "I have one for ya."

The men turned expectant eyes to the lame man.

"Prospector went to heaven," he began.

"Didn't know miners could get past the pearly gates," Dan Butler countered with a snort.

The men laughed.

Rivalree glanced up, inspecting the smiling faces around her. How could they be so unconcerned when their friends and leader were out God knew where, possibly dying or injured?

Buckley held his hand high in defense. "Didn't say he didn't have trouble gittin' in. In fact, once he reached them pearly gates, old Saint Peter stopped him, asked him what he did for a livin', and when the prospector answered, Peter turned him away 'cause there were too many miners in heaven already."

A loud spurt of hilarity split the room, the men shaking their heads knowingly.

"The prospector turned to leave but jest before he got out of Saint Peter's sight, he returned, a plan in mind. 'Saint Peter,' he says, 'I got a deal to make. You let me in and I'll get rid of all them other miners for ya.'"

Rivalree rose and took a turn about the room, unable to sit still any longer.

"Saint Peter agreed," Buckley continued his tale. "And the prospector began circulating a rumor among the idle miners that there was a big gold strike in hell. Within hours, they all pulled up stakes and streamed back to the pearly gates, demandin' to be let out.''

"Ain't never known no miner to ignore news like that," Mace Lockman grunted.

"Meantime, the lone prospector returns to Saint Peter and sheepishly asks to be let out, too. Saint Peter asks him why?" Buckley paused, a big grin splitting his face. "Hell, I might have started the story about the devil's strike, but what if there's somethin' to it? I don't want to be the only one left out.''

Laughter rattled the rafters, as the men slapped each other on the backs, one hopping up and down, hooting.

Rivalree spun, presenting her rigid spine. *Damn them! How can they not care?* She turned to the stove and stoked the fire, setting a kettle on to boil. There was no reason for her action as they had no more coffee, but the familiar movements calmed her shattered nerves.

"Don't worry, Rivalree. They'll be back soon," Joleen offered softly, standing beside her.

"Joleen," she protested, unaware the other woman had joined her. "You should be sitting down.''

"I'm tired of sitting. And I'm sick of those boring stories. Please, let me stay with you.''

Rivalree nodded, patting the girl's hands lying across her swollen middle. "To tell you the truth, I'm glad you joined me. I don't think I can take another one of those stupid jokes, either.''

"What do you think the hunters will bring back? A deer maybe, or perhaps an elk or a moose?''

"As long as they come back in one piece, I don't care what game they get." Rivalree dusted her hands on her apron and settled on a bench at the table.

With a mighty groan, Joleen lowered her overblown frame beside her. "I do wish this baby would present itself. I'm tired of toting it around like this.''

Rivalree stroked the hand resting on the table. "Enjoy it

309

while it lasts. I remember the village women back home used to say, a child is much easier to deal with before it's born, no matter how uncomfortable you feel. At least it isn't crying and demanding.'' She didn't believe a word she said. She'd give anything to have a warm, wiggly baby of her own to love and care for. But more important, she prayed Braven would return soon, safe and whole.

Steam whorled around Braven as he completed the necessary procedures, gutting the deer he had brought down moments before. The heat emanating from the carcass drew him forth, and he was unable to resist warming his hands before sheathing his knife and putting on his gloves. Checking the thongs binding the lifeless deer to a limb, he signaled to one of the men to take the other end, and together they lifted the suspended animal, its head flung back in death, its massive rack of horns nearly dragging the ground. The other men carried bundles of spruce needles. Their task completed, he raised his arm and signaled the hunters forward, and they began the long trek to the cabin.

The pale illumination of the late-afternoon sun dipped behind gray clouds, and Braven glanced up, concern furrowing his brows. Damn! They had a good three-hour walk back to the mining camp. He shifted the weight of the deer on his shoulder and quickened his steps. They must make their way before the weather broke.

Yet as worry pricked at his thoughts, the first flakes of snow settled on his coat and hair. Determined to press on unless the storm made it impossible to navigate the trail, he flashed on Rivalree's face as he had stepped away from the bedroom window. He couldn't let her fret about his safety through the night, as he knew she was bound to do. Somehow, they would make it back to the cabin before the storm became full-blown.

"Braven," called one of the men. "Maybe we should look for a place to hole up."

"We'll go on," he commanded, bowing his head to the flying, white flakes and hunching his shoulders to the wind beginning to shriek a warning to any who could hear. As the cold, wet snow stung his squinted eyes, he hated to admit it, but Rivalree had been right. It had been a foolish idea to go hunting.

Her forlorn words of fear pressed against his heart. "What will I do, if you don't return?" The thought she might have to continue on without him frightened him more than the possibility he might not survive. With her words echoing in his head, he forced his feet to take each step as he whispered, "I'm coming, sugar. Don't worry."

Rivalree's fingers twisted the folds of her skirt until they were limp and wrinkled. Where were the men? Why weren't they back yet? Her gaze skittered around the common room and read similar questions in the faces of the others. A sob of hysterics threatened to burst past her courage-soldered lips. If Pat and the others were concerned, then her fears were founded.

Whirling, she scampered up the stairs for the hundredth time and pushed into the darkening bedroom. Throwing open the sashes, she strained to see through the eddies of snow that danced like maddened demons around trees and bushes.

Oh, Braven, her heart cried. *Where are you?*

Haunting images of his cold, stiff being covered with snow, his hands stretching helplessly to her, crowded out all other thoughts, as well as the freezing wind licking at her uncoated form.

"Damn you, you stubborn-minded man, why didn't you listen to me?" she hissed, her anger speared by the terror curling around her flesh and bones.

311

"Miz Rivalree?"

She whipped her head around, ending her vigilance, at the formal sound of her name spoken.

Mace Lockman stood in the doorway, his hands twisting his pant leg. "I don't think they'll be comin' back tonight. Chances are they'll find shelter until mornin'."

"Mace, it's so cold out there. They'll freeze to death," she choked.

"Braven took matches. If they can find a dry hollow, there's a possibility they can start a fire and . . ." He shrugged, the uncertainty in his eyes pointing out he doubted his own words.

Rivalree presented her back to the man. Tears welled, threatening to spill down her cheeks.

"Please, Miz Rivalree," Mace urged, touching her shoulder with his hands in hesitancy. "Please come back downstairs."

She shook her head in silence, unable to trust her voice not to betray the emotion clogging her throat.

"It's much too cold up here," he pressed, reaching around her to close the window casement. "You can't do him any good standing here."

Her shoulders slumped. "I know, Mace, but somehow it's as though if I leave my post something will happen"—she gripped his offered hand—"something terrible will happen to him."

"I understand, but that just ain't true. Braven's smart and woods-wise. If anybody can make it, he can. He needs your strength, ma'am, not your worry."

"I must stay. What if he should come and the window is shut . . . ?"

"All right, Miz Rivalree. But at least let me get you a chair and a blanket."

She nodded her agreement, turned to the window, and peeked through the casement.

Minutes later, Mace returned, carrying several quilts and one of the chairs that normally graced the hearth. He placed the seat against the far wall and cleared his throat.

Whirling, she frowned. With determined strides, she crossed the room, grabbed the chair and dragged it closer to the window, the portal to life beyond, to Braven. "Thank you, Mace," she offered, taking the quilts from his hands.

With a nod, he retraced his steps to the door. "Reconsider, ma'am?"

She shook her head.

"Be assured, we'll send out a search party if they aren't back by midmornin'."

"Thank you, I'd appreciate that."

As the echo of Mace's steps died, she sat down and pulled one of the covers up over her shoulder. Midmorning. Would she survive that long? She closed her eyes, but horrid images of Braven huddled in a snowdrift projected on her lowered lids. No, she mustn't sleep. That would be the same as deserting her post.

In the still silence the cold seemed to press harder against her body. If she was freezing, how must he feel? She chided herself for being so weak. Mace Lockman was right, Braven needed her strength, and she would give it to him.

The wind began to howl outside the window, taunting her, convincing her that morning would bring disaster in its wake.

"Braven," she whispered under her chilled breath, "come home. I will be the woman you want me to be, if you'll only return."

"Miz Rivalree."

Mace Lockman's gentle voice penetrated the fog of sleep surrounding Rivalree.

With a jerk, she lifted her head, confusion clouding her brain as the light of a lone candle greeted her. Remembering where she was and why, her hand flew to her mouth. Dear God, she'd fallen asleep. She hadn't meant to, but at some point the seductive fingers of slumber had claimed her.

"Is he back?" she demanded.

"No, ma'am. It's not Braven. It's Miss Joleen."

"Joleen?" she questioned, pressing the heel of her hands against her leaden eyes.

"She's moanin' and callin' out. I think maybe it's the baby. I don't know enough about birthin' to be sure."

"Of course, Mace. You've done the right thing by coming to me." She straightened, brushing tangled curls from her face.

The thought that Joleen's labor may have begun struck fear in her heart. She'd never seen a woman have a baby. Would she know for sure if that was what was wrong with the other woman?

Pushing away the warmth of the covers, she rose from her chair, stiff and aching in every joint in her body.

"Please, Mace, while I go downstairs, stay here and watch for me."

He hesitated, then nodded in agreement, resuming her seat by the window.

Please, Joleen, not now, she prayed as she eased down the stairs. She needed to give her full attention to Braven, and if the girl had her baby now, she would have to devote her mind to helping her. How could she turn her thoughts to Joleen, with Braven lost and possibly dead?

Her steps hesitant, she approached Joleen's bed and pulled back the curtain. The girl writhed in obvious agony, the sheet clamped between her teeth.

Rivalree knelt and pressed her hand against the girl's forehead.

"I'm sorry, Rivalree," Joleen rasped. "I tried to be quiet.

314

I tried to make the pain go away, but it won't." She groaned, her eyes rolling back in her skull.

"Hush, Joleen. You can't help what nature dictates." She rolled up her sleeves and shoved the covers away from the girl's lower body. There would be a baby born. If not this night, then by the morrow.

She glanced around the room as the men stirred sleepily. There was no doubt that the bringing of this child into the world was up to her as concerned faces looked her way for reassurance, including the pale, drawn face of the girl helpless to control the demands of her body.

Chapter Twenty-Two

Morning dawned like a sleepy-eyed bear after a long winter of hibernation. Rivalree thought for sure daylight would never arrive, but at last faint streamers trickled in the lone window by the stove revealing dancing dust particles that one never saw unless the light hit them just right.

Again she dipped the washcloth into the pan of cool water and dabbed at Joleen's brow and forehead. For hours the girl has suffered, whimpering with each contraction ripping through her thin body, but still there was no sign that the baby was any closer to presenting itself.

How long could these things take? Rivalree strained to remember her limited experiences with women in labor. Her mother had, at times, disappeared for days aiding a neighbor woman birth a child. She wasn't sure whether she should be concerned or not about the slowness with which this baby entered the world.

The clump of booted feet coming down the stairs whipped her head around. Her heart drummed against her ribs. Braven!

Instead Mace Lockman vaulted toward her, his hair rumpled and his clothes wrinkled from sitting up all night, waiting.

"Are they back?" she asked, knowing in her heart the answer she would receive. Mace's face was too severe to offer such good news.

"No, ma'am, but the snow has stopped and the day is clear. I suspect we'll see 'em in a few hours."

And if we don't? Her heart pounded, but she didn't voice her fears. Instead she nodded and turned back to Joleen, occupying her trembling hands by wiping the sweat from the girl's face.

"Thank you, Mace. I would appreciate a watch being posted at all times by the window."

Dan Butler stood. "I'll take a turn." His large form edged up the steps.

Mace crossed the room to stand over her. "How's Miss Joleen doing?" His brow crinkled in worry.

She glanced up, surprised to see the concern etched on his features. "I'm not sure, but I suspect it can't be much longer."

He nodded, satisfied that as a woman she knew what she was talking about.

Behind her she heard Pat set a platter on the plank table, a meager breakfast that didn't draw much interest. She placed her laced fingers in her lap and closed her eyes, the thin patina of patience covering the ball of raw nerves she'd become obvious to none but herself as she waited. Her life crumbled around her, and she sat there calmly anticipating the further disasters that were bound to befall her.

Joleen's body tensed, and Rivalree eased forward in her chair knowing another contraction began.

"Easy, Joleen," she urged, giving the girl one of her hands and allowing her to squeeze it until she thought her fingers would surely snap under the grip wrought with agony. Seconds later Joleen went limp as a gasp of relief tumbled over her dry lips.

"I be thinkin' this isn't normal," Pat observed. He stood

behind Rivalree so close his breath ruffled her hair.

She glanced up at him in concern.

"I witness my mum birth seven children after me. And Carrie, me own darlin' daughter." A wisp of a smile lifted his lips. "I remember the day of her birth as if it were yesterday." The smile faded and concern took its place. "The pains should be gittin' closer together." He studied her upturned face. "But then you know more about these things than I do."

Reaching up, she clasped his arm. "No, I don't. All I know is the little my mother told me—which isn't much."

The little Irishman cocked his head and eyed her in surprise.

"Rivalree," cried Joleen. "The pain . . ."

She turned, offering what help she could to the laboring woman, but it seemed inadequate in the face of her suffering.

Pat pulled up a chair to sit beside her.

"What do we do for her?"

"Not much we can do," the Irishman stated, "except wait."

Wait? Damn, she was tired of being passive and allowing everything around her dictate her actions. She must take the situation in hand.

"I think not," she declared, pushing up from her chair. She turned to Mace Lockman. "Check with Dan and find out if he's seen any signs of the hunters."

Mace nodded, relieved to be doing something, and scampered up the stairs.

She whirled on Pat. "I'm going to examine her," she announced, heading for the dry sink and the bar of soap. "You can help me or stay back, the choice is yours."

"Do you think that's wise, colleen?"

She began lathering her hands. "It can be no worse than doing nothing."

"I'll help," he stated, taking the soap from her fingers.

She sighed in relief. She could use his assistance. As she dried her hands on a clean towel she studied the Irishman. He was knowledgeable about childbirth, probably more competent than she was. She would leave Joleen in his capable hands and organize a search party to locate Braven.

The solution was so simple. Why hadn't she thought of it before?

Handing the towel to Pat, she glided across the room, back to Joleen's writhing form, determined to bring the girl's agony to an end.

"Joleen," she soothed. "I need to look at you and see if the baby is all right."

The girl stopped tossing her head back and forth and whimpered her understanding.

"Pat's with me, Joleen. He knows a lot about childbirth. I'd like him to stay if . . ."

"I don't care, just help me," she moaned. As Rivalree's hand touched her knees, she willingly allowed them to drift apart.

Surprised by the woman's easy acceptance of the man, Rivalree hesitated for a moment. *But I'm not the one suffering*, she chided herself. *Perhaps I wouldn't act any different if it were me.*

Her examination found nothing out of the ordinary. The child still rode high in its mother's body.

"It's like I said, colleen. There's not much we can do, except give her time."

Time. The one thing she had in short supply. "Then you think it will be a while before the baby comes."

Pat cocked his head. "Could be hours, but then it's hard to tell. Anything might happen."

"Pat," she said, taking his weathered hands in hers. "Here is what I would like to do."

Before she could finish her thoughts Mace tumbled down the stairs. "Nothin', Miz Rivalree. No sign of the huntin' party."

Together, she and Pat stepped away from Joleen's bed.
From the corner of her eyes she could see the Irishman
studying her. *He knows what I want to do.*

"It's time to organize a search party. Pick three of the
best woodsmen, Mace, and we'll leave in a half hour."

"*We*, ma'am?" Mace's brows lifted in disbelief.

"That's correct. We."

"But, ma'am, I don't think it's wise for you . . ."

"Let it be, Mace," Pat interjected. "If the colleen wants
to go, you have no authority to stop her."

Surprised, Rivalree whirled to see if the old man's
support of her position was in earnest. "Thank you, Pat,"
she murmured, still somewhat skeptical that he would
take her side.

Mace drifted away to see to the gathering of supplies for
the rescue party. She turned her attention to Joleen, as
the girl began writhing on the bed. Chanting words of
encouragement, she stroked the damp hair and forehead.
The suffering of childbirth seemed harsh and cruel. Why
did women go through this pain again and again?
Yesterday she had envied the pregnant woman's condition. Now, she didn't.

The contraction eased, and Joleen's sobbing breath
slowed, too. As her eyes opened and focused on Rivalree,
gratitude was clearly visible in her gaze.

"Joleen," Rivalree whispered, leaning forward,
"Braven still has not returned."

The girl's head dipped once in understanding.

"We must look for them." She paused as the girl's eyes
fastened on her. "I need to go with the search party."

Joleen's stare implored, yet she never uttered a sound.

"Pat is here. He can help you. He has witnessed many
child come into this world." She drew the Irishman into
the circle of the girl's vision, and rising, settled him in the
chair beside the bed.

321

Rivalree eased away though she could sense the girl's silent pleading.

"Rivalree," Joleen called, her voice hoarse with pain.

She stilled, praying in her heart the girl wouldn't ask her to stay. If she made such a request, she wasn't sure what her answer would be. Braven or Joleen, which would she choose? Which obligation pulled stronger? She squared her shoulder and faced the prone woman.

"God go with you," she breathed.

Rivalree's shoulders slumped in relief. "Thank you, Joleen. God be with you, too."

The girl smiled weakly.

Something lurched in her heart. It was as if their words were a final farewell. What an inane thought. Women had babies every day. Joleen would be fine. She pinned her attention on the preparation for the outing as the girl began to whimper with the beginning of another labor pain.

A half hour later, wrapped in her warmest coat, her feet stuffed in three pairs of woolen socks inside her sturdiest shoes, her hand encased in a pair of Braven's gloves at least three sizes too big, she checked the supplies strapped to the backs of the men. They were as prepared as possible. It was time to leave.

Her hand cupped the newel post. The remaining men uttered good-byes and good lucks to the departing group as they ascended the stairs.

Reaching the first landing, the ramification of her actions beat frantically inside her stomach. What if they didn't find the hunting party? What if they got lost, as well? Her heart drummed in rhythm to her queasy middle. The possibilities were too numerous to consider.

Glancing down at Pat, the unreadable expression on his face puzzled her. His eyes sparkled, gleamed with excitement. Then he hooded them, and she assured herself she had to have misread him. He was worried, that was all.

Concerned for her, and for Braven and for Joleen.

The men below her on the steps shuffled in impatience, their bodies heating in the enveloping clothing they wore. Why did she hesitate? Was she afraid of facing the elements? Or was she frightened to confront the truth that waited for her on the outside? If she found Braven dead . . . The vision sent her heart tumbling to the pit of her stomach.

Refusing to succumb to her fears, she renewed her convictions to lead this search party and marched up the stairs.

"Rivalree!"

The pain-inflicted call ripped through her.

"You can't leave me. I cannot have this child alone."

"Joleen," she breathed, frustration and relief battling inside her. Elbowing her way down the steps, she approached the frightened girl. She knelt beside the bed, looking up once at Pat, who frowned in response. "Joleen," she repeated, taking her hand. "I need to go."

"I need you to stay," Joleen retorted. "Please, Rivalree. I tried to keep my fears to myself, but it's impossible. I need your help."

Rivalree's head dipped in acquiescence. Taking one final glance at the line of men on the stairs, she waved them on. "All right, Joleen. I'll remain with you."

Tears trickled down the girl's angular face.

She stood, her hands clasped tightly before her. "Mace," she called. "Bring Braven home to me."

The man stared down at her from the top landing. "I'll do my best, Miz Rivalree. Don't worry. We'll find him."

Pat's gnarled hand covered hers. "'Tis probably best this way, colleen. The men can move much faster without a woman along."

"Perhaps you're right," she answered with a sigh, but whether of relief or longing, she wasn't sure. She watched the last man of the search party step through the bedroom

323

door and close it softly behind him.

Everything will be all right, she told herself with a lift of her chin. *Braven will be home for Christmas. Joleen's baby will be born then, too.*

Slipping off her coat and gloves, she lowered herself back into the chair to wait, her heart knocking savagely against her ribs, her resolve keeping her breath deep and even.

"Push, Joleen. Don't give up. The baby's nearly here."

With her elbow Rivalree brushed sweat-dampened hair from her forehead and watched, fascinated, as the tiny, wriggling form struggled forward. Then as if a magic button had been pressed, the infant rushed from its mother's protective womb into her waiting hands.

"Joleen," she said in wonderment. "You've done it." Taking the clean towel Pat offered her, she dried the squalling newborn, then wrapped it in a blanket.

"My baby," Joleen whimpered, her arms outstretched and shaking with fatigue. "I want to hold—" She looked up, questioning.

"Her," Rivalree supplied. "You had a little girl."

"A daughter. Judd and I have a . . ." The girl's face reddened as she glanced at Rivalree.

"It's all right, Joleen." Rivalree placed the now placid child in her mother's arms and gazed in awe as Joleen inspected each and every part of her: hands, feet, ears, and face.

"She's perfect," Joleen cooed. "A Christmas child. I shall name her Christina."

The tiny face screwed, and a wail of unbelievable volume erupted from the infant.

Christmas. Rivalree's eyes shot to the mantel clock. It was Christmas morning and still no sign of the hunting or of the search party. Where were they? Why were they not back?

She twisted the lap of her skirt into a ball wanting nothing more than to race up the stairs and out the window into the snow calling Braven's name. Instead she glanced around the ill-lit room at the other occupants. Very few had rested this Christmas Eve, and the lack of sleep registered on tired faces.

The baby's cries ended as abruptly as they began, the silence bringing Rivalree's attention back to the bed. Mother and child both slept, nestled nose to nose, a deceptive picture of tranquility.

Her mind moved sluggishly, thoughts slipping away before she had a chance to grasp them. For two nights she'd not closed her eyes except in short snatches. Exhaustion tugged at her red-rimmed lids, but she couldn't sleep, not until she knew Braven was safe.

"Come, colleen, you need some rest." Pat touched her shoulder.

Her chin snapped up from its perch on her chest. "No. Not until my husband is home."

"It's several hours until daybreak. The men won' attempt to return until the sun is up. Come. A few hours sleep will do you good," he urged.

Her mind struggled against the Irishman's insistenc yet her body followed willingly as he led her to the bed Fully clothed she dropped across the coverlet, the fain scent on Braven's pillow filling her senses and sending he thoughts plummeting into incoherent dreams of her lyin in his arms, his lips against hers.

Persistent wailing penetrated Rivalree's sleep-drugge mind. For reasons she couldn't quite put her finger on, sh struggled to awaken. A sense of guilt bombarded he reproach for falling asleep in the first place. But why?

Braven. She jerked up so quickly her head spun. Her fee hit the floor with a soft thud. Glancing down sh discovered her shoes placed neatly beside the bed, onl socks covering her icy toes.

How long had she slept? Her eyes darted to the timepiece on the mantel. Nine o'clock. Morning or evening? A fire roared in the hearth as if someone had recently refueled it, yet a glimpse at the lone window in the room revealed darkness. Had she lost an entire day? Dear God, where was Braven? She clasped her hands over her ears. Why didn't Joleen console her crying child?

She stumbled toward the curtained bed where the mother and child lay and pushed back the barrier. Joleen struggled to lift herself up and bring the sobbing infant to her breast. The sounds she made could only be described as motherly little coos and gurgles as she gave her babe the nourishment it demanded.

"Joleen," she whispered, clinging to the bedpost.

The girl glanced up, a radiant smile of joy parting her lips as she suckled her child.

Something lurched inside Rivalree at the sight, a desire to have a little one of her own to cuddle. Confused by her feelings, Rivalree turned away, trying to combat the hollow sensation lurking in her heart, yet the smacking sounds Christina made kept the images of Joleen fresh in her mind. Pain brought love and joy, she realized. She shook her head in agitated denial. Yet as she considered that everything in her life she cherished, including Braven, had come to have meaning only after suffering hardship and agony, she accepted the truth of her words.

"Rivalree, are you all right?"

Twisting, she faced Joleen. "Yes, of course. How long did I sleep?"

"Not long, only a couple of hours."

"It's still morning?" She glanced again toward the kitchen window seeking signs of daylight.

"Yes, of course." Curiosity tainted Joleen's voice.

"Then why is it still so dark?" She whirled, probing each corner of the room. "Where are the remaining men?"

"I'm not sure."

Panic brewed in the pit of her stomach, churning and bubbling until she couldn't swallow. The darkness outside, the empty room, bode ill. Anxious, she glanced again at the clock.

"Look, Rivalree," Joleen murmured. "Isn't she beautiful?"

Tearing her eyes from the mantel, she glanced over at the other woman. The sleeping child curled in the crook of her mother's arm, an innocent cherub, still smacking her lips in satisfaction.

Rivalree's heart melted. "She's the most perfect child I've ever seen," she agreed.

Joleen looked down and traced Christina's downy face with a thumb. "There's something I have to tell you. Something I've needed to say for a long time."

Sensing the girl's distress, Rivalree offered her full attention. "You needn't thank me, Joleen. You would have helped me had the situation been reversed."

"I do thank you. You chose to stay with me rather than look for . . ." She choked, unable to complete her sentence.

Rivalree reached out and took Joleen's hand in hers. "No need for guilty tears. You were scared. I understand."

"No you don't. When I came looking for Judd, I knew about you. I figured you would be here. He told me you were coming to California to marry him. Aware my presence would cause an upheaval, I came anyway. I didn't care about you or what you would feel seeing me large with his child." She stuffed her clinched fist in her mouth stifling a sob.

"Joleen, that doesn't matter now."

"Yes, it does. You have to know. There was never nothin' between me and Judd, just a companionship. He spoke constantly about you, and before I learned to care for you, I envied you, hated your very existence. I thought perhaps, if I let Judd—no, I encouraged him," she said venomously. "Maybe he'd forget you and learn to love me instead." She hung her head, long suppressed guilt

327

misting her eyes.

Rivalree released a pent-up sigh. "Oh, Joleen. Don't you understand? Judd is behind me now. There's only Braven for me. I don't begrudge what you had with Judd. Knowing Judd and meeting you, perhaps he did come to love you. You are the kind of woman he needed. I was always too headstrong, too . . ."

"Do you really think so?" Joleen's eyes glimmered with hope.

"I do." She rose, the fears that had been festering since she'd awoken coming to the surface.

"Rivalree," Joleen reached up and touched her arm. "There's one more thing. If anything should happen to me . . . Christina. Please take care of her. She should have been yours all along."

"How foolish, Joleen. Nothing's going to happen to you. Your child is born and you are fine."

"Please, just say you'll take care of her."

Rivalree paused, seeing the sincere request in the other woman's face. "Of course. As if she were my flesh and blood."

Joleen fell back against the pillow and closed her eyes.

The clammer of booted feet upstairs brought Rivalree to her feet. Dear God, the men were back.

Snow-covered forms stumbled down the stairs. Mace Lockman. Dan Butler. The seach party. She studied each figure emerging from the bedroom door. Braven? Where was he?

Mace halted at the foot of the steps, clutching the newel post, his breath coming in deep gasps.

"Mace. Please. Did you find him?" Her pulse sputtered and stilled.

"I'm sorry, Miz Rivalree. Nary a sign, and the snow is comin' down harder than ever."

A light-headed feeling sent her mind soaring. "Braven," she mouthed, her throat so tight she couldn't utter a sound. "God in heaven, I have lost him."

Chapter Twenty-Three

Braven slapped his arms with his hands and hunched a little closer to the snapping fire. Observing the four men with him, each a huddled form with nothing showing but eyes, red cheeks, and nose, he suppressed the shudder winding his spine like a watch stem. The cold was almost unbearable. He glanced up, checking out the godsent shelter they had stumbled on yesterday as the snow had encased them in blinding eddies. The ground dipped at the roots of the giant spruce tree and the bottom limbs formed a natural roof over their heads, keeping the snow and the wind out, but, unfortunately, retaining the choking smoke of the small fire he had managed to build and keep going over the long hours.

It was as if some strong, immortal force had led them to this particular spot. What he had discovered as they had stumbled into the hollow left a chilling fear embedded in the pit of his stomach. Jack Quincy's body—a bullet lodged in his chest. Quincy, the man who had supposedly left the camp last fall in a hurry, according to Pat who had gotten the information from Jacobs.

Braven's gaze shot to that man across from him now, as cool as an icicle, Jacob's stare didn't flinch as their eyes met. Had Hank Jacobs been the man responsible for the deaths and accidents plaguing the mining camp all year? Though the evidence indicated the possibility, there was no way for him to be sure.

The only thing he could be certain of was that whoever wanted him out of the way was still among them. He could never let his guard down again, not until spring return. Pushing ice-ladened branches out of his way, he glanced beyond the shelter, watching the whirling, white flakes slant to the ground. *If* he managed to survive this ordeal and lead his men back to the protection of the cabin.

The limb snapped into place as he released it and settled back on his haunches. What a horrible way to spend Christmas. He would gladly eat beans and salt pork for the rest of his life if only he could return unscathed to Rivalree before the day was out.

Rivalree. The thought of her soft body clinging to his warmed him. Was she frightened? She should know him well enough to realize he was safe and waiting for the right moment to return.

Jesus, he wished the storm would let up. They weren't that far from home, maybe an hour at the most. He had planned this day, Christmas, with the utmost care, and now, because he had rashly gone off hunting to satisfy a selfish whim, the day was ruined. The toboggan he'd constructed with the help of all his crew sat abandoned in the mine. Their first Christmas together, and Rivalree would remember the holiday as one without him.

"It's over," one of the men declared, pushing up from a squat.

"What?" Braven muttered, pulling his thoughts to the present surroundings.

"Listen, the wind has died down."

Braven pushed to his knees, brushing away the limbs heavy with snow. White flakes drifted in a zigzag pattern like feathers falling from the clouds. "You're right," he exclaimed, examining the gray, low-hung sky. It couldn't be much later than noon, and if they hurried there was still a good portion of the day left. Appointing two of the men to hoist the slung deer on their shoulders, he snuffed out the fire and shouldered one of the packs on his back. With a shout of excitement and a chorus of "Joy to the World" bursting from his throat in a resonant voice, he led the way through the winter wonderland.

"They're back!"

Mace Lockman's trill of exuberance skirted the gloom encompassing Rivalree. For the last four hours she had gone from overwhelming terror to a numbness that had left her mute, unable to cry or express any emotions whatsoever. Braven was lost, and she was again alone. Had she told him she loved him before he left? She couldn't remember. Dear God, how could she have forgotten to tell him how much he meant to her?

Large hands cupped her shoulders and shook hard. "Did you hear me, Miz Rivalree? Braven has returned."

"My husband? Back?" She pushed aside the curtain of shock and forced her mind to function.

"Braven," she cried in a loud, relieved voice as she shoved past Mace and dashed up the stairs. Her feet possessed wings as she raced to the landing and into the bedroom, grabbing her coat hanging on the railing post as she sped by it.

Suspended over the window ledge, she drank in the sight of him directing his men dividing up of the deer into small enough pieces to bring inside. Like a departing passenger on a ship, she leaned lower waving her hand.

"Braven," she called again, nearly tumbling out the window into his uplifted arms.

"Hello, sugar." His smile beamed brighter than the emerging sun. "Merry Christmas."

"Christmas?" She giggled uncontrollably. "Of course

Christmas." She blew him a kiss. "And to you, my love." She remembered the folded sweater slipped under the bed she had made for him. "The merriest of all Christmases to you."

Within minutes he stood beside her, his arm wrapped protectively about her, and she willingly accepted his strength. The laughter of moments before congealed in her throat, choking her, leaving a sob in its wake.

"Dear God, I thought I had lost you," she admitted against the muffle of his jacket, her hands entwining about his neck.

"Oh, ye of little faith," he whispered in the shell of her ear. "Heaven and earth couldn't have kept me from you. Not today, our first Christmas." He swung them about, and with a sweep of his arm he indicated the quartered venison. "See, the mighty hunter has returned bringing an offering to the fair maiden."

His mood was infectious. How could she resist his crooked grin and his shining eyes? How could she have ever withstood his charm? She colored with embarrassment as the crowd of men filling the room waited for her response.

She dipped a curtsy and replied. "How would you like a venison roast with black pudding to celebrate the holiday?"

"Fit for a king," he replied with an exaggerated smack of his lips. "Oh, before I forget." He reached in his breast pocket and pulled out a small packet and placed it in her hands.

The smell of mint and wild garlic wafted upward filling her excited senses. Her eyes widened in disbelief as she carefully unfolded the piece of cloth. "Where did you find these?"

"While sitting under a tree waiting for the storm to end, I discovered these bits of culinary delight beneath a layer of snow."

As if he had showered her with diamonds, she squealed in glee. "Oh, Braven, this is wonderful. We shall have a feast the likes of which we haven't seen in a long time." She threw her arms about him. "I have something for you, as well."

"There's only one thing I want from you, my unpredictable wench," he purred against the column of her throat.

"Braven," she answered, slapping him on the shoulder, aghast at his bold words in front of their gawking audience.

"I promise I will sample your delights before the evening is out." He spoke softly so only she could hear. Still she reddened, but her heart beat wildly in anticipation of his pledge.

Bustling about the stove, Rivalree attended to chores that women for generations have done. But to her, the tasks were brand-new and exciting as the babe nestled next to Joleen. Her first Christmas dinner prepared on her own, for her husband. Even Pat backed off, giving her free rein with the pots and pans.

"I should be helpin' you," Joleen offered weakly as she pushed up from the pillows with a groan.

"Nonsense," Rivalree replied, waving the girl back down.

The painful rush of air that followed her words brought her head around. Joleen's pale face seemed lost on the pillow, her lips bloodless, her eyes sunken in. Perhaps it was normal for a woman to be so . . . feeble after giving birth. Rivalree wished she knew for sure, but her lack of experience in these matters offered no assurance.

Glancing at Pat, she was alarmed to find him watching the new mother, too. But he looked away before she could catch his eye.

I'm being foolish, she thought, placing the cut of venison in a pan and surrounding it with some of the precious wild garlic and mint. *Joleen has gone through a long, tiring ordeal. I can't expect her to jump up and do everything right away.*

Over the heads of the men, she encountered Braven's gaze. He grinned, his eyes sparkling with delight. He was enjoying the tradition of their first holiday together as much as she was.

She wiped her hands on an apron, pushed back stray curls from her forehead, and issued a contented sigh. The roast was on, and it would be a matter of hours before the meal would be ready for consumption. This was as good a time as any to pass out the presents she and Joleen had made for each man in the room.

Without a word, she skirted the arc of chairs and stooped to retrieve the calico-wrapped packages from under Joleen's bed. As she rose, her arms ladened, she managed to give the girl's wrist a squeeze.

Joleen offered a wan smile. "I'd forgotten. Merry Christmas."

Eyes soft with concern, she lifted the top gift and placed it beside her friend. "Merry Christmas, Joleen. Thank you for being here."

She rose and sailed away before the girl could protest and began distributing the gaily wrapped presents among the surprised men.

"Merry Christmas," she chimed as she placed presents in outstretched hands.

"Thank you," each man mumbled, the embarrassment obvious in their voices as they accepted her offering. Even the Irishman was silent, apparently at a loss for words.

Approaching Braven, she smiled shyly, stepped over to their bed, and reached underneath. She pulled out the special package she had slipped there several days ago and placed it in his lap.

334

"Looks as if you've been busy, wife."

"Not just me. Joleen had a hand in making the presents." She cast a sidelong glance at Mace Lockman. "And yours, Mace, Joleen insisted on doing all by herself."

Joleen reddened. So did Mace, but Rivalree could see them peeking at each other from lowered lashes.

"And mine," asked Braven as he untied the string and lifted up the sweater she had spent long hours knitting. "Did you insist on making mine all by yourself?"

"From me to you," she answered softly. "I love you."

The shuffle of feet and the squeak of chairs as the other men opened their gifts broke the spell between them. Excitement crisped the holiday air as they tried on mittens, scarf, or hat, whichever the women had made for them.

Braven stood, pulled his sweater on over his head, and as he straightened cuffs and collar, he grinned down at her. "What do you say, boys. Do you think we should show the ladies their Christmas present?"

Rivalree flushed like a child, caught up in the spirit of giving and receiving. Mace scooped up a protesting Joleen, and though Rivalree could see the telltale signs of pain around the girl's pinched mouth, Joleen never once stopped smiling at the man who held her frail body crushed to his chest.

Minutes later two of the men emerged through the front door dragging a large toboggan behind them.

"Braven," Rivalree chortled, clapping her hands in glee. "What a delightful surprise. When can we try it out?" She hadn't been sliding since she was a child. She turned willful eyes on her husband.

"Why not right now?"

"Now? What about the dinner?" she protested.

"I can keep an eye on the roast," Pat offered.

"But Joleen? This is her present as well. We should wait until she can join us."

"Go, Rivalree," the woman insisted. She looked conten

supported by Mace Lockman's strong arms. "I can go another time. Right now, you try the sled out for me and tell me all about it when you return."

"Are you sure?" Their gazes met and held.

"Of course, you silly goose. Besides, Mace and Pat will keep me company."

Little Christina let out a squall as if protesting that her mother had forgotten her. Laughter sealed Rivalree's decision.

"And Christina. She'll keep me company, too."

Rivalree cast a doubtful look at Braven, then turned to retrieve her coat.

"Rivalree," Joleen called. "The leggin's. They're perfect. Thank you."

With a flashing grin, she shrugged on her coat and captured Braven's arm. "I'm ready."

Braven grabbed her about the waist as she preceded him up the stairs. "I challenge you to a bet. I'll get this toboggan going so fast you'll beg me to stop."

"No, never," she countered. "I was the fastest sledder in my village when I was a little girl. You'll never beat me." Squeaking a protest, she darted up the steps avoiding his swatting palm.

How quickly things change. Hours ago, she'd thought her life was at an end, and now she was on top of the world.

The light sled skimmed over the well-chosen course like melting butter slid down a hot skillet. With a carefree laugh, the likes of which he hadn't known since childhood, Braven clutched the lithe figure in front of him tighter when he stuck out his left leg to turn the vehicle as they reached the bottom of the slope. The toboggan spun in the powdery snow sending a shower of crystalline cold over them, and as the coaster came to a sudden stop the world continued whirling as they tumbled from their perch.

They landed in an embarrassing sprawl, Rivalree wedged between his thighs. At that moment he decided she had never looked more enticing, snow dusting her hair and lashes, her hand reaching up to push to wet tendrils from her face, her mouth open in exhilaration as she breathed her delight. How right she felt captured between his knees. His body's response to her pressing warmth confirmed what his imagination demanded. The need to possess her, share in the intimacy of their love, drove rational thoughts from his head.

Rolling in the soft snow, he held her beneath him, a knee planted by each of her thighs, and, much to his surprise, she didn't resist the thorough kiss he pressed on her frost-reddened mouth even when the others approached. In fact, her arms drew him closer. He was tempted to stretch out against her and take her there and then.

Until the lump of icy snow pressed against his exposed neck.

With a roar, he flipped away, reaching behind his head to try and dislodge the snowball stuffed in the collar of his coat. "Rivalree, you little minx, I'll get you for that."

She giggled, flopped on her stomach, and attempted to rise in the slippery white, but only managed to kick loose flakes in his face with her scampering feet.

"Braven, no," she shrieked as he clamped her ankle in his strong grip. She bucked like a wild mare as he tugged her down beside him a grin of calculated revenge curling his lips.

"If it's a snowball fight you want, sugar, you've got it," he boasted, as he draped himself across her chest and formed a clump of snow with his freed hands.

Her eyes sparkled with mischief and she giggled, a

short, nervous sound.

Balancing the missile in one hand, he reached down and began unbuttoning the front of her coat. The impish delight melted to disbelief on her face. "You wouldn't," she dared.

"Wouldn't I?" His gaze glinted devilishly. His fingers came to rest on the swell of her bosom. He raised his hand as if to toss the cold snow down her front, but instead he dropped it to the side. His other hand still molded to her tightening breast, he kissed her instead, his tongue plundering her willing mouth as if he were dying of thirst and she offered relief.

Her hand crept up his sleeve to work its way around his neck, but he caught her arm and pinned it to the ground. "I'm not foolish enough to fall for that trick again," he warned, neatly scooping up a handful of snow and dumping it on her as he jumped to his feet.

"Braven," she sputtered, slapping the cold from her face and chest as she pushed up from the ground.

From his position above her, he laughed, but began backing up, knowing full well she would never let it rest with him one up on her. She would plan her revenge well.

The weight hit him hard from behind, and before he could regain his balance, he fell face first into the deep snow. Multivoiced amusement rippled above him, and as he rolled over to locate his attacker, snow pelted him like bullets.

"No one bullies our Sierra Angel," bellowed Dan Butler, raining more snowballs at Braven's unprotected form. "Not even her husband."

A spurt of laughter followed the declaration, and Braven could single out Rivalree's higher-pitched giggle as he protected his face in his gloved hands. "Does this mean my crew is committing mutiny?" he demanded as he gathered ammunition.

"In the fullest sense, sir," Rivalree replied, emerging

boldly from the circle of men. "Your men have found they prefer my genteel ways instead of your heavy hand."

"Heavy-handed by all means," chuckled one of the men.

"The cruelest of bosses," jested another. "We demand fair treatment."

The circle closed tighter around him, and he bided his time. He would get that minx for her actions. Waiting until the second was right, he twisted, showering snowballs at the group above him. A hail of return fire rained down on him, but he worked his way to where his rebellious wife stood, poised for flight.

Her shriek of protesting merriment was like music to his ears when he brought her tumbling down in the snow in front of him. How fortunate he was to have such a woman. The flying snowballs never let up and soon he found himself protecting her as well from the volleys of cold, wet rockets. Her arms entwined about his neck, she laughingly huddled beneath his larger form, letting him take the brunt of the assault.

"Coward," he whispered as a well-aimed missile knocked his hat from his head.

"Not at all," she countered, drawing him closer, oblivious to the men about them. "I would say I was rather smart to let you suffer the worst of the attack."

"Think so?"

She nodded, wariness creeping into her gaze.

Scooping her up, he turned them about, leaving her exposed to the myriad of snowballs. Squealing her protest, she plummeted his chest with her fists.

"Rivalree. Braven," lilted a faraway voice.

The playful antics ceased, and Braven lifted them to a sitting position. The crowd parted as he cupped his hand around his mouth and shouted, "What is it, Pat. We're over in the pasture."

"It's the girl and her babe."

Rivalree jumped to her feet. "Joleen. No, it can't be."

Fear rang sharply in her voice. Without hesitating she ran toward the cabin.

"Rivalree, wait," Braven called, pulling his feet beneath him and following her. "I'm sure Joleen is fine."

"You don't understand," she said, never slowing her pace. "She knew something was going to happen. I must be with her. I promised."

She scurried toward the building, never once looking back. A profound sadness invaded his heart, whispering an ominous message. Words of doom he had no desire to hear set his heart to racing.

The smell of the mint-basted venison invaded Rivalree's senses as she made her way down the stairs. The sound of Christina wailing incessantly brought her to a halt on the bottom landing.

"Joleen?" she called, fearing no response.

"Rivalree" came the barely audible reply, the pain evident in the hoarsely spoken word.

Throwing off coat and gloves, and shoving aside the memory of the joyous hour she had spent with Braven in the snow, she drew a chair beside the bed where Joleen lay. Beads of perspiration dotted the girl's blotted face. Shivers rocked the thin body as if an earthquake resided deep in the fever-racked limbs. What malady struck so quickly?

"Child-birthin' fever."

She whipped her head around to find Pat standing close behind her.

"Puerperal fever? But that can be fatal," she breathed. She lifted the squalling baby and cradled her to her chest, cooing softly.

His elfin face screwed tight and his chin dipped once. "I know. Carrie's mother died from it."

"Are you sure that's what Joleen has?" Her eyes pleaded with him to deny his words as her rocking arms stilled.

340

Christina began whimpering.

"The symptoms are right. I don't know what else it could be."

She brought the child to her lips and laid a kiss on her down-soft cheek. Christina needed her mother. "What do we do?" she asked, helplessly. "There must be some way of stopping her from . . ." She stuffed her knuckles in her mouth. She had almost said dying.

Pat shook his head. "The fever must run its course. All we can do is wait—and pray."

"God wouldn't be so cruel," she protested under her breath, rising to her feet in order to bounce the still unhappy infant. "Your mother will be fine soon. You'll see," she crooned to the child, needing to reassure herself as much as Christina.

Within minutes the baby slept peacefully and Rivalree laid her alongside her mother. She wouldn't give up. Joleen couldn't die, not when she had so much to live for now.

Stifling a sob of frustration as much as sorrow, she stumbled away from the angelic picture the slumbering mother and child made. Braven met her in the middle of the room, his broad chest offering comfort as she buried her face in the warm flannel of his shirt. She clung to him, absorbing his strength and quiescence, wanting so much to explain how she felt. "I can't let her die. Not now."

"You've done your best, sugar. You can't blame yourself. It's up to Joleen to come through this on her own. All you can do is be there if she needs you."

Lifting her chin, she gazed into his worry-specked eyes. Perhaps there was good reason to find the fault within herself. Reasons Braven knew nothing about.

"Please, Joleen. Try."

Rivalree urged the girl to take another sip of the clea▸

venison broth she held to her cracked lips. "For Christina. She needs you."

The thin soup dribbled down Joleen's chin to join the puddle forming on the coverlet. With a sound of frustration Rivalree sat down the cup and lowered the slim, fevered body back down on the pillow. It was no use. Joleen grew weaker by the hour. Where once she'd spoken coherently now she moaned and begged forgiveness from unknown people.

Rivalree sniffed the air. A strange stench fouled the room near the bed, evidence of the infection eroding the dying woman's insides. Fear gripped her heart and twisted. If Joleen should succumb to this illness, what would become of Christina?

Her gaze riveted to the tiny figure, now lying peacefully in the crate Braven had pulled from the storage room and lined with blankets. She had seen the compassion in his eyes as he had observed the helpless little creature, but would he accept the child into the circle of their love to become part of them, a child perhaps not of their bodies but of their hearts? He would have to; she had promised Joleen. And though she had made the pledge light-heartedly without realizing the implications of what she agreed to, she would keep her word. Christina would be raised as if she were flesh of her flesh.

An overwhelming need to hug the child to her bosom shot like an arrow into her heart, but she held her body, as well as the maternal instincts growing steadily inside her, in check. Christina belonged firstly to Joleen, and needed her mother's protection above all other, including herself.

"Rivalree."

Her name spoken so softly as if the wind had formed the word startled her. Joleen's gaze, though misted and far away, held hers with steady determination.

"Christina, where is she?"

She touched the girl's limp fingers, shaken by the

lifeless iciness of them. "She's fine. The men made her a cozy crib out of a crate. You'll see once you get better."

"I need to see her now—one last time."

"No, Joleen, don't say that." She placed her fingertips against the dry lips. "Don't give up."

Joleen didn't resist. Her lids lowered once over her doe-brown eyes and lay there twitching as if refusing to obey the command to reopen. "Please, bring me my baby," she pleaded wearily.

Lifting the sleeping bundle, Rivalree's arms ached with longing as she placed the child gently into the crook of her mother's arm. She waited, breath held. Was she too late? Relieved, she detected the slight rise and fall of the girl's chest, the only evidence that life still battled to remain in the thin body.

Her eyes opened, and a frail hand pushed back the swaddling blanket from the baby's cherubic face. "She's beautiful, isn't she."

A sob lodged in Rivalree's throat. "Yes," she eked out.

"She will be a beautiful woman when she grows."

"Oh, yes. Absolutely." Grief roughened her voice, but Joleen didn't seem to notice.

"What do you think she'll be?"

"What do you want her to become?" Tears leaked from her saddened eyes.

Joleen's gaze locked with hers. "I want her to do whatever makes her happiest."

The pain in her throat kept her answer mute. She could only nod in agreement.

Gathering the baby in her arms, Joleen offered her up to Rivalree. "You have so much. Don't let your pride get in your way." As the child left her mother's fingers to lie in the secure clutch of her protector, Joleen sighed, the sound as tiny yet final as a faraway bugle playing taps.

"Joleen," she keened. "Dear God, Joleen."

The shuffle of feet invaded her grieving as the others

gathered around them.

"I'm sorry, my love," Braven said, kneeling beside her and gathering her close to his heart.

Sobbing, she raised Christina, almost as if the child were a sacrificial lamb. "She's ours now, Braven. Joleen gave her to me. I must see that this child comes to no harm, ever. I promised Joleen."

Pity and pain radiated from his eyes. Was he refusing to accept the baby? Dear God, no. She wasn't sure she could forgive him if he turned his back on her newly discovered joy.

Chapter Twenty-Four

For two days Braven watched Rivalree's unending determination begin to flag. How could he tell her she wasted her energy? Without maternal nourishment, even if they'd been lucky enough to have a milking cow or goat, the baby's chances of survival were thin, at best. He didn't have the heart to hurt her so, though he knew deep inside the loss would be much harder for her to bear when the child died.

"Rivalree." He reached out his hand and caught her arm.

Hours before, Christina's lusty wails had turned to weak whimpers. The child lay limply in the crook of her arm, barely sucking on the improvised nipple soaked in venison broth, the only form of nourishment available.

Her eyes met his, defiant, daring him to say the words they both knew he thought. He couldn't destroy her last ray of hope.

"Give her to me. Let me try," he insisted, reaching out for the baby.

She clutched the child tighter, almost fearing to turn her over to his care.

Did she think him capable of doing the infant harm? He renewed his efforts to relieve her of her burden. "Please?"

he asked, pain and pity gripping his heart.

Accepting the child from her reluctant arms, he began rocking it in imitation of the way Rivalree had done hour upon hour for the last two days. She dogged his steps, and though his patience wore thin, he said nothing to her, allowing her to inspect his every movement as he pressed the bit of broth-soaked cloth into the baby's mouth and watched its pitiful attempt to nurse.

His heart contracted, feeling a moment of agony for the doomed infant and a large surge of love and respect for his wife. Someday it would be their own offspring she would coddle and protect, and that child would be the luckiest in the world to have her as a mother. He wanted so much to share his feelings, but now was not the time. She wouldn't understand, but would think he rejected Christina.

Finally, Rivalree's stiff shoulders relaxed, and she took a seat by the fire. The child fell into a fitful sleep, and Braven placed her in the makeshift cradle on the chair near where she sat. How much longer before they placed the tiny body next to its mother in the shallow grave in the mine? As he watched Rivalree's head nod in mindless exhaustion, he feared for her heatlh, both mental and physical. Dear God, let her be strong enough to accept the demands of fate.

Rivalree drifted in a tiny boat, the rise and fall of the ocean lulling her, tempting her to forget all the problems that bore down on her with the weight of the earth upon Atlas's shoulders. For days she had snatched moments of restless sleep wherever she could, until she'd forgotten what it felt like to sleep in a real bed. Somewhere in the distance a tiny voice called to her, begging her for help. Or was it only hiccuping wails she heard?

Crying? Her head snapped up. Christina. Thoughts of the child tore her from her dreams. She found herself in her bed, the curtain carefully drawn in privacy, her dress

346

folded on the edge of the coverlet.

"Hush, hush, little one." Braven's deep baritone reached her ears. The rhythmic squeak of the rocker joined his voice, and the baby's wails quieted to little, pitiful catches. "You mustn't awaken Rivalree. She needs her rest."

Creak. Creak. The rocker moved back and forth. "I wish life could be easier for you, punkin." Then he let out a great rush of air and continued with the nonsensical cooing a parent makes to a beloved child.

Rivalree blinked in the darkness. Braven did care for Christina. How could she have so misjudged him? With guilt, she thought back on tired moments when she had felt it might be best if the baby didn't survive. But Braven wanted and loved Christina as much as she did. Now, more than ever, it was important the baby thrive and fill the empty spot in both of their hearts.

Rising, she drew on her dress and pushed back the curtain. She spied Braven, his head resting on the rocker's backrail, his eyes closed in weariness. The wrapped bundle lying in his arms could only be Christina, silent and unmoving.

She tiptoed across the floor, one board bowing in loud protest as she stepped on it. Breath held, she paused, hoping she hadn't awakened any of the sleeping figures in the room.

Reaching the quiet pair in the rocking chair, she leaned over and peered down into Christina's face. The sweet smell of newborn drifted up to fill her nostrils. So still and doll-like she lay, one tiny fist pressed to her mouth. Lifting the bundle from Braven's curved arm, intending on placing her back in her cradle, Rivalree brought the miniature face to her lips. She paused, her mouth caressing the baby's forehead. Something was wrong. Bringing the child back into view, she studied her. Nothing moved, not her eyelids, nor lips. The small hand

347

dropped limply against the blanket wrapped around her.

A whimper of protest formed in the back of her throat. "No, not now." Her eyes shot upward. "You cannot take her now." She hugged the lifeless body to her heart as she cried out her angry protest.

Braven stirred, his arm seeking the burden of the child he had held. His head lifted, and he met her tear-filled eyes with confused ones. "Rivalree, what's wrong?"

She settled on the floor, her hands working frantically to remove the blanket around Christina. "Please, baby, wake up. Cry for me," she sobbed.

As Braven took the lifeless child from her, she wanted to scream angry words at him. She hurt deep inside and needed someone to feel the agony tearing her apart. Instead she directed the accusation inwardly. All of the horrible things that had happened were her fault. Her inability to be truthful, not only with herself but with her husband, had caused first Joleen and now Christina to die. God punished her through the lives of others innocent of her sins.

She crammed her vacant palms against her ears and rocked in silent mourning, memories of Silas Guntree clawing at her clothing and the distasteful words thrown at her afterward by the women of Charity crowding down against her aching head. She had been a coward to run then, unable to face up to the truth about herself. And upon reaching San Francisco, she had continued her uncourageous flight and had accepted the easy route of escape—marriage to Braven Blackwood.

Her gaze shot up to find him staring down at her, a helpless pain registering on his beloved features. How could she have used him so cruelly?

He knelt beside her and drew her to his broad expanse of chest. It would be so easy to crumble and let him erase the burden of her many transgressions. It would be so simple to continue to live the falsehood that bridged the roaring stream separating them. But she couldn't. If she wanted the disasters to stop, the horrible waste of innocent lives to end, she had to tell him the truth about her past. Now, before God saw fit to destroy him as well. She was a woman raped by a vile man, soiled and tainted, unfit to be a wife to anyone.

She dragged herself from his embrace and pushed up to her feet. "You don't know, Braven," she choked. "You can't understand. This is all my fault."

Shoving him away, she raced toward the front door and threw herself onto the enclosed porch, to crumple into a pitiful heap.

"We need to talk." Braven's eyes caressed the huddled figure of his wife. She was taking the death of the infant much harder than he had imagined.

Her tear-streaked face lifted, and his heart shattered into uncountable pieces at the agony he saw residing there.

"Rivalree," he said softly, bending down to clasp her shoulders and bring her to her feet. "How could you possibly think that you are responsible for what has happened?"

"I have lied, Braven. Cheated everyone of the truth, especially you." She glanced down, shame clouding her amber eyes.

He quirked his brow in surprise. What could she have lied about that could have caused such disasters? Nothing. She was too good and gentle and caring. Placing a curved finger under her chin, he raised her face until she had no choice except to look at him. "Be reasonable, sugar. Whatever it is, it's not as horrible as you think."

"But it is. You don't know." She spun away.

Grasping her shoulders, he whirled her back around. "Try me."

Uncertainty leapt into her stare. She swallowed hard.

Whatever she had to tell him took all of her courage. "I did not come a virgin to your bed."

Of all things for her to say, that statement took him by surprise, threw him off guard. Had she lost her mind? What nonsense was this she babbled? His brows angled in a frown. "Whatever are you talking about, woman?"

"The slave hunter. Silas Guntree." Her words fairly tumbled over themselves. "The men who murdered my parents. I . . ."

"You gave yourself to him?" he asked incredulously.

"No. Not gave. Not willingly. He forced himself upon me."

"Are you saying you were raped?" He shook his head bewildered. Remembering that first night in the wagon with her, she had been untouched. Of that one fact, he was positive. Why was she telling him this wild story?

"He pushed me down. Tore my clothes. I hit my head on a rock. I don't remember much else except the women telling me what had happened."

"And you believed what they told you? For all of this time you have taken their word as fact?"

"Don't you understand, Braven. I am not what you think I am. I came to you soiled, the leavings of another man, if you can call him that."

He frowned, perplexed. Did she think he was some kind of ogre? What reaction did she expect from him? "What do you want me to say?"

She swayed, chaos fusing her features until he could no longer read the emotions playing across her face. "What any decent man would do. Punish me, toss me to the side, but, please, don't stand there staring at me. Do whatever you're going to do and get it over with."

He reached out. She flinched as if he would strike her. His hand drifted back to his side, curling and uncurling in anger.

Not at her. She was a victim and wasn't even aware of it.

But at all those unknowns, slave hunters and village women, especially those old biddies, who had left their scars deep in her soul.

"What if I was to tell you that you are wrong?"

Her brows furled; her chin lifted with defiant spunk. "Why would you taunt me that way? I have learned to live with the truth, so must you." She whirled and marched back into the cabin, leaving him standing there, disoriented.

She believed a bunch of damned old busybodies over him. Then she categorized him as a man who would be so insensitive as to actually blame her for what had happened. If it had happened, which it hadn't. A sound of frustration slipped past his lips as he shook his head. How was he to deal with such stubborn single-mindedness?

Rivalree sat before the crackling fire, rocking, her hands lying idle in her lap. The loneliness was unbearable. Even the comfort of Joleen's and Christina's graves were denied her. Braven insisted she remain in the cabin, declaring it was for her own safety, while he and the men renewed their efforts working the mine. He could not have condemned her to a worse punishment. Why would he forbid her that one source of solace unless he thought to give her ample time to repent her sins? How could he be so cruel as to leave her alone, day in and day out, isolated from any human contact?

She lowered her head into her hands. Was this a prelude of what her life would be like with Braven? Or would he, once the snow melted and freed them, desert her? Either alternative would be hell in itself. She must take matters into hand, and decide her destiny for herself. But there was only one choice she could make. Leave Braven on her own accord, something she found impossible to even consider. She needed him and the love he had once offered her.

Perhaps if she tried one more time, he would forgive her and make matters right between them.

Moving to the stove, she checked the meal in progress. With quick strokes she stirred the stewed venison, her nose wrinkling in distaste. Now weeks into the new year, the idea of eating deer meat was as unappetizing as salt pork. If spring didn't arrive soon, she would go stark raving mad.

The mantel clock chimed, and Rivalree counted the bells with eager anticipation. Six o'clock. The men would return at any moment. She wiped her hands on a dish towel and touched her hair checking for stray curls, then ran her palms down her dress front attempting to remove the creases.

Straightening, she rushed to the front door and waited, anxious as a neglected pup for Braven's return. Tonight would be different. He would sweep her into his arms and tell her how much he loved her and that he didn't care about her past. Oh God, if only he would.

As the men filed through, she scanned over their heads for a sign of her husband. His blond head, inches higher than any of the others, popped into view, and she had to hold her arms rigid to keep them from reaching out to him.

Their eyes locked and held as he approached. She tried to smile, but her mouth refused to do more than work nervously. For a moment she thought she saw a spark of something, a reminder of the man she had come to love, then his gaze grew formal. His smile was perfunctory, a mere shadow of feeling. Cold and uncaring, his mouth touched her cheek in a whisper of a kiss, if she could call the gesture by such a kind name.

"Good evening, Rivalree," he stated with as much emotion as a wagon wheel contacting with a dusty road.

"Braven," she answered in the same calculated tone. "Dinner will be ready in a few moments." Her fingers gripped her thighs; unshed tears stung the back of her throat. *He can barely tolerate my presence. How could I ever think the love lost between us would return?*

Lifting her chin, she turned her back on the man who held her very essence in his hand and didn't seem to care. She desired his love and yearned for a child, but if she couldn't have those things, then she demanded her freedom.

Spring couldn't come fast enough. As soon as the roads were passable she would demand to be taken to La Porte. From there she would make her own way. She would begin her life again, and never, never would she tell another soul the sins of her past. Braven's rejection had taught her one thing. She was responsible to no one but herself.

"What is it, me boyo?"

Braven twisted, tearing his gaze from the snow-hung bushes that sparkled in the setting sun as though someone had tossed a handful of diamonds in their midst. Closing the bedroom window, he leaned back against the sill and crossed his arms over his chest. He studied Pat O'Grady, criticizing himself for doubting the man who had never once given him a reason to suspect him. But suspicion haunted him nonetheless, not only of the Irishman, but of every man who shared the cabin with him. Someone had murdered Jack Quincy as well as Judd, and that person wouldn't stop until he was dead. That was why he kept all of the men occupied, insisting they return to work the mine. There he could keep an eye on them as well as avoid Rivalree's self-righteous condemnation. She refused to hear what he had to say. He had every right to be frustrated by her inability to trust him.

He chuckled softly as he shook his head. "Am I that obvious, Pat?"

"I know ya well, Braven. I can read the worry in your eyes."

"Jack Quincy."

Pat's brows furled. "The man who left last fall. What about him?"

"I ran across him when we were lost in the storm."

"How could you have seen him? I would have bet my bottom dollar he was enjoying a warm, cozy room in Marysville about now."

Braven searched for an uncomfortable reaction from the other man—darting eyes, worried mouth—but Pat stared back, a look of bewildered disbelief slashed across his face. "I found him hastily buried under a tree—a bullet in his chest."

"Jack Quincy? Are you sure? I swear one of the men, I think Jacobs, told me he saw Quincy leave the camp."

"Jacobs says he knows nothing about it."

Pat stared him straight in the eyes, his glare never flinching. "Jacobs told me different last fall."

Braven looked away. "That doesn't matter now. I'm watching every man in this camp. I can't trust anyone."

"By all that's holy man. I don't blame ya. If I was in your place, I'd even suspect you." The Irishman grinned and slapped him on the back.

The tension inside him ebbed away, rounding the edge of doubt for the old man with it. He could trust him. "Thanks, Pat, for understanding. Help me keep an eye on the others, will you?"

"You got it, my boyo. Relax. You know you can always count on me."

If only he could make Rivalree understand the situation, maybe he could ease up on both of them. Being cooped up in this tiny cabin with all these men was reason enough for anyone to behave strangely, and he sometimes wondered at his logic for bringing her up to the mine in the first place.

With a sigh of acceptance of what he couldn't change, he gripped the older man's shoulder and headed out of the empty bedroom. He knew without a doubt once he got Rivalree out of this environment, took her home to Louisiana, and settled her into a genteel life, she would feel differently. She would come to realize how much he cared for her.

Squaring his shoulders, he descended the stairs prepared to face the icy reception she would give him. Spring couldn't come fast enough to suit him.

Chapter Twenty-Five

April 15, 1852

With the inevitability of the seasons, spring thawed the white silence of the mountain but did nothing to ease Rivalree's frozen heart. Canyon Creek roared in protest as the rushing waters from higher up filled its bed to capacity. Multicolored wildflowers peeked their fragile heads up wherever the disappearing snow left bare ground and berry vines—raspberry, gooseberry—wound about wild strawberries patches, the white of their flowers clean and innocent.

Rivalree took a deep breath of mountain air, reveling in the newborn smells around her and feeling as if someone had unlocked the bars of a prison and released her. The steady drip-drip of liquefying snow combined with the trickle of rivulets working their way downhill brought a smile to her lips. At last she could escape the loneliness of the Sierra Mountains and the disappointment of a love gone sour. Her relationship with Braven had deteriorated with each passing day, until they barely spoke to each other.

She clutched the rolled newspaper to her chest, its print smudged from the many who had skimmed its pages, and released her pent-up breath. The answer to her prayer lay at her fingertips, a small advertisement for teachers at the English school in Los Angeles. Though the publication was nearly a year old, she knew in her heart she could find a job there, respectable work. The notice asked for female applicants only. How many women of good reputation would answer the request? Not many, as there were few in all of California that spoke English and had a good education.

She slanted her eyes at Braven, busy with some of his crew removing debris from the mine entrance, which was no longer blocked by the covered walkway. She would show him she was capable of taking care of herself and that she didn't need his reluctant support. She refused to be a burden to anyone, much less a man who despised her as much as her husband apparently did.

Something sad twisted inside her as she remembered the numbered nights of passion they had shared. What had gone wrong between them? Though their courtship had been anything but normal, the love that had sparked between them had overridden the conflicts. She dipped her head to stare at her hands still gripping the newspaper. But the blaze of their love had died an instant death the moment he had learned of her past.

How could she have been so naive as to tell him the truth? She shook her head in well-learned cynicism. She had been a fool of the worst kind, but no more. As soon as Eloy Jackson appeared with the wagon and team, she would leave, taking only what she'd come with—her trunk and the five hundred dollars still hidden there. That would be enough money to get her passage to Los Angeles. Her proud mind made up, she turned and headed back to the cabin.

"Yahoo," came a cry of excitement behind her.

She whirled to discover what had caused the commotion, lifting the rolled paper to shade her eyes. She watched as the men threw down their tools and dashed around the cabin toward the road. Even Braven tossed aside the shovel he'd been using and sauntered in the same direction.

"Hee-ya, you lazy nags," called a faraway voice. The creak of harness leather and the crunch of wagon wheels caught her ear.

Dear God, the storekeeper was here with the wagon. She swayed, as fearful indecision ripped through her. All of her inner confidence scattered like sand dunes before a wind. The time was now to prepare to leave.

On silent feet she approached the milling crowd surrounding Eloy Jackson. The burly man jumped down from the wagon seat, secured the reins to the brake handle, then slung a satchel of mail to one of the miners.

"Why you ole son of a galoot," he bellowed, slapping Braven on the back as he grabbed him in a rough embrace. "I knew you were up to more than spoonin' with your woman, unless you have strange ideas about marriage I know nothin' about."

The crowd laughed and snickered.

"I would have told you, Eloy, but I didn't want to put you in an awkward position," Braven answered, returning the back-pounding.

"Damn it, man, did you strike it big?" The man's eyes glistened with envy.

"Enough color for all of us to go home wealthy."

"Oh, hell, you have all the luck. But I should have known. The Sierra Angel would bring her man the mother lode." Eloy smacked his knee with his open hand. "I would kill for an opportunity like you have."

"Not the big one, my friend, but enough for me. The truth is, I'm ready to head home, Eloy." He eyed the other man with a raised brow. "I'll give you your golden opportunity. How would you like first crack at owning the Louisiana?"

"Do you mean it?"

Braven nodded, a grin splitting his face.

"How much?"

"Come on inside, man. We'll discuss it, and the terms of obligation."

Steaming, Rivalree watched the crowd of men walk toward the cabin. Damn Braven Blackwood. She owned as much of this mine as he did. Never once did he consult her or ask her opinion about what they should do with it. He would sell it, sign it off, and take the money.

She waited outside until the men returned an hour later. Then she marched to the porch and entered the front door, her plans well detailed. Without hesitation she took the stairs and entered the bedroom, which she occupied now on her own. Opening the lid to her trunk, she began packing all of her belongings, lying them neatly one on top of the other. She would leave in the morning even if she must go with Eloy Jackson. As much as she found the storekeeper distasteful, it was better than staying here where she was ignored and unwanted.

"What in the hell do you think you're doing?" Braven placed his hands on the door frame and leaned into the bedroom, a barrier of sorts to keep his unpredictable wife from escaping.

Rivalree spun around, fear and confusion meshing her features. Her stubborn little chin that he loved so well, lifted, and her gaze hardened before she returned to her task. "Packing. I want to leave right away."

"Rivalree," he said, exasperated. "You know there's no way we can go before a couple of weeks, possibly more. There're too many details to be taken care of to leave any sooner."

"For you perhaps, but not for me." She continued her maddening packing of clothes in her well-used trunk.

Thinking back, he remembered the first time he'd seen

that damn piece of luggage, the evening it had been delivered to his room at the St. Francis Hotel. The same night he had married her full of anger and frustration. Now the chit planned on leaving him, not once thinking about how he felt about her actions. Uncaring, selfish. The desire to shake her until she relented rose like a turbulent tide. He had come full circle, his emotions of that fateful night returning to overpower his logic.

Grabbing her by the arm, he lifted her bodily, forcing her to face him. "I don't think so, woman. You don't leave this camp until I say you can." Now why in the hell had he said that? Threatening her would only make her more determined.

Her eyes narrowed, and she pulled her arm away from his manacle grip. Unwillingly he released his hold, wishing he could start the ill-fated encounter all over again.

"You have no right to tell me what to do, Braven Blackwood. You don't own me." She whirled back, knelt, and closed the trunk with an ominous click. "Leave me alone. I want nothing more to do with you."

Something inside him shriveled and died. God in heaven, she was serious. This was no little spat, but the end of the love he had thought still resided immortalized deep in her heart. He loved her. He didn't want to lose her. If only he could force her to listen, he would make things right between them. He glared down at her rigid back, determined to do whatever he had to to make her see reason.

"Nobody leaves here until I say so, not even you, goddamn it." Holding his fisted hands against his sides, he stormed from the room and to the common room below.

He sat down at the table and lowered his head into his hands. How had they grown so far apart?

Pat eased down beside him, folding a letter and slipping

it back in its envelope. "She seems determined to leave."

Braven lifted his head to study the older man. "You heard?"

"You two were loud enough to wake the damned in hell."

"I can't let her leave. If I do, I'll lose her."

The Irishman stuffed the letter in his shirt pocket, then covered Braven's outstretched fingers with his. "Not true, me boyo. Maybe if you give her a chance, away from you, she'll mellow. This place is enough to make the sanest lose their mind." His eyes flicked over Braven. "Why don't you let me take her down the mountain. That way I can talk to her, make her realize . . ."

"No." Braven stood. "I appreciate what you're offering, but my wife is my problem. I can handle her on my own."

Pat chewed his bottom lip. "Don't you think you're being a bit pigheaded?"

Braven tensed, the muscles in his neck and shoulders standing out. "If anyone but you were to say that, Pat . . ."

"Have you forgotten the killer is still among us. The saints only know what he'll do to get his hands on the gold and the mine. Do you really want the colleen here in danger?"

Braven returned his face to his open palms. Pat was right. Rivalree would be safer away from this place. If something were to happen to her because of his stubborn determination to control her, he'd never forgive himself. He studied the other man from the corner of his eye. Perhaps the wise thing to do was let her go. "How far do you plan to take her?"

Pat hesitated, fingering the pocket holding the letter. "All the way to San Francisco, if you want. Carrie's there. She'd put the colleen up until you could join her."

"Your daughter's in San Francisco? I knew you had one, but I always assumed you'd left her back East somewhere."

362

A crooked grin creased the Irishman's face. "Carrie's not the kind of woman you leave behind."

Braven mulled over his choice. Maybe time with a respectable, practical woman like Pat's daughter was exactly what Rivalree needed. Since losing Joleen, she'd changed. Female sympathy might be what would bring her around. The thought of being separated from her left a void in his heart, but if time away from him would help . . .

"All right, Pat. If you're sure you don't mind."

"Wise choice, my friend. Wise choice." Pat rose, again patting his shirt pocket.

As the old man left the cabin, Braven stood. He would tell Rivalree now. Turning toward the staircase, he caught his breath as she glided down the steps, her chin lifted defiantly, her eyes looking anywhere but at him.

"You still want to leave," he demanded.

She jumped almost as if she'd not expected him to speak. Her gaze riveted, and he knew instinctively what her answer would be.

"As soon as possible."

"Pat's agreed to take you to San Francisco." He waited for a response, but got none. "You must promise to wait there for me."

Her chin climbed a notch higher, then she continued her way down the stairs and sidestepped him.

"Damn you, Rivalree, don't you ignore me. Unless you swear you'll wait in San Francisco, I'm not going to allow you to leave."

A look of confusion crossed her face. Swallowing hard, she glanced away. "I'll promise anything to get away from this . . . place."

She pulled from his grip and continued to the stove.

He watched her haughty sway, and his gut twisted painfully. Was he doing the right thing by letting her go?

He prayed he was, but the choice wasn't his to make. He knew without a doubt she would leave no matter what he said or did.

The steamer's loading dock was a nucleus of activity, but fortunately the crowd was trying to board the boat, not depart. Rivalree crowded next to her trunk, the one familiar thing she could see, and waited, wondering if Pat had gotten lost, or, God forbid, forsaken her.

Jitters, she told herself. Pat had been too attentive for the entire trip from the mine to San Francisco to desert her now. He had told her he would be as quick as he could, but a wagon might not be that easy to locate in the crowded streets of the city. She would give him ten more minutes before she got alarmed.

With a sigh, she plopped down on her trunk to wait, wiping sweat from her temples and forehead as the crowd grew denser around her. Dear God, what madness drove these men to push like cattle to head the line? Like lemmings, a small little creature she'd once read about, they were crowding to their dooms, unconcerned about what life held for them when they reached their destination. Gold fever. The affliction was more fatal than the Black Plague.

"Rivalree."

Her name lilted in Pat's familiar brogue brought a deep breath of relief from her lips. She stood, waving her arms, and caught sight of the little man sitting high on the seat of a wagon, two broken-down nags bringing the vehicle up level with the dock on which she waited.

The commotion she stirred flapping her arm brought attentive stares. She ignored them, not really caring what the horde of perspective miners thought of her as she waited for Pat to reach her.

A hum of excitement buzzed around her, and she

thought for a moment she heard her name whispered. But no, she must be mistaken. Yet as Pat pulled alongside where she stood, he seemed to have no trouble getting help to lift her trunk into the wagon bed. In fact, a scuffle ensued, and she worked her way to the wagon and climbed into the seat. The crowd had turned away from the steamer to stare up at her expectantly.

She blinked, unsure what the problem was until the first man spoke.

"Won't you bless us, Miss Angel?"

"We dun heard about you, ma'am. Please," another stranger pleaded, reaching up his hand to touch her skirts.

"Sierra Angel." The name echoed from mouth to mouth, and a near hush fell over the crowd.

Rivalree was shaken. How could the foolish rumor have traveled so far? She opened her mouth to denounce the false reputation, but lonely eyes waited, hoping for some small words of encouragement. How could she refuse them?

"One blessin', ma'am, and I'll die a happy man."

The softly worded plea twisted her heart. She smiled down. One more time wouldn't matter, not if it gave these poor wretches hope. They were no different than she had been those many months before, seeing the gold fields as an answer to their problems. God bless them, they knew not what they did.

She stood up on the footboard and scanned the crowd. Tall men, short men, handsome ones, homely ones, they all had similar dreams. What right did she have to deny them?

She took a deep breath and collected her thoughts. What should she say to them? What did they wish to hear? Her gaze honed in on one pair of eyes. Hope, their owner asked. Give us fair prospect for the future.

She moved down the row of stares reading the same response in all the faces lifted to her. Brown eyes, gray eyes, blue eyes, she took them all in.

Blue eyes? My God, Braven was in the crowd. She searched out the familiar orbs. *Oh, Braven, you didn't forsake me. You followed. You love . . .*

Her amber eyes locked with the ones she sought. Their harsh scrutiny pierced to her very soul, hate and revenge pouring out of them, then they disappeared, melting in the crowded dock. Her heart leaped to her throat. Those eyes had not belonged to her husband, but she knew them. Why?

Blue eyes? Blue eyes? The only other man who had possessed such a startling gaze was Silas Guntree. Impossible. What would the slave hunter be doing here? He was thousand of miles away in some sultry southern town destroying the lives of humans with every breath he took. He wouldn't be here in California.

But what if he was? Would he remember her? *Foolish girl,* she chided herself, *your imagination has become much too vivid.*

She tore her stare away from the spot the eyes had occupied and swept the crowd with a kindly look. She had been mistaken. Only friendly, pleading eyes perused her, asking nothing more from her than a word of encouragement. How little they asked.

"There's gold in the hills, gentlemen. Follow your instincts and you'll find it. Bless you all."

A cheer shook the pier, and the steamer's captain and crew converged on the wharf side of the paddleboat with curious stares.

Pat flicked the reins over the rumps of the team, and the wagon lurched forward forcing Rivalree to sit. On edge, she searched the crowd one last time for signs of Silas Guntree. She was relieved when the wagon pulled away and that Pat was taking her to his daughter's home. She would be safe there. *Rivalree Blackwood,* she scolded inwardly, *you have nothing to be afraid of, so stop imagining things.*

The wagon threaded its way through the well-remembered muddy streets of San Francisco. Images of Braven lifting her from the mire those many months ago shot through her memory with the pain of an arrow piercing her heart. Why did everything have to remind her of the man who no longer figured in her life?

He didn't give a hoot! He wouldn't have let her leave the mine if he cared one iota about what happened to her. And his words about her waiting here for him—he hadn't meant those, either. He had just been too much of a coward to tell her the truth. Or maybe worse, he didn't want her getting her hands on his precious gold. Damn him!

She concentrated on the passing businesses, attempting to forget her disturbing thoughts. The buildings they passed began to look familiar. The sheriff's office where she had tried to have Braven arrested. There, on the left, the printer's where she'd had the handbills made. And, yes, there, the saloon in front of where Braven had torn those flyers from her hand. They were only blocks from the Veta Madre.

Surprised, she twisted on the bench, questioning the Irishman with her eyes. "Pat, where does Carrie live? Aren't we awfully close to Portsmouth Square?"

The little man studied her, analyzing her. "It's not too much further, colleen. Don't worry, Carrie will welcome you with open arms."

His words did nothing to relieve the uneasiness lurking in her insides. What was wrong with her? She found something to fear in everything around her. She had to stop this nonsense.

Straightening in her seat, she placed her hands in her lap. Yet when they turned in the opposite direction from the rowdy section of town, she couldn't help feeling relieved. She was experiencing a paranoia that made her suspicious even of Pat. She had to get a hold of herself. Taking deep breaths, she soon found herself hopelessly lost in the maze of streets the Irishman guided the wagon down.

She cast a sideways glance at the old man. It was as if he was trying to confuse her on purpose. "We sure seem to be taking a long, roundabout way."

"Muddy streets, colleen. I don't want to get the wagon stuck."

She nodded, accepting his explanation. She knew all about this ungodly city's impassable streets. Damn! She'd done it again. She was thinking about Braven Blackwood.

"Whoa," Pat called, pulling hard on the reins to halt the team, dragging her thoughts back to the present.

The narrow alley in which they stopped was lined with garbage leaving a rancid smell in her nostrils. Pat's daughter lived here? She swiveled to question him, but he was already out of the wagon, a skitter of rats darting in and out of patches of light as his movement startled them.

Dear God, what kind of place was this? What kind of woman was the Irishman's daughter? She considered jumping from her perch and running away. But where? She had no idea where she was. And the rats. A pair of red, beady eyes glistened up at her from a littered corner, daring her to try to escape. She shivered. She'd read about the horrible things rats could do.

"Carrie," Pat greeted as the door to the building on her right opened.

"It's about time ya got here, Papa. I see ya did what I told ya to do in my letter. You brought her with ya."

Rivalree cocked her head. Carrie's voice sounded so familiar, so coarse and demanding . . .

Her eyes searched the darkened doorway. She caught a

glimpse of red hair piled high on the woman's head. Then the gleam of the pistol barrel stopped her further perusal.

"Get down, Rivalree," insisted the voice, the gun drawing a circle in the air in emphasis. "You're as mousy as I remember. I can't figure out what men see in you." The woman stepped into the dim light of the alley revealing her angry face.

Rivalree gasped in fear. "Carla? What are you doing here?"

The woman eyed her, then motioned with the pistol. "Ask Papa that question. He brought ya here."

She whirled to confront the little man.

"I'm sorry, colleen, but it was necessary. We could think of no other way to force Braven to turn over the gold."

"The gold?" she mouthed. "You're doing this for the gold? But Braven gave you your share, didn't he?"

Pat turned away, shame clouding his eyes.

Survival instincts took control of her. Blocking out thoughts of the rats and the garbage, she leapt from the wagon seat. Her foot slipped in mire and she fell to her knees. Before she could rise and escape the nightmare facing her, beefy hands grabbed her arms and lifted her.

"Let me go," she cried, fighting with all her strength. A smelly hand clamped down on her nose and mouth stifling her screams. She struggled to catch her breath, her fingers coming up to claw ineffectually at the flesh covering her face.

The door slammed with a resounding crash and Rivalree battled the arms of her captors. Dear God, didn't these people realize Braven Blackwood would never give up his gold. Not for anything and especially not for her. What would they do with her once they discovered that fact?

Chapter Twenty-Six

The Louisiana Mine
May 1, 1852

Braven crushed the finely scripted missive in his powerful fists. The son of a bitch. John Masters had finally stooped lower than a rattlesnake. Though the ransom note was unsigned, there was no doubt in his mind the gambler had had a hand in its wording. Rivalree's life for all the proceeds from the mine. He had always known the man was ruthless and greedy, but he'd never quite believed until now that he would murder to obtain what he wanted.

But how had he gotten his hands on Rivalree? Was Pat O'Grady involved some way in his sinister plot? Had the Irishman been responsible for the deaths and destruction that had occurred over the last year? He just couldn't believe it was true. No, he had asked too much of the older man by leaving the obligation of his wife in his gnarled hands.

The note dropped unnoticed to the ground as he ran strong fingers through his disheveled hair. He shouldn't have buckled beneath the desires of a distraught woman and the boastings of an injured old man. If anything happened to Rivalree, he'd never forgive himself.

Though her safety meant more to him than life itself, why the gold? The answers to his deepest longings rested in the money's ability to buy a plantation and make it successful without slavery. He'd worked too damned many years to get what he had to turn it over to a greedy bastard like John Masters. How could he return home empty-handed, a failure in the eyes of his father and brother? How could he go on living without Rivalree? The choice was one that left him a loser no matter which he selected. His pride and future or his heart?

There was no contest. He would beggar himself or grovel at the feet of Satan if he had to in order to save the woman he loved.

Kneeling, he retrieved the letter and spread it across his thigh, reading it one last time, hoping beyond reason to find he'd been mistaken about what it demanded. The words read the same as they had the first time. Pulling himself up, he stumbled into the cabin. *Rivalree. Rivalree. I'm coming.*

He threw a few essentials into a canvas sack and approached a wide-eyed Eloy Jackson and Mace Lockman, the only two remaining after the departure of the crew.

"The mine is yours now, my friends. May you have better luck than I." He eyed Mace before he turned toward the wagon. "Are you sure you want to stay on?"

"I'm sure, Braven. I know this mine like the back of my hand. Eloy and I worked out a partnership, and if what you tell me about Masters is true, we'll need our combined strength to keep him at bay." Mace looked down at his hands. "Besides, with Joleen buried here and all, I'm not ready to leave yet. Her spirit is here, with me."

"I understand," Braven answered. And he did. He knew what the love for a woman could do.

Throwing his bag into the wagon bed and carrying

nothing but the sacks holding his, Rivalree's, and John Masters's shares of the gold profits, he scrambled into the seat, slapping the reins over the horses' rumps. Without once looking back, he began his journey to San Francisco anxious to reach his destination as fast as he could and confront the bastard who dared to attempt to control him with extortion.

The rickety, narrow stairs squeaked their protest as Rivalree's captors forced her upward. With each step she took, she left hope further below in the parlor on the first floor of the building. Though she had never seen the inside of a brothel, instincts told her she was in one now. The heavily curtained main room carried a lingering odor of exotic perfume, cigars, and liquor. She could almost imagine the scantily clad women draped across the brocade couches and the men, their ogling eyes soaking up the display of feminine flesh.

What did Carla have planned for her? She cast a furtive glance at the other woman. The fact the redhead was Pat's daughter still sent waves of shock and disbelief coursing through her. Carla had hated her from the moment they'd met, and there was no doubt in her mind the woman would kill her, or worse, when Braven refused to turn over his gold.

Reaching the second story of the house, the procession came to a halt in front of a closed door. Carla fumbled with a ring of keys, searching for the one that fit the lock.

Rivalree swung her gaze on the Irishman, who had followed meekly behind the group from the moment they had entered the building. "I don't understand, Pat," she faltered, "I thought you were my friend."

The old man's face twisted, and his eyes darted to his daughter's figure hunched over the door handle. "Don't worry, colleen, nothing will happen to you once Braven

373

turns the gold over to us."

She lifted her chin and swiveled her eyes away from him, all hope of assistance from him shattered. She had no one, nothing, to look to for help. There was only herself and her overpowering desire to be free.

The door squealed open, and Carla turned, signaling the two men trapping Rivalree between them into the room. She didn't resist as they pushed her forward into the sparsely furnished cubicle, a well-worn bed, a shabby dresser, and a nightstand holding a chipped bowl and pitcher and most likely a chamber pot in the cabinet below the only furniture in sight. A prison of the worst kind. She had no doubt they planned to lock her in this room until they decided her fate.

Without words, the two men shoved her forward, and she stumbled to her knees. By the time she gathered her legs underneath her the barrier closed with an ominous click. Pushing up, she scrambled to the door, testing the handle, but the lock was secure. She pressed her ear to the wooden slab, her palms flat beside her head.

"Carrie, you promised she'd come to no harm." Pat's voice filtered through the door.

"Don't call me that, Papa. You know I don't like Carrie. The name's too soft and weak."

"But, Daughter, your sainted mother gave you that name."

"Mama is gone, Papa. Dead a long time. I'm Carla now. Don't you forget it."

"But, colleen, I . . ."

"As far as the woman is concerned, as long as Blackwood gives me what I want, he can have her back. She's nothing to me but a means to an end. You boys, see to it her trunk is brought upstairs. I don't want anyone seeing it and getting suspicious."

The voices began to fade. She was nothing to Carla, but then, she meant even less to Braven. She turned her back to the door and slid to her knees, fear festering like an untended wound in her heart.

Braven tucked the letter of deposit from the bank in Sacramento into the satchel holding the few possessions he'd brought with him down the mountain. He had left behind many things of endearment to him at the mine, including the mantel clock from home and the toboggan he'd made for Rivalree. They would remain forever at the Louisiana Mine, a reminder of its past owners to all those who followed in their steps through the years.

At least the gold was safely deposited in the bank's vault, just as the ransom note had demanded. It had galled him to have to place it in John Masters's name, but he'd been given no other choice, at least not at this time. Once he confronted the bastard, that would be a different matter. He would find Rivalree then seek his revenge on Masters.

He watched the wagon pull away, sold to a group of miners headed upriver to stake their claims on some wild, rushing river. He shook his head. Out to make their fortune. Not so many months ago, he'd been exactly like them, so confident and sure the easy answer to his every dream lay in finding precious nuggets strewn on the ground. How different he felt today.

All he wanted was the gold that was rightfully his, Rivalree tucked securely in his arms, and passage for the two of them back to his home in Louisiana. And he would have those things, all of them, even if he must strangle the life from John Masters.

"Last call for boarding," cracked the riverboat captain.

His plans well laid, Braven stepped aboard the steamer headed toward San Francisco with vengeful determination his only companion.

* * *

The pretty brunette studied Rivalree from the doorway, the tray of food resting in her delicately made hands.

"You're the Sierra Angel, aren't you?"

She focused on the face with heavy makeup and wondered what answer would be to her best advantage. "I've been called that by some."

"You're as lovely as an angel." The other woman paused. "But then I've been told you were."

What did one say to a comment like that? Thank you seemed inappropriate. She dipped her head and stared at her fingers gnawed raw around the nails from worry. Two weeks had passed, and as far as she knew no word had been received from Braven. She'd been right. He didn't care what happened to her. In fact, he was probably relieved to have her out of his hair.

"Is it true Braven Blackwood is your husband?"

Rivalree's gaze shot up, a small frown creasing her brows. What did this woman know of Braven? What should she answer?

"Yes," she replied in a small voice. "He is. What is he to you?" Interest piqued her voice.

The woman's eyes narrowed suspiciously. "Nothin'." She turned and set the tray on the dresser and studied her reflection in the distorted mirror. "Nothin' at all."

There was more to this woman than simple curiosity, and she was determined to find out what that something was. The one thing she had plenty of was time as she spent most of her days locked in her room, the one window shuttered and sealed. "My name's Rivalree," she offered. "What's yours?"

The brunette turned, her eyes skimming Rivalree's slender form. "Some folks call me Lil, but I prefer Lily."

How different from Carla. This woman preferred the softer name. That must be a good sign. Rivalree rose from the foot of the bed where she'd been sitting and crossed the room to stand near Lily. "I agree, Lily is much prettier."

376

She felt the woman tense, so she turned her attention to the tray of food, picking up a buttered roll and taking a bite. "The food is good, did you prepare it?"

Lily laughed, a soft tinkle of a sound. "Good Lord, no. I don't do the cookin' around here. I'm just one of Carla's girls." Her mouth pursed into a frown as she took a step away from Rivalree toward the door. "Don't you try to coddle up to me," she warned. "Just because you helped my pa and Braven Blackwood always dealt fairly, there's no reason for you to look to me for sympathy. I cain't help ya, even if I wanted to." The woman edged backward until she reached the door, unlocked it, and slipped out, slamming the barrier between them before Rivalree could reach it.

"Wait, Lily, wait. I just want to talk to you," she pleaded, but the turning of the lock was the only sound to greet her.

Who was Lily's father, and how did she know Braven? A ray of hope splashed against her upturned face. If she could find out, this woman might help her, regardless of what she'd said.

She returned to her seat on the foot of the bed. Lily's father. The woman had said she, Rivalree, had aided him. How? She racked her brain trying to conjure a face, a man who reminded her of Lily, but none came to mind.

Standing, she began pacing the small quarters. Lily would come back again. She was positive. If only to make sure she was all right. For some reason the woman felt responsible for her. Her long-doused instinct to survive sprang to life, setting her heart to racing against the prison of her ribs.

Braven crashed through the swinging doors of the Veta Madre, his eyes seeking signs of John Masters in the dimly lit casino. His blood pounded in his temples like strokes of doom as he crossed the room in long strides.

Curious stares followed him, young girls with new faces wondering who he was. Even the bartender had changed, this man's eyes cold and cruel, unpleasant. He glanced around, his fingers caressing the pistol strapped to his hip. No sign of Masters or of his girlfriend Carla, either.

"What do you want, stranger," the bartender demanded, halting his hand that held a rag with which he cleaned the bar.

Braven noticed his other hand slip under the counter. No doubt the man had a gun stashed there, loaded and ready to use. He unfurled his balled fists, crossed his arms over his chest, and struck a relaxed pose, hoping to put the man at ease. "Looking for John Masters. Is he in?"

"Might be, might not be. Depends on who's askin'."

Braven seethed. The saloon owner was surrounding himself with ruffians, evidence that he felt a need to be protected. "Tell him Braven Blackwood is here with the gold."

The man's brow lifted with curiosity. He stepped away from the bar and headed toward the rear door leading to the girls' rooms and Masters's private office. Before he left the room the bartender nodded to another man sitting at a back table.

Braven knew he was still being watched, so he dropped his large body down into a chair to wait.

Minutes later the bartender returned and cocked his head toward the rear entrance. "Mr. Masters will see ya now. His office is at the end of the hall."

"I thought he'd be in for me," he commented dryly as he started toward the door.

The bartender blocked his progress, sticking his hand out, palm up. "The gun. I'll relieve you of your side iron."

Braven eased the pistol from its holster and handed it, butt first, to the man. He didn't need a weapon to handle John Masters. Damn, he was capable of murdering him with his bare hands.

"All right. You can see him now." The man eyed him up and down once, taking his measure.

The long hallway brought back memories. He passed the room where Rivalree had stayed briefly. That door as well as all the others were closed. Was she behind one of them now? He squelched the urge to try each one to see if they were locked. If Rivalree was here, he would first have to find out which room she was in.

At the end of the corridor, he spun to his left and entered the darkened office. Breath held, he scanned the room before stepping in all the way. Masters sat at his desk, his chair cocked back, his hands behind his head, an amused expression on his face. "Wondered when you'd get here, Blackwood. Took you long enough."

Braven crossed the room in three strides, ready to jerk the son of a bitch out of his chair and strangle him, but the ominous click of a gun behind him stilled his feet. He looked over his shoulder to find the bartender leaning against the doorjamb, his own pistol aimed at his heart.

"You sorry bastard," Braven hissed.

Masters righted his chair and placed his hands on the desk. "What the hell's the matter with you, Blackwood? I had every right to expect you last winter. I figured you'd taken my share of the profits and skedaddled."

"I'm not that low, Masters. I keep my word. The day Judd brought you in as a partner, I knew the relationship would eventually come to this. Goddamn you, where's Rivalree?"

"Rivalree? You mean that little slip of a girl you took off with last spring? How would I know where she is? I figured you'd set her up somewhere in the city, a cozy bed to return to in the fall."

Braven's fist lifted threateningly. "You know damn well she's my wife." He took a step toward Masters. "Where have you stashed her?"

"I wouldn't, mister, if I was you," warned the bartender.

Braven dropped his hand to his side.

"Me?" Masters queried, his barking laugh erupting, his brow lifting in amusement. "Why would I have her?"

Braven reached into his breast pocket taking out the ransom note. "Didn't you send this to me?"

Masters accepted the letter, opened it, his brows flexing up and down as he read what it said. He looked up, surprised. "I swear I know nothing about this demand."

Braven's eyes narrowed in disbelief.

Masters rose to his feet and circled the desk. "On my honor, I'm not behind your wife's disappearance. I've done a lot of dishonest things, but extortion and murder? I'm not that insane. Look, Blackwood. All I want is my share of the gold. Nothing more, nothing less."

Braven's shoulders slumped in confusion. If Masters wasn't behind the demands, then who was? Panic gummed his racing pulse, making his heart skip numerous beats. Where was Rivalree?

"Look, man. The note says to send a message to the Gilded Cage. That's a whorehouse not far from here."

"I know, I already sent a note around."

"The Cage is a place Carla started when I kicked her out of the casino last fall."

"Carla? She's not with you anymore?"

"I got tired of her pushy ways. Hell, man. I didn't want to marry her or any other woman."

Braven's brows slashed into a straight line above the bridge of his nose. "You think Carla's behind this?"

"It's possible. The woman's crazy." Masters signaled to the man holding the gun on Braven. "Give him back his weapon. And Jack," Masters directed the bartender, "bring me the one from under the bar. If you want my help, I'll go with you."

Braven accepted his pistol and checked it with the thorough quickness of an expert. "And why would you do that?'' He paused before returning it to his holster, eyeing Masters.

The other man shrugged, his barking laugh ringing out. "Hell, I don't know. Let's just say I'm bored. You won't want to hear I took a shine to your wife the first time I laid eyes on her. You're a lucky man, Blackwood. She's one hell of a lady.''

Was Masters telling the truth, or was this a setup? His fingers caressed the letter of deposit in his shirt pocket. It would be better to take the other man with him and know what he was up to than leave him behind.

"All right, Masters. You can come with me, but I'm watching you. One funny move, and I swear I won't hesitate to shoot you."

Masters grinned as he accepted the gun from the bartender's hand. "Likewise, Blackwood. If this is an attempt to get rid of me, be aware I'd shoot you without a qualm, too.''

Both uneasy, the two men stepped out the back entrance of Masters's office.

Chapter Twenty-Seven

Lily was back. Rivalree watched her under lowered lashes, wanting to do nothing that might frighten the woman away. Her fingers itched to clutch the brunette's shoulders and shake her, demanding to know what was going on. Instead, she clasped them in her lap and waited in silence, her desire for information clawing at the back of her throat.

The woman set the plate, piled high with fresh strawberries, down on the edge of the dresser. "Carla would kill me if she knew I'd brought you these." She studied Rivalree, then shrugged her slim shoulders. "But I figured you deserved some kind of diversion, cooped up in here all day. Personally, I would have gone stark raving mad by now."

Rivalree smiled, her eyes lighting with excitement. She was right. Lily did feel concern for her. "Thank you, they look delicious." She rose from the bed on which she sat, hesitating. "Do you mind if I come get them?"

Pleased, Lily held the bowl out to her. Rivalree resumed her seat after accepting the offering, popping one of the red, ripe fruits in her mouth. She watched the brunette as she chewed. Sticking the bowl out toward the other woman, she offered, "Would you like one?"

Lily swayed, undecided. "Sure, if you don't mind." She joined Rivalree on the bed.

Soon they were sharing the treat like two schoolgirls, the sweet red juice staining their fingers and lips, the camaraderie easy and natural between them.

"Tell me, Lily, who is your father?" Rivalree licked the strawberry juice from her fingers. "I've searched my memory trying to figure out where I met him." She shot her gaze at the other woman. "The mystery's been driving me crazy."

Lily tensed, and for a moment Rivalree thought for sure she would bolt for the door and run. Relief flooded through her when the brunette instead took another berry and whirled it in her fingers.

"I'm not surprised you don't remember him. Last spring you rode on a stagecoach from Sacramento to Marysville with him. You gave him courage and hope. Because of you, we made peace with each other. I owe you, Rivalree, for giving me back my father. I'm now willing to understand his need to strike it rich, and he's accepted what I am." She took the empty bowl and carried it to the dresser. "Not that what I've become is right, but I can't change it now. I'm a whore, and I suppose I always will be."

The kind man in the stagecoach. Rivalree remembered him well. He was the first person to call her Sierra Angel. And this woman was his Lily, the daughter he had spoken of, a victim of circumstances and the times. She'd never thought those few words of encouragement might come back to aid her, but they had. "Lily, it's never too late to change. You can pick up at any time and go on with your life. Your past doesn't have to taint you forever."

The meaning of her words circled round to haunt her. What was she saying? Past mistakes and blunders had controlled her own life. Her fist lifted, pressing to her mouth. Dear God, was she doing the same thing as Lily?

"Do you really think that's true, Rivalree?"

Did she? Her mind swirled in confusion. The words sounded so wise and logical. But could she believe them? Her future would go nowhere if she didn't. *Oh, Braven, what a little fool I've been.* "Honestly, Lily. Don't ruin the rest of your life. Your father would welcome you with open arms. I know it." If only she could be as sure about Braven. If only she'd not left, bitter words between them. She hung her head. How could she blame him for not coming after her? She didn't deserve his love. A lone tear slipped down her cheek.

Lily turned and knelt at her feet. "What is it, Rivalree?" Genuine concern etched her voice.

She glanced up. Should she share her problems with this woman? "Braven. I don't think he's coming after me. I don't know if he cares anymore."

"I know Braven Blackwood. He's an honorable man. I was with him the night he rescued you from the Veta Madre. Believe me, he is driven by love for you."

"You were with him?" Lily was an old flame? A flare of jealousy ignited, and she fought to squelch it.

"He came to me angry and wounded by things you'd said to him. I was nothing to him, but he was always a true gentleman." Lily placed her hands on Rivalree's shoulders.

A smile of absurdity bowed her lips. A man of honor to the core, yet he hadn't bothered to come to her rescue. But could she blame him? She had deserted him at a time when he needed her the most. She had wounded his pride and masculinity, all because she was caught up in feeling sorry for herself as a result of an event that had taken place long ago.

She stood, gripping the other woman's arm. "Lily, did you mean what you said earlier about owing me?"

The brunette's eyes widened, and Rivalree feared she would deny her words. "I owe you, Rivalree, but please I can't do anything . . ."

"Yes you can, and you must." Gently she shook Lily. "I must escape. I can't do that without your help. Please, Lily."

The woman's head wobbled from side to side. "You don't understand what you ask. Carla would beat me, then throw me in the streets," she whispered. "I can't."

"Listen, we'll go together. I have five hundred dollars in my trunk in the corner. The money's yours. It'll be enough to reach your father."

"I don't want your money, Rivalree. Honestly. It's not because I don't want to help, it's just I'm afraid."

"So am I, but together we'll find assistance." She willed the other woman to gather the strength to agree.

"But how can we get away together?"

"You leave the house now and then, don't you?"

"I can, but I don't much."

"And Carla, she must go out, too."

"Every day, around two, to the bank. About an hour from now."

"Are the other girls aware I'm here?"

"No, but . . ."

"Paint me up. Cover my hair. Maybe they would think I'm one of them."

"But the bullies Carla keeps on hand."

"They would never expect me to try and walk out right under their noses."

"Perhaps if you wear one of my dark wigs." She sighed, the sound deep and resigned. "We can try."

"Thank you, Lily. We'll succeed. I know it."

"Wait here, and let me get some makeup, hairpieces, and a dress. Jesus Christ, Rivalree, I hope you're right."

Lily slipped out the door, locking it. Her footsteps faded down the hallway. Rivalree paced the room, praying the woman would return as she'd promised and their plan would work.

Whorehouses always had a certain look and smell about them. The Gilded Cage was no different. Braven scanned the shabby building across the street highlighted in the late-afternoon glare, willing his plans to go smooth. He glanced at John Masters standing on the wooden sidewalk beside him. What were the man's motives for coming along? Whatever the gambler's reasons, he couldn't be trusted. He couldn't imagine what had possessed Judd to bring Masters in as a third partner. Well, he was Eloy Jackson's headache now. He chuckled inwardly. Maybe he should say Eloy Jackson was Masters's problem. No one would push the burly storekeeper around, at least not for long.

As he got a feel for the layout of the house, the front door opened, a woman in an ornate feathered hat stepping out.

"Carla," Masters whispered, touching Braven's arm and signaling him to step back into the shadow cast by the porch on which they stood. "Chances are she's headed toward the bank. She should be gone for at least a half hour."

Good. The timing was right to enter the building and check around. Was Rivalree being held somewhere inside? Or had Carla used caution and left her somewhere else? He knew the answers to his questions lurked inside the dilapidated structure across the road.

He glanced up at the sun. Couldn't be much past two o'clock. Chances were most of the occupants inside the brothel were still sleeping. Moving to the edge of the porch, he scanned the exterior of the whorehouse looking for windows and doors. A narrow alleyway, barely wide enough for a wagon to enter skirted the left side. With a jerk of his head, he directed Masters to follow him as he darted across the thoroughfare and down the darkened alley.

Masters tapped his shoulder. "What are we doing, Blackwood?"

"Sneaking in," he replied.

The gambler snickered. "Somehow I imagined you more the bust-in-the-front-door-guns-blazing type."

"Only if it serves my purpose. I don't think theatrics are the answer now. I just want to find Rivalree."

As he spoke from his vantage point pressed against the corner of the structure, he saw the front door open again. This time two figures exited. One he recognized immediately. Lily, the tall, willowy brunette whose acquaintance he had made last fall. The other woman held her head down, a stiff pile of black hair swirling on her head, her gaudy dress proclaiming she was another one of the whores. He seriously considered stopping Lily and asking her for help, but what if the whore was in on the kidnapping? It would be better to let the two women pass.

The women stepped down from the building's porch to cross the narrow lane, and the rustle of their skirts filled Braven's ears as he squatted behind a barrel not more than two feet away. His breath eased out slowly as the ring of heels faded.

Shifting his position, he touched Masters's shoulder and pointed toward a window at the rear of the building low enough to the ground that they could slip inside without trouble.

The sash was open in invitation, nothing but a strip of mosquito netting hastily stuffed in the opening to keep the pests out. Braven pushed his way inside, stumbling over a hassock on which silk stockings and a robe were draped.

Masters slipped in behind him. Both men surveyed the room trying to decide where they were.

"Carla's bedroom I would say," offered Masters,

picking up the robe, rubbing the material between his thumb and forefinger. "This looks familiar."

Braven nodded, then began a systematic search. How lucky could he be? Carla's room. A likely place to find evidence of Rivalree's whereabouts.

Minutes later, he tossed down a pile of scarves and trinkets. Nothing. Damn. Where was Rivalree?

Masters opened one of the three doors leading out of the room. "Over here," he hissed, motioning with his hand. He swung the door wide, revealing a small office.

Braven joined the gambler, and they continued their search, riffling through stacks of paper on the small desk in the corner.

"Look, is this your note?" Masters held up a scrap of familiar-looking paper.

Braven took it and read the words he'd written only hours before. "Yeah, this is it." He folded it and stuck it in his pocket, next to the letter of deposit for the gold. "Maybe we should have followed Carla. She might have been headed to where she's holding Rivalree."

Masters cocked one brow. "Maybe, but I still think she was going to the bank. That's a habit she's had since I've known her."

Braven nodded, accepting the other man's reasoning as fact.

"Now what do we do?" Masters asked.

"Keep looking until we find her." He stepped toward the other door in the office and poked his head out. A hallway. He looked both directions seeing no one, then waved Masters to follow as he left the office. He would check behind every door in the building if he had to. Rivalree was somewhere.

The click of a pistol hammer being drawn back brought him up short. "What in the hell do you two think you're doing?" demanded a gravelly voice.

Braven spun, his fingers gripping his own gun, but he

came to a stiff halt halfway around as the cold steel of the gun butt pressed against his back.

"Customers normally come through the front door," the voice insisted. "I don't think Miss Carla is going to be too happy with you boys. If you're trying to rob her, you're too late. She's already gone to the bank. Now turn around, slowly."

Braven complied, discovering Masters standing in the doorway, readily giving up his pistol to the ruffian who'd caught them. The damn, cowardly son of a bitch. Masters could have easily overpowered their captor if the gambler had tried. He scowled, shooting his accomplice a sour look.

Masters shrugged. "Wasn't worth getting killed over."

Braven didn't agree. Finding Rivalree was more important than anything in his life, including all the gold in California.

Rivalree gripped Lily's hand as if it were a lifeline. Dear God, they had made it without a hitch. She giggled, the sound made in nervous relief as she thought about how she must look, the chalky black wig pinned to her head, the makeup thick and overpowering on her face, the dress she wore—her hand came up to cover the bare expanse of chest the low cut bodice exposed—the gaudiest she'd ever seen.

"Now what, Rivalree? Where do we go now?"

She turned to Lily and squeezed the woman's fingers. "Which way to the sheriff's office?"

"I'm not sure, exactly, but I know it's north of here."

"All right. We'll cut through alleys and head in that general direction. No sense taking a chance of running into Carla."

Lily nodded in agreement.

"But first," Rivalree said with a shake of her head, "I

ave to get rid of this wig. The pins are pulling my scalp so
aard I have tears in my eyes."

"I'm sorry, Rivalree. I just didn't want the damn thing
o fall off before we got away."

Rivalree smiled in understanding as she stripped the
uncomfortable hairpiece from her head, and stood,
ooking at the shaggy thing, unsure what to do with it.

"I don't care about the wig. Toss it in that garbage can."

She turned to rid herself of the false hair, then paused. A
shuffling sound. Rats! She scrunched her nose in distaste
and snapped her hand back from the can. The sound
continued, steady, rhythmical, getting louder. The noise
was made by boots.

A small gasp escaped her lips. Were they being
followed? "Come on." Grabbing Lily's hand she headed
down the alley, cut behind a store, nearly tripping over a
ine of garbage cans, and scurried down another narrow
street, darker and dirtier than any they had entered before
now.

She paused, sure her imagination had gotten the best of
her, and that the footsteps she'd thought she'd heard were
nothing more than the product of the fear twisting her
nsides.

Scuff! Scuff! Silence.

Her eyes widening in panic, she pulled Lily after her as
she stumbled down the littered alley.

"Rivalree, what's wrong with you?"

Again she halted. Their pursuer stopped three steps
after they did.

"We're being followed, Lily. I know it. And my instincts
ell me we don't want to get caught, no matter what!"

Carla caressed the certificate of deposit as if it were a
over. Her eyes widened. "I didn't know it would be so
much money." Her gaze shot to John Masters standing by

the door. "Did you see, Johnny?" She shoved the letter toward the gambler. "It's enough so we can both retire and go somewhere to live a respectable life."

Braven watched the other man's face harden.

"Damn it, Carla. Don't you understand. I have no desire to marry you, not for all the money in the world. I'm happy with the life I have."

"No, can't you see, Johnny," she continued, her eyes begging him for approval. "I did it all for you."

"All of what?" Braven demanded, tension coursing through his body.

Carla glanced at him, almost as if she were surprised he was still there. "Why, everything. Papa and I planned well, the accidents, the mishaps, they were supposed to scare you away leaving the mine to Johnny." Her eyes narrowed in anger. "But not you, courageous Braven Blackwood." She spoke his name as if it tasted foul in her mouth. "You had to stay even after the boy died and that uppity woman from back East showed up."

"Rivalree?" he questioned, realizing the redhead wasn't aware of what she said. "Carla," he demanded softly. "Where is Rivalree?"

A small frown creased her brows, then her gaze shot up, anger smiting her features with its heavy hand. "Why is that damn woman so important to everyone? You? Papa?" She honed in on Masters. "And you, Johnny? Even to you?"

With the speed of a striking cobra, she grabbed a captured pistol from one of her ruffian's hands and tore out of the small back parlor where they stood. "But no more. I'm tired of her mooning calf eyes."

Disbelief shook the remaining occupants of the room. Braven's heart did a somersault in his chest. Carla was going after Rivalree with *his* loaded pistol. If he didn't stop her no one would.

Taking advantage of the guard's inattentiveness, he

struck without hesitation. His fist smashed into the hand leveling the weapon on him. The man grunted and the gun went flying to thud against the wall and land spinning on the floor.

Lunging, Braven reached the revolver first, seconds before his opponent. The man landed on top of him, struggling to rip the weapon from his fingers.

"Let go of it, you son of a bitch," the ruffian demanded.

Instead, Braven jabbed him in the ribs with his elbow forcing a yelp of pain to tumble over the man's lips. "Like hell I will," he replied through gritted teeth.

Rolling in a jumble of arms and legs, they struck a chair, which fell to its side with a thud inches from his ear.

To his left the sound of another tussle kept the adrenaline pumping through his veins. If Masters could keep the other man occupied until he overpowered his assailant, there might be a chance of gaining control of the situation and stopping Carla. He must prevent the crazed madam from following through with her threat. Rivalree, dear God, Rivalree. He must rescue her.

With the strength of the righteous, he pinned his adversary to the floor and pressed the pistol barrel to his heaving chest. "If your boss lady commits murder, I'll see you're arrested as an accomplice."

The man relaxed under Braven's clutch and lifted his hands in surrender. "I don't wanna hang for murder."

"Good." Braven released his hold on the man and stepped away allowing him to rise to his feet. He turned to assist Masters to find the gambler had his opponent under control as well.

"Go on," Masters said with a dip of his head. "I'll watch these two. Careful with Carla, she's capable of doing anything."

Braven nodded and tore from the parlor, down the narrow hallway that ran the length of the house to the front room. Shrieks and grunts accosted him. Carla was fighting with someone. Rivalree! His feet picked up speed, racing toward the sounds.

The scene that greeted him sent a spark of surprise bolting through his chest. Pat O'Grady and Carla held the pistol between them, each trying to keep the other from gaining control.

"Stop it, Carrie," Pat demanded. "By all the saints, what's gotten into you, colleen?"

"Let it go, Papa. I have to kill her. That's the only way Johnny will come with me," she sobbed hysterically.

"No, Daughter, you go too far. There's been enough death because of this gold. No more. Not like this. On purpose."

Carla seesawed, the muscles in her arms straining to overpower the small Irishman. Assessing the situation, Braven barged into the room, determined to take the gun away from the struggling pair.

The explosion of the firearm reverberated around the walls. Pat's eyes widened, disbelief shading his usually tanned face a sickly white. "Carrie, what have you done?" he groaned as his fingers released the gun and he slid to the floor, his hands clutching his middle.

"Papa?" Carla whispered, the weapon held limply in her fist. She dropped to her knees beside him. "I didn't mean to. Why did you have to try and stop me?" Her face contorted, twisting the sensual features into a snarl. "You," she accused, spinning to aim the gun at Braven. "You caused this." She pulled back the trigger with her thumbs.

"Carla, no," rang out John Masters's voice. "If you shoot him I'll never go with you."

Her attention diverted to the man she loved. "Johnny," she whimpered, her voice soft and feminine.

Masters stepped forward, his hand outstretched. "Give me the gun, Carla."

"Then you'll come with me?" she asked.

"We'll talk about it. Give me the gun."

Her eyes narrowed. "No. You're with them. You're just trying to stop me from killing your precious Rivalree." She swiveled her arm from Braven to Masters.

Bunching his muscles, Braven slammed into the gambler knocking him to the floor as the second shattering explosion rent the room. The crash of glass behind him sent a shower of broken shards cascading through the air, showering the men on the floor.

"Carrie, no," gasped Pat, the old man reaching out to grab her ankle.

Carla twisted, stumbled through the room toward the front door, the pistol and the letter of deposit crushed against her breasts.

Braven let her go, watching his future, the gold from the Louisiana Mine go with her. He dropped to his knee beside the old man. "How bad is it, Pat?" He moved the Irishman's unresisting hand from the wound in his stomach.

"Braven," he choked, "it was never meant to come to this. No one was supposed to die, not Judd or Jack Quincy. The accidents were only meant to frighten, not kill." Pat coughed, blood foaming on the fist he held to his mouth. "Carrie means everything to me. I'm sorry, I never meant to hurt . . ." Another spasm struck leaving the old man speechless.

Masters knelt beside him. "Go on, Braven there's not much you can do for him now. I'll take care of him until . . . Go find your Rivalree."

Braven nodded and started to rise.

"Braven, me boyo," Pat rasped, "Rivalree—third room to your left." A small sound of pain escaped the blood-flecked lips. "Please, find it in your heart to forgive me."

He stared down at the dying Irishman, his emotions battling within him. Too many lives sacrificed because of one woman's crazed desires. How could he forgive Pat for the crimes he'd committed all in the name of love? Yet he found himself doing things he'd never thought possible because of his love of Rivalree. He could sympathize with the old man's predicament.

"I understand, Pat. I do." He twisted away, heading toward the stairs, taking them two at a time. As he raced down the upstairs corridor, relief washed through his pumping heart.

"Rivalree," he called, crashing through the door to the room Pat had indicated.

He stared into the empty quarters, his gaze darting around seeking signs of his wife. Her trunk stood open against the far wall, a blue dress he knew well was draped over the bed, her sturdy shoes dropped casually on the floor below the clothes.

"Rivalree, where are you?" he demanded, willing her to appear.

She was gone. Only God knew how, and he hadn't a clue as to where to begin looking.

He stumbled past the door, sweeping the gown from the bed as if he thought touching her possession might bring him a vision of her precious face. "Dear God, where have you gone?"

Whirling, he retraced his steps determined to search every hovel in San Francisco in order to find his missing wife, no matter if it took him the rest of his life.

Chapter Twenty-Eight

Rivalree held her breath so still in her lungs she thought her heart would stop beating. In fact, she prayed the pounding organ would cease the loud racket it made as she feared their pursuer would hear and discover their hiding place behind the stack of crates. She squeezed Lily's damp hand, hoping she conveyed confidence, and even in the dim light of the alley she could read the fear shining in the other woman's eyes.

Lily's mouth opened to speak. Rivalree shook her head and pressed a finger to her lips in warning, then she scanned the access lane seeking signs of whomever had made the noises she had heard.

Her brow furled into a frown. Who followed them? It had to be someone from the Gilded Cage, someone who suspected their hasty departure was not as innocent as they had tried to make it appear.

The stillness and the silence around them unnerved her. She was sure she had heard footsteps moments before, but now—nothing moved but a piece of paper caught in the breeze.

Scratch. Scratch.

There. Her eyes riveted to her left. What was that? She waited, clutching Lily's hand as the noise continued with a steady regularity.

A small dog poked its nose from behind a barrel, its front paws scraping at bits of refuse.

A starving cur seeking scraps of food? Was that all she'd heard?

The mongrel cocked his head and stared in their direction, his spine stiffening, and he barked, challenging them to intrude further into his territory.

Lily released a tiny yelp of fear. Rivalree clamped down hard on the brunette's fingers to silence her. The dog looked behind him, tucked his sparsely haired tail between his legs and scampered away.

Shuffle. Click.

A long shadow fell over a stack of barrels and cans at the end of the alley. Rivalree felt the fear rising in her throat nearly choking her.

Craning her neck as far as she dared, she assessed the situation. The other end of the alley was at least two hundred yards away. The shadow moved closer, a stack of crates crashing to the ground just ahead.

"I know you're here somewheres," drawled a determined voice. "Goddamn it, I'll find you."

What should they do? If they remained in hiding, eventually their pursuer would locate them. If they ran, he would see them and give chase. Lily's breathing hissed in terror inches from her ear, echoing the indecision shredding her own courage. The thought of waiting to be found by whomever sought them frightened her more than taking a chance on flight.

Run! Her heart pounded, pressing hard against her ribs and temples. She tugged on Lily's wrists and pointed down the alleyway. The woman nodded, her weight shifting in preparation to dash to freedom.

Taking a deep breath, Rivalree rose on the balls of her feet, forcing her appendages to move as fast as they could. The bright afternoon sun spilling into the alley's mouth grew closer. They were going to make it. She glanced back to check on Lily's progress to find the woman right on her heels. Three yards behind them came another figure, slowly closing the gap between them.

"Run, Lily," she shouted, making her legs pump faster as she gathered her skirts up in an unladylike clutch to keep her feet from tripping over her hem.

Lily screamed as their pursuer grabbed her arm shoving her to the ground. Rivalree stumbled in confusion as the man raced right on by the downed woman—after her! He didn't want Lily, he wanted her.

"No," she blurted, continuing to try and outpace the man chasing her. "What do you want?"

The assailant's fetid breath stung her senses as he drew closer. "I want what was denied me," he growled, something in his speech pattern striking terror in her heart. A hand clamped her arm, spinning her around, slamming her hard against a heaving chest.

Cruel, blue eyes bore into her as a strange offensive smell filled her nostrils. Fish and seaweed. A flood of memories spewed from the recesses of her brain. "Silas Guntree," she whispered, not believing her own words as she spoke them. "How . . . ?"

"I see you remember me, li'l missy." His unforgettably piercing gaze squelched her courage into mush.

"Dear God, no." Her knees turned to rubber, buckling under the weight of her body.

Holding her up by her wrists, he shook her violently. "I remember you, too. Very well. Because of you I had to leave behind the comforts of my life. Rivalree Richards." He spat out her name as if it fouled his mouth. "Word of your rape reached everywhere I went. No one would hire me, so I came seekin' my fortune in the gold fields. Did it give you a thrill to lie about me?"

Rivalree shook her head, denying his words and their implication. Braven had been right all along. Silas

Guntree had never touched her. Because she'd believed gossiping rumors instead of the man she loved, she'd ruined her life and her marriage.

"I've dreamed of my revenge. But never"—he pressed her face to his—"never did I think I would get a chance to see my fantasies come true. Fortune was with me to find you like I did." He raked her struggling, underclad body, leaving her feeling dirty and used.

"Please. I never accused you of anything. I . . ."

"If it's rape you want, li'l missy, I'll be glad to oblige."

A drop of spittle collected in the corner of his mouth. Rivalree convulsed, sickened by the sight.

Weight struck him from the rear, and his body slammed hers into the wall behind them, knocking the breath from her lungs.

"What the hell?" Guntree grunted as he loosened his hold on Rivalree and turned to eliminate the annoyance plaguing him from behind.

Palms flat against the wood siding, she struggled to inflate her aching chest.

"Run, Rivalree," Lily shouted as she clung monkey-style to Silas Guntree's back.

She obeyed the command, pushing away from the support of the structure, her lungs still sawing in and out sucking at air that seemed nonexistent.

Like a bear with an exuberant hound clamped to its hide, Guntree roared his angry resentment for the woman on his back who had fouled his vengeful plans. "Damn you, bitch," he bellowed, reaching around with one powerful hand grabbing a fistful of brown hair.

Lily shrieked, her teeth biting down on his arm. Guntree spun like a discus thrower flinging the woman off. She slammed to the ground, but gathered her feet underneath her body to launch a new attack.

Guntree was ready for her, and the moment she neared him he struck her another blow, sending her sprawling at

400

his feet.

"Lily," Rivalree cried, concern for her friend blocking the need to escape from her mind.

The woman pushed up on hands and knees, disoriented, a small groan bubbling from her lips. Guntree's airborne foot swung at her, setting Rivalree in action.

"No," she screamed, throwing her body against Guntree. Offbalance, his aim missed, but Rivalree found herself again in his clutch.

"You're nothing but a whore, like I suspected when I saw you ridin' in on that wagon as big as you please. Sierra Angel. Mountain Harlot sounds more likely. You don't deserve to be treated no better." He forced her around, her back to his chest, her arm twisted behind her until she thought the bone would snap.

"No," she groaned, the pain shooting up her arm, her feet dragging in the dirt of the road as he pushed her along. Angling her head to see behind her, Lily's sagging form did nothing to dispel the helpless terror numbing her mind.

This time Silas Guntree would follow through with his threats, and the odds of escaping his wrath again were not in her favor. Dressed as she was, even if witnesses saw him forcing her down the street, who would care what happened to one more nameless prostitute?

His palm clamped across her face to keep her from screaming, the nauseating odor of cured fish on his hands assaulting her senses. Bile rose in her throat.

Oh, Braven, where are you when I need you most?

At least Braven knew he searched for two women, not one. How could he have been so unobservant as to let Rivalree walk right past him and not recognize her? The dark-haired woman who had left the Gilded Cage with Lily had to have been Rivalree. None of the other women

401

were missing. Damn his stupidity not to have stopped and checked them out.

His search took him in the direction the two women had traveled earlier. So far he'd found nothing, not a clue, that indicated where they were headed, almost as if the back alleys of San Francisco had swallowed them up. Where could two women have gone and not have been noticed? He shoved his thumbs in his belt and continued his march down the street.

Stepping down from the sidewalk to cross another shadowed alley, he stopped in the middle of the street to stare down the garbage-littered lane. Just like all the others. Barrels and crates lined building walls. A small dog at the edge of the far structure stuck his nose against the ground, sniffing, as if trying to locate something. Braven paused, watching the animal's wary approach, its near-hairless tail thumping against the ground as it crouched, growling. Then the dog turned to run back the way it had come.

His breath hung suspended in his lungs. There was something in the alley. The mongrel had seen it. A scraping sound reached his ears. He stepped into the dark shadows, easing his gun from the holster on his hip.

Not knowing what he'd find, he feared the worst. Rivalree dead, the victim of murder. What if he never found her? It wasn't uncommon for people, even strong, capable men, to disappear in this cesspit, never to be seen again, much less two women dressed in the getup of whores.

Rivalree, where the hell are you?

He vividly recalled the two women walking past him, their steps decisive, as if they knew exactly where they were headed.

A soft groan invaded his hearing. He glanced up, inspecting the alley again. Several crates were overturned in the middle of the alley suggesting a struggle had taken place.

"Rivalree?"

The moan whispered again.

Slipping his pistol back in his holster, he scrambled over the refuse until he discovered the huddled form lying on the ground.

Lily. Dear God, it was Lily. His gaze darted around seeking signs of another body. Nothing. He knelt, gently touched the woman's shoulder, and rolled her to her back.

The woman sucked in her breath as if moving created an unbearable pain.

"I'm sorry, Lily. I don't mean to hurt you."

Her eyes fluttered open and locked with his. "Braven Blackwood? Is that really you? Rivalree was sure you'd never come. I . . ." She bit her lip, and a gasp of pain slipped past her lips.

"Where is she?"

The woman shook her head. "I'm not sure. He dragged her down to the other end of the alley and to the left. She was fighting and kicking, so they couldn't have gone far or someone would have seen them." She pulled up to a sitting position, her arms cradling her middle.

"He? He who? Who has Rivalree?"

"She called him Gunny or Gunner. Gun something."

"Guntree? Silas Guntree?"

Lily nodded. "I think that's what she said."

Silas Guntree, the person who had destroyed her family and home. The man she thought had raped her. Impossible. How would he have found her here in California? He remembered Rivalree's hysterics the night he had carried her from the Veta Madre. She had mistaken him for Guntree, as well. Someone else had her, but who?

"Lily, can you stand up. I've got to go after her."

She lifted her chin and reached her hand out for his assistance. "I'll manage. Get me to someplace public. I'll be fine."

He lifted her up and set her on shaky legs.

She touched his cheek with a thumb. "You know,

honey, she's given up on you. But I knew you'd come fo her sooner or later. I tried to keep her at the Gilded Cage but she was determined to leave on her own. I figured she' be safer with me, but I guess I was wrong." She dropped her eyes down.

"I'll find her. Don't you worry."

His hand under her elbow, they moved down the alle and onto the main thoroughfare. He turned his attention in the direction Lily said they'd gone. The street was lined with low-class warehouses. Her assailant could have dragged her into any one of the buildings. Which one? He didn't have forever to search. He had to find her in the nex few moments.

"Fish. He smelled of fish," Lily piped out.

Braven gripped her shoulders. "Are you sure?"

She nodded in confidence.

"Stay here. Don't you move."

The woman's shoulders slumped. Braven was positive she would do as he said. He raced down the street, seeking signs of a warehouse holding barrels of salted fish. No much of a clue to go on, but it was all he had.

The smell assaulted him as he neared the third building If Lily was right, Rivalree was somewhere in thi structure. His running feet came to a halt. What was hi best plan of attack? John Masters had pegged him well The time was right to bust through the door, his gun blazing.

Tossed in the dark corner as if she were no more than a sack of old rags, Rivalree gathered her feet beneath her prepared to spring the moment Silas Guntree stepped closer. Glancing up at the barrels of salted fish stacked high around them, she found no easy route of escape Nothing short of death would make her give in to his cruel demands. Not this time. She would fight him with the last breath of her body.

"You're makin' this hard on yourself, li'l missy. What's ne more hump for a whore like you?"

She didn't answer, just watched his every move. His and moved down to the buttons on the front of his denim ›ants. Swallowing hard, her heart beat erratically in her hest. *I will stop him*, she chanted over and over in her nind, fanning the sparks of courage residing there.

Guntree grinned, the expression so sure and confident othing would interfere with his plans. With determined trides, he closed the gap between them. She pushed up, ossing her body against his, hoping to throw him off ›alance. Grunting, he grasped her unbound hair and vound it about his fist then laughed as she fell to her .nees, helpless, servile before him.

His hand clawed at the green satin of her dress. There vas no doubt in her mind he meant to strip her bare.

Squeezing her eyes shut, she prepared for the sounds of ipping cloth. When it came, she screamed, for her scalp vas nearly ripped from her head. Then, to her surprise, he was free, her ears ringing, her dress in shreds at the left houlder. But somehow, miraculously, she was no longer eld in his cruel grip.

Without questioning the reason, she rolled to her tomach and pushed up, angling toward the front of the varehouse. The sounds of a struggle taking place behind er slowed her down, but she decided against stopping to nvestigate. She didn't care why she'd escape; what nattered was that she had.

"You sorry son of a bitch. You're lucky I got here when I lid. Otherwise you'd be dead now."

The rich timbre rattled around in her brain. She came to an abrupt halt, her breath rasping in her ears so loud she vasn't sure she'd heard correctly. That voice. Braven? It :ouldn't be. Whirling, the air rushed from her body in a ›reathless huff.

Two figures struggled on the floor, Guntree on top, his arge frame disrupting her view of the other man.

"Braven?" she whispered.

"Don't stop, Rivalree. Get out of here," the beloved voice commanded.

Her head nodded in acceptance of his authority, but she couldn't tear her eyes away. The two men grappled, each trying to best the other. As if from nowhere a gun appeared between them and a tug-of-war commenced, the grunt each man emitted as they battled for supremacy of the weapon left her wondering if Braven would prevail. If Silas Guntree won . . .

The horrors of the possibility sent tremors of fear rushing through her. Concern for her own safety was there, but Braven would be the first to die if Guntree gained the upper hand. She couldn't allow that to happen.

She launched herself, slamming against the slave hunter with the force of a gale storm. Guntree toppled like a giant, uprooted tree, his cry of protest so close to her ear, his hot breath blasting her. Her neck cracked as they rolled, his weight crushing her, leaving her unable to fill her lungs with much needed air.

A vise clamped around her neck, and she was dragged to her feet, her heart pumping so hard she could have sworn it had taken up residency in her ears.

"Braven," she cried, but the sound was no more than a rasp, indistinguishable from the other desperate noises rattling in her throat.

The world blackened, leaving pinpoints of light in the center of her vision. *This is death*, she thought with the calmness of an eye of a hurricane. The hands around her neck tightened.

"Throw down the gun, mister, or she's dead," Guntree threatened.

No, Braven, don't do it, or you will die, too. Her fingers clawed at the hands around her throat.

Cr-r-rack!

The sound that had begun this segment of her life

would bring it to an end. Blanketing her in warmth and comfort, the darkness became complete.

"Rivalree?" Braven's heart drummed a protest. He was too late. The few seconds of indecision he had taken had cost Rivalree her life. Lifting her limp body into his lap, he cradled her head against his chest, rocking.

Her chest expanded, her lungs grasping at the air. For the only time he could remember in his adult life, Braven fought the urge to cry out his relief.

Laying her gently down, he bent over her, taking deep, cleansing breaths with each rise of her breasts. Her lashes fluttered, divided, then embraced again.

"Sugar," he urged softly, running his hand through her golden hair.

Her amber orbs stared back at him. She threw herself up, clutching his neck with all her strength. "Oh, Braven, you came," she sobbed. "I'm so sorry I've been such a fool. Please forgive me."

"Forgive you—whatever for?" His arms mimicked hers, holding her tight.

"From the moment you met me at the wharf, you've always been near, protecting me. I have made such a mess of our lives. If I could have seen the truth in the beginning, our marriage could have been so much easier."

"That doesn't matter now, sugar. The past has never held much light for me."

"I know, my love." Her finger traced the line of his jaw. "Now, it no longer matters to me, either. Only you and our future together has any meaning."

"A future with me might look bleak." His brows dipped in a frown.

"What do you mean?"

"I turned the gold over to Carla in order to find you." She pushed back from his embrace, her gaze studying him in awe. "For me? You gave up your dreams?"

"For you I would have given my life, if necessary. Don' you know that yet?"

"But the gold? What will you do about your plans to return to Louisiana and convince your family a plantation can be successful without slavery? How can you do that without the money?"

"I imagine I can't." He grinned. "But I can teach them something much better. North and South is not like vinegar and oil. There's room for understanding and most of all"—he lifted her chin with his finger—"there's room for love." He placed a tender kiss on her lips. Taking her hands in his, he urged her to her feet. "Come on, we need to . . ."

"Oh, Braven," she gasped, the back of her hand against her mouth. "Is he dead?"

He whirled them, turning her away from Silas Guntree's body lying in a pool of red. "He's dead. And if you're up to it, I think it would be best if we went straight to the sheriff's office."

She nodded, burying her face in his shoulder as he led her from the warehouse.

Rivalree glanced around the tiny office. She remembered it and the sheriff well. Then she had been here accusing Braven of murder, now she was here to defend his reason for killing a man.

The sheriff glanced up from his report and motioned to his deputies. "Go on down to the warehouse and retrieve the body. Take the deceased to the undertaker." He turned to Braven. "I best have the pistol, Blackwood. I'll need it to verify that this was the weapon used."

"I understand," Braven answered, unbuckling the holster from his hip and placing it in the lawman's outstretched hand. "There's another dead man at the Gilded Cage. I would like to claim the body for burial. He was a friend of mine."

"You've had a busy day, I'd say," the sheriff grunted. "Name of the deceased?"

Braven glanced down at Rivalree, then placed his arm around her shoulder. "Pat O'Grady."

"Oh no, Braven. Not Pat," she whispered, tears of true sorrow springing up in her eyes. "What happened?"

"Carla shot him. I sincerely think it was an accident."

"Accidental, you say?" the sheriff interrupted.

"His daughter. They argued, then struggled over the weapon. He was trying to take it away from her, to keep her from killing someone else."

"Who?" the sheriff demanded, writing as fast as he could.

Braven tightened his hold on her. "My wife."

"Me?" She slumped against his side.

"The woman escaped with a letter of deposit worth a fortune."

"Yours?" the lawman queried.

"Partly."

"Gold?"

Braven nodded.

"Man's foolishness, I'd say."

"I'm inclined to agree with you, Sheriff. But if we find her I'd like to get it back."

The sheriff shook his head. "Don't expect miracles. People come and go in droves from here."

The front door of the office flew open.

"Damn you, Johnny. Let go of me." Carla's unbound hair whirled about her face as she tried to extract her arm from John Masters's grip.

The gambler pushed her forward and closed the door behind them. He twisted her arm against her back. "Give the bank deposit back to him, Carla. Now."

"Don't you see, Johnny, it's all yours. It's what you wanted."

"Perhaps," Masters answered, "but not this way. Give it

to Blackwood."

Carla reached into her reticule and pulled out the letter. She spun and slapped it into Braven's hand. "Here, I hope you choke on it." She shook off Masters's relaxed grip and headed for the door.

"Not so fast, little lady," the sheriff barked. "You're under arrest for kidnapping, extortion, and attempted murder." He grabbed her by the elbow, pulling her toward the back room.

"You'll pay for this, John Masters," she screeched as she disappeared through the doorway.

Masters turned to Braven. "Now what?"

"That's up to you. This deposit is in your name."

Masters hesitated, a small gleam resting in his eyes. For a moment, Rivalree thought he would take the certificate and run. Braven must have thought so, too, as his mouth flattened into a hard, bitter line.

"I think we agreed to one third." Masters put out his hand in a gesture of friendship. "You're a high-minded son of a bitch, Blackwood, but you're honest. I've not known many like you. Let's head to my bank. I'm sure we can work the details out."

Braven placed his hand in Masters's and shook it. "If you think I'm difficult, wait until you meet your new partners. Eloy Jackson and Mace Lockman will make you wish you had me to deal with instead."

Masters's barking laugh rang out as he slapped Braven on the back. "Leave it to you to make my life more difficult than ever."

Rivalree watched the two men banter, and she offered up a radiant smile. Yes, it was best to forget the past and think about tomorrow. Life's happiness dwelled in one's dreams and plans for the future and a golden fervor to see them all come true.

Epilogue

Bentley, Louisiana
April 3, 1855

The warm, moist southern breeze caressed Rivalree's neck as she swept her hair on top of her head. The cane-back rocker squeaked softly, a lullaby of sorts, as she watched the tiny figure in the crook of her arm purse her lips and emulate a sucking motion. Her child. Hers and Braven's. The true symbol of their undying love. The baby she had yearned for for so long.

The click and shuffle of Braven's familiar footsteps cut across the wide verandah on which she sat rocking her daughter. She glanced up, placed one finger to her lips in warning as she saw him come around the corner.

Braven's tall figure came to a halt a few feet away. "I thought I'd check and see how my girls were doing."

"Wonderful," she beamed, angling her arm slightly so he could view the sleeping infant. "How's the planting going?"

"The cotton seed is in the ground. We're ahead of schedule and at least a week before our neighbors. If all goes well, sugar, we could have another record year." -

"I knew you could do it, Braven. And the workers. I feel

411

guilty for not making my normal rounds to all the houses."

"The people understand, Rivalree. I'm constantly bombarded with questions as to how you and the baby are doing. They love you."

She looked down and smiled. All their plans had gone so well. The plantation thrived, more efficient than any other in the parish. She glanced back at Braven, the love she felt for him spilling from her eyes.

"Miz Rivalree?" A tall, dignified black woman stepped from the house. "Ya'll have callers."

Rivalree straightened in her seat. "Show them to the verandah, if you would, please, Elisa." She almost wiggled, hoping the visitors were who she expected.

The elegantly dressed brunette floated across the porch, her hands gloved and a feathered hat cocked on her head. "Rivalree," Lily breathed, a touch of southern accent creeping into her voice.

Braven placed another chair near where she sat and offered it with a gentlemanly flourish to Lily. With the grace of a woman born to the life-style, she accepted the seat, then twisted to inspect the little stranger in Rivalree's arms. "She's beautiful, absolutely angelic." She reached to clasp the hand of the well-dressed man standing behind her. "Have you named her yet?"

"Braven and I agreed, unanimously. Rivalree Aileen. She's the firstborn girl of her generation."

"Of course. Family traditions. I'm still acclimating myself to my new way of life." She squeezed the tall gentleman's hand. "Arthur has been so patient with me."

"And why not," Braven piped in. "You're a beautiful lady, Lily. I wish there were more like you in the South. I'm sure your husband agrees."

She smiled shyly at him. "Thank you, Braven. You always were such a charmer. I was wrong about what I said so long ago about southern men. You're gentle and kind

412

and caring." Again she cast adoring eyes at Arthur.

Rivalree watched the silent communication between her husband and her friend. Not once had she regretted bringing Lily back to Louisiana with them. She had been an undaunted partisan and confidante over the last three years.

Yes, she was lucky. She had it all. A husband who adored her, a friend to share the ups and downs of her life, and a child to keep the dreams alive. She turned her gaze to the baby. *Rivalree, my daughter, may your life be as rewarding and full as mine has been.*

GIVE YOUR HEART
TO ZEBRA'S HEARTFIRE!

COMANCHE CARESS   (2268, $3.75)
by Cheryl Black

With her father missing, her train held up by bandits and her money stolen, Clara Davenport wondered what else could possibly go wrong. Until a powerful savage rescued her from a band of ruffians in the Rocky Mountains and Clara realized the very worst had come to pass: she had fallen desperately in love with a wild, handsome half-breed she could never hope to tame!

IVORY ROSE   (2269, $3.75)
by Kathleen McCall

Standing in for her long-lost twin sister, innocent Sabrina Buchanan was tricked into marrying the virile estate owner Garrison McBride. Furious with her sibling, Sabrina was even angrier with herself—for she could not deny her intense yearning to become a woman at the masterful hands of the handsome stranger!

STARLIT SURRENDER   (2270, $3.75)
by Judy Cuevas

From the moment she first set eyes on the handsome swashbuckler Adrien Hunt, lovely Christina Bower was determined to fend off the practiced advances of the rich, hot-blooded womanizer. But even as her sweet lips protested each caress, her womanly curves eagerly welcomed his arousing embrace!

RECKLESS DESIRE   (2271, $3.75)
by Thea Devine

Kalida Ryland had always despised her neighbor Deuce Cavender, so she was shocked by his brazen proposal of marriage. The arrogant lady's man would never get his hands on her ranch! And even if Kalida had occasionally wondered how those same rough, powerful hands would feel caressing her skin, she'd die before she let him know it!

Available wherever paperbacks are sold, or order direct from the Publisher. Send cover price plus 50¢ per copy for mailing and handling to Zebra Books, Dept. 2367, 475 Park Avenue South, New York, N.Y. 10016. Residents of New York, New Jersey and Pennsylvania must include sales tax. DO NOT SEND CASH.

<u>FREE</u> Preview Each Month and $ave

Zebra has made arrangements for you to preview brand new **HEARTFIRE** novels each month...FREE for 10 days. You'll get them as soon as they are published. If you are not delighted with any of them, just return them with no questions asked. But if you decide these are everything we said they are, you'll pay just $3.25 each—a total of $13.00 (a $15.00 value). **That's a $2.00 saving each month off the regular price.** Plus there is NO shipping or handling charge. These are delivered right to your door absolutely free! There is no obligation and there is no minimum number of books to buy.

TO GET YOUR FIRST MONTH'S PREVIEW...
Mail the Coupon Below!